World on a String

Based on the Memoir of Charles Stark

To DRE ad JOHN —
— HEARTFELT THANKS FOR
Yur SUPPORT and
FRIRNDSHIP —

Karen Stark

♡ Karen

FOR

Sally and Zoë

FOREWORD

In 1910, Charlie Stark was born into abject poverty, his immigrant parents and American-born five siblings crammed into a tiny tenement apartment in Brooklyn. A few years later, they moved to 58 East Third Street in Manhattan's Lower East Side, into a miniscule two-room flat where three more children were born. The teeming sidewalks of East Third Street notwithstanding, they at least provided Charlie air to breathe and space to move his arms and legs outside such cramped conditions, eleven people living in just two rooms. However, on these sidewalks he describes: "By the time I was five years old, I witnessed dozens of rapes, murders, stabbings, shootings and people being thrown off rooftops." Charlie's prospects of surviving the violence and squalor surrounding him relied solely on an innate artistic talent. Before he was sixteen, he had collected and conned his way into an assortment of eclectic art jobs that eventually led to a short-lived set design career in the Yiddish and other mainstream theaters that flourished on the Lower East Side -- short-lived because the bootleggers offered him bigger bucks to decorate their speakeasies. Suddenly, Charlie's business associates became the likes of Bugsy Siegel, Joe Masseria, Owney Madden, Dutch Schultz and a motley jumble of other infamous characters that lurked throughout the Jewish, Italian and Irish slums.

But Charlie was everyone's favorite boy. Not just a painter and designer, he sang in the underground bootleg clubs, told jokes and entertained the masses until the day he witnessed a violent and bloody act.

World On A String is the fictional presentation of my father's astonishing memoir, illustrating a young man's unique ability to survive poverty and despair, with ensuing triumphs and tragedies spawned from his boundless wits and comparable naiveté. And yet, despite the hardships, my father loved his life in New York; so much so, he wouldn't stop talking about it. From the day he set foot in Kansas City, Missouri in 1932 at the age of twenty-two, until his last, eighty-seventh year, it was by far his favorite topic of conversation. Even into their old age, my mother and her sisters would reminisce about the incessant tales of New York, Charlie Stark would recite relentlessly.

"Your father simply would not shut up. We heard the stories of his adventures with Bernie Poster, the gangsters, the theater and Molly Picon ten thousand times."

Whereas many children would be told stories of three pigs, or bears or princesses at bedtime, I heard endless, bountiful accounts of his escapades with friends Bernie Poster, Tollie Oppie, Schmutz, Hey Hey Goldberg, Kishke Breines, tales of his many childhood romps and explorations of New York City, so many loving stories of his adored Music School Settlement House, and exhaustive details of his hard life in the tenements.

In 1983, on his seventy-third birthday I told my father he needed to chronicle all these wonderful tales. He started with one long, yellow legal pad, and wound up with twelve.

"This is great!" he'd call up and tell me. "I'm having a ball! I started at the beginning but am going only up to 1932."

From the faintest memories of his birthplace on Jerome Street in Brooklyn, his memoir moves to East Third Street, where the journal spotlights his childhood and teen years, then ventures into accounts of his unique associations with celebrities and gangsters. Everything was written out by hand, meticulously and in copious detail on those twelve legal pads.

Shortly after my father's death in 1997, I typed his long memoir and thought about donating it to perhaps a museum or historical society in New York. But then I thought differently. I thought about all the amazing tales of his pals on the street, his pals Cab Calloway, Molly Picon, Paul Muni, and Jimmy Durante on stage, his "pals" in the dangerous .speakeasies, of his huge, impoverished family living in that tiny apartment, and all of Charlie's Huck Finn-like exploits. I thought about how this unusual little boy, who lived in such poverty and faced so many hardships, could adapt, prevail, embellish, survive and find himself cavorting within the circles of the rich and dangerous. How could I not turn this into a novel?

World On A String contains much of my father's actual memoir in the first-person "Charlie" chapters. Alas, for the sake of fiction, I had to exclude many details and much information. Fortunately, since those twelve legal pads were so thoroughly abundant in facts, descriptions and observations, the reader will have no difficulty understanding Charlie's multi-dimensional life as he moves through the Depression, the slums, his adversities and joys, and all of the challenges the roaring 1920's afforded.

Of the book's five central characters, who have their own third-person chapters, four are based on critically significant people in my father's life. The aforementioned Bernie Poster was Charlie's dearest childhood friend. Though my father so often recounted their many adventures, and featured him in his memoir, I regret that I know very little of Bernie Poster. But I could so easily imagine these two ragamuffin Third Street boys, escaping their stressful lives in the tenements for the spirited adventures my father would concoct, and racing in and out of the Poster family's candy store on the corner of East Third Street and Second Avenue.

Like Bernie, "Miss Wilson" is someone I know little about. I don't even know her first name. I do know she was one of Charlie's many beloved mentors at the Music School Settlement House directly across from my father's tenement building on East Third Street. Originally founded in 1894 to provide musical instruction to neighborhood immigrant families, the Music School Settlement House eventually offered a variety of social services to help quell the growing concerns of the poor on the Lower East Side. Of this beloved enterprise, my father writes:

"The Music School Settlement House was four stories high. It was red brick and white wood-trimmed with a high iron fence the whole width of the building. It was the widest building on the block. It was run by a half dozen women appointed by a Fifth Avenue group, a charity thing, I think, for the kids on the east side who were musically inclined. Violin, cello, and piano lessons were offered, and older people studied vocal. The staff of women lived at the school, so you had to have a kitchen. Miss Mary Birnie was the head of the school. She was an Eleanor Roosevelt type. Miss Fisk, second in command, was a Charlotte Rae type. Miss Rainey, a tiny gray-haired lady, was assistant to Miss Fisk. Miss Kibbee, a tall gray-haired lady, quite buxom, was the music librarian. She wore expensive looking glasses. Miss Wilson was, I think, the liaison between the Fifth Avenue alumni and the school. She could have been the treasurer. My brother Harry and his high school friends did their homework most nights in the Music School library. There were never any music students there at night. When I was little, I used to love sitting around the big library fireplace with them, reading Grimms fairy tales, sitting in a cozy Morris chair, and taking in all their big talk."

What an oasis for a tenement kid. The warm, welcoming Music School and all its loving employees were held in the utmost reverence for the rest of Charlie's life. He would be thrilled to know it still exists and thrives in Manhattan, now called the "Third Street Music School," though it has moved up to 11th Street. But for the sake of fiction, "Miss Wilson" has become the school's librarian, and Charlie's greatest advocate.

The character of "Opal" presented many challenges. She is never mentioned in Charlie's memoir, and I doubt she was ever mentioned to many people at all. Only once, late in his life, in a conversation with my sister Julie, did my father recount his relationship with an adored, young African-American woman whom he claimed was his greatest love. Absolutely nothing is known about her nor their brief relationship, except, my father said, for the great intolerance they endured. Thus, the character of "Opal" is entirely fictional.

"Mama" is Clara Schwartz Stark, my father's mother, caretaker of her meager home, and diligent custodian of her nine children. I never met my grandmother, but it was easy to imagine her trials, defeats, and arduous attempts to survive such taxing conditions. Yet, with greatest love and supreme reverence, my father wrote and always spoke of her as being a spirited, optimistic, jolly woman, who was the cornerstone of their family foundation. I never met my grandmother, but I know her so well through her equally resilient and vivacious son.

Lastly, the character of "Joey" is entirely fictional, though in some ways he is an amalgamation of many scurrilous personalities mentioned in my father's memoir. Dozens, if not hundreds of seedy, scandalous, quirky, cruel and dangerous scoundrels lurked in Charlie's neighborhood and within his circle. But Joey is purely imagined, and does not represent any one individual.

The remaining real people used as minor characters - Charlie's father, siblings, his Aunt Annie, set designer Alexander Chertov, impressionist painter Charles Hawthorne, and renown mobster Joe Masseria --are strictly fictional representations, though are based on my father's relationships with them as he describes in his memoir. Their dialogue is wholly based on what I have imagined what might have transpired between them and Charlie.

Any other descriptions and accounts of well-known people are historical and documented.

Creating *World on a String* has been a true labor of love, paying homage to the life of my father, to the lives of so many who survived the immigrant tenements on the Lower East Side and to those who supported them, to the Yiddish theater, Vaudeville, the city of New York, and to those who endured and outlasted the Great Depression.

Scores of people have been invaluable in helping me realize the fruition of this novel, especially: Joshua Allen, Lynn Andrews, Arturo Ciompi, Lisa Creed, Normandy Davis, Susan Elia, Catherine Fletcher, Christopher Hyland, Vedia Jones-Richardson, George Koch, Antonia Lilley, Bill Neal, Jonathan Nyberg, Kathy O'Connor, Hal Sandick, Julie Stark, Cynthia Sturges Strull, and Rebecca Wellborn. I cannot begin to thank them for their professionalism, guidance, encouragement and friendship.

Joey   **1932**

Joey "The Pimp" Rotollo felt the rat squirm in his pocket.

"He ain't gonna do it!"

"I told ya he wadn't gonna do it. Chicken! What kinda bullshit is this?"

Beneath the brim of his white Panama hat, smudged gray from too many nights absorbing exhaust fumes on Allen Street, Joey, a diminutive, twenty-one year old with a baby face more reminiscent of a pre-teen if not for two jagged scars excavating each cheek bone, squinched his blank, black eyes and shot a crocodile sneer toward his companions, one slightly used hooker and her John. The pincers on Joey's left hand gripped the opening of his pants pocket to keep the rat securely inside, while his right hand flicked at a throbbing, partially severed thumbnail, acquired from the previous night's brawl he'd instigated on Stanton. Along his pocket's frayed, cotton seam, and against his bony, hairless upper thigh, Joey could feel the rat's tiny, frantic claws searching spastically for an escape route through the gabardine.

"I still say it's disgustin!"

Joey felt the rat's claws catch the threads of a small hole his switchblade had punctured the night before. He started to reach inside his pocket for the knife, an habitual motion when he needed confidence, the assurance he wasn't any negligible, mere Gumbah from the slums of East Third Street, but he stopped, remembering he'd broken it. *Damn, if I hadn't've stuck that fucker in the ribs, I wouldn't've broken my shiv.* Though *thinking* wasn't Joey's usual prelude to action, he did realize the rat would be tearing through the hole and scampering out the pocket, down his leg to the street and down into the sewer if he waited much longer. He couldn't put it off. A bet was a bet. Whether leaping a six-foot split between towering roof tops, lying on subway tracks and bolting just before the train, or biting off the head of a rat, Joey was more than eager to accept a challenge. A buck was a buck. And Joey needed bucks. He'd already cleaned out his old man, a drunk of a father who, after collapsing on the splintered wood floor of their flat every night of every pay day, never quite knew where his money had disappeared. All Joey had to do was wait for the old man to pass out with his bootleg bottle of gin, and pinch the old sot's weekly ten bucks. Joey did consider himself a commendable son, however, by leaving his pop with a fiver. He would have taken it all, of course, if not for the necessity to keep his father thoroughly smashed, knowing most of the remaining five bucks would be spent on hooch, again to repeat the Friday night bender and Joey's subsequent pilfering week after week. Still, those five measly bucks pinched from his father's gin-soaked pocket, and another twenty finagled from his hookers, were hardly the weekly cut he owed big boss Joe Masseria, a boss with a particularly bad temper who expected that C note.

"Sure kid," Masseria had said when he and Joey were first negotiating the terms of his employment. "I'll letcha work on some of my broads. You just work real hard, pal, or I'll be workin' on you."

Joey worked very hard.

"Ya wanna make me puke or somethin'?" said the young prostitute in a red satin dress."Let's get outta here!" she added, spewing smoke from an ivory cigarette holder. She brushed ashes off the rabbit fur collar of her coat, and spread back the lapels to reveal shiny, silver sequins attached to the plunging neckline of her tight red satin.

"C'mon Joey, quit stallin'. We ain't got all night," whined the John, one sweaty hand around the girl's rabbit fur and his other sweaty hand caressing her ample hip.

The rodent's tiny, cold nose pushed through the hole in Joey's pocket, leaving a slimy wet dot on the skin of his upper thigh which froze almost instantly in the thirty degree wind chill, giving Joey the odd sensation that he'd somehow wet his pants.

"C'mon, Doll, let's breeze," yapped the John. "Your boss is a nut job. His choo choo's off the track."

"Yeah!" giggled the hooker. "Let's us blow this station!"

All at once, because even in an endless Universe, worlds, stars, moons and galaxies do collide, two distinctly different but similar incidents occurred at the corner of Allen and Houston on Planet Manhattan. And much like these events in the heavens that create monumental alterations to the cosmos, even as they remain mere specks in an indifferent vacuum, two men faced Joey "The Pimp" Rotollo on the opposite street corner. Their spontaneous arrival at that one scrap of sidewalk under the new electric lamppost on a cold night in the cold Depressed universe of 1932 New York City had its own cosmic effect. One of the men was black. Dressed smartly in a full length brown suede coat and matching suede hat with a wide brim, the black man plucked a long, expensive cigar from his vest pocket and lit up.

"Forget the ten spot, Joey. The bet's off." The John pocketed a crumpled ten dollar bill.

But Joey couldn't take his eyes off the black man, who was blowing a steady stream of cigar smoke up to the shiny new electric bulb in the street lamp. In the glow of the dazzling incandescence of modernity, illuminating the corner of Allen and Houston like no mere gaslight could ever do, Joey could see the black man also removing from his vest pocket a bulging leather wallet. The man tipped his hat, pointing his cigar right at Joey's hooker.

A chill raced up Joey's back, sliced through his neck and landed in his throat like a hot coal. *Niggers?* he thought, *I'm supposed to pimp for a nigger?!*

Since the War, it was one thing, Joey believed, to see the Bowery fill up with *all those fuckin' soldiers,* limping around on one leg, throwing up blood from their drinking binges, and begging for dough night and day. On one hand, Joey could understand cripples needing a handout, but not "nigger cripples." *Let 'em bum off their own kind in their own slums* was Joey's way of thinking. But it was quite another thing altogether, he fumed, for some black dandy to swagger past Lenox Avenue and down into *his* territory, in his own neighborhood for Christ sake, acting all hoitiy-toity like this nigger was Somebody in his fancy clothes, and him expecting a piece of white ass? *Like I'm gonna turn a trick for a nigger? Like I'm supposed to let a nigger ball one of my white girls?*

Extreme rage started to boil inside Joey's chest. He could feel his heart pounding, slamming against his ribs. The black man on the corner even wore a diamond cufflink on each wrist. *I'm gonna let a nigger show me up?*

"Don't squeeze the merchandise, Honey," said Joey's hooker, her John cupping one of the breasts ballooning past her sequins. "Ya might bruise the apples."

Joey reached into his pocket and grabbed the rat, clamping his fingers around its neck. As if the seething fury inside him weren't enough, as he watched the black man grin superciliously and flash his diamonds, Joey's wrath only swelled and bubbled that much more when he saw the Jew Charlie Stark also standing underneath the lamppost. *Bastardo! Here's another asshole wantin' to show me up!* He gripped the rat tighter. It didn't matter that the Jews on Joey's block were just as poor as his Italian family and friends were too. They all shared the same mold-ridden, garbage-ridden and insect-ridden tenements. They all wore the same thread-bare, thread-worn, and shredded hand me downs. They even shared the same fuming hallway toilets. It didn't matter. Not to Joey, who'd clung to vivid childhood memories of him and his six brothers having to crawl through the school garbage cans every single day looking for their lunch while Charlie and his brothers could sit in the cafeteria savoring their slices of bread. Joey and his family had stale noodles and green-tinged cheese every damn day, while the smell of roasted chicken floated out the Kike Charlie's window every Friday night. Charlie and his brothers could play stickball in shoes, Joey and his brothers only had shoes for winter. And now the Jew son of a bitch was always flashing money like he was the Rockefeller of Third Street or something. The son of a bitch!

"Yeah, it's true, I'm doin' a job for Big Joe," Charlie had bragged one night from his stoop, flaunting a new pair of white linen trousers and flipping through a fat roll of one dollar bills.

Right! Like Joe Masseria's gonna give you, a faggot Jew painter the time of day? Joey had steamed. That big boss Joe Masseria would actually hire Charlie Stark and pay him good dough just to draw stupid pictures and slap some pansy ass paint onto a speakeasy wall stuck in the pit of Joey's stomach like his own switchblade. *When I been pushin' Masseria's broads and makin' squat?* Joey was supposed to get twenty-five clams from that weekly C note he forked over to his boss, but he hadn't seen Masseria in three weeks. They had a new "arrangement" where Joey would make the pay off to one of Masseria's flunkies, who every week would only say, "I ain't got your dough, kid, get it from The Man." Joey had way too many debts to pay to way too many guys to be making squat, guys who wanted to squeeze him just like the rat he clenched in his pocket. And now the Kike Charlie Stark was rakin' in *his* cash? But Joey figured he had the goods on Charlie Stark alright. One night, he'd been way uptown, pulling one of his hookers away from a nigger blow-job on 135th Street, when he saw it all. Clear as day, in the crummy dust beam of a dingy Harlem gaslight, Charlie Stark was walking down the sidewalk hand in hand, all lovey-dovey, with a black, nigger dame.

Joey now squeezed the rat even more tightly. *The fucker! Him rakin' in the dough, my dough! Him thinkin' Big Joe's wrapped around his little finger and I'm gettin' jack?! And the bastard's datin' niggers!!*

Dodging traffic, the well-dressed black man and Charlie Stark simultaneously stepped off the curb and shuffled through the mob of pedestrians toward Joey.

Charlie Stark and niggers! Joey felt the rage in his chest erupt into full-fledged fury, boiling, bubbling, exploding into one dark singular thought. Cold-blooded murder.

"I said, the bet's off, Joey. C'mon, Doll, let's make tracks."

"Sure thing Honey, it's nooky time."

"Don't move!" Joey snatched what was left of his broken knife, thrusting it toward the hooker, slicing several silver sequins from her neckline and nicking off a shred of skin above her left breast.

"Hey!" she screeched.

"I said, don't move!"

Joey "The Pimp" Rotollo constricted his rat, digging his fingernails into the fur so violently, he instantly broke its neck. He yanked the limp rodent from his pocket, jammed it between his teeth, crunched off its head, and spat it out.

"Gimme my ten bucks!!"

Charlie *1932*

Even from the back of the room I could see she needed some fixin' up. I wanted her to be perfect, a goddess, the golden diva of my dreams, every inch a ravishing, Old World beauty, better than any Renaissance painting, better than the Madonna. The Mona Lisa would forever be one jealous broad, and the Venus de Milo herself would only be remembered as a show room dummy. I was creating a true masterpiece in form, shape, color, in every glorious dimension. Every stroke of my brush and drop of my sweat was an act of passion, not of labor but true love. Now, after five solid weeks of traipsing up and down ladders like a yo-yo, covering myself from head to toe in rainbows of tempera, and exhausting every muscle of my body to capture each loving detail, finally, my opus goddess radiated a life glow that proclaimed not just her own vibrancy and vitality, but ensured that the two of us together, painting and painter, would achieve immortality. She had to shine like the sun, like the stars, she *must* shine, and with one more flick of my brush, a caress of cadmium red like an infusion of my own blood, I would make her shine alright. But not be too shiny. The one spotlight hanging above the stage would cause a bad glare. One spotlight! Jeeze, there shoulda been a hundred spotlights on my diva, but what did I expect from a two bit speakeasy?

I leaned back on my chair, stared up at my goddess on the wall, and tried to think, puffing on my *Cremo* and gulping hot coffee. Was she finished? Was she really about to leap off the wall and embrace her creator?

Maybe not.

Yellow ochre, yeah that's it, I thought, pulling tobacco off my tongue.

Her cheeks were definitely too white, she looked more like a China doll than an olive- skinned Talyena. That wouldn't do. I wanted to impress the boys, even if they were two low-life, scum-bag hoods thinkin' they could run a business. I'd make Dominic and Carlo think my diva was like *Carmen* or like their mothers when I finished. And they would. I knew these Italian guys worshipped their mothers and loved opera. Even the Italian janitor in my building loved his opera. The *janitor,* for God's sake.

I dunked out my cigar in the coffee cup and walked to the stage, grabbing the paint brush I left on a bar stool.

"What putzes," I muttered. "I'm creating these crimulniks a masterpiece, not just any old stage backdrop, and all Dominic and Carlo can think about is running booze and how many dames they can bring into the joint."

I studied my mural. It covered the whole back wall behind the stage, if you could call it a stage, a bunch of old two-by-fours nailed together. The boys wanted a class joint, not just some hole in the wall speakeasy like all the others near 52nd Street, but they were hardly dishing out enough dough to make it real class.

My mural *made* it class. I painted right onto the brick, covering up all the crumbling mortar and water stains which had been that crummy basement's main attraction. Of course, a speakeasy had to be in a basement, but with the three coats of indigo blue paint I shmeared on the walls, and with the burgundy velvet fabric I hung, it would look sensational. I'd gotten a deal on four dozen gold-painted side chairs with blue velvet seats, I hung twelve brass candelabra wall sconces with pink silk shades, I even varnished every damn slat of the old scuffed up oak floor. It took five weeks alright, but the joint was gorgeous, a knockout. Those mugs got a showplace for twenty bucks a week. They shoulda paid me twenty bucks a day.

And now my diva was almost perfect. I painted her standing on a marble balcony of a stone palace, over-looking a quaint Italian village. The square below her was full of people, fruit peddlers, fancy gentlemen in top hats, organ grinders, and old ladies sitting at the edge of a sputtering fountain selling flowers. Without a doubt, this was the greatest mural I'd ever done. I wondered who the hell was gonna appreciate this? Dominic swore Bugsy Siegel himself would be in there some nights, and Carlo promised they would have a first class clientele.

"We'll make a fortune," Carlo had bragged just yesterday, his big tuchis leaning back on one of my gold chairs until I thought it would break. His hairy hands circled his fat belly like it was already full of money.

Yeah, right. Dominic and Carlo, two schlemiels still clinging to their mama's Sunday linguini, thinking they were big time operators. But who knew? Maybe we would get the high rollers.

"*I've got the world on a string,*" I sang at the top of my lungs. I didn't care who heard me. "*Sitting on a rainbow, got the string around my finger, what a world, what a life, I'm in love.*"

Eight tin cans of paint sat in the back alley doorway just to the left of the stage. I took the can of dark yellow tempera, swirled my brush in the thick ochre and climbed back up the ladder to my six foot high Madonna. We were cheek to cheek as I dabbed the yellow ochre under each eye and down her face. Caresses, my caresses of affection, the paint brush was like my palm cradling her face in my hand. The yellow ochre blended with the damp white paint, still moist on her cheeks like the morning dew, and it all smoothed out evenly. I stopped and rested my elbow on top of the ladder. Almost perfect. Her black hair fell down to her bare, creamy shoulders, the top of her breasts mounding up from the hot, low-cut red dress I painted her in. One of her hands held a white rose-petaled fan to her lips, the other hand held the hem of her dress out to the side, suggesting any tiny movement would reveal great legs.

*"And life is a beautiful thing, as long as I hold the string,
I'd be a silly so and so if I should ever let go."*

Now the finishing touch, cadmium red blended smoothly, but just a dot on each cheek bone. *My goddess,* I thought, *sure as hell ain't no whore in thick make-up.* Just a kiss of cadmium red would give her the life glow she deserved. Spiritual, sensual, my Madonna would be absolutely revered.

I hopped off the ladder and went to my paint cans, pushing open the back door and peering up the short steps into the alley. A cold September wind gushed from 52nd Street, spewing tin cans and newspapers along the bricks. For a second I thought I saw someone scrunched down behind some egg crates, thought I saw the glimmer of a white Panama hat. The only guy I knew who wore a Panama hat was scuzzball Joey The Pimp, a punk kid from my neighborhood always with his grubby fingers into grubby business, but a creep like him wouldn't be up here in the high class district. Joey was always scrounging in some alley alright, making trouble up and down my block on Third Street for years. I didn't care if it was Joey or cared what he was up to. I wasn't gonna let a jerk like Joey "The Pimp" Rotollo spoil my day. Not on this day. This was my Consummation Diva Day.

An 8 by 10 manilla envelope suddenly blew into the alley. Perfect! I grabbed it and scurried back inside the joint. I used the envelope as a palette, pouring on a few more drops of cadmium red and mixing in just a touch of the ocher to give it a hint of orange.

"But I don't just mix colors," I said out loud, "Hell, I am a *painter.*"

This had to be true, Alex said I could be a great painter, and he knew talent.

Alexander Chertov was a well-known set designer in the Yiddish Theater, and in the 1920's the Yiddish Theater was booming. I lived on East Third Street, just half a block from Second Avenue where all the great Yiddish Theaters hung their marquees, and we'd see the actors and playwrights and producers frots up and down the block every day. The Café Royale, where they'd all kibitz and nosh, was right in my neighborhood. "Royal" was right. The Yiddish theater people, great Russian and German Jewish intellectuals, classic stage actors, directors, producers and artists, were practically royalty to us poor shmos in the tenements. There were dozens of comedies and dramas every week, and we flocked to the theaters whenever we could. Alex had worked with some of the top set designers, too, like Boris Aronson who became a big Broadway designer, and Joseph Urban who designed opera houses and palaces all over Europe. So Alex knew what he was doing, and if he liked me, I must be okay.

"We will work like Joe Urban," Alex had told me in his thick Russian accent, "little strokes of the brush like Van Gogh. This will create magnificent scenery."

At first, Alex had hired me just to be an errand boy, some chump to run back and forth to the basement under David Kessler's Second Avenue Theater, bringing him his paints on stage. But on my first day of work, I brought in some of the posters I'd made to decorate the Colonial Friends social club in my neighborhood, big 3 by 4 foot cardboards with my paintings of young girls and boys embraced on a dance floor, or scenes of lovers in a moon-lit forest. He was impressed.

"You are too good just to fetch and mix the colors. You will paint with me."

For Kessler's next vaudeville show, Alex had me size the flats, giant wooden frames with canvas stretched tight over them. To make the sizing, I boiled pans of water with pieces of chipped glue until it got good and sticky, and with a wide brush gave the flats a good shmear. When they were dry, I'd sit back and watch the master. Alex, looking so intellectual with his high, furrowed forehead and close-cropped black beard, would take a long bamboo stick with charcoal on the end, and proceed to outline the details for the backdrop. You don't need a lot of details in painting scenery, with the proper lighting everything should look great. But Alex was a stickler for details. To him everything had life, a tree "moved," buildings moved, sidewalks moved. To him everything had a flow. He wanted to honor even a tree with detail. A little crazy, but I got the hang of it. We'd fill deep saucers with dozens of paints, dry temperas mixed with glue-size, every color in the book. The first time I picked up a brush, dipped it into a saucer of burnt sienna and ran it over Alex's charcoal outlines, I knew I was working with a master. Whether he was creating a city skyline, a Russian village, or even a farm field, you felt you were part of the backdrop, like you could jump right into that field and roll in the hay. He was a master alright, it was like working with Picasso. What an inspiration!

And if that wasn't enough, I got to see great shows at Kessler's for free. I could stand in the wings or sit up high where the drops and curtains were fastened with heavy sandbags and see everything. It was 1924, vaudeville was at its peak, and Kessler brought in the biggest acts in the business. He had been a big wig actor in the Yiddish theater and was now a big wig vaudeville producer. Every great singer, comedian, musician, family act, magician, acrobat, juggler or trained seal played Kessler's. Fanny Brice, Bert Lahr, W.C. Fields, Eddie Cantor, Sarah Bernhardt, Nora Bayes, Phil Silvers, I saw them all, and not only the shows, I saw plenty of chorus girls, too. Some of those dolls would change from costumes to naked right in front of me. This was great and a heck of a lot better than sweating upstairs in Kessler's farshtinkener projection booth everyday where I'd been a crummy projectionist, threading movie reels in the dark for two years. But if it wasn't for that lousy job, I never would have met Alex.

I was fourteen years old when I got the projectionist job. At first, the job wasn't so lousy, not with getting to see free movies all day long. In my neighborhood, the silent movie theaters were your second home. We were absolutely nuts about the movies, for one thing, the tickets were cheaper than stage shows, just a nickel. You couldn't wait for flyers and posters to announce the next coming attraction. When I was a kid I caught every picture show on the Lower East Side. Every week hundreds of us kids would try everything we could to sneak into balconies to catch a show. I saw everything, all the Lasky studio silent movies with Mary Pickford and Douglas Fairbanks, everything with Charlie Chaplin, Buster Keaton, Harold Lloyd, Jackie Coogan, Keystone Kops, and absolutely everything with Lon Chaney. But I must have seen Fairbanks in *The Thief Of Baghdad* a dozen times. I loved seeing him soar through the clouds on his magic carpet, what a thrill! To me, every movie was like being on a magic carpet cause every movie transported me like magic somewhere else. For a few hours I could gaze into the dreamy eyes of Greta Garbo or watch cowboys and Indians fight it out in the western desert, or sail to a south sea island, or dine in the palaces of Europe, or sit at the steps of the Taj Mahal and completely forget about the infested rat trap of my neighborhood slum.

On Sundays, the movie people let you bring your lunch to the theater, but all the different immigrant kids with all their strange nosh would stink up the place big time. Sausages and salamis and potatoes and sauerkraut and stinky cheeses, who could have an appetite? The whole place reeked. Then the guy with the "schpritzer," a flit gun with some perfumed water, would go up and down the aisles, fumigating the joint. He had to. Between the stink of lunches, the leftover garbage and the smell of every tyke who pished or shaysed in his pants, it stunk worse than the city dump. The popcorn guy would come next, and some joker would stick out his leg and popcorn would go flying A hundred of us crazed kids then scrambled for free popcorn like it was gold. We ate it right off the floor. What a madhouse! There was never a dull moment at the picture shows. And though they may have been nonstop chaos, to me it was a nonstop carnival and a never-ending paradise. Who wouldn't want a job workin' in the movies?

So I asked my pal Louie From Fourth Street if he could swing a deal. Louie From Fourth Street, just fourteen years old like me, had been lucky to land a small part in one of Kessler's vaudeville shows. In those days, David Kessler's Second Avenue Theater showed silent movies as well as vaudeville and Yiddish classic stage shows.

Louie said to me, "Meet me at the exit door, Charlie, at the top balcony. I'll leave it unlocked."

Right before the afternoon show, I climbed the fire escape up to the exit door, and Louie let me in. "The picture's almost over, Charlie," Louie whispered. "I gotta get back stage and get my make-up on. Go talk to the projectionist, he also is the lighting guy. I think he needs an assistant," and Louie took off down the stairs.

Did I really want this job? The balcony smelled awful. Every little kid in the neighborhood must have sneaked into the balcony to take a leak, and the guy with the shpritzer obviously never made it up there. The smell of stale pee was suffocating. At the end of the dark, dingy aisle I found the dark, dingy projection room, and I could see why the lighting guy needed an assistant. Five minutes before curtain, and instead of getting the spotlights and gels ready for the stage show, the shmo was making out with his girlfriend.

I tapped on the glass window. "Hey, my friend Louie in the show says you need some help," I said, wondering if I'd ever get to assist with the kissing.

"In here kid," the guy said, looking up from his frumpy blonde, gooey spit all over his face. He leered at the babe and tried to act all suave like he was Mr. Casanova when he stood up from the chair. How the guy could think he was suave when his face looked like it had sloshed through a pig trough was anybody's guess. I don't know how the heck I kept from bustin' out laughing. But I figured it wasn't such a good idea to laugh at your boss. At least, not on the first day of work.

"I'll give ya the list of cues," he said, the slime around his upper lip and chin shimmering in the dark. "It's easy. If you can read."

He grabbed a handful of the blonde's big boob, opened the door to the booth, and held out to me some crumpled papers.

"I can read," I snapped, entering the smelly booth and snatching up the mangled script.

"At the end of some of the dialogue there's a note to change the gel from red to blue or yellow, or whatever. A moron can do it." He thrust a pile of colored gelatin sheets at me. "Just stick them into the lamp and turn it on. There ain't nothin' to it."

He planted another sloppy kiss on the blonde and led her out of the projection room with his hand glued to her ass. "Wait for the warning bell after the movie," he said over his shoulder, then he and the blonde disappeared.

I sat down on a leather stool, still warm from the blonde's hot tuchis, and waited. I thought, *what a cinch, I can do this easy.* Peering through the glass window past the empty balcony and down toward the stage, I saw *"THE END"* come up in huge white letters on the big black screen. The movie was over and the curtain slowly closed, blanketing the stage. A piercing bell clanged in my booth and I jumped, knocking the colored gels to the floor. From below, the house lights came on and a small orchestra in the pit started playing some jazzy music. I frantically picked up the gels and tried to figure out the script. Thank God, it was pretty straight forward. I rushed over to the two big carbon arc lamps pointing toward the stage. The clunky Kliegl No. 5, a piece of junk from the 1890's, swallowed the yellow gel I hurriedly fed it, but nothing happened.

"Music, yellow spot," the script read. Okay, now what?

Still nothing. The music continued from below, then the house lights dimmed and the curtain started to open on the darkened stage. I panicked. What was wrong? I punched myself and realized there must be a switch on this ancient flashlight. I finally found the button and clicked it on. Nothing. I clicked and clicked while down on stage, Yetta Swerling, a buxom songbird from my neighborhood launched into singing *"Lover, Lover of Mine,"* in Yiddish and in complete darkness, and the whole first floor audience was laughing. Howling.

The make-out artist ran back into the projection room still with goo on his face, but now his shirt and fly were open too. "It's okay kid, they think it's part of the act."

He fiddled with some cords. Yetta kept warbling like a canary in a hooded birdcage and people still screamed with laughter, when finally a yellow beam, all twenty-five amps, shot to the stage. Everyone cheered. I got a standing ovation.

Jeeze, I thought, *they're clappin'! They're clappin for me! Heck, I could do this forever!*

There ain't no business like show business, except maybe the gangster business, and in my neighborhood your best choice for making it big was one of those two. But me? Forget it. Get mixed up with gangsters? Like Joey "The Pimp" Rotollo? Fat chance. Yep, I'd stay in show biz forever.

Miss Wilson   *1915*

She rose from her desk with a start and hurried to the window. On the sidewalk below, another angry brawl was erupting on East Third Street, this one sounding particularly ugly. Corralling ashen curls having escaped the tight bun at the back of her neck, fifty-nine year old gaunt and graying Miss Wilson raised the glass and strained to get a better look from her second story office at the Music School Settlement House. Her knees squeezed into the cold, hard ridges of the steel radiator clamped beneath the window, bright red grooves hollowing the skin behind her thin, gingham blue dress, but she had to see just who was fighting this time. Not even the early morning's golden mist of Spring, illuminating a host of chimney tops, glistening above the city like birthday candles could contradict what was happening below. It was only eight o'clock and already the rosy-fingered dawn had clenched its fist.

After fifteen years on the Lower East Side, Miss Wilson had witnessed so many bruising fist fights, she was almost immune to the screaming, shattering windows and sirens. The small town, Finger Lake library she had relinquished in order to serve destitute immigrant families in the city seemed more than fifteen years away. It seemed like a century since she departed from the stone-walled, picket-fenced, pine-covered calm of Newton Falls. But she had to leave. Nothing was left for her there save the monthly wreaths of white carnations posed on her parents' tombstones, and no one left behind save for tediously numbing children demanding only occasional assistance with a book report, none of them her own children. The likelihood of spawning her own remained, at best, remote. Although she could not claim great beauty, yet defied homeliness, the fact she'd turned prematurely gray at age twenty-two did not help her quest for a mate. And though she'd unregrettably sacrificed friendships for dedication to career, ever bound to her Yankee sense of duty, she certainly had not renounced the idea of matrimony. Nonetheless, she soon began to detect empathetic stares of pity when shopping at Fletcher's Five and Dime or at the A&P, while the eligible young men, even older men, of Newton Falls, continued to move on. For twenty more years she endured their piteous glances and an empty bed. But the day Mr. Fletcher's teenage grandson rang up her bag of bobby pins, bicarbonate, toilet water and Sen-Sen with a *"thank you Ma'am"* and *"can I help you with that heavy bag?"* as if she were one step from a nursing home, was both symbol and symptom. Hence, after spotting the "Librarian Wanted" ad in the *New York Times* she resolved that the withering of Miss Wilson must come to an end. The irony, however, in leaving Newton Falls had not gone unnoticed. From day one at the Music School, forty-three years old and spouse-less, Miss Wilson had noted, with wry observation, how she'd abandoned her search for a young man up-state, only to find a plethora in downtown Manhattan.

"You goddam schmuck! I know you took my dough! Where's my money?"

"Vos art es mikh?"

"You fuckin' shtik drek! I said where is it?"

"Zol ikh azoy visn fun tsores!"

"Zolst es shtupa in tokhes! Shove it up your ass!"

Miss Wilson watched two scuffling teenage boys tumbling down the steps to a basement apartment, yanking out clumps of curly black hair, shoving fists into teeth, knees into groins, their immigrant screams barely decipherable, but at least they were boys unknown to her. Too many other Third Street boys she did know, sweet decent boys, had metamorphosed from butterflies into angry bees, from delicately fluttering to savagely swarming the neighborhood. It was enough to make her weep. Indeed, Miss Wilson had wept a thousand tears in fifteen years.

"Fuckin' mamzer! You bastard!"

Anguished mothers, apron strings flying, poured from the apartments above, raced to the street and pulled the brawling boys apart, not soon enough, however, to prevent two butchered broken noses.

"Screw you!"

Miss Wilson sprang from the window. This latter scream had blasted from her own library. She bolted out her tiny office.

"What on earth are you thinking? This is a *library*!" she hissed, spying only the backs of three dark-haired hooligans sprinting away from the roomful of undeterred children immersed in Zane Gray, sleeping by the blazing stone fireplace or tackling their Hebrew lessons. One of the impudent hooligans actually leapt over a little girl sitting on the floor Indian-style, scanning pictures in the Encyclopedia Britannica volume "D." The girl was almost kicked in the head. Fortunately, the hooligan's high-jump hurdle left her unscathed, though the same could not be said for Miss Wilson's immaculately catalogued reference shelf which rudely discharged Britannica volumes "F" through "M."

"Looks like they got away," chirped a little red-haired boy sitting alone at a table, scrawling pictures in black crayon on plain sheets of newsprint.

"Maybe this time, Charlie, but certainly never again! Did you know those boys?"

"Nope. Just one. Joey Somebody."

"Well," huffed Miss Wilson, tightening her barrettes and reorganizing her book case. "We just can't have it. This kind of behavior is inexcusable. If you find out who those boys were, you must tell me."

"Yep."

Assured she had re-seized control of her dominion, Miss Wilson smoothed back exasperated wisps of gray hair and began to march back to her office, when her curiosity flickered down to the five year-old Charlie Stark, the epitome of a non-hooligan, clutching two fat black crayons, so deeply absorbed in his picture.

"Charlie, is that the city skyline you're drawing?"

"Yeah, my brother tore out a picture from his newspaper so I could copy it."

Behind him, Charlie's older brother Harry and his Jewish pals wrestled with *khof* and *kof.*

"I usually see you here in the afternoons, Charlie, not so early in the morning. Are you also studying Hebrew?"

"No ma'am, I'm just in kindergarten."

Almost every afternoon, Miss Wilson had noticed Charlie in her library, outfitted in his dog-eared pair of scruffy boots, faded brown knickers, and stained shirt, lounging in the big Morris chair by the fireplace, sometimes thumbing through a Tarzan adventure book or *Robinson Crusoe* or Grimm's fairy tales, though she couldn't imagine he was already reading at age five. Sometimes she'd see him just sitting quietly by the fire, taking in the older boys' conversation, then peacefully falling asleep. It was obvious Charlie considered her library his second home, as did countless other boys and girls throughout the neighborhood. Very early into her fifteen years at the Music School, Miss Wilson learned their original mission of offering musical instruction and a bit of culture to wanting immigrant families had veered far off its course. Miss Wilson, and the other teachers and staff who lived at the school, simply had no choice but to engage in a perpetual effort to mitigate every squalid dimension of immigrant life on the Lower East Side. The school provided employment counseling, housing information and medical care. They constructed a playground on their roof, they established a summer camp in New Jersey simply to prove to the children trees really did exist. They even provided an occasional bath. The ties between Miss Wilson and so many neighborhood families, mostly Jewish and Italian and a few Polish and Hungarian, had become as personal as if they were part of her own family. And it was impossible to avoid the personal life of Charlie and his family, floundering in their postage stamp flat directly across from her Third Street office window.

Charlie's two parents and his eight siblings existed in just a two-room apartment. Miss Wilson believed, only by the grace of God, could the Starks, as well as the other neighborhood fertile families, maintain survival. With a herd of children, a chronically ill son and a husband who could only obtain wages by peddling trifling commodities from a pushcart, she deemed Mrs. Stark an absolute magician, conjuring up a happy family foundation seemingly out of a hat. The healthy Stark children endlessly scoured the neighborhood for whatever pennies they could earn and contribute to the family income, pennies that were few and far between.

But the Starks were no different from the Rosens nor the Rotollos, the Bernsteins and the Bonatuccis, the Moskowitzes and the Martellis, and all the other layers upon layers of families, teeming from the hundred year old decrepit tenements, bearing insufferable and constant cacophonies, inhaling the collective fumes of every sausage, meatball, pot of sauerkraut and bloated hallway toilet night and day, anguishing over the decision to purchase food for the family or medicine for the family, and forever scrounging for the most demeaning employment with barely a nickel left over for the endless diapers to swathe the bottoms of endless infants. Miss Wilson guessed her Music School library, quiet, uncluttered, with its cozy fireplace and vast reserve of adventures, fiction and non-fiction, must have seemed like paradise.

"My brother gave me some crayons and paper today so I wouldn't get bored," Charlie added, "but I never get bored here at the Music School."

Miss Wilson studied Charlie's extraordinary drawing. In black crayon, he had drawn an exact likeness of the Woolworth building and its surrounding structures, shown within the newspaper photograph. Disregarding the photo's washed out shading and dim contrast, Charlie's drawing was an exact image. With his little black crayon, Charlie had even been able to depict the building's Gothic ornamentation.

"This is very, very good, Charlie. You must draw a lot of pictures."

"Yes, Ma'am." He pulled out a ragged, folded newspaper he'd been sitting on. The newspaper was riddled with Hebrew characters and crayon lines. "I keep my pictures in my Pop's old Yiddish newspaper."

Charlie unfolded the paper, and out popped a quirky collection of animal drawings, cartoons, caricatures of his siblings and neighborhood pals, an assortment of Model T's, copies of newspaper ads and photographs, all drawn in black crayon, and an odd array of colored abstracts.

"What are these?" Miss Wilson asked, studying the latter, multi-colored designs.

"My teachers tear out patterns from wallpaper books, and they give me colored crayons to copy them during recess."

"Remarkable, Charlie, quite remarkable."

Miss Wilson examined and re-examined each of Charlie's

astonishing pictures. She wondered if she'd ever observed a more creative child.

"Child!" she suddenly remembered from thirty-eight years back in Newton Falls, "stop that doodling! You were supposed to help me snap these beans!" In a not-forgotten yet buried space in the far reaches of her mind, as if filed in the "W's" under "waste," Miss Wilson saw a pig-tailed, thin girl, clutching the stub of a lead pencil. The girl was drawing flowers on paper grocery bags, finely detailed stalks, leaves, stamens and pistils of tiger lilies, daisies, chrysanthemums and jonquils growing along the edge of her back porch, poking up between the wringer-washer and the wheel barrow in the yard, and encircling the base of the towering blue spruce behind their family well. "You finish the beans, Dora," her father was saying to his wife, "the Child must do her figures. Off the porch now! Enough with these foolish pictures, and get to your arithmetic!"

Consciously and unconsciously, Miss Wilson acknowledged this ancient subjugation with the bud of an idea beginning to germinate. "Charlie, is an old newspaper the safest place to keep your portfolio?"

"What's a profolio?"

"A portfolio, Charlie, is a valuable collection. Come with me."

"Am I in trouble?"

"On the contrary, my boy, you are in luck."

The hooligans notwithstanding, saturating her neighborhood, her school, her own library, here was one boy she would manage. Under her watchful, hawkish eye, Charlie Stark, she resolved, would in no circumstances become a hooligan. Though her womb had spawned no child, her library had fostered a thousand progenies and a thousand opportunities for maternal fulfillment, but in fifteen years, there were few triumphs. Yet, with Charlie, she vowed, she would not fail. She'd already failed to mold one other regular afternoon attendee, the once bright-eyed Willy Pearlman who'd grown into the dead-eyed Willy the Red. And the Kaplan boys, she remembered, who had once sat by the hearth contentedly listening to her readings of Jack London now emulated Jack The Ripper. They had grown into jackals. They'd sold their souls for a chance at easy money. Now they wielded knives and guns in gangs, and far too often traded their infested tenements for infested prison cells or the cemetery. Books, Miss Wilson so frequently bewailed in the privacy of her small Music School apartment, were impotent weapons indeed compared to the arsenals of jackals. Books had done nothing to sway Nathan Kaplan in particular, now serving seven at Sing Sing prison. But she would not let this happen again, especially to Charlie. She would not let this one get away. Though the Music School could not offer classes in art, at the very least, she herself would offer Charlie an arena, pencils and paper, and more importantly the advocacy, an advocacy that had eluded a child on that long-ago Newton Falls porch, whose paper bag pictures were reduced to wrapping compost.

Miss Wilson led the boy to her office and emptied out the bottom desk drawer. "You may house your drawing in here, Charlie, to keep them clean and secure. Until that is, we can find you a proper valise."

"Gee thanks!"

"Any pictures you draw, Charlie, whether sketched in our library, at school, anywhere at all, I want you to come in at your leisure and store them right here in this drawer. Is that a deal?"

"Deal!" Charlie dropped the folded newspaper-load of pictures into the drawer and took off running. "I gotta go tell Harry!"

But before she could savor the possibilities of fostering her latest charge, beneath her open window, Miss Wilson heard yet again, the distinctive quake of her neighborhood and the smashing of glass.

"Ya touch me one more time, Frankie Rotollo, and I'm gonna stick this broken bottle right in you and your little brother's fat fuckin' face! Rape! *Mama!*"

"Jackals!" Miss Wilson hissed. She slammed down the window, resolving only to think of Charlie Stark whom she would nurture and protect from the persuasions of neighborhood wolves no matter what.

She marched straight back into her library and returned to the grind of the Dewey Decimal System. But, utterly confounded, she wondered how in fifteen years at the Music School, her thinly paned office window, looming just two floors above the jackals, somehow, remarkably, had remained unbroken.

Joey   *1932*

Wiping the splatter of blood from his lips, Joey "The Pimp" Rotollo reached to the pavement and snatched up his winnings. He pocketed the crinkled ten dollar bill, kicking aside the bleeding torso of a headless rat and its oozing, furry skull he'd just gnawed. He shot another crocodile sneer at his hooker and her John who raced away holding their stomachs. The audacious brown man in the brown suede coat, presuming to be Joey's client, had also raced away, having witnessed the bloody atrocity on the corner. Several other repulsed pedestrians crossed to the other side of Allen Street, but some continued on, having paid zero attention to the scruff in the Panama hat in the first place. Yet one man in a flashy new, blue pin-stripe suit chose to engage.

"Still playin' games, huh Joey? Why ain't ya in knickers?"

Joey grabbed the headless rat body, and shook its damp red fur at Charlie Stark before he could hurry away. " 'Want some supper, Christ Killer?"

"You go ahead. I know how ya love those rat sandwiches," said Charlie, and he coolly strolled on, holding back his own gagging reflex, refusing to give Joey a second of satisfaction. Though on one hand, he almost wished he could feel sorry for the guy. When they were kids, Charlie once saw Joey sitting on his rump in the hallway outside the Rotollo's apartment, finger painting in cat pee. And the Rotollos were so poor, Charlie'd heard rumors they were actually collecting the alley cats and eating them. Charlie knew everyone on Third Street was miserably poor, including his own family, but he hadn't known anyone on the block more wretched than Joey's family. On the other hand, it was no excuse. The guy was a creep. If you saw Joey on the block at night, you made damn sure your sister was safe in the house. Besides, this wasn't the first time, Charlie'd seen Joey spitting out rats' heads just to make pocket change. Who could feel sorry for a maniac? Charlie couldn't walk away fast enough.

Joey tossed the half-rat into the gutter and watched the detestable Charlie Stark saunter away. The ten dollar bill crunched into his pants pocket hardly seemed worth it anymore. Not with that cocky Jew boy showing him up, filching his cut from Joe Masseria. *If only I hadn't broken my fuckin' knife,* Joey simmered, *I'd show the Jew bastard it's me that rules Third Street.* Just like he'd shown those shits on Stanton the night before.

"You pimpin' now, Joey?"

"Yeah, he can only *sell* the broads cause the dumb fuck can't ever lay one himself."

"How many pennies does Joe Masseria let ya keep, kid?"

Savoring last night's sweet memory, Joey believed those smart asses, the Kike, the Polack, even that Wop from his own building, had caught on fast not to mess with him, when they each had caught the tip of his knife as part of their education. *Too bad Jew Charlie wadn't there, he'd've caught one too.* But he will soon, Joey thought, watching the back of Charlie's pin-stripes mosey away down Allen Street. He watched the Jew's fancy cigar spewing cocky clouds of smoke up to the street lights. *Ya can walk away from me now, pal, but you and me's gonna get real close,* Joey sizzled, sinister wheels spinning through his brain. *'Think I'll get me a new shiv and leave a couple of flashy new scars on your mug to match your flashy new suit.*

Joey stroked the two jagged seams of rough skin that marked his own face. "Yeah real close. So close, you sucker," he whispered, "people might think we's brothers."

Charlie   *1932*

I stayed at Kessler's running his projection booth for two years. After the first year, I quit school, right after eighth grade. Why not? I was making real good dough. Eight bucks a week was big money to me. I gave most of it to my mom and pop. Lots of guys did that. And my poor family needed all the extra dough we could get. I still had time before and after the job for a little art work, I couldn't give that up. I'd been drawing and making pictures since I could walk. I'd even made a few bucks drawing posers for a few shops and social clubs. I still had plenty of time to see girls, too. I sure as heck wasn't giving them up, and the book learnin', well, I could always get that lounging in my favorite, cozy Morris chair at the Music School library right across from my building. Who needed school?

Like I said, seeing hundreds of movies for free wasn't bad neither. All the silent movies I'd seen ten times a month, I now saw ten times a day. But the biggest thrill was getting to see bigger than life, my heartthrob Lillian Gish. What a doll! I practically swooned every time I saw her light up the screen. How could I not with those haunting, big brown eyes? She was gorgeous, the greatest actress around. Her cousin lived in my neighborhood, and I thought for certain I'd get to meet her. It didn't matter Lillian was seventeen years older than me. I figured I'd waltz her over to the Café Royale all suave and debonair, just like Douglas Fairbanks or Rudolph Valentino. We'd hob-nob with the hoity-toity theater crowd, I'd light her cigarette, we'd dine on pheasant and drink champagne out of tall thin glasses. And if I couldn't wine and dine Lillian, someday I'd wine and dine some other classy doll in a fancy joint. Watching Kessler's movies all day long made me feel like I could be anyone or be anywhere. Sometimes I didn't know if I lived on East Third Street or with Greta Garbo at the Taj Mahal.

I also fell completely overboard, hook line and sinker for the silent cartoons. When I was a kid, I couldn't go a day without combing the gutters for a paper to read *Happy Hooligan, Mutt and Jeff, Boob McNutt, The Yellow Kid, Krazy Kat* or the *Katzenjammer Kids*. But when the animated comics started popping up in theaters I went nuts.

Gruberman, the head projectionist with his lips always in a pucker for broads, I never even learned his first name, knew some of the guys doing the animation. He said Winsor McCay and his boys made 4000 drawings for his *Little Nemo in Slumberland* cartoon, even more for his *Gertie The Dinosaur*. Paul Terry was cranking out Terrytoons, there was Felix The Cat, we even started getting cartoons from Kansas City of all places. Some hick named Disney was making something he called "Laugh-o-Grams."

Fabulous stuff, all of it, the cartoons were absolutely the greatest. So one afternoon, Gruberman grabbed what I thought was a new cartoon. "Wait'll you see this, Charlie," he grinned mysteriously, slapping on the reel and dimming the house lights. But live action started up, some artist was sitting at his drafting board, his pen in an ink well. Then the camera moved in on a close-up of his hand on the paper. He was drawing a cartoon clown, when all of a sudden the clown popped off the paper and stood in the room as big as the artist himself. It was my first glimpse of Koko The Clown, absolutely amazing live action and animation combined. I flipped.

"The Fleischer boys are doin; these," Gruberman said.

I was tongue-tied, couldn't speak a word. A cartoon was shaking hands with a real man! In the dark, I could almost feel the flickering black and white cartoon Koko dancing right across my face. I'd never seen anything so clever in my whole life.

"They got a patent for some stupid machine that does this stuff," Gruberman added, all matter of fact, like he was just describing some run of the mill butter churn. "Dave Fleischer dressed up like the clown and then his brother Max somehow traced him on the film. But I don't see it goin' nowheres."

"How do I meet these guys?" I finally was able to ask, my eyes glued to the screen.

"Beats me, but who cares?" Gruberman said, lighting up a smoke. "They been working at J.R. Bray's, but I hear they're goin' out on their own. I still don't see no cartoons havin' no shelf life. They're just a flash in the pan."

Goin' out on their own, I thought. All these guys doing fantastic, creative art, crazy cartoons, live-action cartoons, clever as hell, it was wild, incredible. Even some hick from Kansas City was creating sensations, and there I was, stuck like a shlub, changing reels, threading reels, running spotlights, running around a cold balcony that smelled like piss, and covering the ass of Gruberman who hardly did a thing but sleep and make-out with dames.

Gruberman snuffed out his cig and strolled away from the booth, leaving me with Koko, who just leered at me as if to say *"Sucker!"* and he danced off the screen.

I changed the reel for the afternoon feature film with my stomach in a knot. I was wasting away in a farshtinkener projection booth. As I threaded reel after reel after reel, I started feeling threaded to the damn reel myself like I was in prison chains. I could almost feel my head wrapped around the back reel spinning and spinning, my arms stretched tight and wrapped into the front reel with my legs dangling wildly over the lens. I could see the light projecting my flapping legs right onto the screen. My hands went to my neck, I could hardly breathe. I thought I was having some kinda heart attack. The stench of stale popcorn and pee and rancid soft drinks floated up from the audience. And even when my all-time favorite, Lillian Gish appeared on the screen, I couldn't see nothin', not with Koko The Clown dancing in my head, still staring right at me yelling *"Sucker!"* I even forgot to turn up the house lights after the movie until people started screaming.

"Turn on the lights!!"

Some jerk threw a half-full root beer bottle at me, and the whole booth became a disgusting mess of broken glass and sticky soda. But the crummy booth was always a stinkin' mess. Hell, and so was my life. Nothin' but a goddam mess. So what I could watch free movies all day? I was nothin' but a friggin' robot. There was absolutely not one damn creative thing about changing metal reels in the dark and cleaning up the stinkin' mess of slobs. I had talent, goddam it! But there I was, buried in a morgue full of root beer.

Dragging myself over the broken glass to fetch a mop, I saw below the crowd filing out of the theater, then here came Alex Chertov, pulling back the curtain to finish his set for the new act coming to Kessler's that night. Alex had a bucket of paint and a brush, and went to touch up the backdrop where he'd painted a big beautiful library scene. Now that guy had talent.

Suddenly, a big bright window opened in the morgue. Butterflies flew in, flowers, fresh air and perfume. I could breathe again! My brain clicked on like the spotlight, and a huge neon sign flashed right inside my head. *Working on the stage would be a helluva lot better than working above the stage.*

I quickly cleaned up the glass and root beer then hurried downstairs. I'd convince Alex Chertov he needed an assistant. I'd convince him I could make that library look so real you'd want to pull a book right off the canvas, sit on the stage and read. I had to convince him, I was going nuts. More important, I was going nowhere. My life was about making art, not about watching other shmos make art. I was an artist, not a machinist. What was I thinking? For two years I'd sacrificed my art for a damn machine. But that was over with a capital "O." Alex Chertov, hell the whole world, was gonna know Charlie Stark.

Mama   *1917*

Clara Schwartz Stark removed her wig. She placed it neatly onto a pile of graying tissue paper inside a wooden hat box, covered the chocolate brown hairpiece with another layer of tissue, positioned the lid, then shoved the box under her bed. From atop the bed, she removed a cast iron skillet and crossed the room to store it away in a free-standing oak cupboard, but not before smoothing her hand over the cotton sheet lest one tiny wrinkle should remain. She placed the skillet on the shelf with the cooking pots, plates, saucers, and tea cups, then bent to pluck a faded, yellow silk scarf from a pile of skirts and blouses off the cupboard's bottom shelf. She wrapped the scarf around her long, thick, auburn hair, tying a firm knot to the back of her neck, the folded edge of the scarf plastered tightly to her forehead, not a hair out of place nor dangling onto her pale, freckled cheek bones.

At the enameled white, iron sink next to the cupboard, Clara wrung out the final drops off a soaking rag mop, crossed the room again to the one window, opened it wide and lay the head of the wet strings to dry on the sill.

"It's a butterfly!'

"No it ain't! It's a bee!"

"Is so!"

"It ain't!"

Clara peered out the window, one story down to the alley below, expecting to see the wayward Rotollo boys from down the street, up to their usual mischief. Only yesterday she'd spotted them in the alley, all three of them, playing "doctor," with an unsuspecting three year old girl.

"What a schlemiel! Bee's got stingers!"

"Sha!" Clara yelled, but at her own children playing in the alley. "Ya think ya don't got a sick brother asleep up here? Sha!"

She watched her four year-old son Benny and his three year-old sister Loretta dash away with the Freiberg twins from down the hall. She had long given up admonishing her children for playing in the filthy alley behind their building. Her children called it "the yard," but to Clara it was nothing but a receptacle for every foul piece of garbage thrown from the windows above.

Gevalt, she sighed, spying all four children leaping over wooden egg crates at full gallop. *They will break their necks! If I don't break them first!* But she was relieved to account for the whereabouts of at least two of her eight children, which at any given time was a considerable challenge. Clara counted off on each finger. Hymie, Moe, and Harry, she believed were off to their Saturday boys' club at the Music School Settlement House across the street. Baby Eva she had to retrieve from the care of Mrs. Freiberg. *Two and three is five and one is six*, she counted. Turning from the window, she stepped quietly into the doorway of the apartment's only bedroom. In there was child number seven, her son Louie, thankfully still asleep, his six year-old infested, frail lungs rasping softly in quick menacing rhythms. Clara tip-toed away from her slumbering sickly boy, and closed his door. *Butterflies and bees! Okh un vey!* she scoffed, and went to attend the chicken she'd just bought from Breines the butcher. From the one table in an apartment that served as kitchen, bathroom and toilet, she grabbed the small chicken tied in wax paper and string, removed its wrappings, and suddenly realized that living surrounded by brick and pavement on East Third Street, she hadn't seen a butterfly in sixteen years. Not since her husband, Sam, had carted her off to the train station in Jassy, Romania had she scarcely seen a blade of grass. Clara shrugged her shoulders, and tugged at four white chicken feathers stuck between the leg and thigh. *No wonder the kids play in the farshtinkener alley*, she sighed, *maybe just for the sight of a piece of grass in the dirt.* The appearance of either butterfly or bee, she thought, would indeed be the subject of a worthy debate not in the least bit childish.

"Please Mama?" she remembered her son Charlie begging her. "I wanna keep it right here on the kitchen table so everyone can see it! Please, Mama!"

Clara remembered the time Charlie stormed through the front door like he'd found buried treasure. A little white butterfly, no bigger than a nickel, had somehow escaped the church cemetery on Second Street behind their building. Charlie had found a milk bottle in the alley and snatched up the butterfly when it had landed on a tiny tuft of grass growing at the base of the two-story brick wall separating their tenement from the church. He had stuffed the bottle with dirt and twigs and whatever grass he could pilfer from the cemetery, and cherished his butterfly for three glorious days until it shriveled up like a white raisin and died. It was not easy to acknowledge that the only place in the neighborhood to view a patch of green grass was in a place of death, and in a Christian place of death for that matter.

"The dead Christians, they get grass, us living Jews, we get cement," Clara now grumbled. She tried to shake the butterflies from her thoughts and reached inside the chicken

"Gonnif!" she suddenly yelped. "Breines the thief! Where are mein giblets?!" She scraped her hand along the slimy inner ribs and all around to the back of the bird, but it was entirely hollow. "Thief! Breines the thief!"

Back into its wrappings, she slammed down the chicken, furious there was no time to go back to Breines's and claim her chicken livers. Louie would surely wake soon, she had to fetch Eva from Freiberg, round up Benny and Loretta, then - "Mein Gott! Where is Charlie?"

She had absolutely no idea where her eighth child, her seven year-old boy, could possibly be. Not in the alley, maybe at the Music School? On the roof? In some farchadat movie theater? Not, God forbid, in a pool hall with the gangsters! It was just like Charlie to give her relentless quaking shpilkes every single afternoon, Clara never knowing if he were run over, lying at the bottom of the East River or sold into slavery. A nervous breakdown and heart attack would surely be inevitable, she agonized, ransacking through sheets of soaking, brown wax paper in search of giblets. Why did her most clever child have to be the most impossible? One afternoon she had to scour the entire Lower East Side until she found him dangling off the rolling roof at the Majestic Theater.

"Charlie Chaplin is worth your neck?" she had scolded, dragging him back to Third Street.

"But all the kids do it!" Charlie had whined. "Everybody sneaks up there! We can watch the picture shows for free!"

"Free is good! Living is better!" she'd said, and slapped his tuchis good.

But loud tapping at the front door now interrupted Clara's anxious, mental search for her son.

"Who is it?" Clara hollered, grabbing a hand towel to wipe off feathers and chicken fat.

"You should forget your sister was coming to call today at three o'clock? It's three o'clock!" came her sister Annie's voice behind the door.

"Come in already! It's open!"

Clara turned to the pot-belly stove consuming most of the apartment and grabbed a heavy tea kettle off the burner.

The door opened. Annie, short and thin, wearing a bright green wool suit tightly tapered at her small waist and sporting a matching green hat, walked silently into the little room.

"Looks nice," she finally said, but disingenuously, placing a brown sack on the table.

"I'll make the tea," Clara said curtly, filling the kettle at the sink.

Annie pulled a chair away from the table and sat. "Here's your *Manischewitz*. I couldn't get it by Shabbes," she said, inching the sack toward Clara. Annie removed her hat and made a few vain attempts to reposition her lush black wig, knowing full well it was both beautiful and perfect.

30

"No problem. We had grape juice last night."

Tap water surged in manic spurts down into the kettle, the faucet and kitchen pipes growling, moaning like a sick fog horn. Clara returned the kettle to the stove, lit a match, and swung to the cupboard where she seized two china cups, two saucers, spoons and a sugar bowl, and brought them to the table. "You want a cookie?"

"No, I'm watching the pounds."

Clara wrapped up the chicken and pushed it aside. For several long moments the two sisters exchanged no conversation. In the duration, Clara's thoughts were mostly focused on the whereabouts of Charlie, but they were also intent on dispelling the discomfort perpetually evoked by her sister's visits.

For Annie's part, it was one thing to shlep all the way from the Bronx to the filthy Lower East Side with crimulnik gangsters on every corner, but it was quite another thing all together to watch her own flesh and blood be mired in such squalor. Annie's eye circled the room. Standing next to the clattering sink and pipes, the doors to the cupboard could barely shut. It teemed with pots and plates and bowls and glasses, bottles and cans of all descriptions, innumerable piles of clothes and shoes. On the other side of the sink was a heavy oak ice box with a pine plank on top holding two wooden bowls of potatoes and onions and one carving knife. *One knife!* Annie scoffed to herself, *nothing but potatoes and onions! And that ice box is complete rust!* She scanned the rest of the jam-packed room lined with bursting shelves of household goods, linens and more clothes, openly sneering at the scratched and dented mahogany wardrobe, a rickety bed, and a small, stained porcelain commode. A fully loaded laundry line hung just inside the only window and led to the next equally teeming tenement across the alley. And the very table at which Annie sipped her orange pekoe was not a table at all, but just a faded green slab of linoleum slapped over a claw-foot bath tub. Conversely, quite irrelevant to Annie were the shining, pristine-clean black and white squares of tile under her feet, the crystal clear tea cup she brought to her lips, and that every single utensil, shirt and shoe in the acutely crowded apartment was immaculate and in its place.

"So nu? How are you?" Annie finally asked, folding her arms into an irritated clench.

"Fine. And why not?'

"I want to be getting right at my point, Haika," Annie announced. "Look at you!" and she waved her arms like a wand before her sister, a sister she believed had grown too plump from too many pregnancies.

"What look at me? I am fine, I tell you."

"Where is your wig?"

'In the box. Who needs a wig to pluck chicken?"

"My point," Annie grunted, a finger wagging, "is that I know what is going on here."

"Ah, you're meshugie," Clara said, but she plopped more than her usual one sugar cube into her tea. She plopped in four.

"Hah! I knew it! So many sugars? Last week you ate up half the challa I brought, before you could put it on your Shabbes table! You are pregnant again! I know it!"

Clara slapped her right hand on the table so hard the spoon jumped out of her cup. "Is nine children such a crime?"

Her left hand, however, slipped under the green linoleum table top, her palm cupping the soft expanded knoll of belly beneath the poof of her skirt, so warm and supple. And no matter what Annie or anyone could say, here she was growing the bud of her and Sam's passion, a bud that would surely bloom once again a great blossom, Clara believed, for all potential butterflies.

Joey   *1932*

Benny Weinberg's Eight Street Cabaret smoldered in a murky mix of stale cigarette smoke and the languid jingle of a jazz piano. It was a slow night. Autumn in New York had bequeathed the usual gush of showers, but this night's deluge had only channeled three customers through the door. Teddy Kratz and Herb Mendelman, each of them too old to appreciate the club's usual raucous bee-bop but too young to consider the grave, played cribbage at a small round table in front of the bar, gnawing crumbly cheesecake and slurping mugs of rice-brewed bootleg beer.

"Would ya watch it?" griped Herb. "Youse gettin' cheesecake in the peg holes!"

"Ain't I paid for it? Shaddup and deal," said Teddy, plucking crumbs from the cribbage board and sucking them off his fingers.

"Ya know, I like this kid," said Herb, jerking his thumb toward the piano player.

At the ivories, nineteen year-old Leonard Finkle stroked the sticky keys, dreaming of Carnegie Hall while pounding out honky tonk.

"Aww, he's just a punk. Benny'll be in Dutch plenty. The kid's under-age."

"What's this tune, Lenny?" Herb shouted. "I ain't never heard it from nowhere."

Teddy shoved the deck of cards across the table. "That's cause youse from nowhere, shmendrick. Would ya just do the cards?"

"What's the point? The cockamamie peg holes are all shaysed up with sour cream!"

Behind the bar, Arnie "Spigot" Cozinsky tugged a damp dish rag from the bottom of a high-ball glass, inspected it warily, then stuffed the rag back down to swab out two remaining drips. He accompanied Leonard's sultry piano.

"I gotta right to moan and sigh.
I gotta right to sit and cry.
Down around the river............"

"Spigot! Suds my mug!" shrilled a scruffy guzzler at the end of the bar.

"I know the deep blue sea
Will soon be callin' me...."

"Fifteen two, a pair is four, knobs is five and how the hell can I peg through cream cheese? Hey Spigot! What's the name of this song?"

"Herb! Forget the fuckin' song and play your crib!"

"It must be love, say what you choose.
I gotta right to sing the blues....!"
"Everybody shut the fuck up!" snapped the scruff, crashing his glass mug on the bar. "You too, Big Nose!" and he shook his fist at Leonard. "Gimme another fuckin' beer, Spigot, before I shove this goddam mug between your goddam eyeballs!"

Ruefully, Leonard wiped at the vast hunk of cartilage holding up his black-framed eyeglasses, and he raised his incomparable fingers off the keyboard.

"Awright awright," said Arnie, grabbing the windbag's empty glass. "I'll get your friggin' beer. But Lenny, you don't stop that piano playin', ya hear me?"

"See what I mean!" Teddy chided. "Youse causin' a tsimmis, and ya got gornish in your crib. Just gimme the deck!"

"I ain't causin' nothin'!" said Herb.

Arnie dabbed the dish rag at beads of sweat bubbling beneath his double chin, his beefy, bare forearm seizing a loop-handled rope at his feet. He pulled up a heavy trap door. From under the floor boards he snatched a dusty brown bottle, lowered the door, then chinked off the cap with an opener. Leonard returned his silky fingertips to the piano keys, Teddy and Herb licked their plates to a glittery blast of *"Four O'clock Jump,"* and Arnie loathingly passed a refilled, frothy mug of beer to Joey "The Pimp" Rotollo.

"That'll be two bits."

"Fuck you, Fatso." Joey slammed a coin on the counter and resumed excavating the grime beneath his fingernails with the glimmering tip of his new switchblade. Three solid days of gray smoggy rain had done nothing for the world's oldest profession nor for Joey's piece of the pie. *What's a goddam street walker without a goddam street in this fuckin' rain?* he glowetred, checking his watch. *And where's that mother fuckin' Hennigan?*

Joey had just twenty-two bucks, there quarters and four pennies buried in his pocket. Twenty-two bucks and seventy-nine cents were all he had to his name. But Johnny Hennigan owed him a hundred. He had bought one of Joey's dolls for a little party to woo prospective whiskey distributors, saying it was for big boss Owney Madden. Joey didn't care if it was for Franklin Roosevelt. If Hennigan was a no-show with his C note, he'd take care of Hennigan *and* Owney Madden. *I can handle these cock suckin' Irish Micks,* was Joey's typical refrain. Hennigan, already an hour late, might have been more punctual if he could see Joey trimming his fingernails with the razored edge of his knife, down to the quick until red and oozing, slicing into his own appendages like he was practicing for butchering, perhaps, a small animal. He needed that C note.

"Fifteen six and a double run is fourteen and I win, boychik!"

"Aww your tuchis is hangin' out!"

And I've just about had it with this Jew bar, Joey continued to boil, chewing off the crag of a hanging cuticle. The shard now clenched between his upper and lower front teeth, Joey began to gnaw menacingly as if the scrap of masticated skin were Hennigan himself.

The front door to Benny Weinberg's Eighth Street Cabaret then opened with a whoosh of wind and rain, and closed behind Charlie Stark.

"Hey Spigot! Where's Benny?" Charlie shouted to the bar, flapping a soaking wool topcoat and a saturated wool hat. "Jeeze, it feels like winter out there."

"No Benny and no customers neither, Charlie. You'd think we's havin' a blizzard or somethin' not just a little shpritz of rain."

"What about these two alter kakers? They's customers ain't they? Hey Teddy, hey Herb. What's the ante fellahs?"

"Jesus, Charlie, like we'd be playn' poker with just two guys? Youse a Greenie or what?"

"C'mon Herb, I'm a Reddie," Charlie smirked, tussling his furry wet mop of auburn hair. "Look at all that!" He leaned over the cribbage table and shook his wet head like a happy dog.

"Cut it out, wise guy!" barked Herb, his face getting sprinkled. "You say youse a 'Reddie' too loud and some cop'll think youse a Commie. Then you ain't got no head left at all, putz!"

"Aww, Herb, your tuchis is hnagin' out."

"See? I was right!" Teddy wagged a finger.

Charlie tossed his sopping hat and coat over an empty table. "Fill me up with some hot java, Spigot, and Lenny, stop with the dance tunes already and give me somethin' I can sing to!" Charlie forked a cigar from his shirt pocket and sidled up to a bar stool. "Hey Lenny! You shavin' yet?" he added, swinging his leg over the seat. "Whattuyuh say, Joey? Got a match?"

Joey closed and pocketed his switchblade with a look that said he'd prefer closing and pocketing Charlie. "Yeah, I got a match, Jew boy. My ass and your face."

"Big laugh. Where's your action tonight, Joey? Your girls home knittin' raincoats?"

Arnie burst out laughing. "Ya hear that, fellahs? Raincoats! Is that a scream or what? Hookers knittin' raincoats! Get it?"

"Yeah we get it," Teddy groaned, re-shuffling the deck. "But not Joey's broads. They don't like no raincoats. That's why all their Johnies got the clap."

One bar tender, one musician, two middle-aged men and a red-haired wise guy rocked Benny Weinberg's Eighth Street Cabaret with uproarious laughter.

"Here ya go, Charlie," Arnie choked, dabbing laughy tears from his cheek with the affable dish rag and pouring out hot, but day-old coffee.

"Never mind, kid," Charlie said to a seething Joey. He fumbled through his trouser pockets, pulled out a wad of crumpled one dollar bills, and retrieved a match box within the stash of cash.

Like a buzzard circling the soon to be dead, Joey licked his proverbial chops. "Must be nice to have so much cabbage, Stark, that ya don't even know what else ya got in your pockets."

"It ain't so much," Charlie said, sloshing half a pint of cream and four sugars into his cup. "I never like to fold dough. I wad it up, it feels like more, know what I mean? But I'm doin' okay."

"Uh huh." *More than okay,* Joey salivated.

"C'mon Lenny!" Charlie gulped a slug of sweet coffee and hopped off the stool. "Enough with this jive! Gimme a real song!"

Leonard's fingertips quickly shimmied down the keyboard with a feisty flourish then shifted to a softer tempo.

"Now that's more like it!" Charlie said, his fingers snapping in wistful rhythm.

"After you've gone and left me crying
After you've gone there's no denying ...."

Something inside Joey "The Pimp" Rotollo's sullied skull began to ignite. *A wad of cash.* The wheels spinning beneath his frayed, faded Panama hat, wheels of fortune, wheels of torture, scheming wheels of steel, Joey seized upon the brief memory of crinkly bills erupting from Charlie Stark's pocket. *Fives? Tens maybe? Nah, they was all ones.* But cash was cash, and to Joey, Charlie Stark always seemed to have himself a shit load.

"You'll feel blue you'll feel sad,
You'll miss the dearest pal you've ever had....".

Joey took out his new switchblade and recommenced carving his cuticles *The Kike's just playin' it smart,* he figured. He supposed Charlie was flashing ones in public, but keeping the big bucks back home. *The punk's workin' for Joe Masseria for Chrissake. He's gotta be loaded.* A jagged beam of muted gray light sharpened Joey's dark meditation. A scheme was surfacing. It rose from the cesspool of hell, bubbling up like hot lava. And it would be so pathetically easy, he drooled, child's play, fool proof. This sinister, singular mission could keep him rolling in easy money for months, maybe years, he thought. Hell, as long as he wanted, as long as he could keep sticking it to Charlie Stark.

The question was, who would be the fall guy? For sure, some chump close to Charlie. But who? Charlie had a lot of friends, he had a lot of family too. Then bingo. *Oh yeah,* Joey plotted, *the dip shit brother* The idiot child Benny Stark, the clown of Third Street, making like he was Charlie's right hand man, bird-dogging him all over the neighborhood like a hungry puppy as if just standing next to Charlie could give him the most remote hint of clout, when for years Joey and everyone else on the street knew undeniably Benny Stark was the world's biggest sucker. He could get to Benny alright, get to him fast, and get to Charlie Stark too as swift as the speediest arrow from Robin Hood's bow, pop, right in the heart, steal from the rich. But should he pop Benny Stark now and promise more of the same for the other dip shit brothers if Charlie didn't pay up? Or maybe, Joey schemed, running his thumb along the spike of his knife, just a little nick and scratch here and there to Charlie himself would show him Joey meant business. Weekly payoffs or weekly bump-offs. *Cute, very cute!* Joey snickered to himself. Then again, what about the dip shit sisters? A little *nick and dick* could be just as effective on those broads. Or maybe, yeah, there should be no one fall *guy* at all, but one fall *girl.* What about that nigger bitch he'd seen with Charlie? Oh the things he could do to her.

*"There'll come a time, now don't forget it, there'll come a time, when you'll regret it....*C'mon Lenny, pick up the pace!" Charlie crooned, finger-snapping and toe-tapping.

"Some day when you'll grow lonely
Your heart will break like mine
And you'll want me only
After you've gone, after you've gone away ...."

Joey closed his knife and edged away from the bar. Fastening each of the big buttons on his long, black trench coat, he eyed the singer contemptuously.

"You'll feel blue and you'll feel sad
You'll miss the dearest pal you ever had.........."

Joey pulled the brim of his Panama hat down over one eye, straightened his collar and swaggered past the tinkling piano. *Doncha worry, Charlie Stark. I'm gonna be your dearest pal forever.*

The door opened and closed to a howling wind and pelting rain, but inside Benny Weinberg's Eighth Street Cabaret, the carefree revelers romped aimlessly, not knowing they should consider themselves lucky to be safe and warm.

Bernie   *1920*

In his brand new, shiny Buster Brown boots with real leather laces, Bernie Poster raced down the twelve steps of his granite stoop, leaping over the last four and tumbling onto a hot summer sidewalk. He wasn't hurt. He immediately stood and wiped off dirt and three potato peelings from the back of his corduroy knickers, a soft wad of freshly chewed *Beeman's* from his right knee, and cigarette ashes from the palms of his hands which had already started to sweat in the blazing heat.

One tenement building away, a gaggle of sweaty boys, also in short trousers, huddled near the corner of East Third Street and Second Avenue, one of them kicking a can against the curb. None of them had noticed that on this particular morning Bernie had come out of his house having graduated from leaping three steps to four without drawing blood on either knee.

"Hey Bernie!" came a cry from the gang. "Wanna get in the game?"

Bernie flicked the sticky *Beeman's* into the street and stared at the boys. *Maybe*, he thought, hesitating, inching slowly toward the crowd, the shout of this one question completely eradicating the elation of mastering his stoop.

"Yeah, and bring us a Twist!"

Bernie shrugged his shoulders. *Oh well*, he grumbled and merged into the pack. He knew the boys would never really let him play, they just wanted candy. For the entirety of his ten years, the kids on his block stuck close to Bernie simply to get closer to his father's corner candy store. Bernie was little and scrawny and so awkward he could hardly kick a ball without falling over, but a pocketful of lemon drops always seemed to at least allow him to temporarily belong.

"Who's up? Oh no! Not Bernie!" was the typical groan among his friends. "You wait, Bernie. It's Howe's turn! But how 'bout some licorice, pal?"

Everybody likes to be my friend, was Bernie's only thought when the boys on Third Street clamored for his company, *but nobody really wants to be my friend.*

"Way to go, Bernie! Four steps, ya finally made it!" yelled a freckle-faced boy kicking the can.

Charlie Stark stood in the middle of the pack, his fists shoved deep into the pockets of his short pants, his red hair slicked back, soaked with sweat. "Help us out, Bernie," he shouted, "we can't start Skelly until I get some chalk to draw in the squares! Can you get us some?"

No one would ever really be his friend, that is, except for Charlie. Charlie was different. He always let Bernie play. When it was Charlie getting up the games, you played by his rules because the games *were* Charlie's, he invented them. "Alleevio Aleevio," "One Foot Off, Two Foot Off, Three Foot Off," "Skelly," "Liberty Liberty Passball," they were all his. Even the tough kids begged to get in his games, even the tough Italian kids, like the Rotollos and Tony Corsitini who was sixteen and already working for bootleggers. Most of the time no one even started a game until Charlie came out of his house cause Charlie let everyone play.

"Sure Charlie!" Bernie smiled, and headed for his pop's store. "Ya want I should get ya some Dots or a Malomar?"

"No thanks, Bernie, I don't need no candy, just chalk! We gotta get the game goin'!"

Charlie was a real friend. In the summer he'd take Bernie everywhere he went, and Charlie went to all the great places.

"We're goin' on a hike tomorrow, Bernie," Charlie announced after taking a clammy white chalk stick from Bernie's sweaty fingers. "See if you can find two nickels for the subway and have your mom pack a roll with butter in a sack."

"What do you mean, a *hike*, Charlie?" Bernie asked happily, even as Sollie Schreiber, Kishke Breines and Mel The Meydl had pushed him far away from the fresh chalk lines on the sidewalk.

"We're gonna hike to Central Park, to the zoo," Charlie said casually, eager, rowdy boys lining up behind him.

"Are you nuts? Fifty blocks? In this heat?"

"That's why we got two nickels. If we get tired we ride home. It's like this, not only do we got an adventure we can brag about when we get back, but everybody'll be jealous of our tan. We'll look all brown and healthy just like Tarzan."

Bernie stood back and watched the mob push and shove to the Skelly squares. He wondered what his mother would say to this. She wouldn't even let him go to the movies without a chaperone. Fifty blocks? All the way to Central Park? Charlie acted like this was just a happy jaunt over to Orchard Street.

"He's out! He jumped the line! Sollie's out!"

"No I ain't! Take over!"

An elbow jabbed the small of his back, and Bernie was knocked off the curb into a soft, steaming mound of horse manure, recently deposited from a passing milk cart. Bernie instantly started scraping each new Buster Brown against the concrete curb, quite certain his mother would now make him stay inside for a week. His shiny new shoes his mother had saved for, all through Purim, Passover, Lag B'Omer and Shavu'ot were now caked with horse shit. Luckily, stuck in a wad of tar at the base of the curb lay the wooden stick from a Good Humor Bar. Bernie grabbed it and furiously dug out the tiny grooves in the soles of his new shoes.

"No way, Sollie! Youse out!"

"Bernie! Get over here! Forget your cockamamie shoes! It's your turn!" Charlie yelled.

"It's okay, Charlie!" Bernie yelled back. *What's fifty blocks?* he shrugged, and meticulously excavated every scrap of dung in every infinitesimal furrow in the soles of his new shoes.

The next day, he and Charlie set out, marching up Broadway, at Charlie's insistence, like Doughboys.

"Sound off! One-two!"

"One-two!"

"Three -four!"

"Three-four!"

"One-two, three-four, one -*two*, three- *four!*"

"Sound off!" Bernie began the chant this time. The sack with roll and butter dangling at his side became a bayonet, the shiny Buster Browns sans horse dung, having passed his mother's inspection, became heavy waders sloshing through German trenches.

But twenty minutes into their adventure, two blocks past the turn from 14th Street onto Broadway, the blazing sun grew into a blazing hell, and the scraped clean soles of Bernie's boots felt as thin as newspaper against the burning skillet of the city sidewalk. Two more blocks, ten blocks, twenty blocks, passing dozens of movie theaters, Bernie wanted to stop and spend his nickel on a picture show where it was cool inside with six big electric fans blowing, but Charlie said they had to mush on. When they passed dozens of delis and cafes and bakeries with their smells of hot pastrami sandwiches and challa breads and pita breads and pastries clouding up the sidewalks like sweet fog, Bernie wanted to stop and spend his nickel on a kosher hot dog, but Charlie said no way.

By the time they finally got to Central Park, Bernie was fried beet red from the sun, exhausted and starving. Charlie guided them to the shade of a towering elm by the lake where Bernie promptly fell to the grass, wondering how he could ever brag about anything to the kids on his block if he were dead.

But Charlie had found another nickel in a gutter and bought themselves two bottles of celery tonic. They lay on their backs and lunched on their rolls with butter. Sip by sip, bite by bite, Bernie began to revive. Charlie, never wanting to ever admit he was tired or hot or had acquired sore feet, suddenly bolted upright.

"Watch this," he announced, scampering toward a trash can, and singing at the top of his lings. *"Oh I come from Alabammy with my banjo on my knee....!"*

Bernie was amazed Charlie had the energy to scamper anywhere after walking fifty excruciating blocks. He watched Charlie run to the trash bin, stick in his head, frantically poke around, then come back with a glass jar, as brisk and bouncy as if he'd just woken from a long, peaceful nap.

"It ain't got no lid," he said excitedly, like he was holding Aladdin's lamp, "but that's okay." He placed the jar on the grass, grinning like he was half expecting the genie to pop out.

"What the heck you doin?' " Bernie asked.

"Just watch!" Charlie snatched a long hat pin from his shirt pocket and bent it into a hook. He gathered the crumbs from their rolls, and mushed them into a little ball. Then he stuck the crumb ball onto the point of the pin and headed toward the water. "We're goin' fishin'!"

This Bernie had to see. Exhaustion or not, he got to his feet and followed Charlie to the lake. Charlie bent down and gently put his crazy fish hook into the water as deep as his scrawny, sunburned arm could plunge.

"What a view!" Bernie laughed. "I gotta see your big tuchis staring me right in the face?"

"Shhh! You'll scare my fish!"

"You're meshugie!"

"Shhh!"

In one minute, Charlie was screaming, "Got one!" And he pulled up a little sunfish about two inches long. Charlie grabbed the jar, filled it with pond water and dropped in the fish. "So nu, Bernie? Who's meshugie?"

He did this over and over until there were no more crumbs from the roll, but he had three fish to show for it.

On the subway ride home, Bernie hardly felt healthy nor hearty like Tarzan, wincing from the heat of his flaming sunburn on every inch of his exposed skin. Charlie was even more burned up, all freckled and red to match his red hair. But even hotter than his sunburn, Bernie could feel his face grow redder, noticing the shameful gaze from his fellow subway riders.

"Shande! The shame of it! You lookin' like a rag-a-muffin Huckleberry Finn in public? his mother would surely scream. *"And with that royter kop? That red haired devil?"*

Despite the scornful stares, his bright red shins feeling like the skin was about to peel right off, and even with the expected screams from his mother, Bernie's utter bliss could not be quashed. He beamed down at the three dusty brown minnows circling inside the jar on his lap. Charlie was letting him keep the fish.

"You *what*?" his mother screamed on cue when he got back to his apartment. "Two little ten year-old boys all alone shlepping uptown by themselves? You could have been run over! Gunned down by gangsters! Kidnapped! I tell you, that Charlie Stark is a red-haired tyvul! It's a wonder you're still alive! Stay away from him!"

Bernie listened without reply nor reaction. *Nah, who could ever hurt me as long as I'm with Charlie?* he thought, and he headed for his room.

"Gevalt! What are those horrible things in that jar?"

His mother kvetched at him all through supper. Bernie didn't care. Charlie let him keep the fish. And Bernie hardly cared they didn't live through the night. Because Charlie had promised they could go back tomorrow and get some more.

Charlie   *1932*

In a week I was out of that stinkin' projection booth and coming and going to all the great Yiddish theaters on the Lower East Side. Alex dragged me along to set up shop and paint scenery at Billy Minsky's burlesque houses, the McKinley Theater in the Bronx, the People's Theater in the Bowery, and Maurice Schwartz's new Yiddish Art Theater. We even got to do a few theaters on Broadway.

At Schwartz's, the most famous of them all, Alex and me were there when they first started building it from the ground up. If you worked for Maurice Schwartz you worked for the king. And once you set foot on his stage, you could practically write your ticket to Broadway, even to Hollywood. The big hulking Hebe sure had an ego, but there was no doubt about it, Maurice Schwartz was the best producer in town. People went to see his productions in droves. The guy was also a nutso perfectionist, so the sets had to be sensational or he'd let loose a roar you could hear in Queens. But he loved Alex. Alex was his first scenic director. For one of Schwartz's revivals of *The Dybbuk* we had to build several sets depicting a Russian village. But right in the middle of production Alex got the flu and was laid up for three weeks. I had to finish the set by myself. At sixteen, I was suddenly in charge of a Maurice Schwartz production.

For three weeks I lived and breathed one hundred percent pure panic and pure exhilaration. I was a dopey kid and the captain of a ship all at the same time. Lucky for me, Alex had made several small cardboard models of the sets so I had something to go by. I poured over the models night and day, studying every splinter of a wood shingle, each blade of grass, and each leaf on a tree. By opening night, Charlie Stark, set designer extraordinaire, had constructed and painted a stage that beckoned like a sumptuous banquet. At the dress rehearsal, Schwartz himself and the entire cast crowded around me and thanked me. They said it looked gorgeous. Schwartz, in his big dramatic booming voice said "Charlie, you've saved the day!" You coulda heard it in Queens.

I was on top of the world, meeting all kinds of big machers who thought I was something special. But to me the biggest macher of 'em all was Molly Picon, and nobody was more excited than me when Alex said we would work on her next musical. Me, working for Molly Picon? What a cute little thing she was, our very own Jewish Mary Pickford, our first great Jewish star. I loved her, she was everybody's sweetheart, and we were thrilled for her when she and her husband Jacob Kalich bought the corner of 12th Street and Second Avenue, boasting a grand new façade

with her name splashed across, *"Molly Picon's Second Avenue Theater."*
It made me all the more excited to work with Alex. It was more like
working for Molly herself.

We did most of the painting in the huge musty basement under
the theater. Another smaller basement, directly under the stage, was
where the musicians could exit the orchestra pit, or for the stage crew, or
where chorus girls could kibitz with the stage crew. Chorus girls would
fool around with anybody. I'd see them fondling anyone in pants every
time I'd come and go from the basement to the stage. Finally, after weeks
of sizing, and mixing colors, and painting and building sets, and tons of
shlepping, it was opening night. There was great excitement in the air just
before curtain, and I was looking for a viewing spot in the wings, when
here came Molly. Right before curtain and she wasn't too busy to find me
back stage and say, "Charlie, you're a great kid. Thanks for everything."
And earlier, her orchestra leader, Joseph Rumshinsky actually rubbed my
red hair and said, "This is for our good luck tonight, Royter Kop!"

Holy cow, I was beginning to think I'd become a macher, too.
All the greats in the Yiddish theater became my pals: Jennie Goldstein,
Max Gable, Bella Finkle and her husband Muni Weisenfreund, who
changed his name to Paul Muni for the pictures. I knew them all. I even
got to meet the great producers Jacob Adler and Boris Thomasshefsky,
he was Bella Finkle's uncle, and Samuel Goldenberg, Irving Grossman,
all the big wigs. Heck, even singer Frank Fay, who later married Barbara
Stanwyck, used to give me rides to the theater, and once he introduced
me to Jack Dempsey. I thought I was hot stuff. Celebrities were always
hanging out in my neighborhood, I'd always see 'em, but working with
Alex, hell, I wasn't just a fan, I was a goddam crony.

After a couple years though, I started to get restless. I was worn
out, going up and down ladders all day long, going up and down from
basements to stages, shlepping all over town to get stuff for Alex, and the
old Russian had a temper.

"Charlie!" he'd scream, "Get me the magenta! This is no
magenta, you moyshe kapoyer ! Go to the Village! I need the magenta,
now!"

Sheeeeesh! And off I'd run all the way to Greenwich Village to
shlep paint. He was running me ragged. Get up in the morning, get to the
theatre or some warehouse or basement, run around the building or all
around the whole Lower East Side like a maniac, barely having enough
time to grab even a knish for lunch, then go home covered in a million
shades of paint, get to sleep, and then start all over again the next day at
the crack of dawn. Alex's fifteen bucks a week was almost double what I
was making as a projectionist, but a hundred bucks a week wouldn't have
made things any better.

Then I started hearing it from my buddies. Tollie, Oppie, Moishe Pickles, Bernie Poster, Galumpta George, Hey Hey Goldberg, Schmutz, Kishke Breines, even from Itchy Frend who was two years older and really my brother Moe's pal, they all started in on me.

"So Charlie, how come we don't see you in shul no more?" they'd say.

Funny. They never went to shul. They meant our social club.

Our social club, the Colonial Friends, was next to the synagogue across the street from my building. Social clubs were everywhere. You'd get a group together, get a charter and license from Albany, find an available spot, spend a few bucks decorating, and you're in business. You had a place to play cards, shmooz, and meet girls at weekly dances. Joe Haber, one of the founders, had a brother with a leather factory called the Colonial Leather Goods Company, and so we got our name. I'd been a regular for years. You had to be twenty-one, but I was the only underage kid they let into the place cause I pumped away at the player piano and entertained the members with my singing. And besides, I did all the decorating. When I was just sixteen they paid me a hundred bucks to spruce it up real good. I'd gone to the New York Public Library and got books with scenes of Colonial America. I painted our club walls with big illustrations of the New England countryside, then I took thin strips of wooden molding to frame them in to look like real fancy paintings in some New England hunting club. Six of these smaller murals I put in our dancing area. But what really knocked them dead was the huge twelve by eight foot mural I painted in the entrance hall, a real tally-ho hunting scene with horses and fancy red-capped riders in a snowy winter wonderland background. The whole thing was framed by huge green and gold damask curtains I hung on either side. When you walked in, it was the first thing you saw. It was gorgeous. It was the best looking social club on the Lower East Side. Everybody thought so. The Colonial Friends gave me a permanent key, I was an honorary member. It took me two months to finish the job, but for a hundred bucks it was well worth it. I was loaded!

"Everybody's been askin' for ya," Itchy Frend said to me the first night I'd spent at the Colonial Friends in months. "I guess you're now too big a Broadway celebrity to be hangin' out on Third Street with us chumps."

Okay, so maybe I was busy as hell, that was one excuse, but, maybe I just didn't want to hang around my block much. My pals were great guys, but what the heck was so wrong about rubbin' noses with some real class?

"Yeah, and I hear you've been up in Harlem," Bernie Poster said. "Your pal Cab Calloway is makin' a name for himself. Has he brought you up on stage with him like Sophie Tucker did when you were five, Charlie? Did you sing *My Yiddishe Mama* for Cab like you did for Sophie?"

People always remembered my one time gig with Sophie Tucker at my pop's social club, the night she called me up on stage to sing with her. I could belt out a song even at age five.

"Are you and Sophie cuddlin' up at the Cotton Club, Charlie?" Bernie went on.

"Cut it out, Bernie." This was starting to sting.

"Maybe Molly Picon will dump Kalich and marry Charlie," Bernie laughed and started dancing around the club, singing "*Yiddle With A Fiddle*," aping Molly's famous act.

I knew it was hurting Bernie I was never around. He and I went way back. I wasn't snubbing him. I'd never do that. He and his dad had gotten me my first artistic job. Sam Poster had a candy store a few doors down from my building. When I was a kid, it was my favorite place on the block, especially in summer when old man Poster would raise the front pane-glass window, and the rich smells of fresh preserves would waft out onto the street. He'd have jars and jars of fresh jams, all kinds, cherry, peach, raspberry, strawberry, and chocolate syrup to mix with seltzer. A two-cents plain with chocolate and seltzer was my favorite. The seltzers with jams were a nickel, but I rarely got those, they were too expensive. Sam Poster also had a machine in a barrel of ice that churned sweetened water and lemons into a slush he called "Icis," which was the very best thing on the Lower East Side on a sweltering summer day. When I was a little tyke I was at Poster's candy store every day I had a penny, and I played with Bernie almost every day.

"You know all those nice blue and red *Fan Tan* chewing gum signs around town, Charlie?" Mr. Poster had said. "I wanna have some signs in my shop, too. The man who does 'em needs some help, and Bernie tells me you got artistic abilities. Think you can do it? He'll pay you fifty cents a sign."

"No problem!" Hell, I was thirteen. I could do anything.

So this Spanish guy, Romero, that's all I knew, met me the next day at Poster's. Our job was to go around to the shops and paint *Fan Tan* signs right onto the shop windows in water colors. It sounded fun, plus I got paid, and got all the *Fan Tan* I could chew. I'd meet Romero after school, work a few hours and be home in time for dinner. This went on for two weeks, until one afternoon he said he'd wanted to show me a mural he was painting at his house. I hopped in his Ford, a pretty big thrill, who had cars? We drove to his apartment house all the way to Coney Island. The mural was sensational, a big bullfight scene with matadors in red caps and capes, roses being tossed their way from gorgeous girls throughout the coliseum, painted right on the wall of his front room. I met his young dark-haired Spanish wife and new baby, we kibitzed a little, they gave me a glass of tea, and then the baby started crying like a banshee, so he took me home. But on the way back, he started talking strange, started in on how his sex life had become so lousy with his tired wife and new baby and all. He started asking me all kinds of strange stuff about my sex life, private stuff. Then he put his hand on my leg. I knew something was up. I could smell a rat as soon as he started talking. So many artists I knew had turned into feygelehs, but not me. That was something I was always having to prove. I was no sissy, all my friends knew that. But other guys were always making the wrong assumptions about me. It drove me nuts.

"Stop the car," I'd shouted. And before it came to a complete halt, I bolted, falling onto the pavement, busting my knee and bloodying my pants.

Bernie had felt terrible. "I'll make it up to you Charlie, I promise!" he'd said when I saw him the next day. "You can have all the Icis you want for the rest of your life, and I know my pop will hire you for other jobs."

"No problem, Bernie, it wasn't your fault the guy turned out to be a pansy. Besides, now I know I can start my artistic career. I got you to thank for that."

Bernie, my best pal, and now there he was, dancing all around The Colonial Friends making fun of me. I lit up a *Cremo* while he and my other best pals made like baboons at my expense.

"I'm Molly Picon," Bernie was squealing in a squeaky voice, his pants hitched up to his knees, flashing his skinny, hairy legs. "And I'm so hot for you Charlie! You're the greatest artist in the whole world! Come to my dressing room after the show and I'll pose for you!"

"No! Better yet--" Moishe Pickles screamed, "She'll pose for him in the nude!"

The guys were falling off their chairs.

"Thanks fellahs, you're real swell pals," I got the point. I stuck the cigar in my teeth, and left the club, puffing hard on my *Cremo*. Maybe my buddies were right. What the hell, I thought, I could give up show business. Who needed show business? Weren't my friends and family more important than that uppity theater crowd? Maybe I had gotten too big for my britches. And who the hell were show people anyways? Like my Mama always said, just a bunch of dumb machers who wanted to pretend they never came from a tenement. And who needed crazy Alex and all that shlepping? I could get another job, easy. Hell, I was sixteen now, I could find something legit that paid good bucks, and I wouldn't sell out neither and work for hoods running booze or dames like half the guys on my street. Not a chance! I knew better. You wouldn't catch me scrounging for my dinner in a garbage can, like the poor Italian kids on my block, but you wouldn't catch me with my fingers in no dirty money neither. No way. Not in my whole life would I ever work for hoods. Not in a million years. Workin' for hoods was a death sentence.

Half-way up my stoop, I could hear my buddies still guffawing like they were gonna pass out. "Yiddle with a fiddle!" someone shouted.

I'll get my buddies back, I thought. *No one's gonna make a chump outta Charlie Stark. Screw Alex and screw show people.*

It was after midnight. Mom and Pop and the kids would all be asleep, but what a riot it would be in the morning when they'd wake up and find me snoozing on the border bettle. I hadn't slept at home for almost a week. I could smell Mom's Friday night latkes seeping from our apartment, the night air still thick with their oily smoke, but for sure it was a smell better than any high class perfume at some phony theater. I tossed my cigar and snuffed it out with the heel of my shoe, excited to get upstairs and be in my own home. But then, glancing back up the street toward Second Avenue, I just couldn't help thinking.

"Right about now the crowd's just heatin' up at Nauheim's drugstore" I whispered. "The cast and crew from a dozen shows are drinkin' and noshin' and kibtzin' and wonderin' who's gonna take who back to their apartment for wild love makin' and sleepin' til noon."

But another wail of hilarious carousing hit me from across the street at the Colonial Friends.

"Oh well, what the hell. Feh on show people," I sighed, fetching my half-smoked stogie for another day. "And feh on all those chorus girls." Maybe it was time for me to chuck out all those wild girls, find someone steady, someone nice, and settle down. But who had time to look for a decent girl? It was tough enough as it was to find a gem among the cheap rhinestones in my neighborhood. Then again, up on Second Avenue came more blasts of happy laughter from the theater district.

"Damn! On the other hand, Molly Picon said I was a great kid."

The greatest Jewish star of all time thought I was something special. Me, a stupid shmendrick from crummy Third Street. Me! Hell, I guess I was a macher. Was I crazy? What kinda stupid putz would give that up? Give up the theater? Give up those chorus girls?

I danced up the steps to my sweet, warm house. *Not me,* I thought. Pals were pals, but Molly Picon, for God's sake! That was all the girl I needed.

Opal   *1932*

Two entwined black men, their kinky curls plastered flat with
pungent lavender-scented pomade, both wearing rouge and red lipstick to
obscure the blight of their middle-age, jitter-bugged into Opal Thomas,
causing the teal peacock feather in her red hat to abruptly flutter to the
dusty, concrete floor.

"Sorry!" the men chimed in unison and whirled away toward the
center of the dance floor, shrieking saxophones beguiling the mob of
dancers and anyone else who dared to descend the dank, basement steps
to the Sugar Cane.

Opal, having spent the entirety of her nineteen years observing a
plethora of eccentric and sundry characters roaming the streets of her
beloved Harlem, was unfazed at the sight of two men dancing. And she
was quite used to raucous behavior at the Sugar Cane, a motley night club
off 135th Street, where blacks and whites and a flagrant procession of
homosexuals, opium smokers and scurrilous free spirits paraded through
the club on any given night. Still, she had hoped being tucked away far
back by the phone booth might offer some refuge while she stood waiting
for her father, Coney, to finish his shift tending tables.

Wearily, Opal bent to retrieve the feather, wiped a thin crust of
cigarette ashes off the quill and reattached it to her wool hat. It was
midnight, and she was exhausted. She had just finished her own long shift
waitressing at the celebrated nightclub Small's Paradise, nursing a
particularly large and boisterous swarm of Wall Street bankers who, after
being turned away from the sold-out show at the Cotton Club, could only
find consolation at their second choice for Negro entrainment by guzzling
bootleg gin for five straight hours. Her feet ablaze with blisters, Opal
leaned against the phone booth, shifting uncomfortably from shoe to shoe
attempting to distribute the pain from heel to toe. A piercing scream,
more like an ebullient cackle, went up near the Sugar Cane's long rickety
staircase. In the murky back shadows, under tables and brazenly on top of
tables, Opal could both see and hear the feral antics of illicit lovers, the
swish of a zipper, the probing rustle of a pleated skirt, the slapping of
lips. Equally sanctioned at the Sugar Cane, the giddy, hepped-up
musicians were smoking their marijuana right on stage. Opal, as always,
could easily tune this out. Even as Billy Strayhorn, straight from an
earlier Cotton Club gig with Duke Ellington, took over at piano to the
roaring delight of the dizzy crowd, Opal could think of nothing more than
the sheer glory of her welcoming bed.

"Wow, this joint really jumps!" said a white boy, exiting the phone booth, puffing the stub of a cheap cigar.

He was dressed nicely enough in a navy blue suit and sparkling white shirt with a blue and red striped tie. And with the thick crop of slicked back red hair, all that red, white and blue made Opal think he looked more like a Roman candle about to pop on the Fourth of July.

"I'm waiting for my father," she said coolly, hoping to discourage any further solicitations.

"Pardon?" the boy strained over trumpet blasts.

"My father. He works here."

"Oh, that's nice." The boy slid a few inches away.

A slight pang of regret made Opal wish she could retrieve the tone of her words and caused her to squirm on her less blistered right foot. Perhaps the boy, and he was only a boy, he didn't look much older than herself, was not a rogue on the make after all. But one couldn't be too careful in a notorious club like the Sugar Cane where each night she'd go to fetch Coney, she'd have to fend off a hoard of insatiable, nocturnal leeches, lusting, and pinching, for blood. Luckily, her father ambled from the kitchen, freeing her from any further responsibility to conversation with the boy.

"Excuse me sir," the boy stepped toward Coney. "Do you know if Tony Partello's in the club tonight?"

" 'Don't know no Tony," her father said sleepily, using his shirt tail to wipe a smear of mustard off the back of his hand. With wisps of tight gray curls circling each ear, one might guess he was close to sixty, but by Coney's frail wobble one might presume he was ninety.

"Tony, the owner?"

"Nope," Coney yawned, "I thought Jimmy Spriggs was the owner."

"Sorry. 'Guess I was mistaken. I was supposed to meet the owner here about a job."

After a brief fit of coughing, erupting from his choked lungs like a tubercular patient, Coney fired up a *Lucky Strike*, offering a light to the tail of dead ash hanging from the boy's cigar. "Well," he said, wheezing out cigarette smoke, "why doncha just stick around and see if he shows up?"

The boy did not respond. He stood silently with his eyes unabashedly fixed on Opal. So blatant was his stare, she wondered if she looked as tired and haggard as her father. That must be it, she thought, why else would he be gawking at her? Although she believed her red wool suit and matching red hat with the long teal peacock feather were certainly stylish enough, after eight hours on her feet she was certain she looked awful. Opal never felt particularly attractive in the first place. She considered herself too thin, too bony, with a face too long, a mouth too wide and eyes mere splinters, like two withered almonds shaved in half. And her tawny light "high yeller" skin, she concluded, just made her look as washed out as a dish rag, nowhere near the color of dark grand Africa, not even a shade of the bronze Amazon, but the color of a country stained.

"You work here?" the boy finally asked her father, shifting his gaze back to Coney.

"Yep, it ain't bad neither since I get to hear all the bands. What kinda job you lookin' for?"

Opal ignored their conversation, and tried to ignore the boy. She opened her handbag and fidgeted with a veal chop wrapped too loosely in wax paper. The occasional slice of steak or lamb chop she could pilfer from abandoned plates at Small's Paradise was far more sustaining than anything her father could get at the Sugar Cane, even for free, where the wings of a roach were rarely mistaken for roasted onions, but tonight Coney's fare was leaking oozy sauce all over her bag. She searched out a handkerchief and mopped feverishly at the goo in the bottom of her purse. Then Coney grabbed her arm.

"We gonna snag us a table, darlin.' Whatever ya got in that bag, I can eat right here. No sense goin' home just yet."

When Opal looked up from the veal chop, the boy's soft chestnut eyes were twinkling like starlight. The boy's name turned out to be Charlie Stark, a Jew from way downtown near the Village. He dashed to an empty chair, snatched it away from an approaching sailor and dashed back to the table for two where Opal and Coney had already seated themselves.

"This here white boy says he be pals with Cab Calloway!" Coney chuckled, loosening his dinner from the soggy wax paper. "All right, youngin, do tell!"

Coney got a waiter friend to bring Opal a free ginger ale, but he passed him a dollar to fetch two bottles of *"Hennessey."* Her persnickety father had insisted on the *"Hennessey,"* knowing full well the contents flaunted on the fake label erroneously accounted for the contents inside the bottle. Monikered "Smoke," "Monkey Rum" or "White Lightning," this cheap blend of bootleg hard liquor resembling kerosene was guzzled at the Sugar Cane and the thousand other second-rate speakeasies throughout the city like it was magic elixir. Opal often worried it was laced with embalming fluid. It had happened before, maybe not at the Sugar Cane, but toxic, doctored booze was everywhere. People actually died from the stuff. Her father was already hampered by nagging arthritis and by relentless attacks of asthma. Yet, it was impossible for Opal to monitor, much less discourage, Coney nor his penchant for *"Hennessey."*

"....So my pal Ernie Franks, see. Molly Picon's manager, books this young guy named Cab Calloway," the boy Charlie rambled. "He was a smash. He was there for a week, and him and me became buddies--"

Opal tried to tune him out, reluctantly sipping her drink, craving the smooth covers of her warm bed, longing to be rid of the high-heeled shoes pinching her feet and tormenting her blisters, aching to be away from the rowdy jive and jump of the Sugar Cane, and wishing with all her heart the boy would suspend his furtive glances dancing in her direction.

".....Cab and me, we'd hang around backstage, or in between shows we'd go over to Abie Frend's deli almost every night for some nosh. We had a ball."

Oh brother, Opal winced. *What a liar.*

"...Until his last night at Molly's when all hell broke loose. The theater was jam packed, the grips were ready to bring up the curtain, a dozen beautiful dancin' girls in yellow feathers were all in place, and the band was tuned and set for the big intro, when Cab jumped on stage and started screaming. *'Wrap it up! Get packed! We're outta here!'* He started pushing everyone off stage, musicians, dancers, the roadies, everyone. *'C'mon Charlie! Gimme a hand'* he's yellin' cause Ernie never paid 'im. *'I got a line of taxis outside, Charlie! Help me get everybody out!* What a scene! Everybody was crazy, loadin' up trombone cases and music stands, and costumes and feathers, everything. The lobby was packed with customers, and people were lined-up down the whole block for the show, when here comes Cab, storming out to the street with his entire act escaping through the crowd and piling into taxi cabs for a mad dash getaway. But all that's nothin.' I been hangin' out with celebrities at Molly's since I was fourteen."

"Hell, ya don't look much older than fourteen right now," Coney said with a snicker, devouring his veal chop in two ravenous bites.

"No sir! I'm twenty-one!"

Now that is impossible, Opal scoffed. For thirty more minutes, she suffered though the boy's incessant monologue, mired in his lies of supposed encounters with singers, magicians, chorus girls and well-known hoodlums. This braggart, Charlie Stark, also told of a multitude of jobs he'd procured, ranging from projectionist, stage painter, sign painter, cabaret singer, and decorator, to actor and employee of a dozen businessmen and gangsters throughout the city. But these were jobs most men couldn't find in a lifetime let alone by the time they were twenty-one and in the midst of a dire national Depression, when there simply were no jobs. *This white boy is the biggest liar in New York City,* Opal thought.

"....Anyways, it was my pal Cab that got me the job at the Cotton Club--"

However, at the *end* of thirty minutes, Opal had forgotten about her bed, and began to marvel at this character or conman Charlie Stark. Cautiously, she permitted her eyes to drift from the soda bubbles dancing in her glass, up to the freckles dotting the bridge of his nose, which quivered happily with each animation of his endless tales. For sure, the boy was cocky, but that could be discounted by the sheer delight he took in reciting his adventures. He wasn't really a braggart, Opal reconsidered, he was a bard. Stories seemed to waltz off his tongue like Fred Astaire and Mr. Bo Jangles doing a jig.

"...So I walked right into the Cotton Club, and thought, it's nice and all, but holy smokes! I could turn the place into a palace. Egyptian marble and gold leafed columns of red granite, and golden cherubs flying over fountains flowing silvery water right in the middle of--"

Opal quickly looked away. Charlie had noticed she was watching him. But how could she not? He was the most charming thing on earth. But her sense of enchantment suddenly turned to panic. She would not let herself be interested in a white boy, she resolved, remembering the lecture from her older brother Jonas. "*You will not,*" he had threatened one night outside Small's Paradise shortly after she'd started her job, "*ever, and I mean ever, cuddle up to no white man! White man see black woman walkin' down any street day or night, he don't see no flesh and blood! He see poontang and that be all!*" On the other hand, Opal mused, it had been her understanding that at the forefront of every colored *or* white man's living and breathing consciousness dwelled poontang, undeniably and exclusively, in all manifestations and colors.

"Can I get you another ginger ale, Miss?" Charlie interrupted his narration.

"No, thank you," Opal muttered, dispelling each and every dimension of her brother's reprimand. For despite Charlie's ability to charm, it was the little things he did that captured Opal's curiosity like a steel trap. Folding his handkerchief and placing it under a wobbly leg to steady their table, inching the soup can ashtray closer to her father's wanting cigarette, using his jacket sleeve to sop up drops of liquor to keep the table dry, always referring to her father as "sir," scooting their table away from thrashing dancing couples who kept thumping into the back of her chair, and completely regarding the color of their skin as though--

No, that was different too, she observed. The color of their skin was completely *disregarded* by Charlie. She and Coney could have been bright Kelly green and covered in purple polka dots, and Charlie wouldn't have given it a second thought. *He talks with us black folks as though it were as natural as talking with his own kin, as though he were black himself.*

And oh the attention.

"The color of your dress, Miss, is really, somethin'. I sure wish I had a paint color like that. It's better than red, it's cardinal. Yeah, that's it. I wish I had a color called cardinal to match your beautiful dress. Ya know, the peacock feather in your hat gives me a great idea to feather and texture the wall I'm paintin' downtown. 'Course, it does look great in your hat. 'Sure I can't get you another ginger ale, Miss?"

But she could not think about this. How could she possibly ever think of being with a white boy? Jonas or no Jonas, the rest of the world would be far more threatening.

"......Are you kiddin'? Sure I know the Duke!" Charlie chattered through a cloud of cigar smoke. "Well, at least I've met him once or twice when me and Cab was at The Cotton Club. I was way up high on a ladder paintin' a palm tree--"

Charlie's hand rose off the table to indicate the height of the ladder, his other hand plucked the cigar from his teeth and brandished it like a paint brush, making wide, sweeping strokes. *But he's not interested in me at all*, Opal thought, thrashing herself for thinking such absurdity, picking off bits of melted candle wax and rolling them into little exasperated balls.

"...I'd already taken paper mache and chicken wire and a whole bucket of brown paint--"

All at once Charlie grasped her hand. "Ya know," he broke-off his story, "you can make little toys outta melted candle wax. I used to do it all the time, 'make little things for my brothers and sisters." He took the tiny wax balls from her palm and instantly fashioned them into a little dog with ears sticking up like a terrier. "See?"

Opal was certain the ticking hands of her Timex froze on the dial. Time itself had suddenly encased her in an isolated block of space, frigid, yet melting, like she was sitting in a giant ice cube both icy and hot. Through a fog of swirling slow motion, Opal watched Charlie's broad white hand, textured in a maze of pink freckles and plush tufts of soft red hair, envelop her palm like a warm glove. Despite a few smudges of cakey blue tempera paint and blisters, she marveled at the rough stubs of fingers that looked so hard yet held such capability and felt so soft. Absolute magic, exhilarating and mystifying, diffused the incredulity of a tiny wax dog's leap into existence, and utterly propelled Opal's heart to the moon.

Charlie smiled and set the wax dog before her, turning back to Coney. "So my palm tree, right, was popping like a firecracker. I mean, it was positively radiating the place--"

Again, his gnawed, pale fingers rose above the table, arms, hands and pearl cufflinks in a constant carnival of motion. Opal believed she could actually start to see the bark of Charlie's tree and the fan of large green palm fronds rising up from the dust of the Sugar Cane.

"....And so the Duke himself says 'Charlie, that tree's sensational!' But then, who should walk in the joint but Jackie Handleman, straight from Sing Sing! Seven years he got for manslaughter, but he says to me, 'get down off that ladder, Charlie, I got a job for ya'--"

As Charlie continued to recite, illustrate and perform, interspersing the flash of a smile and a jaunty glint in his eye across the table toward her, Opal found herself stuck in a befuddled battle between enchantment and denial. Finding a boyfriend had been the furthest thing from her mind, much less finding a white boyfriend. It was preposterous to consider a liaison with a white boy, a Jew, an elf, this impetuous rascal Charlie Stark. She would not under any circumstances contemplate this boy.

"Time to go, darlin,' " Coney finally announced, in another fit of raspy coughing. He knocked back the remaining dregs of Monkey Rum, snuffed out his cigarette, then lit another. Coney grabbed Charlie's hand and gave it a vigorous shake. "Ya sure do tell a lot of tall tales, boy! Movie stars and gangsters seem to be your best friends! Good night to you then, Mr. Celebrity Boy!" he laughed, and staggered off through the mob of dancers.

In a flurry, Opal stood up too, and, before she could temper her actions with reason, she saw herself shaking Charlie's hand, and incredulously hearing herself proclaim, "I liked your stories, Charlie. I'd like to hear more of them some time."

Boldness, much less brazenness were seldom part of Opal's nature. Perhaps the intoxicating fog of marijuana smoke hovering above the dance floor had revised her senses, perhaps the fumes drifting from so many pungent spilled pools of Monkey Rum had altered all rational thought and had transformed her usual introversion, or perhaps it was Charlie himself whose charms had cast such a powerful spell. It was impossible to elude enchantment. Regardless of origin, Opal's burst of audacity drove her from the table, running for her father before Charlie could respond. *Oh God, what was I thinking?* She hurried up the dark dungeon steps ascending the tomb of the Sugar Cane, fearing she was already dead and buried.

Joey   *1932*

"The stupid Wops on my block've been gettin' up craps in the alley behind my house," Benny Stark was saying to his pal Solly, underneath the glare of the streetlight on the corner of East Third Street and Second Avenue. Benny stood up tall to straightened the wide lapels of his brown suit and spread them wide to flaunt his new, big and bold, grape-purple tie, hand-painted with screaming orange and yellow daisies. "And every goddam time," Benny laughed, seizing a pack of cigarettes from his vest pocket, "the suckers, they get raided. Dumbshit Talyenas!"

Unbeknownst to Benny, his remarks were being carefully monitored by Joey "The Pimp" Rotollo, five paces away in front of Poster's candy store, pretending to be interested in the *Atom* comic books dangling inside the glass. *Youse be the dumbshit, Christ Killer,* Joey snickered, glimpsing the scene only in his periphery. He believed there was no need to stand closer to the tall, lumbering idiot, Benny Stark, with that sloppy blonde hair, dressed in those dizzy clothes like some moronic clown in a circus, when the loud-mouth Jew boy was broadcasting everything clear as day.

"These greasy Italian dopes don't realize they gotta pay somebody off. I slipped my janitor twenty bucks to keep an eye out. Thanks to me, we can shoot dice for hours, untouched, no more raids." Benny plucked a *Camel* from his pack and lit up, grinning like he'd just figured out how to beat odds at The Aqueduct. "So stick with me, kid. Watch this, Solly!"

"Forget it, Benny, youse gonna lose your shirt," said his chum, also dressed in a wide-lapeled suit with a flashy flowered tie. Solly peeked tentatively into the dark Third Street alley at a swarm of rough-looking guys throwing dice.

"Relax, kid, I've already raked in forty bucks. Look." Benny flashed a wad of bills.

"Jeeze Benny," said Solly, " youse playin' with the down-the-blockers? Ain'tcha outta your league? These guys are playin' ya for a sucker, pal. They's lettin' ya win now, and settin' ya up later for a kill."

"No way, Solly, these guys are my friends."

Listen to your chum, Benny. Joey smirked, smashing a wandering moth from the streetlight, squishing it into sticky pulp against Poster's window, and massaging the switchblade in his pocket. He'd wait to make his move when the dumbshit Benny was more vulnerable, as soon as Benny lost that wad of forty, which Joey knew would be soon indeed. Just a few knicks here and there, Joey envisioned, and then, *Let's us go find your big brother, Benny, unless you like the feel of all this bleedin'.* Joey happily ogled the trickle of moth pulp oozing down Poster's window, and opened his knife.

"Yeah, well good luck, Benny. Youse gonna need it!" And Solly strolled away from the street light into the darkness of his neighborhood.

"Aww , youse a dumbass, Solly!" Benny shouted after him, waving his wad of cash. "I'll see ya tomorrow, pal, in my new Packard!"

"No, *youse* the dumbass, Benny!" said his brother Charlie, who'd suddenly breezed around the corner and snatched the wad from Benny's hand.

"Hey! What the hell, Charlie! That's my dough!"

Joey turned from his pulverized moth to see the despicable Charlie Stark then scoot into the alley with the cash. Both Benny and Joey, each with differing perspectives of displeasure, watched Charlie march straight toward the dice-throwers.

"Hi fellahs, ciao ragazzi," Charlie managed in his meager Italian. "Listen I gotta talk to ya about my brother Benny, uhh, mio fratello is stupido, uhh, abbio pazienza con mio fratello grullo." he said, handing back the money.

The crap shooters all stood up, laughing and patting Charlie on the back like he was a hero. Puffing on his cigar, Charlie strolled back to his brother.

"Get this, Benny, you're okay for now, but no more craps with these guys, ya hear me?" Charlie pushed Benny hard in the chest and dragged him toward their stoop three doors down.

"Where's my forty bucks?"

"What'd ya start with?"

"Five! I was doin' good!"

"Uh huh." Charlie pulled a five spot from his pocket and gave it to his brother. "Ya were doin' real good, alright. Alright for a sucker."

"What the hell did you say to those guys?"

"Nothin.' Trust me. Just stay away from 'em."

"Hey, I can handle those Talyenas!"

The two brothers passed their stoop at building 58, Charlie grabbing Benny's arm. "C'mon, boychick, I'll buy ya an egg cream."

Back at Poster's, Joey "The Pimp" Rotollo crushed together his back molars, grinding away what little enamel was left. He flicked shut his switchblade. This exasperated procedure inadvertently pricked a tiny, trickling hole in his thumb. Joey sucked off the drop of blood, but he had to laugh. It occurred to him, he was suddenly thirsty. And not for an egg cream.

Mama   *1917*

Clara swirled a spoon through her tea, making slow idle whirlpools. The four sugar cubes had dissolved into a thick sticky elixir she hoped would give her a boost of energy. It was true. She was pregnant yet again, only two months gone, and she was exhausted. Although it was way too early to feel a tiny foot jab her spleen, or for a tiny elbow to punch the breakfast from her gut, she could reliably detect the insurgent germination rushing through her body, her belly, her blood, so familiar after eight previous journeys, so fatiguing the excursion. The bud of life sprouting in her womb, however, was not the only thing sapping her strength.

"No, Clara, it is no 'crime' to have another child, but meshugie? Absolutely!" her sister Annie barked, her cheeks flushed with unsympathetic rage. "What kind of moyshe kapoyer would bring nine children into this poorhouse when eight was plenty bad already?"

"I don't think like this. I think instead about the Good Book and the Good Book says to me, '*Each child carries his own blessing into the world.*' "

"Hah! It also says children *and* money make a beautiful world, sister! Kinder un gelt iz a shayne velt!"

"We will be fine, Annie," Clara said, trying to assure her sister and herself. She was no moyshe kapoyer, she was not backward, she was no topsy-turvy mixed up schlemiel. She was fully aware of the heavy, debilitating months ahead of her and the draining, worrisome months that would follow, but she was also fully aware of how one more child just might carry a blessing into her world, into her lacking yet justifiable family. "Sam, he's got six months to save a little, and the big boys bring in gelt too, she added."

"Clara, Clara," Annie sighed and bent her head low in a whisper, as if they were not alone. "How do you and Sam get your privacy? 'Know what I mean? Don't you think your children can hear the hanky-panky?"

"We get our privacy. Harry and Hymie are always out working, Moe and Charlie are in school, Louie sleeps all day, and the others are so little, they know nothing."

"Don't be so sure," Annie said, clicking her tongue in disgust. "And don't you know Louie sleeps all day because the boy is sick?"

"This you tell *me*, his own mother? I know something is not right with Louie!"

Something was more than not right. Night and day, Clara feared it was the dreaded tuberculosis, but the doctor had said no. Maybe Louie was born with bad lungs, maybe a bad heart, he couldn't be sure, but even an operation, he'd said, would probably not help. Every little breath Louie could puff sounded like an ocean inside his lungs. And yet he hardly complained, even when he'd wake up from the half dozen naps he took each day and find blood on his pillow.

"I go to the dispensary every week to get some kind of pill to make him be more awake. The druggist says it's the asthma that's making him a bad heart. 'He needs to eat better,' the druggist says to me. Feh! The doctor, the druggist, who knows from what?"

"Of course he is sick, Clara! Look how you eat!" Annie waved her arms at the only visible food in the apartment like she was waving away a bad smell. "Onions, potatoes and one scrawny chicken!"

"We eat fine. The other children are fine. It's not for lack of food Louie is a sleeper."

"Take him to a different doctor!"

"Like I can afford doctors? Yes, if something bad happens, I have no choice. For right now, I let him sleep."

"And so another child is going to help the mishegoss in this cold water flat?" Annie scolded, her finger still wagging under Clara's nose. "Stop making children, or next time I come not with *Manischewitz* for you, but with nine leashes!"

"My children are not dogs! I tell you, they are my blessings! They give me naches. Ain't it a blessing my boys bring home a few dollars every week?"

"Feh! They slave like dogs in a filthy sweatshop just to make pennies, and your husband makes like a village mule for what? Bobkes!"

"We make our rent," Clara held her ground. "The baleboss always gets her dollars."

But this too, Clara knew, was a stretch. The dollars trickled in by dimes and quarters. Even though Sam, himself no Mr. Atlas, he was such a scrawny thing, was up every morning at dawn to get his blouses, soft goods and materials by the yard from Mr. Shor's fabric shop on Orchard Street, then load up and drag his heavy pushcart all over the Lower East Side, he'd come home exhausted and with hardly any commission after paying off Mr. Shor. One day he told Clara he had to give half his commission to some punk kid who worked for big boss Joe Masseria.

"You don't give away your hard earned money!" she had screamed when Sam showed her the four measly quarters he had made for the day.

"Fine, I don't give half, and I give away my life next," he'd said. "You want one dollar or one dead husband? You choose. The gangsters don't take no for an answer."

But her Sam, he had a brain. The next day he had parked his pushcart on Chrystie Street right in the middle of Little Italy.

"Vestiti belli!" he had shouted out in Italian. Clara hadn't even known he could speak Italian. "Beautiful clothes! Beautiful fabrics by the yard! Twenty-five cents to a dollar!"

He did this all day long, kibitzing with the Italian housewives in their own language. He'd said the Italian hoods started kibitzing with him too and they left him alone. There were no more pay-offs to the shtick drek gangsters. Then in the same breath, as if this would go down easier, he had said, "Charlie came with me."

Clara's heart had almost jumped right out of her chest. It was bad enough Sam often took Charlie to Orchard Street, a place you couldn't even see with the entire street draped in laundry lines, and stores, sidewalks, streets jammed with people teeming like maggots, screaming children everywhere fighting, stealing, shenanigans of all kinds. You couldn't breathe on Orchard Street. You couldn't even find the sidewalk without having to crawl under a pushcart or horse wagon. Clara supposed a thousand, maybe a million pushcarts sat hemmed in against each other selling everything under the sun from pickles to clothes, to pots and pans and shoes and fruits and vegetables and toys and sauerkraut, even wedding cakes. Kids got trampled on and died every day on Orchard Street.

And this is where he takes our little boy? she had fumed. *But, no, he has to take him to the hoodlums too?*

"Charlie was a big help," Sam had said, "a genius! He figured out if he takes a stick and knocks away the manure and garbage off my wheels, I save time not having to stop and clean every five minutes. I worked in three extra blocks, Haika," and he'd handed Clara six bunched up dollar bills wrapped around two nickels.

A little genius, huh? Clara now thought, licking sugary tea off her spoon, remembering Charlie was still missing. Should she race to Orchard Street and look for him trampled beneath a horse wagon, or continue consenting to be the butt of Annie's condemnation?

"A sweatshop," Annie kept ranting, "where they bust the union and then they bust the heads! Your sons will come home bleeding, mark my words!"

"What they care about some union? They just work," Clara answered, anxiously glancing at the clock above the door. *Where was Charlie?*

"Unions, gangsters, in this farchadat neighborhood, everyone gets a knock on the head. And now you got the Communists? So nu? Where is your boarder, the Bolshevik?"

Clara and Sam had taken in a boarder to make an extra dollar a week. They had to, even with ten of them living in only two rooms. Everyone on Third Street took in boarders from time to time.

"You never know what kind of crackpot tuchis will be sitting at your kitchen table," her neighbor Mrs. Freiberg had once said, a family of seven themselves, after taking in a Greenhorn Polack right off the boat. "But you, Mrs. Stark, you had to get yourself a radical tuchis!"

The radical was Levinsky, Clara never knew his first name, straight from the Ukraine, straight from the revolution, and constantly bellowing she and Sam had to take sides.

"Sides for what?" Clara had asked him, which only made Levinsky bellow louder.

"Are you Red or White?" he had yelled at her, bedding down the very first night on the bettle they'd placed over the bath tub.

What a fool! Clara had thought. *I'm white, all else I know is black like a Schwartze. What can he possibly mean, red or white?*

Then he'd screamed that it wasn't enough for her and Sam to be Jews.

Oy vey! How long can I put up with this nudnik?

For two weeks, every night Harry and Hymie would drag themselves home from the sweatshop, the nudnik preached to them. "You fools! You have to form a union!"

"Mama, why does Levinsky want Harry and Hymie to get married?" Charlie had whispered.

"Not a marriage union, a union-union, Charlie. Go to bed."

Then Levinsky started in on Sam. "You pushcart peddlers are slaves!" he had screamed when Sam came home from Orchard Street with the pep of a limp rag. "You think you're being a good Jew because you don't criticize? You think God is going to increase your wages? Hah! Forget your religion! You're no different from the Italians or the Irish, or the Germans or the Poles! You're all workers together! Unionize! Organize! Help liberate all the workers! That's what your life must be, Sam Stark! Otherwise you have nothing! You *are* nothing!"

Clara had watched Levinsky's short-cropped black beard fill up with little drops of spit from his ranting. Sam had tossed him the towel he'd just used to wipe Orchard Street off his face, and said all calm, "Clara, do we have any grape wine in the house?"

Clara had handed Sam the bottle and a short glass. He sat, poured himself a meager inch and picked up Charlie, setting the boy down on his lap.

"This is what my life must be, Levinsky," he had said. He threw back his head and gulped the *Manischewitz* in one swallow. Then he ran his hands through Charlie's thick red hair, giving him an affectionate whack on both sides of his head. "This is what my life is."

But that was not enough for Levinsky. He and his Communist cronies were everywhere, on every corner, in every tailor shop, even in the synagogues upsetting the rabbis, saying all the neighbors had to organize, saying they had to give up their religion.

"This crazy Litwak thought just because we got a mezuzah on the door we must be Galitzianers," Clara now tried to explain to her sister. "We got no money to be so very religious like the Galitzianers. But Levinsky, he believes it brings shame to be any kind of Jew. Would you believe, he wouldn't even speak no Yiddish. Remember Papa, back in Romania, remember him saying, *"He who knows no Hebrew is an ignoramus but he who knows no Yiddish is a Gentile*. So I got to thinking, Levinsky must be both."

Annie nodded. "So what next? Did he steal from you?"

"No, but then he says we gotta fight the government, says democracy, even socialism is some kind of evil. 'Sure,' I say to him, 'we want better wages but not at the expense of our necks. There are protests and arguments and fights constantly all over the block. People are getting bloodied, Levinsky!' But does he care? He gets my boy Charlie to pass out his Communist *Freiheit* newspapers all around the neighborhood. Charlie said Levinsky paid him fifty cents to distribute the papers in Little Italy when he goes there with Sam."

"Fifty cents? Not a bad wage for a boy!"

"Fifty schmifty! Last night, I finally get the nerve to say, 'Levinsky, you're turning my son into a capitalist.' "

"You didn't!"

"I did. Today, he is gone, thank God. And good riddance."

"See? And now a dollar you don't have to raise another child! Between the gangsters and the Communists how will you survive, Clara?"

"And I tell you, between the gangsters and the Communists, we are surviving very well."

"A klog iz mir! My own sister, she understands nothing! Farshteyst gornisht?"

Annie's reprimand carried on and on until Clara simply gave up. She knew there was no convincing Annie, but she also knew Annie would continue to come on Fridays with bread or wine, and that her husband Joe would sometimes come too, bringing pennies for the children and letting them climb onto his back for "pony" rides around the room. But, she sighed, it was obviously just charity. Whatever their gifts or occasional gestures of good will, it was clear Annie and Joe viewed them as animals.

Tuning out her sister's unrelenting lecture, Clara's attention turned to waking up Louie. It was time for his pill. She needed to fetch baby Eva from the Freiberg's, grab Benny and Loretta from the alley, then, bundling them all up, go scour the streets for Charlie, hurry home and bake a chicken. A sudden spasm quaked her lower abdomen. *Can't be,* she thought, resting a hand upon her swell of belly. *It's too early to feel the baby.* She believed she was probably just hungry. She hadn't the time to get lunch. But there was no time to eat that leftover cold potato just now.

"If I've said it once, I've said a thousand times, Sam Stark would turn out to be a pauper. How much gelt does he even--"

Clara resolved to give her snooping sister fifteen more minutes, then go round up her brood. She knew Sam and her three older sons would be home very soon. Onions, potatoes, and yes, she thought, one scrawny chicken without no giblets, thanks to Breines the butcher, the gonnif. But giblets or no giblets, they'd all be hungry and expecting her dinner on the table.

Miss Wilson   *1924*

Her Irish Setter solid brass paper weight, her pewter cup of finely honed lead pencils, her porcelain dish of paper clips, even her four-inch volume of Bartlett's Quotations shuddered with the slam of the morning headlines onto her mahogany desk. Recoiling from the 80-point banner, screaming across the *Journal-American*, Miss Wilson felt an urgent, overpowering need to calm herself by pouring a second cup of Earl Gray, though upon raising the teacup to her lips she could see the cream had oddly begun to curdle. This, she surmised, was the apparent effect of what the newspaper's front page reverberated. Jimmy Walker was going to run for mayor. The garish headline notwithstanding, the tawdry photograph said it all. The infamous state senator stood smiling impertinently, bedecked in shiny top hat and tails, a diamond brooch on his lapel, a voluptuous blonde on his arm, with a caption reading, *"Mr. Walker will do everything possible, he says, to become 'the People's Mayor.' "*

"Balderdash!"

The wealthy people, the Tammany Hall people, the corporate people, and the bootlegging people, Miss Wilson fumed, would now surely determine the results of the fall election. The rest of the people, most notably the *poor* people, she believed, detecting the stench of festering diapers and rotting fish bones rising up to her open office window, these people had already lost the election.

She supposed Mr. Walker's awareness of real people was inhibited by the gleam of his diamonds, by the glare of his limousine's headlights, by the gaudy shimmer of so many Broadway marquees hawking the shows whose openings he habitually attended, held more priority than the state's business. Though the November election was still months away, Miss Wilson already felt the sting of defeat. She believed Mr. Walker as mayor would be an overwhelming, consummate disaster. It was one thing for her to constantly labor at shielding her Music School charges from the diamond-studded gangsters and their rhinestone-studded molls who rapaciously prowled the Lower East Side, enticing, beckoning her boys toward immorality, but with a *mayor* Jimmy Walker perpetrating the notion his road to debauchery was a path to wealth and fulfillment, how would she compete? The vulnerable boys and young men of East Third Street, she anguished, would most assuredly deem the depraved, flashy new mayor a role model.

She crumpled all of the newspaper into the tiniest, most compact wad possible, thrust it deep into her waste can, raised one heel of an Oxford and applied an accompanying solid squish. But she would not be dissuaded. Now more determined than ever to thwart the wiles of degenerates, she resolved to increase her efforts to influence, nurture and mold character within the boundaries of her own authority. She plopped back into her swivel desk chair, scanned the ticking clock above her office door, and waited for her most visible triumph, Charlie Stark. Though late as usual, Charlie was living proof her diligent cultivation had not been in vain.

She tugged out the bottom drawer of her desk, surveying a bulging leather valise. It was stuffed with dozens of Charlie's drawings and small posters she'd been housing for over eight years, during which time, thanks to her steadfast encouragement she believed, the valise had continued to grow and bulge. She rifled through the drawings with blissful gratification. The younger Charlie's Model T's had now become sleek Cadillac sedans, his caricatures were now detailed portraits, and yet he had experienced not one hour of artistic instruction. Miss Wilson marveled at how so many drawings, paintings, calligraphy, almost anything requiring pencil or brush, seemed to flow from Charlie's fingers. Her devotion to her school's fine music notwithstanding, amid the hymns and harmonies, arias and librettos, etudes, fugues, sonatas and concertos, Miss Wilson lamented on a daily basis that within the Music School's expansive world of culture they could not offer Charlie one class in the visual arts. Nevertheless, Miss Wilson maintained confidence she had at least successfully cocooned Charlie from the neighborhood's loathsome influences.

"Miss Wilson?" came the voice of her superior with a rap at the door.

"Come in, Miss Birnie."

Reviewing a list clamped to her clipboard, the Music School's chief administrator marched into the office, a freshly sharpened pencil stuck between her ear and sandy-gray permanent wave. "I've just been apprised you've selected Charlie Stark to decorate our concert hall for the Spring recitals. Do you really believe a mere thirteen year-old boy is up to this task?"

"You have my assurance that he is, Madam. You may recall the Thanksgiving pageant when we awarded Charlie first prize for his stunning mural of the Pilgrims landing at Plymouth Rock," she beamed, then pointing proudly to the valise. "There is also this remarkable portfolio, and surely you must know of the work he is doing for the Eltons?"

In her quest to distract Charlie and the other boys from straying toward hooligan behavior, Miss Wilson had overseen the formation of recreational clubs. On Wednesdays after three o'clock and all day Saturdays, the boys could use the Music School to hold their meetings, collect their ten cent weekly dues, play checkers or chess, or plan for dances.

"Charlie has designed their emblem and illustrates their newsletter," Miss Wilson continued.

"I am aware of this, however I have not yet determined that--"

"And did you also know the Sollats and the Stalwarts have gotten Charlie to design *their* club newsletters?"

"Yes, I did know," Miss Birnie replied skeptically, turning to the open window, where the screech from the organ grinder, his chattering monkey, the milk man's clanking delivery, the junk man's bellow for scrap and the thick smoky aroma of rendered chicken fat now wafted up from Third Street. "Charlie has indeed overcome much of the chaos of this neighborhood and has become such a school mascot, I believe his freckled face could adorn our school stationery, but this is an important event, and I am not convinced."

"Well, I *am* convinced, convinced more responsibility and discipline are crucial for Charlie to continue developing his artistic skills. To so publicly display his talents will only further build confidence and encourage him."

"All right," Miss Birnie sighed, snatching the pencil from behind her ear. She struck a checkmark to her list. "You may hire Charlie Stark, but you know we cannot pay him. We can only offer reimbursement for materials."

"Thank you, Madam. You will not be disappointed in how our Charlie will represent the Music School."

"Five dollars!" Miss Birnie added, turning her back, stalking away, and closing the office door. "And not one penny more!"

Miss Wilson gazed eagerly up at the clock, willing the second hand to usher in her Personal Triumph. She could hardly wait to tell Charlie the news. In contrast to the morning headlines, this was news exceedingly more palatable.

The door burst open, and a panting Charlie, beads of sweat tickling the faint, new red hairs of a pubescent upper lip, lunged toward her desk. "I just saw Miss Birnie! But she didn't say nothin'! Did I get the job?"

"Yes, Charlie, you did!"

"Holy smokes!" he bubbled, excitedly twirling his newsboy cap around and around in his hands. "I really got it! Wait'll the kids hear about this!" he cried, leaping for the door.

"Just a minute, Charlie. There are some conditions. First, you only have three weeks for preparation. Can you please try to be on time for a change? This is a deadline to which you must adhere."

"I will!"

"Second, as you know, our Spring recitals are our most significant. You'll have to do your best work."

"Ya can count on me, Miss Wilson! I'll make it look terrific! Can I go tell the kids now?"

"No, I'm not finished. I want you to consider this assignment very seriously. The concert hall will be set up for the usual student performances, but afterward we will be graced by the appearance of Mr. Raymond Dittmars and Miss Rae Lev who also will be performing. They are professional concert musicians, Charlie. There will be many important people here."

Charlie grabbed her hand and shook it vigorously. "I promise! Everybody'll love it! You'll see!" and he bolted for the door.

"Wait, Charlie! You forgot your stipend!"

He turned back, grinning so broadly the freckles on each cheek stretched as wide as the Brooklyn Bridge. "Money? I get money?"

Miss Wilson plucked a five dollar bill from the cash box in her top drawer. "I trust you will be responsible with this. It's strictly for materials, not for you as payment."

"Yes Ma'am!" and he rocketed away.

In a matter of minutes, over the shrieking whine of the organ grinder's monkey below her window, Miss Wilson could hear the elated, uproarious screams of thirteen year-old boys.

Within three days of dispensing her orders, ten large white posters had been tied to the wrought iron fence in front of the Music School. A few days later, a euphoric Miss Wilson had been informed every school and social club in the neighborhood were also adorned with Charlie's handsome announcements. In all four corners of each poster, he had painted large red eighth notes and black quarter notes on a musical staff. The accompanying text was especially clean and clear, simple block letters, yet every character was drawn with such proficiency one would have thought Charlie had studied calligraphy for years.

Three weeks later, her euphoria exceeded even titanic proportion. The concert hall was stunning. Reams of black and white crepe paper, meticulously cut into long four-inch wide streamers, hundreds of them, had been woven, tied, criss-crossed, braided and shaped into the most exotic patterns. The streamers hugged the span of the entire ceiling, and were draped from ceiling to floor along every wall, sporadically dotted with ten-inch wide silver-glittered paper stars. The effect was dazzling. Miss Wilson believed it was like sitting inside a giant, sparkly, silver birdcage.

From cinder block to silver, from drab to divine, Miss Wilson mused, noting throughout the performances the upturned heads ogling Charlie's magnum opus. Afterward, as the large crowd of proud parents, relieved recital students, and devotees of chamber music gathered for refreshments in the corridor outside the concert hall, Miss Wilson stood back and waited for the accolades. Although the overheard conversations centered mostly on Shuman, Charlie's name kept streaming through the excited babble. Even Miss Birnie was duly impressed.

"Well, I must say Charlie certainly came through for you," she admitted, idly studying the back page of the evening program. "Charlie's decorations were quite attractive and were most appropriate for this evening's musical fare."

"Oh no, Miss Birnie, he came through for *himself*. Charlie takes great pride in his accomplishments,"

Still, Miss Wilson wondered if Charlie had even seen the program since he'd spent the entire night hiding in the cloakroom. She doubted he ever saw the large print *"Thank you Charlie Stark for advertising, promotion and décor"* first among the acknowledgements on page two. Gratefully, Miss Wilson observed Charlie's older brother, Hyman, dragging him from the cloakroom and stuffing him with cucumber sandwiches. But before she could approach Charlie with her own plethora of compliments, he was intercepted by the renown Mr. Dittmars.

"Charlie, I want to thank you for the beautiful ambience you created tonight," Miss Wilson heard him say. "It was a real pleasure to perform in such an attractive setting." Mr. Dittmars reached into his coat pocket and took out two tickets. "Miss Lev and I would be honored if you would attend our upcoming concert in Carnegie Hall."

I knew it! Miss Wilson quivered, jubilation dancing between heartbeats. Charlie was getting genuine public accolades, credible accolades from those who knew real artistic talent. Engulfed by the throng of admirers, a beaming Charlie finally caught her eye, and Miss Wilson returned his appreciative glance with the biggest, warmest smile her lips could carry. A puffed-up Charlie strutted over and held out his hand.

"Here ya go, Miss Wilson," he said, handing her three quarters. "Seventy-five cents left over and the receipts for four twenty-five."

"Thank *you*, Charlie. Your work is absolutely magnificent."

Racing off to the punchbowl and mobbed by adoring fans, he never heard her compliment. Regardless, thanks to Bartlett's Quotations anchoring her desk, Miss Wilson recalled a particular verse. *Victory is not a name strong enough,* she recited. She would indeed savor this victory forever. For more than the night's mere triumph, Charlie's success was a down payment on his future. She began to imagine thick, vibrant volumes of *"Paintings By Charles Stark"* gracing her library shelves, inspiring, motivating, and transforming future deprived children who would wander through her door. She could see the "Charles Stark Retrospective" of oils on canvas and his two-story high murals embellishing the storied stone walls of the Metropolitan Museum. But her own personal accomplishment, she glowed, her supreme achievement she believed was incalculable.

Tickets to Carnegie Hall! Miss Wilson dabbed the corner of her handkerchief at the droplets seeping from one eye. Nearly blinded by unparalleled fulfillment rather than mere tears, she watched Mr. Dittmars, Miss Lev, the oboist, the violinist and all of the Music School staff continue to envelop her yearling. "Victory is *not* a name strong enough," she whispered. For indisputably, this night confirmed now and for always, she had eluded the influence of jackals.

Charlie   *1932*

Enough was enough. Alex Chertov was driving me nuts. I'd had it up to here with the crazy Russian screaming and yelling and ordering me around. And with every single one of my pals making me out to be the world's biggest heel, it wasn't a hard decision to finally quit. Molly Picon or no Molly Picon. Besides, I wanted to paint what I wanted, not just fill in Alex's outlines on backdrops and shlep paint for him all over town. Seeing the free shows didn't even seem worth it anymore. Those cheap chorus girls, caked with gaudy make-up in their sleazy costumes, were driving me nuts, too. "Hey Charlie, does that fiery red hair mean you're always hot and horny?" they'd tease. "Hey Charlie, are you still a virgin? Let's find out," and even worse things. Jeeze, I was around tramps twenty-four seven. I'd had it. Anyway, the union was breathing down my neck. I was underage, it was only a matter of time before I probably got canned. So yeah, I quit. Maybe I blew a big career in set design. Maybe I would have been the biggest thing on Broadway. Who knows? What the hell! I just didn't want to be somebody's chump, especially Alex's chump. I was gonna be a great artist alright, but on my terms. Nobody was gonna own Charlie Stark. It was time to move on, even if it meant giving up the good dough. But I didn't care if there was a Depression with people standing in bread lines, I'd get me another job, and I'd get more than Alex's fifteen bucks a week. I had to. Pop was getting on in years, it was tough for him hauling his bulging pushcart up and down the Lower East Side. The guy could have a stroke. And my poor brother Louie kept getting sicker and sicker. We found out it was asthma and some kind of heart trouble. It wasn't good. He had to quit school too, not like me to get work, but because the goddam teachers wouldn't let him come no more. They thought they'd all catch what he got, like my poor kid brother was some kinda leper or something, the dirty rats.

And Hooverville's were popping up everywhere, Depression families with no place to go living in cardboard boxes or crates. Central Park was full of 'em. But I'd kill before my mom and pop and brothers and sisters slept in a box.

For the next two years I kicked around the city, scrounging for whatever design jobs I could get, painting signs for stores and doing a few more theater jobs here and there, but there wasn't much around. I did find some work at the YMCA in the Bowery, painting health education posters on venereal disease. World War One was long over, but hundreds of soldiers, still homeless, maimed, most down on their luck, would hang out at the flop houses and twenty-five cent a night honky-tonks in the Bowery, and hang out with all the cheap whores there too. VD was rampant. I thought I might be doing a good thing helping these poor guys learn how to protect their putz, but drawing nasty red VD sores? Sheesh!

I left that job and went lookin' further uptown to Eighty-Second and First Avenue, to the German section of town called Yorkville, where I'd heard some German sign painter needed an assistant. He hired me straight away. In the crowded front room of his first floor apartment on Eighty-Third Street, we painted signs for illegal haufbraus and a few shops. Though every extra buck this guy made he spent at a crummy German speakeasy around the corner. I'd go to work in his smelly apartment that always reeked of sauerkraut, but he was drunk most of the time and beating up on his wife and kids who had to stay in the back so we could paint. So much for Prohibition, huh? Those sermonizing white-bread gals of the Anti-Saloon League and their stupid law were supposed to prevent bums like him from getting drunk all the time and beating up their wives. Prohibition! What a joke!

So one time when he was out, his plump pasty-faced wife, always in tears complaining about her schmuck of a drunk husband, made a pass at me.

"I need a man, Charlie. A real man," she slurped over me, while I was painting on their cold, chipped tile floor. Then she started stroking the back of my neck. "Wir gehen jetzt weiter, ja?" She nodded toward the bedroom.

No dice. I was outta there fast. Of course, the other "joy" of Yorkville was wallowing in my fair share of anti-Semitism. "Hey Jew boy! Go back to your slum!" I'd hear that plenty. In one smoky, stinky underground haufbrau, I was hanging some posters when the fat bartender actually said to me, "We'll let you work in here, Christ Killer, but don't expect a drink."

I stomached Yorkville for just two weeks. Thank God I saw a *"boy wanted"* sign in a dusty store window on Fifteenth and Fifth Avenue. This was much closer to home than Yorkville, and that suited me just fine. The shop was the *Ad-Win* advertising company, and the job was for art work help with their displays. Perfect! This was a job that screamed for Charlie Stark. I hesitated and walked around the block a few times wondering how I could land this job 'cause there must have been two dozen poor shmos waiting in a long line to get to the interview upstairs. I came back around the block with an idea. I went right up the stairs and knocked on a door that read "Irving Meyers." The door opened, and Meyers, the Ad-Win owner, scowled and said, "I'm not ready for interviews yet, kid. I told everyone two o'clock." The clock on his wall said 1:45.

"Yes sir," I said, groveling. "Sorry Mr. Meyers. I'll come back later." I closed his door and walked nonchalantly down the steps, and, chock full of moxie, took the "*help wanted*" sign off the window.

"Fellahs, the boss has taken sick," I lied. "He's not interviewing today. Come back tomorrow."

"So you're a smart ass, huh?" Meyers glared at me at two o'clock when I told him what I'd done, and all the other applicants had scrammed. "Why would I want to hire a punk like you?" he growled.

It took just five minutes of me explaining my experience with Alex and all the sign painting jobs I'd done, plus Meyers had been at the Colonial Friends and seen my work.

"Maybe I could use a spunky kid like you," he grunted, clearing stuff off his desk to show me some layouts.

And easy as that, I got the job. For twenty bucks a week, five more than what Alex was paying me, I silk-screened posters, designed display windows for French-Shiner-Urner shoe stores, other ladies' specialty shops, and for Landay Music stores. I stayed with Irving Meyers and his brother Sam at Ad-Win for eighteen happy months. When I got paid every Saturday at noon, Sammy Meyers and I would stroll over to a great little kosher restaurant on Fourteenth Street for our usual meal, beet borscht with sour cream, chopped liver, meat and potatoes and all the sour pickles we could eat for thirty-five cents. Or I'd walk down the street to the RKO Jefferson Theater and for forty cents see a movie or a great act when they were still doing vaudeville. I'd take the subway home from Ad-Win or I walked, glide into our flat like I was somebody, slap down my ten buck contribution on the kitchen table and make Clara Schwartz Stark one deliriously happy Jewish mama.

It was a good life. What Depression? But then my pal Milton Kraus told me I should work with him up in Times Square at the Laco studios, making similar kinds of displays I was doing at Ad-win. It would make me a few more bucks a week, creating big displays of movie stars and posters for theater lobbies. So I bid a sad farewell to Irving and Sammy and headed back to the theaters. It was a ball to be working with Milty, who I'd hung out with since we were kids, and to make a little better money and, yeah, to be hob-nobbing again with theater people. I guess they weren't so bad after all.

Georgie Jessell even started drinking coffee with me every night when he'd finish his show at the Grand. I'd met him there one time when me and Milty were putting up displays. Me and Georgie became good pals.

"I'm leavin' for the coast, Charlie," he told me in that nasally voice of his, when we were noshing at Nauheim's drugstore. "The theater's gotten snobby. I need these phonies like a loch in kop.

Hollywood's gotta be more real than this," he said, gulping down his java. "You should come too."

Not a chance, I thought. *I'm making great money and living it up. This ain't no big city, hell, this town's my village. I'll never leave New York in a million years Never.*

One night after an all day grind behind Laco's drafting table, I was sitting at Nauheim's with a crowd of celebrities. I was shmoozing with two decent chorus girls for a change who seemed nice, not at all like the tramps I'd see at Kessler's, when who walked in but Alex Chertov. He nudged his way through the crowd to my booth.

"Vie geyts, Charlie?" he panted, helping himself to my pastrami on rye and cream soda.

"I'm great, Alex, how ya doin' ?" I answered, circling my arm around my plate.

"I need you, Charlie. I got more work now than ever." He stood there shvitzing right onto my food. He looked like he hadn't eaten in days. Alex snatched up my bottle of cream soda, finished it off, and took another bite from my sandwich. Then he pushed my cute chorus girls right out of the booth and squeezed in next to me, close, too close, pastrami was heavy on his breath.

"Charlie, give a listen," he whispered. "I got the new Menashe Skulnik comedy at the Art Theater, the new musical at the Grand, and if I play my cards right, I got Gershwin's *Of Thee I Sing* at the Music Box! Big time Broadway, Charlie! Joe Mielziner's turned it down! Don't be a fool, you'll get good money! Gershwin, for God's sake!"

That's a lotta crap, I thought. I knew Joe Mielziner. He'd never turn down a set job for a Gershwin show. "I can't do it Alex, I'm sorry. I can't be married to the theater no more. Theater lobbies are about all I want to handle right now."

"For what? A few lousy quarters a week for pickles? " He grabbed the dill off my plate and started crunching. "That's bobkes. I'll pay you thirty dollars a week," he insisted. "That'll buy you crates of kosher pickles!"

It was hard to turn down. Thirty bucks a week? Broadway? I could do Broadway easy. This could be it. My old fantasy of wooing Lillian Gish at the Café Royale floated through my head. I could see the champagne corks popping and could almost hear the bubbles dancing in the glass. "I'll have to think about it," I said, whisking away the last big dill off my plate just as Alex gave a reach.

"Don't think, *do!*" he begged.

I got up and threw my tip change on the table. "I know how to find you, Alex, " I said, and pushed my way out through the crowd.

"Find me? I'm already here! Don't be a schmuck, Charlie!"

I left Nauheim's and headed for home, thinking I really would be a dumb schmuck to turn him down. As I turned onto Second Avenue, I saw four guys I knew who stopped to say hi and tell me how they couldn't find no jobs. Two were married already with kids, the other two were still living with their parents, everybody hungry and wondering where the money was gonna come from. Me, there I was, in the middle of the goddam Depression for God's sake, already making twenty-five a week and then I get a thirty buck offer. Was I crazy? Guys would kill for that. I puffed hard on my *Cremo*. Workin' again with Alex would be a pain in the ass alright, but I'd definitely be crazy to turn down dough like that.

As luck would have it, good or bad, and you never quite knew on the Lower East Side about mazel, whether you had luck or if you should make luck, or if some luck might put you in an early grave, my questions were soon answered. When I turned down Third Street, I saw Joe "The Boss" Masseria sitting on my stoop, smoking a big fat Cuban cigar. Joe was a big hood, one of the biggest, and he sometimes took up residence in my building. His mom lived on the top floor, and Joe used her small apartment as his safety net when he wanted to lay low from cops and other gangsters. He was one rough son of a bitch. He started out in the Morello Gang, bootlegging, racketeering, knocking off any mugs that threatened Morello's territory, but then Joe personally rubbed out all his bosses so he could be number one. I knew him well enough to kibitz with him on the block, but a guy like that, you made an effort to stay out of his way.

I headed up my steps, but Joe grabbed me. "I need some boxing posters, Red. Ya think ya can handle that? I hear you're an artist."

The fear in my gut exploding up to my brain seemed to melt away when I heard his next magic words. "You'll make good dough, kid. Fifty bucks for one little paint job."

And that's all it took. Yeah, I guess I was a little crazy.

Bernie   *1924*

Bernie Poster jostled his way through a mob of frenzied school mates exploding out the door from P.S. 20. It was the last day of eighth grade, summer time again, time for another three whole months of explorations and exotic journeys through alleys, up and down fire escapes, scuttling through basements, culverts, or along railroad tracks, and hopping from roof top to roof top. Time for him and Charlie to pursue the magic of their city. Throughout the school year, the two friends had only weekends for adventure, but when Bernie's father had insisted on him working in the candy store, those weekends came few and far between. He had to buckle down, Bernie's pop had said, and take life seriously, especially with his Bar Mitzvah coming up. Bernie was heartbroken. To him, there was nothing more serious than a rousing escapade with his best pal, Charlie. So when summer came around, and the teachers opened the school house doors to a hoard of ecstatic, screaming kids, Bernie was the most euphoric. For three whole months he could be with Charlie.

But where was he? Bernie stood at the door, watching every jubilant kid race past him, but Charlie wasn't one of them. Finally, he spotted his pal lost in the pack, walking slowly down Eldridge Street.

"Hey Charlie!" Bernie shouted, running up to him. "It's fishin' season!"

"We'll see, Bernie."

"What's with the 'we'll see?' It's summer! We got three whole months of adventure!"

"Three months is right, Bernie. It's all I got."

"Whatcha talkin' about? Ya ain't movin' or somethin'?"

This worried him. It always worried him. Lots of Bernie's pals had been moving to the Bronx or Brooklyn when their folks got a little more money. The Beckers in 46 building moved last month, and Tollie Oppie left just last week. At least Charlie's family was dirt poor. Bernie didn't think they'd ever have the money to move. They hardly had enough to care for Charlie's brother Louie who was always sick as a dog. The last time Bernie had been at Charlie's house, he'd heard Louie wheezing and coughing from the bedroom, making gurgling noises in his throat, and he saw bloody towels in a waste basket. It made him want to throw up. But as much as Bernie never wanted Charlie to move away, it killed him to see his pal so poor.

"I'm goin' to a new school in the fall," Charlie mumbled, looking like he was about to cry.

"So? That's no big deal. We all get moved around to different schools. So what?"

"Yeah, but this school's in Massachusetts."

"You kiddin'?" Bernie felt his heart fall into his shoes.

"Miss Wilson wants me to go to some art school in Massachusetts. My mom thinks I should go."

"No way!" Bernie was barely able to speak. Miss Wilson and all the teachers at the Music School had always been his friends, he thought. How could she do this to him?

"I dunno. My mom thinks the school's in the Village, but Miss Wilson says it's in Provincetown. She says some guy named Hawthorne runs it and he's a big wig painter. She showed him some of my art work and he liked it and wants me at his dumb school."

"Is your mom really makin' you go?"

"Every time I talk to her, even in Yiddish, I tell her the school's far away, but she don't understand."

Charlie stopped abruptly, then took off running. And Bernie, panting like a dog from the shock, didn't have the breath to go after him.

The next morning, the first day of summer and normally a day Charlie would be waking him up at the crack of dawn to drag him off to someplace wonderful, Bernie lay in bed. He'd hardly slept. He'd been awake most of the night wondering if this were the last summer he'd ever get to see Charlie again, thinking of all the glorious summers he'd had Charlie all to himself, thinking of Coney Island.

"Whatever you do, don't tell your mom!" Charlie had ordered on last year's first day of summer, fully aware of Mrs. Poster's ardent misgivings about any collaboration between her son and Charlie Stark. Too many summers of peeling sunburn, oozing blisters, scuffed up shoes and torn pants had determined that.

Trekking to Coney Island, however was worse. "Sodom By The Sea," his mother called it. She and his pop had once taken Bernie there, but when they went to the "Blow Hole Theater" and his mom's dress flew up from he blast of wind shooting from the floor, she said she'd never go back. It wasn't that a hundred people in the audience saw her bloomers, she'd said, it was because of the dimples in her knees.

"I don't show my knees to nobody!" she had screamed, and took Bernie by the hand and dragged him away.

His pop was mad too. He'd said, why should a bunch of goyim get to see his wife's knees when he hadn't seen them in years?

So they'd left and Bernie never even got to ride the Loop-T-Loop.

But on last year's first day of summer, Charlie didn't take him on the Loop-T-Loop either. He'd said the boat ride was more fun, and they wouldn't throw up from being upside down. They rode the boat ride three times, shooting down the steep track and splashing into the cool water. They got soaking wet, but Bernie didn't care. Later, they saw a man get shot out of a canon, and a side show called "Annie the Alligator" a lady who had skin like a crocodile. Charlie had said she should be careful cause some nut was gonna kidnap her and turn her into a suitcase or alligator shoes. Bernie couldn't stop laughing.

That day it was almost 100 degrees outside, and Bernie had wanted to go to the beach for a swim, but from the top of the Ferris Wheel they couldn't even see a beach.

"Are you crazy?" Charlie had said, sweat pouring down his neck like a faucet, even though the Ferris Wheel had come to a stop and they were sitting way up high in the breeze. "That ain't no beach, Bernie, it's a giant shvitz hole! There must be a million people down there!"

For half a mile up and down the beach, Bernie could see nothing but a huge sea of people plastered on the sand, mingling and slithering side to side like the waves sloshing up to the shore. It was enough to make him sea sick. So instead, when the Ferris wheel deposited them back on earth, they each had gotten two Coney Island red hots with mustard and shared some cotton candy and a bottle of cream soda. They strolled through Sodom as they ate, staring into saloons with dancing girls in fishnet stockings.

"Now ain't this better than baseball?" Charlie had leered, noting how Bernie originally had told him he was saving for tickets to the Polo Grounds, not on a shlep to Coney Island.

"See?" he leered again, more wickedly, honky-tonk piano music screeching through old-fashioned, swinging saloon doors. "I told you Coney Island would be more fun than a stupid baseball game. Ain't it better to see a babe in fishnet stockings than seeing fat ol' Babe hit home runs?"

Suddenly, Bernie had thought he'd never be interested again to watch a Peckinpaugh to Pratt to Pipp double play. Instead, his eyes were glued to the giant doubles bouncing up from the chests of dancing girls.

"C'mon, Bernie," Charlie had said, dragging him away. "I can convince your mom we spent the whole day playin' stickball, but not if I bring you home with a boner!"

By the time Bernie did get home, he was burnt to a crisp, and his mom had said he could have an extra lemonade Icis after dinner to cool him off. But when she'd asked him what he'd done all day to get so sunburned, he didn't dare tell her Charlie had taken him to Sodom By The Sea. It wasn't the probable potch he minded, a spanking was nothing, he just couldn't live if she wouldn't let him play with Charlie.

The next day, just to be on the safe side, Bernie had suggested they stick closer to home.

"Okay, Bernie, let's go on a halvah hunt. No offense, kid, but your pop's halvah is too oily. It's gotta be dry and chewy so it can stick to your teeth."

Bernie had no money leftover from Coney Island, but Charlie was loaded. After scrounging underneath the Loop-T-Loop, sifting through trash that smelled from all the pukers, he'd found five quarters, three dimes, eleven nickels and a handful of pennies that had fallen from people's pockets when they went upside down. He'd also found a dozen pairs of eye glasses and a set of false teeth.

So they'd set off exploring lower Manhattan looking for the best halvah in town. They searched the Bowery, tramped up and down Houston, and hit every side street on the Lower East Side looking for any deli or candy store that sold sticky slabs of halvah by the slice. Charlie had three rules. One, it had to be dry, two, it had to be plain, no chocolate, marble or pistachio, three, it had to stick to your teeth. After four hours and seventeen penny slices of halvah, they both had gotten the runs and headed back to Bernie's house. The winner? Sam Poster's candy store.

Charlie had just smiled and shrugged. "Eh, what do I know?" he'd laughed, and they'd raced for the bathroom.

But that was last summer, much like the summer before, and all the summers before that. Now, he'd never ever ever have a summer like that again, he ached, staring at the plaster cracks in the ceiling above his bed. He'd never have Charlie again.

And then, he heard a commotion at his door.

"Good morning, Mrs. Poster," Charlie was saying in Yiddish. "Is Bernie awake yet?"

Bernie leapt from his bed. In ten minutes he was hurrying down Rivington following Charlie to the East River.

The Delancey Street Dock clanked and whirred with the morning's catch. Burly dock workers, like frantic pistons in a frenzied jack hammer, wrestled tackle, gear, grappling hooks, ropes and cables. Heavy crates full of fresh cod tumbled off their blistered fingers. Portuguese fishermen warbling sultry ballads sliced through fat tuna with razor sharp cleavers. And haggling buyers from delis, markets, restaurants, and cafes in all five boroughs scrutinized tail, fin and scales.

"The perch, the cod and the red snapper! Get 'em in the truck! The mussels look like shit! Move it!"

Two loaded ice trucks rumbled over fractured timbers and headed for the Fulton Fish Market. A thousand shrieking seagulls circling voraciously, dived, snatched, grazed, devoured and insatiably circled again in a cacophony of flapping feathers and relentless screams for carnage and carrion.

But below the Delancey Street Dock, Bernie watched his friend Charlie angrily glare into the black water and fidget with the big box and rope he'd hauled from East Third Street. It was a dramatically different Charlie than the one who's taken Bernie fishing under the dock last year. Then, Bernie's only concern had been trying to survive the pitiless, choking smell of fresh fish and their carcasses, worrying the rotting fumes were surely seeping into his skin. Down to his underwear, he had stood at the water's edge, searching out a clear spot in which to jump between the floating tin cans and dead fish. Surveying the streaming mess of beer bottles, soggy newspapers and fish heads floating by, he thought if he could just swish some of it away he might have room for a swim. It had been so hot.

That day, Charlie had been happily yanking his rag-tag fishing gear from the bundle he'd tied-up in a red handkerchief.

"Oh I come from Alabmmy with my banjo on my knee--" he'd sung, when they'd taken off from Third Street. He had attached his bundle to a long stick, laid it over his scrawny shoulders, and had marched away singing and whistling like his favorite comic strip hero, the hobo Happy Hooligan.

"Give me your stick, Charlie, so I can push away the garbage."

"I ain't swimmin,' I'm goin' after guppies and jelly fish."

"Aww c'mon!"

"Tell ya what," Charlie had said, abandoning his load of hatpins, string, glass jars and bread crumbs. He slid down the slippery bank toward Bernie. "I'll watch ya swim for a while, and then I'll fish--"

Bernie pinched his nose and took a big breath.

" -- 'Cause there's lots of rats in the water."

Bernie never went swimming that day. Instead he chose to watch his pal catch eight tiny guppies and be happy as a clam.

"Next time I'm gonna catch me a whale, Bernie! *And I've gone to Loo-ziana for my true love for to see....*"

But today, Charlie was no Happy Hooligan, he had no handkerchief tied to a hobo stick, no hatpins, and no happy singing. All he had was that strange, big cardboard box, as big as his arms could carry, and all that rope.

"Sure you did," Charlie was rambling nervously, unpacking his gear. "You saw *Terror Island* with me at the Loew's Delancey. I snuck you in, remember? The projectionist is my friend."

"All the projectionists are your friends, Charlie. I saw that Houdini picture with my mom and pop," Bernie reminded him.

For weeks, Bernie had noticed Charlie going nuts over Harry Houdini. Charlie'd seen *Terror Island* nine times, and scrounged and saved pennies to buy Houdini magic books. Bernie thought the books were dumb and only tricked people into thinking they could be real magicians, but Charlie hungrily poured over them or read newspaper stories about Houdini every afternoon in the Music School library. Bernie wondered how long it would be before Charlie tried to saw him in half.

"Well, I know you saw *The Grim Game* with me. Did you know Houdini does all his own stunts?"

"I know, Charlie."

"Remember the scene when Houdini's plane crashes and he and the girl get to the ground in one piece? Did you know Houdini really is a pilot?"

"Yeah, Charlie, you told me already, during the movie."

"My pop saw him down at the Battery." Charlie went on, fidgeting with the ropes. "You know his most famous trick when they dropped him in the harbor? My pop said the packing case he was in was all tied up in chains, and though they dumped him all the way down to the bottom, he was up and out in 59 seconds."

"Yeah, but *my* pop says he does it with keys. He hides keys in his mouth and swallows 'em on strings. Then he just uses the keys to open the locks and get out. I think the guy's a fake."

"No way! Did you know he's a Jew?"

"My mom says Houdini's the anti-Christ."

"Now why would your Jewish mother care about Christ, Bernie, let alone the anti-Christ?"

"She said he married a Catholic and he says he can talk to his dead mother. Mom says Houdini's meshugie."

"Fuck you, Bernie! Houdini's a genius!"

Charlie grabbed the box and rope, and slid down the muddy river bank. "Okay, Bernie, this is it," he shouted. "Get down here!"

Startled, Bernie sat on his rump and slid toward the dreaded trash and stinking fish fumes.

"I think I figured him out," Charlie rattled on. "I'm gonna get inside, you tie it all up good and tight, and push me in."

"Are you crazy?"

"Yeah, I may be a little crazy. But I think I can do it. Now come on."

Charlie climbed into the box and crouched down, pulling the flaps over his head. "Come on, Bernie!" he yelled. "Tie me up!"

Bernie was scared. "No! I ain't gonna tie ya up in no box and push ya in a river! Ya ain't no Houdini! Ya ain't no genius! Ya can't be no Houdini just cause ya read his stupid magic books!"

"Don't mess with me, Bernie! Tie up the fuckin' box!"

"No!"

"I mean it, you little shit! Do it!"

"I said, no!" Bernie kicked over the box and Charlie tumbled out. He scrambled to his feet and lunged at Bernie. Without thinking, Bernie's left fist caught Charlie's throat, his right fist cuffed his chin, and Charlie fell flat on his back.

"You schmuck!" Charlie screamed, he was crying hard. "I really think I can do it!"

"Ya can do a lot of things, pal!" Bernie was crying too, the knuckles on his left hand bleeding. "But not this time! I won't let ya!"

Charlie stayed on the ground. "I can't do it, Bernie! I can't go to that school!"

"Ya can't?" Bernie wanted to smile, but knew better.

"I can't leave my family!" Charlie sobbed.

"I don't get it. Ya ain't hardly at home anyways."

"You're right, you don't get it. I gotta sick brother, remember? My pop hardly makes a dime off his stupid pushcart. I just can't up and leave 'em."

"Okay, then stay home. What's the problem?"

"I know I should go, it could be a real adventure. And maybe it could lead to somethin'."

"So go," Bernie said, not believing what he was saying and feeling very confused.

"If I go to that fancy shmancy art school everybody on the block'll say I think I'm better than them," Charlie said quietly, wiping his nose.

"Maybe you are better than us."

"Shut up, Bernie, you ain't no help. I'm just a poor schlemiel from the slums. What business do I got goin' to a school with ritzy kids?"

"Wait, you got a chance to leave these farshtinkener tenements, and you're afraid you'll let down your family, but then you're sayin' they'll be jealous? But you're also sayin' you don't think you're as good as anybody else? I still don't get it."

"Never mind, Bernie. Just forget about it. Forget I said anything."

"No, I ain't gonna forget about this. Stay or go, it's your damn life! I can't figure it out! But I tell ya, if ya stay here, ya ain't gonna spend the whole damn summer tryin' to kill yourself! That ain't gonna happen! I won't let ya."

Charlie wiped his nose again. "So, you've become my protector, huh, little Bernie Poster?" He got up and dusted off his pants. Bernie thought he heard him say, "No one's ever wanted to protect me before."

"What?"

"Nothin'," Charlie grumbled and kicked the cardboard box into the river. Rolling up the rope in a ball, he brightened. "Maybe if I get a big enough hook, Bernie, I can use this rope to catch me that whale."

They walked back down Rivington in silence, and then Charlie announced, "I ain't goin', Bernie."

"That's good with me, Charlie."

They walked the remaining blocks back to their tenements not saying another word.

The next day, Charlie had a different plan. "Ever been on a ferry boat, Bernie?"

They were sitting on Bernie's stoop, crunching a long roll of candy dots on paper he had snagged from his pop's store. Before Bernie could answer, Charlie declared, "Save your allowance the next two weeks, pal, cause we're goin' out to Englewood."

Two weeks later, just as the milk truck rambled down East Third Street with its six A.M delivery, Bernie's buttered roll was packed in a sack, and Charlie was at his door.

"I promise to have him home by supper," he assured Mrs. Poster, who didn't look so sure.

They raced down Houston to the west side and hurried to a ferry docked at the Hudson River. Bernie marveled at the big boat's shiny grand deck and glittery reflections from the river, flickering on its bow.

"This'll be great!" Charlie bubbled, hopping up the gang plank.

At the Music School library, Charlie had seen two pictures of the Palisade cliffs in a book about oil paintings. Both were titled "Sunset Over The Palisades."

"Gorgeous," he had said, "looks just like Washington Irving's Sleepy Hollow! Even better!"

Bernie had told him his mom would never let him stay out past sunset in New Jersey. So Charlie had said they'd go see the sunrise instead.

"What if I get sea sick?" Bernie asked nervously, when the deck hand locked the metal gangplank gate and loud engines started up. Other than the ride at Coney Island, he'd never been on a real boat.

"Forget about it! This is a river not an ocean, shmendrick! Ya can't get *sea* sick on a *river*."

As always, Charlie was right. Chugging away from lower Manhattan, the ferry glided through placid waves and gently swirling eddies, and Bernie didn't feel like throwing up at all. It was now way past sunrise, but Charlie could care less. He scampered up and down the deck, scavenging for crumbs to feed the flocks of circling seagulls. And when the boat bumped through choppy water, Bernie loved the waves splashing up on deck. Charlie made a game of this, and they raced to each swell sloshing over the guard rail, and dashed away just before they'd get splashed, the squawking seagulls racing along with them. Bernie watched the city skyline, magnificent, and more spectacular than he'd ever imagined, start to disappear, then fade and merge into a ridge of dark tree tops shrouded in the morning mist. Then off in the distance, giant green cliffs came into view.

"See `em?" Charlie shouted over the ferry's engines. "Ain't they grand?"

They got to the Jersey shore and began their hike up the Palisade cliffs. After a good bit of huffing and puffing, they found a spot to eat lunch where they could view the great rolling Hudson.

A bi-plane flew over head.

"Hey! I bet that's Lindbergh!" Charlie said, a blade of grass stuck between his teeth.

"How do you know?"

"Because, dummy, Lindbergh lives right here in Englewood."

"How do ya manage to know so much, Charlie?" Bernie asked, savoring his buttered roll, his bare toes tickling a mound of soft pine needles.

"Cut it out, Bernie, you know I get around. Stick with me kid and you'll get an education."

There was no talk of art school. There was hardly any talk of anything. Charlie took the blade of grass from his teeth and placed it flat between his two thumbs. He blew on his thumbs and sent out a blasting high-pitched screech.

"Yeah, I stick with you and you take me for a swim with water rats."

"Hey, I show you a good time and you know it. Remember when I took you and Louie From Fourth Street to the Majestic Theater? We saw 3 movies for free."

"But we almost got arrested!"

Once, Charlie had shown Bernie and Louie From Fourth Street how to climb to the top and lay flat at the edge of the theater's open, rolling roof. They'd been watching a comedy and trying not to laugh out loud and get caught. But Charlie had passed around a plug of chewing tobacco, and when Buster Keaton fell on his face, Bernie had burst out laughing, ejected his wad, and horrified, saw the plummeting tobacco glob fall right onto a man's bald head. The man screamed, looked up, and then the rest of the audience looked up and saw them. For half an hour they ran from the cops.

"But we didn't get arrested, Bernie. That's the whole point," Charlie laughed, remembering the scene. "That was kicks!" He blew another loud squeak from the blade of grass in his thumbs. "Ya gotta admit, Bernie, this is kicks, too."

Sprawled on soft, cool grass with his best pal, Bernie gazed over the towering Palisade cliffs at the wide, shimmering Hudson. He thought the sunlight sparkling on the river looked like diamonds. Above him, a flock of sparrows, not a bunch of dirty pigeons, he noted, was merrily singing and tweeting among the green pines and shady maples. There were no filthy tenements nor crowded streets, no pushcarts, no cops, no dirty alleys, no rats, no swarms of people, no nothing, just him and Charlie lying in the summer grass under a clear blue sky. Bernie deemed this exceptional state of being more peaceful and gorgeous and absolutely perfect than anything he could ever remember in his whole life. He couldn't imagine what would be more perfect.

And Charlie's not goin' away to no art school, he thought. *I got him all to myself. Just me and Charlie like it's always been. Like it's always gonna be. I got him forever.*

Bernie had to admit. This was definitely kicks.

Charlie   *1932*

With Joe Masseria's iron grip still clamping my shoulder in a vice, I tried to be as cool as I could. He had on a three-piece, blue silk suit that must have cost two hundred bucks, and would have made him look as slick as a seal if not for the bulge of a Forty-five under the jacket.

"You want boxing posters?" I said, trying not to sound terrified.

"Not for me, kid, they're for Bugsy."

He smiled like he had a snake between his teeth, and I about swallowed my cigar. Bugsy Siegel was worse than Joe. He was the biggest and roughest mug in town who'd knock off his own mother if he needed to. I heard Siegel actually raped a girl in a speakeasy, in broad daylight, in front of people, just because she didn't fall for one of his passes. People wanted to help her, one guy tried, and he was shot through the head. Joe was about as bad as they came, but Siegel was a maniac. Something didn't sound right about all this.

"Bugsy Siegel wants me to make boxing posters for him?" I asked, hoping I wasn't gonna pish in my pants.

"Yeah, they're for Bugsy," Joe said real cool.

I knew something was up. *"My friends call me Ben, strangers call me Mr. Siegel, and guys I don't like call me Bugsy, but not to my face."* Everyone on the entire Lower East Side knew that. And it was no secret him and Joe Masseria were not exactly friendly. Before I could answer, Joe slipped me a fifty dollar bill.

"I want twenty posters, kid, maybe thirty. Mickey Walker's fightin' Vince Forgione in Newark. Big ol' Vinnie's gonna be the next middleweight champ. Trust me. A lotta dough's ridin' on this fight, kid. I'll give ya one week. If I like your stuff, I got a joint that could use some fixin' up, too. I'll give ya a call." And that was that. He handed me his cigar, went up our stoop and disappeared.

Fifty bucks for one week of work? I put out my *Cremo* and puffed on Joe's sweet Cuban stogie. The smoke was smooth and buttery and made my lungs feel like they were being perfumed. It was one great cigar. Fifty bucks would buy me even better cigars. I stared down at the fifty dollar bill in my hand like it was a magic lamp with three big wishes coming my way. Well, if that's where the money was, I guess I'd take it. I knew Siegel didn't handle Walker or Forgione, those weren't his boxers. I didn't know what was up, I'd just be doing a little art work. If Joe and Bugsy wanted to bump each other off who cared? And if I could land some jobs decorating speakeasies, what the hell, I wouldn't run the booze, I'd be making masterpieces and on my terns. Those mugs knew jack about art. *Fifty bucks for one week of work?* It sure would put plenty of food on the table, pay for my brother's doctor bills, and make my mom so happy. Bringing home some gelt was more important than how I made it, as long as I did it legally of course.

I looked down the street. I saw guys wearing cardboard shoes, panhandling on my own block, as if any of us poor church mice on Third Street had a dime to give away. I had to take this money. I was so tired of seeing Louie coughing up blood all the time and my mom and pop not having an extra nickel to get him a real doctor. With every extra penny Mom got she'd run to the dispensary to get Louie some medicine, but it never seemed to help. With six of us kids still at home, who had gelt for doctors? Mom had to wash dishes in the same big tub in the kitchen where we also bathed, and that same tub was turned into a "boarder bettle" at night for some strange shmo who slept on the board and gave us only one crummy dollar a week for rent. But did I really want to get involved with a big time hood? Not me, I wasn't no chump. The chumps got themselves thrown off buildings or just disappeared from the block when they signed up with hoods. Making easy money was never that easy.

I stood on my stoop jingling three quarters in my pocket trying to decide if I should give Joe back his fifty bucks. But when he'd opened the door to our building and went upstairs, the stinging fumes of urine from the hallway toilet just slapped me right in the face. The smell of pee still lingered on the stoop like rain and seemed to drip right down on Ben Franklin as I stared at the fifty. What I wouldn't give to get my family to the Bronx and out of this rat hole, I thought.

I stopped jingling change and pocketed the fifty. The bill felt warm in my pocket, like those hot baked potatoes me and Pop would put in our pants pockets in the winter when I'd help him with his pushcart. It was the only way to stay warm. Even then I froze. Those lousy potatoes always got me thinkin' about making real money someday. I swore, when I grew up I'd never have potatoes in my pockets again as long as I lived. If I took Joe's offer, I thought, I wouldn't really be working for hoods. I was no crimalnik. I'd be okay, I'd be safe. Who'd want to bump off an artist? With fifty bucks sizzling hot in my pocket, I took the plunge.

In the next week, I gathered up my supplies and made the posters. On each one I painted two hulking, sweaty brutes going at each other like tigers. They looked nothing like Walker or Forgione but it didn't matter. Boxing fans cared more about half-naked men spewing sweat and blood all over the ring than anything else. I exaggerated the muscley biceps on each fighter, their arms looked like boulders. A drop of cadmium red in their eyes made them look on fire. Who'd not want to go to this fight? And I asked no questions. You didn't ask Joe Masseria questions. I just delivered the goods, all thirty posters done on time.

After that, Joe found me and told me about the little club he had off 52nd Street. It turned out to be a real dive that reeked of whiskey and too much sex. There were hardly any tables, just boards on cinder blocks and a few chairs, and a hell of a lot of mouse droppings. I'd need at least a month to get the place decent. He paid me thirty-five bucks a week to spruce it up. Five bucks a week more than what Alex had promised for shlepping in the theaters. Yeah, it was a dump and an illegal club with plenty of dirty money flowing out from bootlegging and racketeering and whoring, but I was no criminal, I was a painter. I closed my eyes to everything around me, the shady money, the shady women, the ever present fistfights, and just painted. If I had to interact, I was all friendly, telling jokes or singing a few tunes. Joe's lackies seemed to like having a funny Jew boy around to entertain them and make their joint look sensational. Sometimes they even let me sing a few numbers to open the show.

For the next month, I worked at Joe's, and with his thirty-five bucks, I was loaded. I bought Mom a big beef brisket from Kishke Breines's butcher shop every week.

"We got now the brisket every Friday night," I'd hear Mom brag to the neighbors, "and not just for Pesach!"

For that alone, making Mama happy, it was worth it.

In a few months I was working a dozen clubs and speakeasies. My reputation spread fast, and soon I was working not only for the low-life but for the high-brows. On 52nd Street, Sherman Billingsley owned a bootleg joint before he started the Stork Club and hired me to fix it up. My pal Spunky from my block opened a real posh spot near ritzy Central Park West, and I decorated that too. I did Cherkis's Jewish cabaret on Third Street, the Gypsy Tavern in Greenwich Village, dozens of Italian bistros on Mulberry Street, seafood houses in Brooklyn, Romanian and Turkish restaurants all over the east side, and of course a ton of speakeasies. But none of them came anywhere close to the magnificent marble palace and gorgeous diva I was now painting for Dominic and Carlo Cormenti.

"Ya break me up, Charlie!" Dominic sniffed one night, after I'd sung my rendition of "Ave Maria" for the Pizans. He took out his handkerchief and wiped his eyes. Big sentimental tears streamed down his cheek as he casually picked up two bloody teeth off the floor. Dominic had just landed his fist into the chops of some sucker he believed had ratted on him. The sucker fell down in a heap, minus two incisors. But I knew I was never the main attraction, I was the main *distraction*.

"I love your singin,' Charlie," Dominic had sniffled again and blew his nose into the handkerchief. "Keep it up," he added, and walked away rubbing his knuckles.

Sheeesh. The mobsters loved me. They loved my singing as much as they loved my art work, but it was my art work getting me the reputation. Some of those mugs would even take me around to other clubs, bragging about me. "Yeah! Charlie's gonna do all the decoratin.' He'll make my joint gorgeous!"

So, yeah, I could ignore their hanky panky, even the big time rough stuff. Then again, I was used to it. Since I was five years old, maybe younger, I'd seen plenty. Rapes, knifings, shootings, people tossed off building. Rough guys were everywhere, and now I knew the roughest, Meyer Lansky, Abe Wagner, Legs Diamond, Dutch Schultz, Louis Lepke, Kid Dropper Kaplan, Owney Madden, Lucky Luciano, Little Augie Orgen, and a ton of other guys. Some of those guys I saw right on my own block, certainly in the joints I was decorating, and some of those guys I saw dead.

Two weeks after I started working for Dominic and Carlo, there was a murder right in front of the club. Some pal of theirs had just been released from Sing Sing after doing five for armed robbery. I actually saw the creep run into a Jewish bakery, grab a big bread knife, and for no reason at all, run to a horse drawn wagon, climb up and stab the Negro driver to death. What bastards these mugs were. 'Gave a lot of good Italians and Irish and a lot of us good Jews a bad name.

But these characters were just a bunch of big mamas' boys with guns. And if you sang a few songs or told 'em jokes, they thought you were a genius or something and left you alone. I guess I must have been a genius. Take that very morning. I'd come early to Dominic and Carlo's to finish up my diva, when some uptown dame traipsed into the club with a manicured poodle. The dame was checking things out to see if the place was "respectable" enough for her and her hoity-toity guests. While she was grilling Dominic with snooty questions about "propriety" and "privacy" like she was a princess or something, I took the Tootsie Roll I was munching and placed it on the floor right behind her dumb dog. When they finished talking, and Carlo had showed her out, he turned around and stepped right in it.

"Che cane stupido e dannato! Stupid goddam dog! "

Dominic laughed till he cried. "It's just a Tootsie Roll dog turd!" He practically choked.

Jeeze, they loved that kinda crap. Like I was a genus or something. Hell, maybe I was.

Joey   *1932*

Holding his nose, Benny Stark stepped onto a narrow, wooden plank over the five foot space separating the rooftops of buildings 56 and 58. Between the two tenements, eight flights down, the warm stench of rotting garbage was suffocating, propelling more than the usual rancid odors from the alley below, sending up clouds of noxious compost all eight flights. Benny tried to stifle the gag at the back of his throat. Wiping down the lapels of his new camel wool blazer as if the putrid smells had caused a smudge, he hopped off the board and found the crap game he was looking for. The guys from 56 had already started, and dice and cash were flying fast. Benny believed this time they'd let him in the game. *One look at this get-up, and they'll see Benny Stark's no shlump,* he smiled, and nonchalantly hitched up his white linen pants so everyone could get a real good look at his new, snow white, kid glove leather shoes and bubble-gum pink argyle socks blazing beneath his trouser cuffs. He reckoned anyone cavorting on the 56 rooftop would surly behold his new duds and see he was a real true, high-class macher. Alas, completely unobvious to Benny was the strident reek of herring with Swiss cheese breath emanating past his tongue.

The tenement rooftop, filthy, dusty, plastered in a slick glaze of old tar and ever-fresh pigeon dung, was the usual bustling, crammed-to-the-teeth, sky-high playground on that balmy Spring morning. Benny elbowed past two boys flying a kite, pushed aside an accordion player, and stepped over Reba Pinsky who, while making-out with Danny Bloom, was oblivious to the skirt riding up to her waist, providing an ample view of her goods. Benny sauntered past a pimply teenager who had tied up a screeching cat in a burlap bag, and was tossing it off the roof. Undeterred, by neither pussy, Benny strutted toward the circle of four crap shooters.

"Hey fellahs!"

"Whassup, Benny?"

"Whattayuh want, kid? "

"Snake eyes!"

"Ya been eatin' herring, kid?"

No one looked up. Unfazed, and blissfully comfortable in the shelter of his own oblivion, Benny flexed his knees with a jerk to flash his dazzling new shoes and socks.

"Move back, kid, youse in my throw," said Sherman "Sherm The Slick" Turtlebaum.

Benny slid a mere two inches away from the pack.

"C'mon, baby sevens! Baby sevens...*now*!"

Benny leaned in and watched Slick's dice turn up a pair of twos.
"Fuckin' piss! I said, move back Benny, you putz!"

Benny watched thee more throws, then cleared his throat. He
cleared his throat   two
more times. He cleared his throat a fourth time, and noisily jingled the
change in his pants pocket.

"Mother fuck! That's another ten I lost!" Slick griped. "And
what the hell's that
goddam clinkin' and clankin'?" He knocked an elbow into Benny's shin.
"Go on, Tinker Bell, am-scray!"

But whatever was oblivious to Benny, was acutely apparent to
Joey "The Pimp"   Rotollo. Joey had been leaning
against a crumbling chimney, picking off bits of ancient brick and
shamelessly tossing chunks down to East Third Street with zero regard
for whosoever head would absorb the bombardment. *What a sucker!* Joey
snickered, gnawing two sticks of *Black Jack* and waiting to make his
move.

" 'Got my own bones, today, gentlemen," Benny was saying,
snatching a pair of dice from his breast pocket with an affected sashay.

"Uh huh."

" 'Got a pocket full of gelt, too, ready for action. See?" Benny
pulled a wad of crumpled cash from his pocket.

"Maybe we should lettim in, Slick,"

"Whattayuh think, Moie?"

"That's good by me."

"Irv?"

"Why not?"

All four men, at least thirty years to Benny's twenty-one, inched
aside to give him room.

"Scoot on in here, Benny ol' pal."

Elated, Benny clamped his knees to the tar and shook his dice,
tossing a few crumpled bills onto the pile of cash. "Alright, alright! Let's
go, let's go! Shake it out!"

"Whoa, kid, we got dice. Save your bones for another day."

Cackling uncontrollably, Joey watched Slick, with just a hint of
slight-of- hand, ridiculously obvious, slide his "Tops" from under his coat
sleeve. The "Tops" dice were not numbered 1 through 6 like regular dice,
only 3, 4 and 5 appeared on the ivory faces. Slick passed the doctored
dice to Benny's anxious hand.

"Call it Benny!" Slick yelled.

Benny threw. "Snake eyes!"

"Sorry, kid."

This went on and on, Joey laughing so hard he thought' he'd be sick. He hadn't had so much fun in years. Even better, just as Benny was about to lose his whole bundle, a great glob of pigeon shit splattered his new camel blazer, and some jerk pigeon-daddy with a chaser pole smacked Benny right in the head.

"Fuckin' A, Mikey! We's shootin' craps! Get your goddam rats outta here!" Benny screamed, grabbing his handkerchief to wipe dung from his shoulder, but only made it worse, the butterscotch, camel wool now smeared with what looked like white shoe polish.

Joey was apoplectic, he couldn't breathe. It was the funniest thing he'd ever seen, Benny covered in shit and some moron sweeping a bamboo pole all over the roof trying to round up a bunch of flying rats. He could at least sympathize with Benny on that. For in Joey's estimation, the morons who kept pigeons might as well have been keeping rats. They smelled like shit, and left their shit everywhere. You couldn't shoot dice or grab a piece of ass on any rooftop in town without wallowing in pigeon shit. And what a goddam waste of time, he believed. There was fuckin' little dough to be made with flyin' rats.

"Coo coo coo!" yelled Mikey the pigeon-daddy, beneath the enormous swoop of fifty fluttering pigeons, the young man's naked arms covered in a thick patina of feathers and sweat.

The crap shooters corralled their pile of cash and scattered.

Joey tried to compose himself, wiping away tears of laughter, and waited to follow Benny out. This would be so easy, he smiled, almost criminal. Was there ever a bigger chump than Benny Stark? Joey figured he'd catch him on the board between 56 and 58, show him the mound of fish heads rotting in the garbage below, and oh so sweetly convince Benny it was his lunchtime. *C'mon, kid, I know youse hungry,* he'd say. He'd escort Benny down to the alley, his switchblade caressing Benny's new blazer, providing some further encouragement. After Benny's "lunch," maybe he'd put a few fish heads in Benny's coat pocket to take back to his brother Charlie.

But Benny didn't leave the roof just yet.

"Outta my way, Benny!" Mikey shouted, tying a red cap to the end of the long bamboo stick in his hand. "Coo, coo, coo!" he shouted again, and begun whistling like a crazed tea kettle. He waved the pole high in the air at the screaming flock of gray and white pigeons circling the roof. "This is it, Benny!"

Joey looked up, scowling. *Jeeze fuckin' Louise, I gotta stand around with a bunch of fuckin' flyin' rats? I got business!*

"Oh Mikey! This is so excitin'!" squealed a plump, platinum blonde sitting on a paint can.

"Ya got 'em!" Benny shouted.

Jesus! These asshole think they's watchin' the Rockettes or somethin', Joey sneered. He went to Mikey's pigeon cage and spat in his wad of gum. *Choke on that, you rats!.*

"Shut up, Benny! Not yet!"

"Which ones are the anipps, and which ones are the teegas, did ya say? Gosh Mikey, and how do ya tell which ones are the tumblers? They all look alike," squeaked the blonde.

"Shut the fuck up, Stella!" snapped Mikey. "Coo coo coo!" he screamed again, flapping his arms wildly.

Three lazy, brown pigeons had been circling the roof when Mikey's flock swooped up, engulfing the three strays. The three birds tried to dart away toward the 54 building then quickly circled back toward 56, but Mikey's flock surrounded them, enshrouding the three birds in their wide net.

"Ya got 'em!" Stella screamed, oblivious to the clots of damp white pigeon dung now adorning her head and shoulder.

"I got 'em! I got Owney Madden!" Mikey shouted, waving the pole like a battle sword. A long sharp whistle blasted from his teeth. "C'mon! C'mon home my babies!"

Joey had been crouching down behind the big pigeon cage to escape the showering shit, but this particular name propelled him upright.

"Owney Madden?" Benny yelped. "You just snatched Owney Madden's pigeons?"

"My ship's come; in, Benny!" Mikey bragged between whistle blasts, luring the birds back down. "I'll get some real good dough when he buys these back!"

I believe I must reassess the situation, Joey pondered, flicking feathers off the brim of his Panama hat. To Joey, it seemed crazy that a big operator like Owney Madden would lower himself by raising flying rats, when Owney "The Killer" Madden owned all of Hell's Kitchen. He controlled just about every pool hall, laundry, night club and theater on the west side. Even the high society types rubbed noses with him. A big cheese like him slumming with rats was just nuts, Joey deemed. But whatever the reason for Madden's odd penchant for pigeons, Joey supposed a visit to Mikey's house was in order when he finished with Benny.

"Look out!"

Thwack!

"Sorry mister!"

Already immersed in a very bad day, his new coat ruined, and out all his cash, Benny was the sudden recipient of a hard rubber ball right to the face.

"Can we have our ball back?"

Benny was steaming. "Sure punk! Go fetch!" He grabbed the ball and sent it soaring high above building 56.

Three men, Mikey, Benny and Joey, each with distinctly different goals for the day, then witnessed the ensuing, inimitable event that would change the course of their afternoon. At first, all three watched the pitched ball sail into an empty sky, when suddenly the clear patch of blue was consumed by hysterical, squawking pigeons. In an instant, the rubber ball had bounced back to the roof, along with one dead brown bird. Mikey ran to the spot and cradled a limp heap of feathers in his palm.

"Holy shit, Benny! Ya got one of Owney's!"

"Big fuckin' deal. Just let 'im buy back one of yours."

"You putz! It ain't like that! He's tagged 'em! He knows exactly which birds is his! When he buys back his three, he'll know in a second one is missin.' Youse dead meat, Benny, and I'm out a hundred goddam bucks!"

Mikey slouched back to his flock and waved the pole until all fifty pigeons swooped back into their cage. Joey could easily see there were two brown tumblers inside with slips of paper tied to their feet.

"Goddam it Benny!" Mikey howled. "And ya threw your fuckin' gum in my seed can! If Owney's birds choke on your goddam *Black Jack*, you can kiss your fuckin' dumb ass goodbye!"

Benny felt himself melt right into his new kid glove loafers. Reba Pinsky, Danny Bloom, the accordion player, the kite flyers the stickball players, and even the cat killer kid, all stared at him as if to say, *"see ya at your funeral, Benny."* And Stella inched away from him like he had a disease. Mikey tossed the lifeless, crumpled bird down to the festering alley between 56 and 58, giving Benny and the dead pigeon the same pitiable glare.

Joey continued to reassess. Benny Stark was now off limits. Having tempted the fate and hostile hand of Owney Madden, he figured, Benny'd be sliced and diced before the day was through. No sense blackmailing a chump who was crossing paths with a killer, and a nutso killer like Owney Madden. Joey'd heard Madden had plugged a guy just for beating him at pool, shoving the cue stick through his ears for good measure.

Joey fingered two more sticks of *Black Jack,* shoved them past his teeth, and hurled the crumpled wrappers at the birds in the cage. Still, he wondered, how did a chump like Benny wind up with new clothes and cash in his pocket? Benny didn't usually have duds and dough like that, Joey knew, and he was too stupid to steal them.

"Fuck you! And fuck Owney Madden!" Benny screamed, lurching through the unsympathetic crowd. Racing back to 58, he tromped across the board as fast as his leather loafers could shuttle him over the wretched refuse smoldering below.

Joey noted the deer in the headlights, deer in the scope of a 22 terror in Benny's eyes, and felt a sharp pang of regret. Not from sympathy did he sense this emotion, but from envy, the covetous hot envy of the sheer horror Owney Madden could provoke. Joey wanted to believe he too could corner some rat-patsy and arouse similar shock and awe just like Owney Madden. He could, and he would, he resolved. If Benny Stark was raking it in from his big brother Charlie, then his big brother Charlie would be forking it back to Joey. So there was no more need for a proxy, he thought, no more need to hustle the dipshit brother after all. He'd go after Charlie himself. Joey spat out his gum, grinding it hard and flat into the rooftop with the heel of his shoe, and walked away smiling.

For the rest of the afternoon, at least a hundred rooftop players would catch their soles on that *Black Jack*, thinking it was just tar.

Charlie   *1932*

So yeah, I guess I was a genius, making good dough, creating my greatest masterpieces, and playing the hoods for suckers. So what if I saw 'em beating up some shmo? The shmo was probably a crook too. So what if they were stealing money from the cash register? The morons were just stealing from themselves. And so what if most of these guys were murderers? I could stomach the beatings, the whores, the teeth rolling across the floor etcetera etcetera etcetera, as long as I had a paint brush in my hand. As long as they'd pay me to paint, hell, I could take anything. Besides, Charlie Stark was their favorite boy, the teacher's pet of Speakeasy 101. The hoods loved me aright, and to one mug in particular, Harvey Berman, I was practically a goddam savior.

Harvey was another in the pack of underworld characters that slithered down East Third Street. A short, plump, baldy guy with a baby face even at forty, that baby face fooled a lot of suckers. Harvey was a baby-faced tiger who used a pair of brass knuckles like claws. And there were plenty of guys in my neighborhood with the scars to prove it. He controlled the corner of East Third Street and Second Avenue. There was no trespassing from Churgin's Drugstore to Abie Frend's delicatessen to Slimy Dave's dairy store if Harvey needed to meet up with his "associates." For some crazy reason, when I was nine years old, Harvey took a shining to me.

"Get a load of this!" he'd once said to some of his pals, all slurping down egg creams one afternoon at Churgin's soda counter. "He's readin'! How old are ya, kid? Five?"

I remember putting down my comic book in a huff. "No mister, I'm nine."

Maybe he felt like a heel. Who knows? But ever since, he'd come find me to read his papers to him. Big tough Harvey Berman couldn't read a word. This went on for years, me reading him the morning *Journal-American,* his mail, his racing sheets, whatever. It got me plenty of candy money. I guess he loved me cause I never made him feel stupid he couldn't read. When I got older, he got me to decorate one if his joints. Harvey had a little dump in the financial district that catered to the Wall Street crowd. I shmeared a little paint around the place and made it look respectable. Then on opening night, I got to open for the band. After one verse of *"My Yiddisha Mama"* Harvey was sobbing. But at the very same time he was blowing his weepy nose into a handkerchief, he'd gone over to the bartender and punched him out for not watering down the drinks. Glass was flying and customers were screaming all the while Harvey was still blubbering from my song. Jeeze Louise, the stuff I put up with! But it was worth it, not only for the good pay, but heck, who knew teaming up with hoods like Harvey would lead me straight into the arms of my greatest love.

The night after he'd sent his bartender to the hospital, I was down at his club sweeping up broken glass.

"Enough with the broom, kid," Harvey said, jabbing a dollar in my pocket. "Take this and go up to Harlem. I want ya to check out a sleaze-hole called the Sugar Cane. Ask for Tony Partello. He owns the dump. He's expectin' ya. You spruce it up good, and I can squeeze the deal to buy it right off his butt. You're not scared of Niggertown, are ya, kid?"

Who me? Hell, I was pals with Cab Calloway!

A packed trolley, two subway trains and almost an hour later, I was climbing down a million steps into the dungeon of the Sugar Cane. Harvey was right, it was nothing but a dark, smoky cave. A real dump, but I soon learned the place could be exciting as hell. Unlike Harlem's swanky Cotton Club, or Small's Paradise or Connie's Inn that didn't let in colored people, both blacks and whites could mingle at the Sugar Cane all night long. What a scene! The place was a madhouse. I didn't think I could ever find anybody, the joint was so packed. Hot sexy couples swayed across the dance floor, saxophones on fire like the music was in flames. I saw girls kissing girls and boys kissing boys in dark, back corners, and everything under a thick cloud of marijuana smoke. But no one cared about black or white, who was who or what was what. And suddenly, in some crazy kind of way, I started to like it. Like it was real life or something.

I wormed through the pulsating crowd looking for that Partello guy, and wound up near the kitchen at the back of the club. I really wanted to forget the damn job and just stand back to watch the wild dancing. Then I realized standing next to me was this tiny Negro girl, maybe only five feet tall and just a teenager. She was a beautiful, light skinned "high yeller" with big dark eyes, dressed to kill in a two piece red wool suit and wearing a red felt hat with a long peacock feather stuck in the top.

"This joint really jumps!" I said.

"I'm just waiting for my father," she answered coldly.

Boy, what a slam. I guess she thought it was a come-on. And maybe it was. She sure was gorgeous, and I could tell this girl had class. Maybe it was time for me to think serious about girls again. I hadn't had a steady girl in over two years. Not since Cookie Klein dumped me for Louie Lepke. Yep, Louis Buchalter Lepke, one of the biggest, roughest hoods in town. Me and Cookie had been inseparable, singing in clubs all over the neighborhood. She was a cute brunette, who could belt out a song too, just like Georgia Gibbs, but better. Posters started popping up every where, *"Charlie Stark and Cookie Klein, The Romeo and Juliet Of Song Will Positively Appear."* We were hot stuff. And in more ways than one, if ya know what I mean. Somehow Lepke got his eye on her, maybe after seeing our act. So he wooed her with big time money and promises of a recording contract, and I lost her. Poor thing. She never got no contract, just a pact with Satan. And you sure as hell don't go competing for the same girl with a devil. I decided to lay off any thoughts of finding serious romance for a while. Cookie broke my heart. Anyways, I was workin' my ass off, I didn't have no time for serious romance, at least not until that very moment in the steamy Sugar Cane.

An old colored man popped out of the kitchen and gave me the scoop on Partello, whose promise to meet me turned out to be nothin' but a red herring. The old guy and me got to talkin.' His name was Coney Thomas, and of all things was the Negro girl's Pop. Before I knew it, Coney and me wound up drinking and shmoozing for two hours. But only Coney and me did the shmoozing. His daughter, her name was Opal, hardly said a word.

"So where'd you get a name like that?" I asked him, too nervous to look at Opal. She was drop dead gorgeous.

"Well," he bragged, dousing his *Lucky Strike* in a soup can ashtray and lighting up another, "I done popped outta my mama right on the Manhattan Beach Hotel front porch!"

He'd said his pop was a bus boy and his mom was a maid, pregnant and still working at the Manhattan Beach Hotel on Coney Island.

"The hotel was havin' themselves a big two-day long Fourth of July celebration. The Naval Band was playin' and crazy fireworks was burstin' and rocketin' high in the sky, and with all that hoopla, well, I just popped outta my mama right onto that Coney Island porch. So that's what they named me."

"Sounds like a tall tale to me!" I laughed, knocking back a shot of the bootleg whiskey he'd conned me into drinking.

"Well, boy, you been tellin' us quite a few tall tales yourself with all your talk of vaudeville stars and movie stars like they was your best friends."

He slugged back one more shot of booze and broke into such a fit of coughing I thought he'd rip in-two. When he staggered up to leave, I figured he was just plastered, but all that coughing didn't sound so good. He shook my hand like he was pumping for water and toddled off through the crowd. Then Opal stood up too. And though she'd barely said a word the whole time, she gently shook my hand and said, "I liked your stories, Charlie. I'd like to hear more of them some time."

You could have knocked me out with the peacock feather in her hat. I didn't even think she'd paid one bit of attention to me the whole night.

"Uhh, sure." I said. I guess I could call on her. Why not call on a Negro girl? It's a free country, I thought, my head buzzing from the booze and all that bumpin' jazz.

For days I couldn't get her out of my head. Something kept grabbing my insides with a funny gnawing feeling, like my stomach was growling, like I was hungry. But I felt it all the time even after I ate and had a full stomach, that hungry feeling wouldn't go away. *I liked your stories, Charlie. I'd like to hear more of them some time,"* just kept singing in my ears.

Wow. She liked me? What was it that she liked? I didn't think I'd said anything so wonderful. And I sure as heck didn't remember telling no stories. I was just introducing myself. Anyway, I knew I had to see that girl again.

I'd been with plenty of girls before, a ton of bad girls who'd spread their legs for any guy wearing long pants. Sure, I'd been one of those guys, but what was the point? They didn't care about me, and I didn't care about them. A quick tumble on a roof top meant nothin.' There was no passion, no romance, no nothin.' And there were girls like Sylvia Frend, who I'd had a crush on for years, who had class and brains. They were moving up in the world, they were gonna get out of these rat hole tenements and make something of themselves. They were goin' places alright, but not goin' for me, cause most girls on my block, good, bad, Orthodox, I mean not one of them, would ever give me the stinkin' time of day unless I was racing down some crazy track looking for success and makin' big money.

But this girl Opal. She was different. I knew that the second I met her. She seemed to like me just for me, not for what I had in my pocket. I *had* to see her again. But could I go through with it? I wondered if all my friends and family would say I was committing a sin to be with a Negro. And the Talyenas I worked for, Jeeze, they hated blacks. Would those scumbags come beat me up? Beat her up? Or worse? But how could love ever be a sin?

"I liked your stories, Charlie. I'd like to hear more of them some time."

Heck, come the weekend, thank you Harvey Berman, I was back at the Sugar Cane in a flash.

Opal   *1932*

Charlie Johnson and His Orchestra put a wrap on *"Sweet Georgia Brown"* with a flurry of trombones and a ka-jing to the final cymbal. Fifteen hundred toe-tapping, illegally-sipping martini drinkers then settled back for the ensuing floor show at a sold-out Small's Paradise. From a cozy, red leather booth near the dance floor, a lanky old man in a tuxedo and his henna-bobbed, buxom young girlfriend had just paid their check and were scooting out behind their table, careful to avoid the passing cigarette girl, when the strap to Opal's tray snapped in-two. The heavy oak tray she'd just restocked, and all forty packs of Old Golds, Camels, Pall Malls, and Luckies came crashing down on the poor man's head. It was bad enough the man turned out to be Mayor Walker's uncle who'd now probably get his nephew to arrange an "unprompted" raid, but the pink Hawaiian lei strap was part of her costume, which Opal was responsible for having repaired or having the cost deducted from her meager salary.

It had been that kind of week. On Monday she'd broken out in hives from a shrimp cocktail she sampled between the Bessie Smith Show and the "Jungle Girl Review," management insisting she and her roseola promptly exit the premises. On Wednesday, with a Spring deluge flooding the sidewalks, Opal sloshed in thirty minutes late when her Lenox Avenue trolley broke down and she had to scramble all seven blocks in the pouring rain. After management's scathing reprimand and the frantic drying of hair and shoes, Opal learned her regular station had been assigned to another girl, the station where Owney Madden and his entourage had given her replacement a pre-paid hundred dollar tip. And now, by Friday, she was assaulting customers.

"I am so terribly sorry!" she gushed, grabbing napkins, the linen tablecloth, even her crackly grass skirt to wipe off the man's head as if her fervent swabbing could eviscerate the small red lump rising above his left ear.

"I'm fine, Miss," the man, seventy at least, grumbled, smoothing back a stray lock of Brylcreamed slick white hair.

"This joint sure ain't like it used to be! I told ya we shoulda gone to Connie's Inn!" whined his companion, at least forty years younger.

Their hauteur in tact, the couple stepped over the debris, sashaying past Opal, past the hula-wriggling Delores and Her Tropical Titillators, and out to their waiting limousine on Seventh Avenue.

Opal smiled repentantly at the indignant glare of witnesses, stooped down to rearrange the cigarette packs back onto her tray and crawled under the table to retrieve a dozen scattered coins. Reduced to her knees, surrounded by judge and jury, she was indeed aware of her crime, and certain of conviction, sentence and penalty, all of which she knew had nothing to do with a knock to an old man's head or to the calamities at work, but had everything to do with her own shameful behavior the week before.

Haunted by her deplorable conduct at the Sugar Cane, she had agonized the entire week, certain she was the Queen Hussy of Harlem, and absolutely convinced Charlie Stark must believe the exact same thing. Everyday since, almost to the hour, almost to the minute, she thrashed, disparaged and crucified herself for her wantonness. Even more crushing was the belief she had so stupidly squandered any chance at love. But that too was preposterous, she grieved. Charlie wasn't interested in her, nor should he be interested in a distinct and manifest, openly wicked hussy. The thrashing only intensified each night she met Coney after work, scanning the teeming Sugar Cane for Charlie, but with no red-haired white boy in sight. *I am repugnant to him*, she would rail inside, *I took his hand. "I'd like to hear more of your stories some time." Oh God, how could he possibly think of me other than a vile, cheap Jezebel?* And even if she hadn't behaved so brazenly, she thought, why would Charlie remotely be interested in a lump of a girl who sat like a stump the whole evening, barely saying one word?

Unable to finish out her shift, Opal retreated to the cloakroom and hung up the broken cigarette tray, promising her boss she'd pay for the shattered strap. Snatching a half-chewed chicken breast and baked potato from a passing bus boy, she wrapped it in wax paper and deposited Coney's dinner into her handbag, then floundered out the back door. All through the five block march to the Sugar Cane, Opal resolved she would only collect her father and go straight home. Not once would she look to the phone booth nor search the crowd nor strain for the scent of a cheap cigar. For the umpteenth time, she reminded herself how determined she'd been *not* to want a boyfriend. Didn't she have commitments? Didn't she have dreams? Wasn't finding a boyfriend the furthest thing from her mind?

She did have one boyfriend. She'd met the boy in high school. She had let him lead her up to the roof of his building and let him introduce her fifteen year old body to romance.

"After a while you'll get used to it," the boy, Maynard, had said.

He was a year younger than she, in ninth grade, but already a self-proclaimed man of the world. He knew everything about sex, he had said, from watching the dogs in his father's junk yard in Queens. Maynard was skinny and cute and had such a kind face, Opal had thought romance with him would also be kind. But she soon learned kindness had its limitations. Kindness, she believed, without care or contemplation could be as barren and arid as any lifeless desert. A kiss, no matter how soft or passionate, was not kindness, the caress of her skin was not kindness. Where was the fervent probing of her heart and mind as well as her body?

Maynard's satisfying himself at her expense ended when he dropped out of school. Colored boys were not supposed to be in school, he'd said, and she never saw him again. She couldn't actually explain why she'd relinquished herself to his sweaty hands, stale breath, and jabbing pelvic bones every Saturday night for over a year, but it was all she had in the form of attention. If sex could translate into being noticed, even for only one night a week, she'd concede her flesh to Maynard. For Opal had been without a mother since age nine. Tuberculosis ravaging Harlem had seen to that. Her older brother, Jonas, was always on the street, finagling odd jobs and losing them, or scrounging the rooftops for his own personal triumphs, and her father had his own survival to think about. Coney had to raise two little ones on the trifling salary he made driving a meat truck by day, and on the nightly pennies he earned waiting tables at the Sugar Cane. So Opal was almost always left alone. At age nine or nineteen, it didn't matter, her dark, small apartment and the profound shroud of loneliness would become suffocating. A room became a cell, the apartment a morgue, and loneliness became a quiet little death, whispering hushed tones inside her head. *"All there is, is you."*

But finding a boyfriend was the last thing on her mind. Her more pressing pursuit was to make enough money, starching shirts every afternoon and on weekends at the laundry across from her building, in the hope of getting to Cheyney Normal Teachers' College when she graduated high school. Her dream of a real career was buoyed when she got the better job, and better money, at Small's Paradise. The girls at Small's said if she were lucky, one tip from the hand of a well-heeled dandy could pay her rent for a month. But Opal's tips dribbled in by dimes and nickels. The big bills went to the girls who served up much more than a bottle of bootleg rum and a match to a Cuban cigar. Opal could have paid her way to any teachers' college in the entire state of New York, in the entire United States if she wanted, if she had only spread her legs for every Maynard in the club.

And she worried about Coney. Her forty-seven year old father, and the persistent, raspy cough knotting his throat, moved through his day with the doddering gait of an eighty-seven year old man. The ever present cigarette, an appendage to his lower lip, was turning his lungs into mincemeat like the beef off his truck.

"It's just the asthma," he'd fake a smile on their midnight walks home from the Sugar Cane.

But each gasp from his lungs would only resurrect visions of her mother withering in rumpled, tubercular-infected bed sheets, coughing up bloodstained phlegm. How long would she have her father, she so often feared?

"I'll be just fine," Coney would add between gasps for air, having to lean against a lamppost, unable to walk just four doors home without stopping at least twice.

How soon would he take his last breath and leave her too? How soon would loneliness become absolute and unconditional, as if her very existence were just another piece of broken furniture in the apartment, as though loneliness were also beyond repair? But despite the ruthless ache of her isolation, no matter how severe the hunger of her own body's desire, she would never again subordinate herself to the Maynards of the world. Never.

Or so she had thought. In one night, over the waning flame of a burnt candle stuck in an empty beer bottle, that Opal would surrender to an ancient hunger was both inexplicable and earth-shattering.

"Ya know, you can make little toys outta melted candle wax."

Now, trudging to the Sugar Cane, Opal fought back the temptation to replay the sights and sounds of that night, dream and nightmare in perfect combination.

"Password, lady."

She tugged at the Sugar Cane's heavy iron door.

"C'mon, lady, gimme the password."

"Oh yes, sorry," she muttered fuzzily at the gatekeeper slouched behind an iron-barred window. "'Teddy Roosevelt.' "

The door screeched open to a blurry haze of smoke and sultry saxophones creeping up the staircase and out to the street. On any other night, the Sugar Cane's billowing, turbulent smog, slithering from the basement like a bewitched cobra, roused excitement and mystery, now it only seemed she was striding through the steamy mists of hell. Opal plodded down the creaky staircase, determined to focus only on finding her father, and not on who might be sitting in the crowd below. Past a pack of love-struck gay sailor boys in navy whites ogling their waiter, through the thrashing dance floor and scattered tables of drunks, Opal kept her nose in her handbag, wrapping and re-wrapping the hunk of chicken. Without once looking up, without even a glance toward that idyllic phone booth where she first saw Charlie, she marched straight to the kitchen. If Coney wasn't finished she'd wait inside with the cook. If he wanted to grab a table to gnaw his leftovers, she'd insist they venture home. Unwavering, face to the floor, Opal fixed her gaze to her own patent-leather red pumps, to the shuffling pairs of oxfords, boots and spiked high heels upon the dance floor, and to the cigarette butts lying limp in spilled pools of Monkey Rum.

"Sometimes I'm happy, sometimes I'm blue.
My disposition, depends on you…..…"

She would let the white boy crooner and his tinkling piano flood her brain and drown out any thoughts of Charlie Stark. She'd stubbornly concentrate on the Sugar Cane's acrid smells of sour beer, French fried potatoes, dime store cologne, and the spicy hot sweat of writhing dancers, rather than allow herself to veer for a second toward any semblance of searching the room for Charlie.

That is, until she was suddenly smacked with the sniff of a cheap cigar. She looked up. There he was. Charlie, one foot resting on the rungs of a bar stool, the other foot tapping to the music, stood puffing his *Cremo* at the kitchen door.

"Good evening," he said, seizing two nervous puffs from his soggy stub of cigar. "Whattayuh think of Hoagy Carmichael?" Charlie yanked a thumb at the lanky, mop-top singer pounding the keyboard.

Thunderstruck, Opal was grateful the enveloping crowd would keep her from sinking to her wobbly knees.

Charlie sang along, *"I never mind the rain from the sky, if I can find the sun in your eyes.* I think the guy's great!"

"He is," Opal stammered, "he's good. Very good." She prayed she wouldn't pass out.

"You gonna meet up with your pop?"

"I am, yes," she somehow managed to say.

"'Thought I'd see if you two wanted to sit and, uh, maybe have another drink with me."

"Well---"

"I really enjoyed meeting you both the other night."

Opal thought she'd faint dead away. "Alright," she smiled. She really wanted to shriek, jump up and down, and dance on a table. " Papa enjoyed meeting you too."

Charlie's elf grin stretched from freckle to freckle. He scampered to find a table and chairs, then, before Opal could sit, he wiped off her chair with his handkerchief.

"How was your night at Small's? Who's the headliner this week?"

She must have answered something reasonable. She was so nervous she hardly heard a word escape her lips.

"Ain't Billie Holiday opening on Monday? Ya know, I might just have to show up!" Charlie yelled over the music.

"I'll try to get you a good table."

"What?"

"I said," she shouted, "I'll try to get you a good table."

"Swell!"

Hoagy ran his fingertips the length of the keyboard and crashed the final note. Then, concurrent with the roaring burst of applause, he eased into a soft ballad. The previously wriggling couples now bound themselves in cozy cuddles and shuffled dreamily across the dance floor.

"Embrace me, my sweet embraceable you...." Hoagy crooned.

Opal glanced downward, snapping open her handbag, and fumbled with the chicken wrappings. Charlie rocked back on his chair and re-lit his cigar.

"Embrace me, my irreparable you........"

Opal wouldn't look up. She spied an escaped garlic glove in the silk lining of her bag and made every attempt to curl herself tight into a ball and dive deep, oh if she could only sink into the secret, hidden folds of that lining.

"Just to look at you, my heart grows tipsy in me....."

She fidgeted for the garlic, pushing away two tubes of lipstick, her compact, her comb, her house keys.

"You and you alone, bring out the gypsy in me...."

Charlie sat forward. "Would you like to dance?"

The resulting lightning bolt delayed her answer. An eternity of questions flooded her mind. Dance with a white man? In public? Just sitting alone with a white man in a nightclub was brazen enough. She shot a quick glance around the Sugar Cane. No one seemed to notice that a white man and black woman were sitting together or seemed to care. But then, across the dance floor, through the sultry sway of dancers, one weasel-faced, greasy-haired white man in a wide-brimmed Panama hat was staring right at her. His loathsome, twisted sneer was all too familiar to a black girl mingling with whites. *What am I getting myself into?* she panicked. Surely this would only lead to trouble.

"I love all, the many charms about you............"

But she so wanted to dance with Charlie. What was one trifling bigot? One prejudiced drunk, she concluded, out of a hundred indifferent, reveling fools was nothing.

"What a dope I am! I haven't even gotten you a drink! Opal, may I call you Opal? Can I get you a ginger ale?"

Now she had to answer two questions. What would be her answers? Yes to both? Did she even dare? *"May I call you Opal?"* He *wiped off my chair before I sat down.* Besides her own father, had anyone in her entire life ever shown her a fraction of these simple acts of thoughtfulness?

"Above all, I want my arms about you.........."

The answer, she decided, would be yes, a categorical and resounding *yes*.

"Celebrity boy! You back? Hello daughter, whatcha got in that bag for me?"

Coney sauntered from the kitchen, his shirt spattered in coffee and ketchup stains. "I could use me a drink!" he announced, collapsing into the chair Charlie had provided. "Four hours waiting on this crazy mob's hard on the feet. Well girl, hand over that lamb chop or whatever you got crawlin' in there."

Charlie looked away from Opal. Opal looked away from Charlie. She saw the sneering creature in the Panama hat gulp down his drink and leave. She nervously slid her handbag to Coney who opened it and greedily extracted his chicken and baked potato.

"I was just about to order us some drinks," Charlie said awkwardly, bolting up to fetch a waiter.

Across the table, Coney just smiled, clumsily tearing paper off his Chicken Cordon Bleu, but deliberately tossing Opal a calculated twinkle from his eye.

"I ordered you the Sugar Cane's finest Hennessy," Charlie said, to Coney, carefully avoiding Opal's glance when he returned. "But I'm stickin' to ginger ale tonight. I was shicker than a skunk the last time I drank this rot gut."

"Huh?" Coney asked, slopping over his dinner.

"Sorry. Shicker means drunk. It's sometimes hard for me not to use Jewish words."

"It's a good word," Opal said shyly. "It sounds like 'sicker' which is what most people get when they drink this bootleg Monkey Rum."

"Don't I know!" Charlie laughed, holding his stomach.

Coney ignored them, wolfing down the baked potato, gobs of gooey sour cream plopping off his lower lip onto the table.

"Is there a Jewish word for 'glutton'?" Opal asked.

"Yeah, 'fresser.' It's Yiddish for someone who likes to eat a lot. Like me, I had three plates of spaghetti tonight at the joint I'm fixin' up."

"You get to work in an Italian restaurant?" Opal asked. "If I did that I'd gain twenty pounds a week."

Their relaxed, cozy conversation flowed on like the calmest stream. Opal felt like she was floating in an open boat, and the incessant banter, shuffling feet and raucous din of the Sugar Cane were merely the chattering of sparrows in the trees. Slowly, as their easy chatter streamed on into early morning hours, the spell Charlie had spun the week before began to fade. Opal was suddenly aware it was not his magic that had previously enchanted her so, it was the comfort, just the soothing easy comfort of being with someone who was content to simply be.

"Lawd, make me a bed!" Coney finally groaned, pushing back his chair. "I don't know if I should be askin' for your autograph or if I should be fearin' that Tommy gun you got under your coat!" he yawned, after two more hours of Charlie's mesmeric tales of days in vaudeville and nights with Lucky Lucciano.

"Nah, I ain't no celebrity," Charlie grinned, "and I sure as heck ain't no hood."

"You might as well be, boy, with the crowd you run in." Coney stood wearily. "So goodnight Mr. Toast of the Town." He belched and started to cough. He kissed Opal's forehead and tottered away.

Opal waited for the *"Is you comin' daughter?"* but it was deliberately, she thought, unspoken. The mischievous twinkle in her father's eye was still there. Clearly, he intended to leave them alone.

"'See ya around, Coney." Charlie tapped flaky ash off his cigar, idly swirling his stogie through a pile of dead butts in the soup can ash tray, and turned toward the sultry singer on stage.

"Night and day, you are the one,
Only you beneath the moon or under the sun..."

Opal took a sip from her ginger ale, parked the glass, then quickly took another nervous sip. Silently, she and Charlie watched two remaining tipsy couples glide across the dance floor.

"Whether near to me or far,
it's no matter darling where you are,
I think of you, day and night........."

"I guess," Charlie said, shyly sliding the cuff of his sleeve over a spot of green tempera smearing his wrist, "we never got our dance."

"I guess not." Opal could feel scorching heat rush to her cheeks. "I probably should be going, too, it is pretty late."

"Can I walk you home?"

"Alright," she answered, this time without hesitation. She'd relish the few minutes they'd have alone, walking four doors down to her apartment, but was relieved, sensing a few minutes would be all her feeble nerves could stand. It wasn't so much the fear of being seen with a white man, it was the escalating fear of her own desire.

"Fresh air feels good, huh?" said Charlie when they stepped out of the murky Sugar Cane into a frosty Harlem.

"It feels more like January than March," Opal said, clutching her coat collar. "Do you think it'll snow?"

They could see Coney up ahead, stopping for breath and staggering in inches toward his building. Opal ambled slowly so they wouldn't catch up.

"I think it does feel like snow," she added.

Charlie didn't respond. *Oh, I'm really enticing him,* she thought, wincing at her pathetic excuse for conversation. *I surely must be the most unremarkable girl he's ever met.*

"It's my birthday today," Charlie blurted out.

"Really? March tenth? Mine is October tenth."

"Whattayuhn know," he mumbled nervously, "we got the same number." Charlie's hand leapt to his pants pocket and clattered something, sounding like a baby rattle.

"By the way," she tried again, "do you know a man who wears a big Panama hat?"

"I know a lotta mugs who wear Panama hats," Charlie muttered.

Opal wished she could gallop to her apartment door. *I'm making him miserable!*

Without speaking, they passed a doorway of solid oak, once the portico to a bygone elegant hotel, now the splintered entrance to a second-hand haberdashery. A raggedy old drunk was curled up in the doorway, snoring through liquor fumes steaming from his breath onto the sidewalk. Opal saw her father ramble inside their building. She picked up her pace, hoping she could shield Charlie from the squalor of her street, fearing he would certainly consider a girl from such a contemptible neighborhood with equal disdain. Two doors down, they stopped and peered through the window of an appliance store where new-fangled, shiny white electric ice boxes gleamed through the chain link fence covering the front glass.

"They're all the rage," she heard herself say, straining to crack the uneasy silence.

"Pardon me? Oh, yeah."

"We have an old one. We still have ice delivered."

"Yeah. Sure. Me too."

Moments before, Opal had wished the night would never end, but just then she scarcely knew how she could bear even the next few seconds. She mentally flogged herself, thinking what a consummate fool she was to believe Charlie's interest was anything more than his expression of good manners.

"Well," she said curtly, struggling to mask her disappointment when they stopped at the fourth and final doorway. "I hope it is a good birthday for you."

His jaw clenched tight, Charlie stared at his shoes. "It's been great so far," he said, not looking up. And then just like Rudolph Valentino, or Douglas Fairbanks, or Errol Flynn and a dozen other dashing leading men Opal had swooned over in so many romantic picture show love scenes, Charlie gently clasped her palm and pressed his lips to the back of her hand. "It sure would be swell if I could see you again."

"I'd like to see you too," she said carefully, struggling to contain utter jubilation.

The lips and jaw clenched so tight, and the cold apprehension in his chestnut eyes instantly softened. "I'll meet you at the club again tomorrow night if that's okay. And this time we'll dance!" He threw a fist into the air, clutching the rattling thing from his pocket.

"What is that?" Opal laughed, believing she might laugh forever.

Charlie opened his hand. "It's my lucky four leaf clover. I got it preserved years ago. It always brings me luck. Always. But I swear to God, I don't think I've ever been as lucky in my whole life as I've been tonight. See you tomorrow then?"

Opal nodded and watched Charlie go off, whistling and dancing a two-step down the street.

Her knees felt weak and her feet like lead when she finally stumbled upstairs to her flat. An hour later, her head clamped to her pillow, she knew sleep would hardly be forthcoming. Her alarm clock kept time with her beating heart and ticked away three-thirty, four o'clock, four-thirty and still her mind recounted every second of their sweet farewell. *"And this time we'll dance!"* Outside her window, the giant pink neon *LAUNDRY* sign blaring from the roof across from her building winked hypnotically. This continuous throbbing glare in her night time window was always a constant reminder of her life chained to servitude. She'd once believed she'd have to slave at that laundry forever. Even after she'd started work at Small's Paradise, the spastic night time flickering still sneered *LAUNDRY LAUNDRY,* as if the rhythmic neon were rocking her to sleep in some sort of sinister cradle. But in the very early hours of that morning on March 10, 1932, what had been a constant menacing beacon of neon flame, invading her room like a marauding moonbeam, had suddenly become a rainbow.

A boy named Charlie had kissed her hand.

Miss Wilson   *1924*

The Gypsy Tavern simmered blithely in its usual afternoon stew of bohemians, intellectuals and lesbians guzzling copious, frothy cups of steamy espresso and wolfing down bushy endive salads. Despite its frequent eccentric inhabitants, the cozy Greenwich Village café on MacDougal Street boasted a literary and artistic clientele Miss Wilson found most inspiring. On any given day she could rub elbows with the likes of Edna St. Vincent Millay, F. Scott Fitzgerald, Walter Winchell, George Kaifman, and Ernest Hemmingway. At night, when the Gypsy Tavern's dark walls became darker still, lit only by diminutive faint candle light, sultry jazz music, pungent hemp cigarettes, and female impersonators were often the norm, and she'd prefer the safety of a Victorian novel in the sedate confines of her Music School apartment. But during daylight hours, the little bistro's cerebral ambiance and a soothing pot of strong black tea could be wonderfully stimulating. That very day, just as the waiter was scooting her up to the table for her two o'clock diversion, Miss Wilson discovered something altogether breathtaking.

> *Unremembered as old rain,*
> *dries the sheer libation,*
> *And the little petulant hand,*
> *is an annotation.*
> *After all, my erstwhile dear,*
> *my no longer cherished,*
> *Need we say it was not love,*
> *now that love has perished?*

The thin lines scrawled on the table cloth were unmistakably penned by Miss Edna St. Vincent Millay herself, who was known to experiment with words wherever she happened to be, riding a subway, attending a ballet, or having lunch. Many a fine linen at the Gypsy Tavern had been blessed with fragments of her verse, but these were the first inscriptions to accompany Miss Wilson's weekly respite with Earl Grey.

"Good afternoon, Miss Wilson."

"Oh Mr. Hawthorne! Look here!" she said to her frequent Gypsy Tavern companion, the painter Charles Hawthorne. "Miss St. Vincent Millay has dined at this very table!" she said excitedly, pointing to the pencil scrawls.

"Quite true," her friend answered, examining the table cloth, "but I'm sure the last line has been changed. I do believe it had been published as '*need we say it was not love, just because it perished?*' The shift from the words *just* to *now* does change the metaphor. But all in all, a rather mournful poem, I'm afraid. Perhaps she was reminiscing."

Their ensuing discourse on the career and habits of Miss St. Vincent Millay continued genially as they pondered the implications of lost love. Still, well before the scones with Devonshire cream and raspberry jam could be delivered on pink-petaled china trays, Miss Wilson eagerly awaited a lull in the conversation for her more pressing concern, how Mr. Hawthorne might help Charlie Stark.

When she was first introduced to the esteemed Mr. Hawthorne at the Gypsy Tavern, the soft spoken and slightly graying gentleman with his casual charm and vast knowledge of the arts had kindled the spark of pure inspiration. Mr. Hawthorne, she happily discovered, was not only a renowned painter, but a lauded teacher of art. Two subsequent tête-à-têtes over tea and scones allowed Miss Wilson the opportunity to veer the topic of conversation toward her Charlie. She believed Mr. Hawthorne was the perfect candidate to provide Charlie with shrewd artistic counsel and to afford the boy principled direction. Most gratifying, she learned, the internationally celebrated, yet humble, Mr. Hawthorne had eschewed the pretentious, lofty circles of Paris and London, rejecting the affectations of high society and the company of savants, for the company of his students. After opening his art academy in Provincetown, aspiring figure and landscape painters throughout the world revered Mr. Hawthorne as the most accomplished art instructor in America.

"My educational mission in no way strays from mastering technique," he had explained one pervious afternoon over tea and petis fors, "but rather focuses on the students' abilities to learn not only how to paint, but also how to see and feel their subjects. Anything under the sun is beautiful, Miss Wilson, if you have the vision. It is the seeing of the thing that makes it so."

Their blossoming friendship, affording her hours of enlightenment and distraction from the dire challenges of Third Street notwithstanding, the serendipity of meeting such a profoundly talented and dedicated teacher seemed miraculous. Thus, the bulging portfolio of Charlie's drawings Miss Wilson had sheltered for so many years was presented to Mr. Hawthorne the previous week.

"Mr. Hawthorne," she now apologized, "I'm afraid I must digress from our discussion of poetry, to turn your attention to the boy's portfolio I'd given you. That is, if you would so kindly oblige the interruption."

"But of course, Miss Wilson," Mr. Hawthorne said graciously, producing the valise, and laying it carefully between the china tea pot and sumptuous pastry tray. "I actually found the work quite promising" He pulled out a few of Charlie's pencil drawings and one of the posters Miss

Wilson had saved from the Music School's Spring recital. "Charlie should enroll in my summer class here in the Village, and after that, if he continues to show proficiency, he may join my academy in Provincetown. By all means, please encourage the boy to attend."

Like a parched gardenia absorbing Spring rain, euphoria flooded her very pores, as if Miss Wilson could sense every follicle on every inch of her exposed skin opening to a thousand aromatic blooms. Indeed, the hairs on her wrist, just beyond the cuff of her tweed suit, stood on end as she returned her trembling teacup to its saucer. Finally, Charlie would now attain true mentoring.

Since the recital, though she had intensified her efforts to nurture Charlie's artistic endeavors, arranging for him to be selected the school's stage manager, Miss Wilson was hardly satisfied. Charlie, of course, had amended the position with his own clever nuances, becoming the Music School's advertising agent, set designer and even electrician. Thanks to his subsequent employment as projectionist and spotlight operator at David Kessler's Second Avenue Theater, the school had procured two magnificent Kliegl carbon arc lamps to light their stage. And all this, the energetic fourteen year-old Charlie had done without one penny of reimbursement. Thus, the job of cloakroom manager, the one coveted, paid position for students, Miss Wilson had also arranged to be awarded to Charlie, although his entire wage depended upon the generosity of those who tipped. And though scores of neighborhood children besieged Miss Birnie with constant requests for this chance to earn a few quarters, it was unthinkable to offer the cloakroom job to anyone other than Charlie whose decorative abilities clearly had enhanced the school's own revenues. Their once meagerly attended recitals had become standing room only events. And yet, Miss Wilson still remained unsatisfied. Charlie's true talents were prime for advancement. It simply was not enough for her to see him languish over mere poster boards and crayons. That Mr. Hawthorne, indeed providence, had now shined upon both her and Charlie at this critical juncture in the boy's development, Miss Wilson considered to be nothing short of divine intervention.

"I am delighted beyond words, Mr. Hawthorne," she gushed, clasping both hands to her bosom as if in prayer. "I believe with all my heart, Charlie will not disappoint you."

That night, while chaperoning the Stalwarts' club fundraising dance, she eagerly awaited a chance to tell Charlie the great news. Assured her teenage charges were behaving honorably, Miss Wilson rebuffed the Charleston contest and anxiously headed for the cloakroom. Elbowing past the hoard of post-pubescent Stalwarts who remained oblivious to their reeking applications of cheap hair tonic, with their dates deplorably dressed like vulgar flappers, Miss Wilson could only imagine her Charlie someday soon outshining them all. His association with Mr. Hawthorne, she was convinced, would result in life-altering, earth shattering success, grace and style. Her Charlie would be the toast of New York. Savoring visions of the Charles Stark Retrospective at *The Louvr'e*, she hastened down the corridor while the Stalwarts' hired bandleader bleated over a noticeably out of tune piano.

> *"What'll I do when you are far away,*
> *And I'm so blue, what'll I do?...."*

She expected to see Charlie, the valiant new commander of the cloakroom, leaning on the wooden counter counting his tip change, but he was not there.

> *"What'll I do when I am wondering who*
> *Is kissing you, what'll I do?"*

Way in the back, behind the jam-packed coat racks swaying softly under the dim light of a dusty bulb, was Charlie, holding a lady's burgundy pleated waist-coat close to his chest. His left arm was outstretched, grasping one cuff, his other arm was around the back of the coat guiding it through a waltz. Smiling, his eyes closed, and humming to the tune, Charlie had seemingly transported himself to the Waldorf ballroom. Miss Wilson cleared her throat.

"Who's that?" he yelped, clattering the hangers and returning his dance partner to the rack.

"You are a marvelous dancer, Charlie. Is there anything you cannot do?"

"Oh, it's just you Miss Wilson," he said, strawberry-faced. "I guess I have a wild imagination when I hear good music."

"Your imagination, Charlie, is precisely why I'm here. I want to talk to you about your art work."

"Yeah, I know, I'm sorry. I went way over budget on the May Day recitals, but ya said I could get a May Pole and decorate it. I just couldn't find one for under five bucks and there were other expenses."

"No Charlie, it's not about your current art work, it's about your future art work."

"Oh okay. What's the skivvy? 'Another uptown concert comin' downtown?"

"Even better Charlie. Have you ever heard of Charles Hawthorne?"

"Yeah, we read the *Scarlet Letter* in school."

"No, not that one, that Hawthorne is long dead. I'm talking about Charles Hawthorne, the renown painter, who is quite alive and doesn't write a thing, although his paintings to me are much like poetry. Mr. Hawthorne has a very reputable art academy in Provincetown but is holding art classes this summer in the city. He would like you to attend."

"Me? Why me? How does this guy Hawthorne know about me?"

"Well, as a matter of fact," she bragged, "I showed your drawings to Mr. Hawthorne, and he was very impressed. He thinks you have great potential as an artist."

Charlie turned away, retreating to the coat racks, clothing brush in hand, and began wiping down the lapels of a black wool jacket. "That was real nice of ya Miss Wilson, but I don't think I can go to no art classes."

"I know what you're thinking, Charlie, but it's not going to cost you a penny. Mr. Hawthorne has agreed not to charge you a fee. And the classes will be held in a flat right off Washington Square so you can easily walk there."

"I hear what you're sayin,' Miss Wilson. I just don't think I'll be able to go," he mumbled.

"Oh Charlie, what else will you do this summer? Sweat on the rooftops? Wait for someone to open a fire hydrant? With Mr. Hawthorne you'll have a lot of fun doing what you like to do most, your art. More importantly, this could lead to greater opportunities. Mr. Hawthorne has openings for the fall semester at his Provincetown academy. Even though you're a bit underage, he is willing to take you on. He thinks that much of you already, Charlie."

"No thanks, I just can't do it," Charlie answered. He looked like he was about to cry, brushing the back of the jacket purposely to hide his face.

"Charlie-- "

"I ain't no art student. I don't know nothin' about art lessons. The kids there will. I just ain't smart enough."

"Rubbish. You are plenty smart. I've watched you read a hundred books in my library since you were five years-old. Besides, the other students won't know any more than you."

"No, I can't …..I'm not….. I'm just--"

"Just what, Charlie?"

"I'm…." he paused, then blurted out, "my parents need me. They need the money I've been bringin' in from Kessler's." He brushed at the jacket frantically, inching further into the shrouded rows of coats and muffs.

"Perhaps so, Charlie, but think of this. Your brother Harry has moved out of the house and has a good accounting job. That's one less mouth to feed. Moe is working at the print shop and making a good wage. They're both contributing to the family income. And besides, you won't have to give up your job at the theater. The classes are just two hours a day and are only for three weeks."

Charlie remained silent, furiously brushing the coat with short, jerky strokes.

"Charlie," Miss Wilson continued carefully, having guessed the real reason behind his trepidation, "there is no need to be intimidated by art classes. You are both smart enough and talented enough to be in any arena of this city. The other students, even the teacher himself, Mr. Hawthorne, are no better human beings than you. But everyone needs improvement, that's why we go to school to improve ourselves. Whether it's you, me, Mr. Hawthorne, or Calvin Coolidge, we all have room for improvement. You artwork is splendid, but with the proper guidance it may become truly great. Who knows? One day your art may hang in museums, Charlie. Please give yourself this chance."

"No thanks."

"Well then, do I have your permission to discuss this with your mother?"

"It won't do no good."

"Charlie, please--"

But there was only silence from the still garments, hanging heavy from their wooden racks.

"What'll I do, when I'm alone with only dreams of you
That won't come true, what'll I do?"

Unwavering, the next morning Miss Wilson marched past the roller skaters, the rope jumpers, the old men playing checkers, the peanut vendor, the organ grinder with his monkey, and a few Orthodox families clutching prayer books on their way to Saturday shul, and crossed Third Street to building 58. Opening the door to the hallway, she was instantaneously engulfed with the acrid fumes of cat spray. Cautiously, Miss Wilson stepped up the befouled creaking stairs, inadvertently cleaving off paint chips along the wall, to the second floor, making a silent, fervent pledge to help emancipate her Charlie from this human kennel no matter what. With a heavy but hopeful heart, she knocked on the Stark's door.

Mrs. Stark, her graying auburn hair tried up in a faded, yellow scarf, was wringing out a soaking rag mop when she scooted Miss Wilson into the apartment.

"Hello and come in! I've only jut washed half the floor, but come sit where it's dry," she said in her Romanian-tinged accent. She escorted Miss Wilson to a green linoleum table-top placed upon a gray, claw-foot bath tub. "That's all I ever do is wash this floor, wash and wash every day. Would you like a glass tea?"

"That's so kind, thank you," Miss Wilson replied, watching Charlie's dogged mother, circumspectly step over soapy floor tile to get to a simmering kettle on the black, pot-belly stove hissing in the middle of the room.

"How are you today Miss Wilson?" she asked, pronouncing the
W in "Wilson" like a *V*. "I hope my children have been behaving
themselves at your school building. Have they?"

"Oh yes, Ma'am, you have raised delightful children with
delightful manners. But I'm actually here today with some good news
about Charlie."

"Good news is always good. What's he done?" she asked,
pouring hot water from the kettle into a sparkling white china tea pot
she'd removed from a cardboard box under the sink.

But with a loud bang, the front door suddenly flew open, and an
exasperated Charlie stormed into the room, not before kissing his
fingertips, and touching them to the tin mezuzah nailed to the doorframe.

"Well?!!" Charlie shouted anxiously, plopping into a chair.

"Well what?" his mother asked, "and mind you the floor! I just
washed!"

"Thank you for meeting me, Charlie. I didn't think you'd come,"
Miss Wilson said. "I was just getting around to telling your mother the
good news."

"Would you like one or two lump sugar with your tea, Miss
Wilson?" Clara asked, scooping loose tea into a tea ball and dunking it
into the steaming pot. "I must apologize, I only got two lump left, but you
may have both," she insisted, bending back under the sink, removing two
pristine white cups and saucers from the linen-covered box.

"No sugar, thank you, just milk or cream if you have it."

"Of course we got. Charlie! The milk bottle And get the good
cloth!"

Charlie sighed, bounced up to the ice box, and returned with the
half-full bottle. Then he huffed to a free standing cupboard and plucked
out a thread-bare red table cloth. As his mother gingerly stepped back
over the wet tile to the table with a tray of tea and cups, Charlie spread
the cloth over the linoleum top. Miss Wilson made a mental note to ask
later of the origins of the odd red tablecloth with a faded illustration of a
large ocean-going cruise ship in the center. The word *"Statendam"* was
embroidered underneath the boat in cursive silk thread. She wondered if
this was the ship that brought Mrs. Stark to America, just as she
speculated Charlie was about to make his own momentous journey.

"Mrs. Stark, as you know," Miss Wilson ventured, "Charlie's
artwork is very promising. I have a friend who is a fine teacher and would
like to offer Charlie free art lessons this summer."

"Mazel tov!" Charlie's mother exclaimed, carefully pouring hot
tea into the cups. "Another good reason to be using the Pesach china! A
toast to you my son!" And she raised her cup.

"I ain't goin'!" Charlie yelled.

"Screaming? Why is there this screaming in front of a guest?"

"I *don't* wanna go!"

"Okay, so don't go. There should be such a tsimmis?" Clara sat back in her chair, folded her arms and stared at her son. "So, nu, tell me, why not?"

"It ain't for me, that's all!" Charlie grimaced and sat back with a huff. He too folded his arms in a tight lock across his chest.

"Mrs. Stark, I've been trying to tell Charlie the classes could help improve his talent and could possibly lead to career opportunities."

"I got plenty career opportunities already," Charlie grunted. "I'm thinkin' maybe I'll make cartoons for the movies. I'm meetin' lots of movie people at Kessler's. Heck, I just might quit school and go to Hollywood."

"Movie people, feh! A klug auf Columbus! " his mother scoffed. " 'You making movies? What you say, 'there will be a fat chance'? Be a real artist, Charlie, take the classes."

"No!"

"Okay, okay, forget about it!" his mother sighed.

"I had hoped, Mrs. Stark, you might- "

"I know what you're going to say, Miss Wilson, but give me a listen. With nine children I do my best to keep them in line, keep them straight and proper. But they do have their own mind. This I cannot change. A parent can only noodge so much. If Charlie can work and make a living without becoming a crimalnik, that's all I care."

Miss Wilson put down her cup. "Mrs. Stark, Charlie and I have been good friends for a long time. I certainly want to remain his friend." She glanced at Charlie whose angry glare had not softened. "I do hear what you are saying, and I do understand. And although I must admit, I am very disappointed, I will abide by your decision. However, they say it's going to be an unusually hot summer, and I still think that if Charlie has a chance to get away for a bit it might do him some good."

"Yeah, yeah, the gangsters and the Communists are everywhere, always worse when the weather is so warm," Clara added. "It's a shoot-'em-up every night."

"Exactly, and even though I truly had hoped Charlie would take the art classes, I do have one other proposition."

"I ain't goin' away nowheres!" Charlie shouted, his face burning skepticism.

"Charlie," Miss Wilson tried again, "the Music School is holding an outdoor camp in Oakridge, New Jersey for the month of July. What do you think?"

"Camp? What is this camp?" Clara raised an eyebrow.

"A nature camp, Mrs. Stark. It's simply recreational, a chance to get the children off the streets. Two weeks for boys and two weeks for girls, and most of the children will be Music School students from the neighborhood. In lieu of the weekly fee, Miss Birnie and I have agreed to waive payment if Charlie is willing to wash dishes. But he won't be a laborer, he'll sleep in the tents like the other boys, hike in the woods, sing around the campfires at night, go swimming and play games. How does that sound to you, Charlie?"

"Wowee! It sounds great! Sign me up!"

"Are you sure you can spare two weeks away from the theater?" Miss Wilson asked with vaguely camouflaged sarcasm.

"Oh sure, that's nothin.' They can spare me for two weeks. I'll get somebody to cover for me easy." Charlie stood up in a whirl, taking a deep swig of milk. "I gotta go tell the kids!"

"Not from the bottle!" snapped his mother, slapping his behind.

Dragging the back of his hand across his milky lips, Charlie dashed out the door.

"So then, we do have your permission, Mrs. Stark, to send Charlie to camp?"

"Sure, why not? If that's what the boy wants." She poured herself another cup of tea and turned toward the one bedroom. "Louie! You want tea?"

"No thanks, Mama," replied a boy's faint voice behind the closed door.

"I'm so sorry, I didn't know Louie was here. Might he also be interested in the camp?"

"Oh no, Miss Wilson, Louie must stay here with me. He is so weak," and then in a whisper, "he has no heart. He can barely breathe. But Charlie, for him it would be good to get off these miserable streets. Know what I mean?"

Miss Wilson knew exactly what Charlie's mother meant. Moments later, outside 58 East Third Street, the monkey in his fuzzy red fez, dancing deliriously around a light pole, screeched wildly at the gaunt, gray-haired woman descending the stoop. Miss Wilson tossed him a penny. *At least one of us has won a prize*, she lamented. Charlie agreeing to escape the tenements for two weeks did not seem particularly gratifying. His willingness to leave home for the first time, sixty miles away in New Jersey, but not allow the same time for his first true love, his art, spoke volumes to her of the harsh realties of her sad neighborhood. The previous night in the cloakroom, she realized Charlie had just used his family and job as mere excuses. That was more than apparent to her now. She knew making money wasn't Charlie's concern. She knew it was fear. At Camp Wauconda, Charlie would be content to be among the known, tenement children like himself. The world of Mr.

Hawthorne, artists, art classes, and museums, what Charlie perceived to be intimidating power and affluence, was a slap in his face, and a perception she might never change. For Charlie *was* the tenement, the tenement was he.

Back in her office, through her open window, Miss Wilson saw Charlie excitedly run up to his chums with his announcement. She couldn't exactly hear their conversation, only the occasional shout of *"New Jersey!"* over the organ grinder's accordion and the junkman bellowing *"throw out your rags!"* Charlie was being consumed by a motley crowd of boys, old and young. It suddenly occurred to her, she didn't even know their real names. The boy "Tollie Oppie," bouncing a rubber ball and repeatedly accosting Charlie with congratulatory back slaps, had been so dubbed since he was a tike and couldn't pronounce "Charlie Chaplin," Murray The Mock, Breitbart, Hey Hey Goldberg, Red The Dip, Moishe Pickles, Galomda George, Slimey Dave, Willie The Polack, Kishke Breines, who were these boys, she wondered, really? And who would they become? Would they forever be roaming the streets? Would their horizons never be broadened past Second Avenue? *These miserable streets*, she agonized, indeed might forever be synonymous with their self-identification. Camp Wauconda might take the boy out of the tenement, but could it truly take the tenement out of the boy?

Between two steadfast leather barrettes, buffeting each ear, denying the flight of her aged, gray strands, the simple refrain from the previous night's melody suddenly streamed into Miss Wilson's head.

"What'll I do, when I'm alone
with only dreams of you,
That won't come true, what'll I do?"

"What a fitting requiem," she sighed, "to the death of my dreams."

She continued to watch the circle of boys swarming around Charlie, knowing how oblivious they were to the aspirations of a desperate woman anguishing at her window. Then the circle parted slightly, only to reveal a ghastly new horror. Charlie was smoking a cigar! That most of the boys standing with him were also smoking could not temper Miss Wilson's unbounded revulsion. She whirled away from the window and sank into her swivel desk chair, mournfully speculating at what else Charlie might be doing.

From the street, she heard a shout go up amid Charlie's entourage of ne'er-do-wells, and heard the uproarious rascals galloping away like a herd of stallions toward some unknown excitement. Miss Wilson prayed the commotion was for the simple gush of an open fire hydrant, and not for a shooting.

Two weeks in July, she prayed, *that's all I ask. Two weeks to*

emancipate my Charlie.
 And then she heard the gun shots.

Bernie   *1924*

When the flagpole began to bend in the wind like a strand of limp spaghetti, Bernie knew this was no ordinary storm. Three brick projectiles from the chimney atop the cook shack bombed-out the dodge ball game, the knot-tying class lost every thread of string blown to the towering blue spruce at the edge of the sandlot, and the sand itself was pelting every single inhabitant of Camp Wauconda like BB's. Bernie certainly had witnessed the wrath of thunderstorms before, seeing garbage can lids soaring like attacks of flying saucers down Third Street, but this storm was different.

"It ain't gonna be like no Grossinger's!" his mother had warned. "Sleeping outside like an Indian, like an animal! Why you wanna go to this meshuganah camp?"

Bernie didn't particularly want to sleep outside like an animal either, but he wouldn't tell his mother the real reason why he'd begged her permission. Essentially, it was all Miss Wilson's fault.

"I'm counting on you, Bernie," Miss Wilson had pleaded one afternoon in his pop's candy store after purchasing her weekly stock of *Sen-Sen*. "I know your father can spare you two weeks away from running this cash register. And I guarantee you will have fun and learn much about nature."

Though Bernie actually preferred the latter by way of adventures with Charlie in the natural environs of lower Manhattan, it had become painfully clear his and Charlie's penchants were no longer mutually shared. Since their ferry boat ride to the Palisades, Bernie hadn't seen Charlie for a month. Bernie hadn't seen Charlie in the candy store nor even on the block much less with a knapsack on his shoulder fishing for guppies. Charlie the schmuck was always at David Kessler's theater.

"Because you are his most cherished friend, "Bernie, I know you'll be able to veer Charlie away from his deplorable decision to quit school. Fourteen year-old boys need an education."

"Right," Bernie had glowered that day, grabbing a push broom to sweep up a canister of *Raisinettes* he'd spilled after handing the librarian her change.

"Charlie," Miss Wilson had ranted on, popping a *Sen-Sen* under her tongue, "has a great appreciation for nature. The camp environment will help nurture his gifts. You have two whole weeks in the country to encourage him, Bernie. He needs to stay in school."

Bernie squished a *Raisinette* with the heel of his shoe, imagining he was squishing the head of Charlie Stark. "I'll see what I can do."

"I have full faith in you, Bernie," Miss Wilson had concluded, closing her handbag with a loud snap. "You will be my chief instrument in swaying his young mind."

Bernie had waited for Miss Wilson to exit his father's store before he griped out loud, "Chief instrument? I ain't nothin' but a goddam second fiddle!"

Now, with tents flying, cots, shoes, knapsacks, and underwear soaring into trees and way beyond the short boundaries of their little sandlot camp, Bernie's thoughts of how to approach his unapproachable friend were quickly supplanted by thoughts of sheer survival. But being one of the older boys, he was obliged like Charlie, Jerry Chalmers, Itchy Frend, Benny Lewis and all the other teenagers to round up the little ones and hustle them inside the director, Miss Stephenson's cottage before they too were blown into the branches of the blue spruce. A screaming crack of lightning and turbulent wind tore off the entire roof to the cook shack just as the frenzied campers bolted shut the camp director's screen porch door.

Young Miss Stephenson, one of the Music School's new piano instructors, was accustomed to rounding up boisterous children for games or recitals at school, but she clearly was unaccustomed to calming the tears of thirty hysterical little boys sixty miles away from home, wailing for their mamas. "It's just a rain storm children! Please try to stay calm and sit down please! Counselors, find your campers and sit in your groups!" she begged through curly, wind-blown bangs in her eyes. "Counselors!"

And then the rain came, buckets, torrents, and hail stones hammering the defenseless cottage like artillery. Amid the resurgent shrieks and ear-splitting pandemonium, it was no surprise to Bernie that the one boy to come to Miss Stephenson's rescue would be Charlie Stark.

"Hey!" he shouted. "As long as we're all together, let's sing some songs! C'mon gang! *Shine on, shine on harvest moon, up in the rain!*" he bellowed above the thunder, his arms waving wildly like a mad conductor. "*I ain't had no loving cause my ugly girlfriend's a meshuganah pain!*"

The terrified tears soon became tears of laughter as Charlie also launched into his rendition of "*Jeepers Creepers*" and "*My Little Margie*" with his own revised, twisted lyrics that had the boys in stitches

"*Jeepers creepers, your frog legs are leapers...*"
"*Margie, I'm always thinking of you,*
Margie, you're always stinking aren't you...."

By the time Miss Stephenson had made cocoa and passed around a box of marshmallows, everyone had long forgotten the storm. Listening to the giddy chorus of his warbling campmates, and slurping down gooey, melted marshmallow, Bernie also had forgotten about the storm, and had almost forgotten how much he hated Charlie. The only reason he agreed to follow Charlie to camp in the first place was not to oblige Miss Wilson, but to somehow get back into Charlie's good graces. He figured two weeks in the country would afford him and his best pal hours of rollicking adventure that would surely rekindle the spark of bygone summers. Since the ferry boat ride, Bernie had only seen Charlie just once, heading up Second Avenue on his way to Kessler's, flaunting his newly acquired taste for cheap cigars.

"Yeah? You goin' to camp too? How'd ya swing it with your Mom, Bernie?" was all he'd said.

But that was a week ago. Bernie never saw him again until yesterday when he, Charlie, and fifty other awestruck tenement boys boarded the giant Pullman, parked and steaming on track eleven in Grand Central. But he and Charlie didn't even get to sit together on the train. Charlie sat with Jerry Chalmers who stared all goo-goo eyed as Charlie bragged incessantly about the twenty movies he saw every day, all the celebrities he'd met, and all the half-naked chorus girls he'd seen changing costumes backstage at Kessler's. And when he wasn't bragging about his job, he was showing off the pocket knife his brother bought him, brandishing it like *Excalibur*, claiming he was going to become the Daniel Boone of Camp Wauconda.

"You just watch! I'm gonna slay me a deer and make moccasins for the whole camp!"

What a joke, Bernie had grimaced, watching the alleys and bricks of Manhattan evolve into country lanes and picket fences through the train window. *Charlie wouldn't know a deer from an East River water rat*. Besides, Bernie knew Mrs. Guyula, the Music School's Hungarian cook who was running the camp kitchen, would keep Charlie so busy peeling potatoes, he wouldn't have time for anything.

But when the mass of excited tenement boys clamored from the Oakridge train station and hiked the one mile to Camp Wauconda, Itchy Frend had corralled Charlie and announced, "Guess what, Charlie? Guyula told me they got a Townie to work in the kitchen. You're off the hook, kid."

Much worse, Itchy, the head counselor, said he needed Charlie to be an extra junior counselor since the camp was over-enrolled. All the way down Route 23 hiking toward camp, the leather straps of his knapsack knifing into his shoulders, Bernie prayed, saying as many bruchas as he could remember, that Charlie wouldn't be the junior counselor in his tent. He'd sooner run away, hop back on the train clinging to the back of the caboose, even die, before he'd be bossed around by "counselor" Charlie.

Upon arrival, while Bernie and two other campers were assigned the silly task to stack mere kindling for the first night's Council Fire, he bitterly watched Charlie, who got to help the big, burly senior counselors set up camp, hammer in stakes, tie-up tent corners, and haul in equipment like they were seasoned lumberjacks. Later that night, after songs and skits and the teaching of Wauconda's secret war chants, Bernie crossed all his fingers and toes as Miss Stephenson announced the tent groups and their counselors. Thankfully, Charlie was not assigned to his tent. Instead, Charlie was dispensed to oversee the seven-year olds at the far end of camp. Love him or hate him, let alone get a chance to counsel Charlie for Miss Wilson, it seemed Bernie would be seeing very little of Charlie Stark.

On the second day, after the storm, and for the next three days, Miss Stephenson cancelled all projects until every storm-strewn tent, crew sock, undershirt, tin plate and flashlight could be found, so Bernie hardly saw anyone much less Charlie. By the time Wauconda's little sandlot filled back up with doubly-secured canvas tents, it was the Fourth of July, a day scheduled for a field trip out of camp.

Eighteen year-old Itchy Frend was leading the pack, and Bernie, with a grind in his chest, spied Charlie marching with him, escorting his seven year-olds to the too familiar refrain of *"Hup two three four, sound off! One two!"* all the way down the dirt road away from camp, just like their good old days up Broadway, except for the fact Bernie was now marching alone. He purposely lagged behind so he wouldn't have to hear Charlie's insufferable drone all three miles to Stockholm. Miss Stephenson had arranged an afternoon of watching baseball. It was Stockholm, whose team featured Scoop Horsheim, a former minor league catcher for the Brooklyn Dodgers, versus West Milford. But Charlie wouldn't shut up the whole game.

"Mill-turds! Mill-turds!" he chanted every time a West Milford Bear stepped to the plate.

"Mill-turds, Mill-tuds!" chanted his charges.

"Knock it outta the park, Scoop!" Charlie screamed when Horsheim was up. "He can do it too! I saw 'im hit three homers against Lefty Grove!"

This was a complete lie. Bernie heard Jerry Chalmers say Scoop had never even made it to the majors. Besides, Charlie hated the Dodgers and had never set foot in Ebbets Field in his whole life.

"Way to swing, Scoop! I tell ya, the guy's a monster!"

After the game and subsequent ear-shattering fireworks, which Charlie swore were real bombs stolen from the Kaiser, and hiking another three miles to a nearby forest where, after Charlie insisted they trek an additional half-mile up a hill to get a better view, they finally put down their bedrolls, and Bernie, like an animal, slept under the stars. Or tried to sleep.

"Look fellahs! It's the Northern Lights!"

"Shaddup, Charlie! It's just a shooting star! Go to sleep!" Itchy shouted.

"Aww, you're tuchis is hangin' out! We's gonna stay up all night and look for shootin' stars, ain't we fellahs?"

In camp, out of camp, all throughout the two weeks of camp, Charlie made every scavenger hunt, every hike, every sing-along, and every single roasted marshmallow pure misery for Bernie. Charlie The Schmuck had barely said a word to him. Charlie The Schmuck acted like he owned the whole damn camp.

By the end of the first week, Charlie had conned Mrs. Guyula to let him go with her in Miss Stephenson's rattling old tin lizzie out to Fitzpatrick's farm to pick cherries. "I picked seven pails!" he said afterward, strutting around camp, refusing to wash his corroborating cherry-red fingertips. "We's gonna have pies for a week thanks to me!"

And the kids flocked around The Schmuck like he was the Pied Piper. He made up games like he did back on Third Street, using pine cones to play *Skelly*, making airplanes out of birch bark, and catching so many garter snakes, no one called him Charlie anymore, but "Snakey Red." Snakey Red never asked Bernie to help him tend the four cardboard boxes full of snakes and dirt sitting out back the kitchen. Instead, he'd picked little eight year-old Henry Zimmerman, a squirrelly runt who lived in Charlie's building, whose shaved, baldy haircut made him look just like the ridiculous bald guy on the *Sapolio* soap can.

"Check it out, Sapolio," Charlie was saying one morning when Bernie's assigned chore was to stack peach crates behind the kitchen. "The snakes don't seem to wanna eat the water bugs we gave 'em. Maybe we should try halvah. Hey Bernie! Run down to your pop's store and get us some!"

Mid-way into the final week of camp, Bernie couldn't wait to be back on Third Street pavement. He was fed up with nature, with sand and mosquito bites itching inside his shorts, with his campmates' dirty feet smelling up their tent, and fed up with Charlie Stark. The Schmuck had practically become a Camp Wauconda hero, and all Bernie had to show for his two weeks was a measly green ribbon for learning to tie a slip knot and half-hitch, and getting to work in the camp candy bank, a repugnance no different than shlepping in his father's store.

The ultimate repugnance, however, reared its ugly head the last two days of camp. The boys, twelve and older, were to pick partners and hike fifteen miles overnight to the Boy Scout camp at Highlands Lake where they'd spend the final night of camp. Naturally, Itchy Frend, a muscle-bound Johnny Appleseed, practically a man, Bernie believed, had picked Charlie to be his partner. Maps in hand, boots laced up, bedrolls tied, and knapsacks packed with food, water and flashlights, at nine AM the explorers swaggered out of camp down Route 23, each boy convinced he and his partner would be the first ones to get to Highlands Lake and win the prize.

Bernie, stuck with Harold "Weasel" Weeseman, a scrawny, blonde milquetoast from Hester Street he hardly knew, could see Itchy and Charlie up ahead, leading the way.

"Hey up, two three four!" Charlie was howling. *"Oh I come from Alabammy with my banjo on my knee....."*

Weasel, though it was almost a blazing ninety degrees outside even at nine AM, fastened the top button of his khaki shirt. "I never been on no hike before," he muttered nervously, having missed the hike to Stockholm due to a self-diagnosed ingrown toenail.

"Uh huh."

"My feet is hurtin' bad already. I dunno how we's gonna make fifteen miles, Bernie. I dunno if I can do fifteen minutes."

Bernie was too shocked to answer, not by Weasel's spineless acquiescence, but by what he saw up ahead. Charlie had hopped off the road, leaping over a drainage ditch, and was ushering Itchy to join him on an old, overgrown logging trail through the woods. Shamelessly breaking the rules, Charlie was thrashing his walking stick at scrub brush to make way for an illegal shortcut off the map.

"What the heck you doin,' Charlie?" Bernie heard Itchy say.

"C'mon! Ya wan get there first, or what?"

No one said a word. Who had the guts to stop Itchy Frend and Charlie Stark? But it wasn't their misconduct that churned the acid in Bernie's stomach, it was the glorious adventure he knew Charlie and Itchy would share for the next twenty-four glorious hours. Mrs. Guyula's fortifying explorers' breakfast of pancakes with syrup, scrambled eggs, bacon (for the non-kosher kids) applesauce, hot rolls, milk and coffee, began to bubble in his belly. Fighting back an escalating urge to throw up, Bernie envisioned Charlie and Itchy, real Daniel Boones, bushwhacking through prickly forests, scaling craggy mountain tops, swimming naked in babbling brooks, fanning the flames of a crackling campfire and sleeping under the Milky Way. Charlie would probably even slay his deer and really would make moccasins for the whole camp. The burning sludge of strong coffee and pancakes began to creep up Bernie's throat.

" 'Think there's any tigers on this road?" asked Weasel.

Five o'clock was the estimated time of arrival for weary Wauconda explorers to greet the designated campsite in a field off route

639. With food breaks, water breaks, and rest breaks, it was assumed eight hours would be ample time to trek the first day's ten miles. Bernie and Weasel, however, staggered in at seven o'clock. The wienie-roast, corn-on-the-cob supper had been over for half an hour, but Jerry Chalmers had saved them four cold hot dogs and a box of pretzels, which they inhaled in seconds, then went straight to their bedrolls. Neither Bernie nor Weasel felt like singing around the fire with their contented campmates.

"Sweet Adeline, my Adeline, At night dear heart, for you I pine......"

Bernie was too exhausted to even pluck stabbing chunks of gravel poking his back through his bedroll, as he pulled the cotton padding up around his ears to drown out the revelers. But it was hopeless.

"I need another marshmallow, mine fell n the fire!"

"Whatta fresser! Ya already had twelve!"

"Sweet Adeline..."

"A Lucky sure would taste good right now!"

"Are ya meshugie? Stephenson'll kick ya out if ya get caught smokin'!"

"Who cares? Camp's over!"

Now Bernie was wide awake. If those mamzers were so concerned about smoking rules, how come no one mentioned the fact that Charlie Stark and Itchy Frend were a couple of dirty cheats? Bernie pulled back the padding and pricked up his ears, praying to hear just one guy mention the obvious detail that Charlie and Itchy were nowhere to be seen, off someplace at their own illegal campsite. But the bile in his stomach, the jagged gravel poking his kidneys nor his sun-seared neck could keep Bernie awake.

The next morning, when every guy in the field was griping about stiff necks, eating cold cereal with powdered milk and having to shays in the woods, Bernie was anxiously packing his knapsack and ready to go. The sooner he could get to the Boy Scout camp, get back to Wauconda and board a train back home the better. He snatched Weasel from his bedroll, dragged him out of the field, and practically jogged the remaining five miles to Highlands Lake. Three hours later, stumbling, almost wilting into the Boy Scout dining hall, not nearly arriving first, but thankful not to be last, Bernie saw exactly what he was expecting. Charlie, sunburned and hearty, freshly showered and looking like he'd been there for days, was sitting on a lunch table like a prince on a throne, bragging about his overnight adventure.

"....I knew all about that bull cause I saw 'im when I went there to pick cherries. He's gentle as a lamb, but I didn't tell Itchy. Ya shoulda seen him run! And that's how I knew about the shortcut around

Fitzpatrick's farm. So when old man Fitzpatrick said, 'you boys wanna ride to the lake?' I said 'Sure!'……. "

Accordingly, and on cue, Bernie rushed behind the dining hall and threw up.

That night, with all the Wauconda explorers sitting around the fire, wearing their *"W"* sweatshirts, Weasel blabbing that the *"W"* stood for him, the final ceremonies for the six camps surrounding Highlands Lake were about to begin, while Bernie's stomach still churned like a cement mixer. The Scouts were letting the Wauconda boys share their tent site at the top of a hill where they could see all the other camps' fires reflecting on the lake. Any other night, sitting around a blazing campfire in a cool mountain mist with his pals, watching the other campfires dotting the glassy lake like jewels on a mirror, Bernie would have been utterly mesmerized. But tonight he was incapable of savoring any of the beautiful view. He knew what was coming. Miss Stephenson, who'd driven up from Wauconda with the younger campers who hadn't made the trek, was trying to quiet the crowd so Itchy could award the Explorer's Grand Prize. She placed the long, flowing Wauconda chief's headdress, packed with real eagle feathers, painted red, blue and green, on Itchy's head, then handed him a box of prizes.

"Well," Itchy started, "I guess I can't really award myself for coming in first...."

The fearless Wauconda explorer's, many unshaven, all burnt to a crisp, sitting cross-legged around the campfire in one big swaggering pack, broke out laughing. Bernie, however, sat listlessly, holding his stomach, trying to keep his intestines in place.

"...Especially since I busted up the rules so bad, no way should I win no prize."

And the gang roared. Bernie agonized that if Itchy gave the prize to Charlie, he would have nothing left to throw up. He'd already lost his breakfast and lunch.

"So to honor the Great Warriors, whose bravery and cunning have made them now our Supreme Wauconda Master Explorers for the year Nineteen Hundred and Twenty Four, the grand prize goes to............."

"Charlie Stark!" is what Bernie thought he heard, stabbing pain shooting through his belly. But what was actually announced was "Danny Pearlnitz and Sam Shakerman!" It wasn't until Sam and Danny claimed their prizes of hatchets painted in Wauconda colors of brown, red and yellow, and leather-bound copies of *Hiawatha* did Bernie fully comprehend and feel his stomach untighten. He looked over at Charlie who was cheering just as loud as the other guys, slapping Danny on the back, and shaking hands with Sam. *Finally, The Schmuck gets shown up,*

Bernie thought, now feeling relaxed enough to turn and view the beautiful, glittering campfires on the lake.

"Spirit of Wauconda!" Itchy began to chant, when the crowd quieted, "bestow upon us your grace and wisdom!....."

Bernie turned back to their fire. Itchy, his arms folded, eyes closed, had taken a dead coal and marked his cheeks like war paint. He stood close to the campfire's flames, and with his face and rainbow-dappled headdress glowing in the blaze, Bernie thought he looked as majestic as an ancient Iroquois, almost forgetting Itchy was just another teenager from East Third Street.

"....Great Warriors come and go with the tide!" Itchy bellowed. "The ever changing cycle of Warriors is like the cycle of life. Like buds on a tree, new Warriors come to Wauconda each summer to grow, learn wisdom and lead!"

Bernie glanced at his campmates. *What's going on?* he wondered. There was such a hush in the crowd, he thought he heard the beating heart of every guy. "What's up with this?" he whispered to Benny Lewis.

"Shh! Itchy's stepping down. He's passing the headdress to next year's head counselor."

"Thus, the spirit of the Great Waconda Head Dress is now passed to.... *Charlie Stark!*"

"No!" Bernie exploded. But his cry was suffocated by erupting screams of joy.

"Snakey Red come forward!"

A deluge of angry tears welling up from his eyes, Bernie frantically dug his fingernails in the dirt. For a fraction of a second, he somehow mustered the courage to glance up, only to see Charlie, now wearing the chief's feathers, jumping up and down like a crazed owl.

"Hail to the chief!" someone shouted.

His eyes stinging, his stomach raging, Bernie glared at the dirt, aching with all his heart he could strangle Charlie with his bare hands.

"Quiet down now, boys!" nagged Miss Stephenson. "The ceremony's about to begin!"

But nobody would stop cheering for Charlie.

"Itchy, Charlie!" Miss Stephenson warned, "Control your campers!"

Bernie could no longer hold back his tears. What for? No one was looking at him anyway, the whole crowd couldn't take their eyes off Charlie. Bernie's soaking cheeks dripped insignificant tears down into the dirt hole he'd dug and formed a tiny pool of mud. Then everything went quiet except for the snaps of their crackling fire, and all the surrounding camps were also shrouded in silence. Bernie sneaked a hand to wipe his eyes and face, but wouldn't dare look up. Even when a blast of trumpets across the lake shook the tomb of their campsite, Bernie kept his eyes fixed on his untied boots. The Boy Scouts and all the other six camps, in unison, had launched into bugling *"Taps"* in different harmonies. The wailing horns howled through the tree tops and up to the stars. Bernie felt goose bumps race up his back, but he couldn't tell if it was from the haunting music or from his own internal fury.

"Day is done, gone the sun. from the lakes, from the hills, from the sky ....."

Bernie recognized the voice.

"All is well, safely rest, God is nigh.........." sang the other voice's joining Charlie's.

One by one, each camp's trumpeter faded away, until there was just one lone bugle echoing over the lake. The last haunting note was held for a few seconds, then it was gone, and again there was silence. Bernie prayed this meant his horrible night was over, but then a harmonica group from the Newsboy camp filled the air with their rendition of *Taps*, and after that the girls from Camp Cowina started in.

"All night, all day. angels watching over me my Lord, all night, all day, angels watching over me! All night all day.........."

As their singing slowly faded away, all six campfires and their reflections on the lake flickered out one by one.

"An-gels watch-ing o-ver me."

Then silence, and finally Bernie looked up to see only one reflection was left on the lake, the Wauconda campfire. Miss Stephenson, her hand held high above the flame, pledging allegiance to some unknown woodland seraph, declared, "Great Young Spirits of Wauconda! We bid goodnight to this perfect day, and bid farewell to this perfect camp season we'll all long remember. Peace be with all our spirits in the days to come until we all return to Camp Wauconda! Counselors! Get your kids to shut up and go to sleep!"

Bernie turned over in his bedroll, away from the fire. *Thank God it's over,* he thought. *I want to go home.*

"Lemme try on that headdress, Charlie!"

"Hey! Who put marshmallows in my bedroll?"

"Sapolio! Stop pissin' on the fire!"

Bernie stuffed his bedroll padding into his ears, but it did little good. He heard Miss Stephenson start up her rattling tin lizzie and chug away down the hill. *Great, now these guys will never shut up,* he groaned. Half awake, half asleep, fully miserable, Bernie began to slip in and out of fitful dreams. Dreams of pushing broomfuls of sand all through camp then into his pop's store, ringing up thousands of green ribbons and hatchets at the cash register, dreams of watching Charlie ride a golden rickshaw being pulled through Chinatown, dreams of pushing Weasel off the Loop-T-Loop at Coney Island.

"Pssssst! Hey Bernie! You asleep? Move over, ya gotta make room."

"Huh?" Bernie asked, half-dead. Then he realized, it was Charlie.

Charlie was squishing his bedroll between Bernie and the trunk of a birch tree. "There's no room anywheres but here, pal. Move over."

Bernie didn't say a word.

"Yeah, like anyone's gonna be able to sleep tonight, huh Bernie? Jeeze, whatta night! Can ya believe? Could ya ever believe in your wildest dreams? Who'd a thunk it, Bernie? Me and you!" Charlie ranted, punching up his knapsack to make a pillow.

"Whattayuh mean, 'me and you'?" Bernie asked, stunned to be acknowledged by someone who'd barely spoken to him for two weeks.

"Camp, you shmo! Could ya ever believe in your whole life we'd be doin' stuff like this?"

"Shhhh!" someone griped.

Charlie thrashed around in his bedroll but reduced his rant to a whisper. "I mean, think of it all!"

"Think of what?"

"Of 'what'? Are you kiddin,? We been in paradise for two weeks! Wienie roasts under the stars, singin', hikin', all the games, and all the snakes, for cryin' out loud!"

"Right," Bernie muttered, scratching one of his forty-seven mosquito bites.

"I gotta be the luckiest guy in the world, Bernie. I got to come to camp, and I got the greatest job in the world to go back to. The head counselor thing is great, but how can I come back to camp when I'm makin' all that dough at Kessler's? I'm makin' so much dough, hell, who knows, someday I might just buy this camp!"

Bernie had long abandoned his charge to convince Charlie to quit Kessler's and go back to school. He'd also surrendered any notion he and Charlie were even friends. Now, it suddenly dawned on him, he didn't give one single damn what Charlie did with the rest of his whole damn life.

"Holy shit, Bernie! I told you I was the luckiest guy in the world. I just found me a four leaf clover right next to your bedroll!"

"I'm goin' to sleep, Charlie."

"Are ya nuts? How can ya even think of sleep on a night like this? Listen to those logs snappin' in the fire, and hey, I can hear the train all the way from Stockholm! Chugga chugga, chugga chugga, woo woo! And look!" he said, jabbing his elbow into Bernie's ribs. "Open your eyes, schmendrick!"

Bernie rolled over on his back and stared up into the meaninglessness void.

"There must be a billion, billion stars up there, Bernie! We must be right in the center of the Milky Way! Hell, we's in the center of the whole universe!"

"Shaddup, Charlie, and go to sleep!" someone else shouted.

"Bernie, look!"

A huge shooting star, like a big bright marble, suddenly streaked across the black sky. In his mournful two weeks of camp, Bernie had seen only one shooting star. Charlie claimed to have seen twenty, but this one was better than all twenty combined. Above the flannel hilltops blanketing Highlands Lake, above the silhouettes of towering pine trees black against the starlit sky, the blazing comet crossed horizontally the entire width of their view with such a long white tail, it was like a long white thread had been sewn through space, like something in the universe had been ripped, but now repaired. It was dazzling. It was magic. And Bernie, for some incomprehensible, excruciating reason, wanted to burst into tears.

"Holy Smokes, Bernie!" Charlie whispered. "That's gotta be the most incredible thing we'll ever see in our whole lives! None of those other shnos even saw it! Just you and me, Bernie!"

"Yeah."

"It's just what I been sayin.' For two whole weeks, we been in paradise. Someday, we's gonna tell our kids about this. Someday I'm gonna tell 'em, for two amazing weeks, me and my best pal got to leave the slums and go to heaven!"

"Sure, Charlie."

"I'm tellin' ya, pal, we'll remember this night forever."

Bernie turned back over to hide the tears rushing down his cheeks. What had been incomprehensible was now crystal clear. It was impossible to love Charlie, it was impossible to hate him. The second gush of tears, however, would not be attributed to this indisputable realization, but to the simple understanding that back on Third Street, maybe not tomorrow, but by next week, back among his cigar-smoking cronies, back among his celebrity pals, his chorus girls, and his darling Molly Picon, Bernie believed in the depths of his heart, Charlie, most likely would forget this night had ever happened.

Mama   *1926*

A regular potato peeler would have been nice. All Clara had was a three-inch paring knife to skin the mound of potatoes sitting before her on the kitchen table, waiting to be dunked into beet borscht. It would still be a five-inch paring knife if the tip of the blade hadn't chiseled off from so many multitudes of potatoes, carrots, parsnips and chicken bones hacked for so many years. However, what used to be a housewife's monotony had become Clara's meditation. The laborious shaving of potatoes, even with an old, dull knife, afforded Clara a benevolent rhythm she found calming, consoling, as if her devoted little knife in its gritty, droning, yet faithful circumnavigation around a mere Idaho spud, generated a celestial purr as comforting as being rocked to sleep in a cradle. For Clara, sleep itself, fitful, agonizing, fraught with unendurable cold sweats, was hardly a relief from the daytime nightmare of knowing her son Louie was dying.

Shave, shave, shave, chop, chop, dunk.
Shave, shave, shave, chop, chop, dunk.

Clara sank her attention into the mesmerizing, unconscious cadence of stripping sullied brown skin from white flesh.

Shave, shave, shave, chop, chop, dunk, one continuous long peel rolling off each potato, then four quick vertical cuts to one side, turn, four horizontal cuts, and plop into the borscht. It was a cherished hypnosis. For a few minutes, even for a few seconds, if she could be distracted from Louie's unrelenting, dissonant wheeze rasping from the bedroom, shrieking from his festering lungs, Clara hoped she could manage at least her own survival.

But s*have, shave, shave, chop, chop, dunk* was utterly defenseless against the one excruciating, merciless question haunting her thoughts, *have I made a mistake?*

"Enough is enough!" her sister Annie had lectured on one of her typical condemnatory visits. "You think Louie will get better in this hovel? You cannot let him just lie here rotting like a fish! Get him to a hospital!"

So Miss Birnie from the Music School Settlement House had helped Clara and Sam acquire financial exemption and an available bed at the state-run hospital in Mineola, an hour's train ride from Third Street. But after depositing a wailing Louie in a steel-framed bed, one of eight in a bleak, gray dormitory full of lifeless children, for a solid hour on the trip back home, Clara couldn't stop sobbing. For the next five weeks, in between scouring dishes, scrubbing the floor, hanging laundry, emptying the ice box drip pan, shoveling ashes from the cook strove, and struggling for sleep, Clara's tortured tears continued to surge incessantly. The ceaseless wringing and washing of her tear-soaked handkerchiefs was as desperate as her son's cries for home, echoing inside her brain on each numbing train ride back to the city. It was a nightmare without Louie, it was a nightmare to go see him. Every week Clara and Sam would bring him fruit, a few peppermints, maybe a comic book, but nothing could appease nor calm Louie's terror and pleading for home.

"I assure you, Mrs. Stark," the doctor would say. "Louie is comfortable and in no pain. The medicine we give him calms his lungs."

"Take me home, Mama!" Louie would sob.

"If we gave him any more medicine, he would sleep too much. We couldn't have that."

"I wanna go home!"

"Mostly, he's eating normally, but we would like to see an increased appetite, wouldn't we Louie?"

"Mama, please!"

"Under the circumstances, we believe, he's doing the best he can for right now. So I guess we'll see you both next week?"

"No! I wanna go home! I wanna go with my Mama and Papa! Don't go!"

"Rest easy, my son. So you can get better, okay? Papa and I will be back soon."

"No, Mama! No!"

"Don't worry, Mrs. Stark. Louie is in good hands."

"No! Please, Mama! *Please!*"

"Nurse!"

Streams of sweat plastered Louie's curly black wisps to his forehead, tiny specks of dark freckles dotting his cheeks and the bridge of his nose, glimmering beneath streams of tears, terror scorching the pale chocolate of his swollen eyes so red and puffy from crying, his frail shell of a body, like a dried-up starfish blistering on a sun-seared beach, shaking and sobbing with despair, were the lingering images shocking Clara's brain and shredding her heart on each train ride home from Mineola and on each and every day her son languished, away from her embrace. Her heart reduced to shards, as if they'd been dispersed throughout her blood in a thousand tiny, cruel slices of fleshy tissues clogging her veins, her legs, feet, her hands and fingers like black molten tar, she wearily crawled through her days in an unremitting black fog.

And for what? she'd anguish. In the hospital Louie only got worse, the blood-phlegmed coughing wracked his little frame constantly, shriveling what used to be an already withered fourteen year-old pubescent body down to the skeleton of a six year-old, like a decaying prune reduced to a raisin.

She had no choice. Clara had stormed to Mineola and re-claimed her son.

Shave, shave, shave, chop, chop, dunk.

It had been a week since she and Sam had brought Louie home from the sanatorium with a sack of medicine to "calm his lungs" and another sack of pills to help him rest. But now he slept constantly, barely able to eat, barely able to breathe past the gurgling undulations snarling inside his chest as loud and strident as the rattling, rippling sludge flowing through her rusty kitchen pipes. Clara's emaciated little boy had shrunk to a bird.

Have I made a mistake to bring him home? she agonized, dumping chunks of potato into the pot of thick beet cream. "Congenital," "congestive," the doctors had explained, and so many other dictionary words Clara deemed were beyond any normal human's understanding. "Mytocardial infraction," "compromised hematocrit," "patent dutus arteriouis," *like I'm supposed to be a biology scientist or something?* "Genetic defect," however, she well understood.

"Simply put," the doctor had said, "this has nothing to do with anything bacterial nor viral, but everything to do with your own family history."

So. It was all her fault somehow. She and Sam, something in their own blood, they were murdering their boy?

Shave, shave, shave, chop--

Clara's heart shot to her throat. A horrifying silence suddenly shrieked from the bedroom. The rhythmic, feral gurgle from her little bird's chest had suddenly gone completely silent. Flinging chunks and peelings to the floor, Clara catapulted from her chair and raced to the bedroom. She found Louie lying still on damp, sweat-soaked sheets, his eyes closed yet furrowed in a fretful scowl. Clara bolted to his side and took his hand. She pressed her lips to his sunken, gaunt-gray cheeks. Both his hand and face were ice to her touch.

"Vey is mir! No!"

A sudden angry, thick bubble of mucous burst from Louie's lungs, breaking the petrifying silence. "Uhhhhh," he moaned, his face remaining in an ashen grimace, his body limp in deep sleep, his lungs once again reclaiming their cruel, yet steady, panting recitation.

"Shhhh, my son. Mama is here. Tsatskele di mames. You are my pet, my Louie, my little bird."

Clara took a wash rag from the water-filled saucer on the table next to his bed and wiped off sweat from Louie's forehead, dabbing off pink phlegm from his lips. She kissed him, pulled the sheet to his neck, and tip-toed back to the table.

Shave, shave, shave, chop, chop, dunk.

A solid week entombed in the apartment, refusing to leave, refusing to leave her son, Clara repeated this race to his side, the gaze into a still bed, and the terror of death, it seemed, a hundred times, never knowing if the sudden, mauling silence would indeed be everlasting. She forced herself to think of something else, but that in itself took the strength of a Samson, an energy she barely had to peel a potato. She strained to focus her attention away from her dying son. She had to. She had to think of her other children and Sam. *Sam,* she sighed, *he is starting to look like Louie. He's a regular bean pole, he's lost so much weight. And how can a bean pole haul a pushcart even one farsntinkiner block?* Hadn't Sam told her just last week he had to stop every few steps on his way back home because of chest pain? And that was without the pushcart.

Clara forced herself not to think of Sam or Louie. She needed to think of her girls. The boys she never worried about. Well, maybe Charlie and Benny, such rascals they were, but certainly not the older boys who worked hard at good jobs. Her girls, however, she couldn't even remember when she last had a conversation with her three daughters. And she hated having to rely on thirteen year-old Loretta to mother little Eva and Kate, but there was simply no other option. When was the last time she'd even brushed Eva or Katie's hair? Clara wanted to take Loretta to get her a new dress, she was becoming such a little lady, sporting real curves and a budding chest below the lush waves of her long black hair. She so wanted to help Loretta through her passage to womanhood, but that didn't happen either. While Clara sopped and washed Louie's bloodstained pillow cases, Loretta had begun her own feminine bleeding without ever telling her mama. Clara had found a blood-tinged Kotex pad sagging among the rubbish in their waste basket, as if Loretta's momentous conversion from girl to woman were as irrelevant as a wadded up newspaper or the wax wrappings from a hunk of cod. But, forgetting most everything these days, Clara could never remember to mention this to her big grown-up girl whenever Loretta was home, "Mazel tov!" she wanted to say to her beautifully transformed daughter. But Loretta was hardly ever home except to make breakfast for the little girls and get them off to school. Loretta almost always spent the night one floor up at the Pinsky's with their daughter, Reba. Sixteen year-old Reba Pinsky, with long, flowing goyische blonde curls, was a looker, a real shayna punim with a body to match. That was another thing Clara wanted to talk about with Loretta. Boys. The boys noticed Reba alright. One boy in particular, that shtick drek Joey Rotollo had attacked her in her own stairwell. Of course he denied it, the little mamzer. Now, Reba hardly left the house. Would the boys now start to notice her Ettie? Or worse? Clara wanted to tell Loretta so many things. She wanted to warn her, to protect her.

"Uhhh," softly groaned her son from his bed, then lapsed into his gurgling slumber.

Shave, shave, shave, chop, chop, dunk.

Except for little Eva and Kate, Clara realized she rarely saw any of her older children. But, she sighed, who could blame them? *The house smells of Louie's shit and pee,* Clara brooded, *and all I do is sob and sob. Who can live with this, let alone the kinder?*

"I can't take it anymore!" Charlie had yelled last night during Shabbes.

Clara had just started the blessing, waving her arms over the Sabbath candles, when she'd burst into tears, collapsing to her chair.

Charlie was crying too, "This house is a morgue!" and he bolted from the table, slamming the door and running down the hall like a racehorse, disappearing into the night and God knows where.

Then again, she pondered, Charlie and Benny were always God knows where. *Hah,* Clara scoffed, *those two Mutt and Jeffs will only wind up to no good,* she thought. Hadn't she spotted Benny playing cards in the back alley with a whole pack of crimulniks? *Gambling at twelve years old? What next?* And Charlie, quitting school to work with that Alex Chertov, shmoozing with the show biz crowd *like he's thinkin' he's a big shot.* How many times had she seen Charlie flashing a wad of cash in front of his pals? Too many times, like he was some Mr. Daddy Warbucks or something just because he had a dollar in his pocket. If she ever caught Charlie gambling in the alley she'd wring his neck good. She needed to yank her Benny and wring his neck too. But she expected meshuganaha Benny to act up, not Charlie. She could count on Benny sneaking pennies from the pushke, or painting moustaches with boot polish on the faces of his little sisters while they slept, but not her haimishe Charlie who'd always been her angel, always stuck so close to home. Her little red-haired boychik, Charlie, where did he go? He was once so content to help her pluck endless grape seeds to make his coveted, jellied puvvaldull, who'd then cozily curl up on the front room floor like a kitten, beneath their old mahogany Sonora, and play Cantor Rosenblatt records, singing along with *Avinu Malkenu* over and over for hours and hours.

"Asei imanu, tsedaka vakhesed,
Vehoshienu
Avinu malkenu.... "

Over and over, Charlie would sing in his hushed, little choir-boy incantation as angelic as a butterfly softly fluttering through the heavens, that was the Charlie she remembered. Not the one whose voice changed and cracked and baritoned into a braggart, a little bonditt who'd become so cocky he was rarely even sleeping at home, and openly preferring the company of celebrities over his own family.

"He's a tyvul!" Annie had once ranted about the seven year-old Charlie just because he accidentally started a fire in the front room. He'd been watching baby Eva while Clara was out shopping. Charlie had said he'd dumped out a box of matchsticks to use as Lincoln Logs, but when his little match stick cabin caught fire, as well as the newspaper he'd used to smother the flame, Charlie had grabbed the ice box drip pan and doused the fire with melted ice. The fire was infinitesimal, but the smoke had engulfed the tiny front room, leaching wafts of smelly gray clouds into the hallway and into the anxious, hysterical noses of first floor neighbors in building 58.

But a tyvul? A devil? The fire was just an accident. Only once could Clara remember Charlie ever actually committing a truly bad deed. And even that was only in revenge for crazy Heckleman assaulting her right on the street. Willie Heckleman, the shlockmeister, sold used, rickety bicycles in a run-down shop on Third Street. He also rented bicycles for an outrageous ten cents an hour. The man was meshugie. He'd have a conniption fit if anyone broke a bottle on the street. Broken glass and the mere thought of punctured bicycle tires made him insane, because he didn't want to be blamed for it and have people wanting their money back for buying faulty tires. He'd vacuum, sweep and scour the whole block from First to Second Avenue looking for nails, glass any sharp things around. He was a lunatic. He called the politzei when Fanny Wisenberg accidentally dropped a hat pin in front of his shop.

One sunny afternoon last month, Millie Gershman had grabbed Clara from her vigil over Louie to get a bit of fresh air. Five minutes into their stroll past Heckleman's, a pencil had fallen from Clara's handbag. Heckleman came screaming from his shop.

"I saw that! You did it on purpose!" the wizened, bald gonnif had ranted, as if he owned the cement. He had pushed her away, knocking Clara off the curb and into a gutter full of horse manure. "Help! Police!" he'd shouted.

Clara was farklemt the rest of the day and all through dinner. When Charlie had come home from work and had found her so upset all he'd said was, "I'll take care of this."

The next day, everyone on the block was talking about Heckleman's broken window.

"'Looks like someone must have smashed a garbage can right through the glass," Millie had reported. "The cops had to get Heckleman out of bed at two A.M. to watch his store. Now he's got broken glass all over everything and he's fit to be tied!"

Shave, shave, shave, chop, chop, dunk.

Clara snickered, remembering Charlie sauntering in for dinner the next night with a shit-eating grin plastered across his face.

"Nu? Whtattuyah know about Heckleman's?" she had asked.

But Charlie, dunking his fingers into the sizzling stew bubbling on the potbelly stove, only stuffed a chunk of carrot into his mouth and remained silent. The rascal! But Clara knew it was Charlie even though he'd remained totally silent all through dinner, not saying one word.

Clara froze. The silence!

She shot a glance at the ticking clock above the front door. What had she been thinking? How could she let herself daydream on and on for almost twenty minutes! Again, the terrifying silence rocketed her from her chair to Louie's bedside.

His eyes were closed, but the usual pained scowl, so frequently the emblem of Louie's fretful dreams, was gone. His forehead was smooth and unfurrowed, his thick, dark, glowering, down-turned eyebrows had now relaxed into a placid balance, the splash of tiny brown freckles rested tranquilly on the bridge of his nose, and the watery, gurgling cacophony inside his lungs was quiet. Habitually, Clara grasped his hand. Again, she pressed her lips to his cheek, and again, both hand and face, as they'd been for the past week, felt like ice. Clara held her breath and waited for the resurgent gasp and gush of phlegm to revive her son.

"Louie!"

Nothing came forth. Clara gripped his hand, squeezing and squeezing in a frenzy to pump fresh cool air into Louie's feeble chest, to inflate his decayed, decomposing little lungs with perfume, a summer breeze, or the impassioned gentle zephyr of a mother's love, as if running through the fervent clench of her hand was a miraculous electric current, a lifeline from her raging heart to her son, a lifeline from Mama, a lifeline from God.

"Louie!" Clara gasped, expelling her own hot breath from her chest. The cold, limp hand she cradled was stony and still. The lifeline had failed. That sacred filament connecting her blood and soul to her beautiful boy, the translucent, titanic magnificence of her love, the spirit of life and love in God and the Universe that had sown Its seed in her womb and had grown her beautiful, beautiful boy, was now severed. Her beautiful boy was dead in her arms.

Clara clutched the gold-chained *chai* at her neck, and whispered the Psalm she recited each and every day of her life. "I will meditate upon all Your works, and consider Your mighty deeds."

And then she began to scream.

Opal   *1932*

For once, Opal had not been in a hurry to get to the Sugar Cane. Usually, she would be anxious to see Charlie. Usually, she would spend many meticulous hours pondering dress, shoes, hat and makeup for their weekly liaison at the notorious night club. Her makeup, in particular, had to be perfect, knowing how Charlie was decidedly repulsed by unwarranted cosmetics on women.

"All that rouge and powder, who needs that chozzerai?" he'd say. "Women already look like women. What's the point of lookin' like a cheap Kewpie Doll?"

Lest she even remotely resemble something fake or cheap, Opal took great care to apply just a swish of mascara to her lashes and a faint coat of "Ruby Garnet" to her lips. But tonight she was anxious for other reasons. Her habitual angst over the selection of makeup and attire was a paltry irrelevance compared to this evening's choice of diversion. Tonight, for the first time, she and Charlie would be leaving the protective shelter of the tolerant, indifferent Sugar Cane, and together, black and white in public, brazenly, she feared, and most likely idiotically, they'd venture out into the world of ordinary people.

Opal positioned a blue wool hat upon her pomade-soft black wave, threw a rain coat around the blue wool suit flaring from its shoulder pads and tapered at the waist, then hurried out to meet her champion on a raw, cold night teeming with gloomy gray rain clouds. Perhaps for one night, she hoped, plodding the half block to the Sugar Cane, she could let herself believe in Charlie. She so wanted to believe.

"I don't wanna just keep bringin' you sacks of cold deli food for dinner," she remembered Charlie scowling one night, across their table, above a particularly raucous crowd at the Sugar Cane, after weeks of handing her paper bags of foil-wrapped knishes or roast beef sandwiches from Delancey Street. "No matter what time I leave my neighborhood, even if I'm workin' uptown, your food's ice cold by the time I get here. What kind of dinner is that for my sweetheart?"

"It's fine, Charlie. Really," Opal had insisted.

"No it's not. And I don't just wanna keep bringin' you meals in crummy paper sacks. I wanna take you somewhere nice. Someplace with class. You don't deserve to be courted in a joint like this with cigarette butts and puddles of booze under your feet."

"Charlie, it's really okay," Opal had lied, so wishing for the same thing.

A burst of wicked laughter had then erupted from the table of four women sitting next to them. Two of the women had been dressed in skirts and silk stockings. But the other two women wore trousers, buttoned-down shirts with ties, and sported short, Brylcream slicked-back hair. These latter two had been staring at Opal the moment she and Charlie had grabbed the next table.

"And I don't wanna be in a joint where butchy dames are oglin' my date!"

"But Charlie, where else would we go? Besides, at least these women ogling me aren't dangerous. And we do have to consider that danger is an issue if we leave the Sugar Cane and go anywhere else."

"Nah, I've been checkin' things out. There's all kinds of swell joints on 125th street that look great. It'll be terrific, you'll see. C'mon Opal, we can't be chained to the Sugar Cane forever."

"Alright, Charlie. I'm willing to give it a try. At least we'll still be in Harlem, close to home if there's any trouble."

"What trouble? I'm tellin' ya, Doll, there ain't gonna be no trouble. Harlem's a lot more hep than you think."

The Sugar Cane was in typical frenzied rhythm as Opal now descended the steps into the cavernous chaos of dancers, musicians, and dizzy drinkers. She squeezed through the crowd, found an empty table and plunked herself down to wait for Charlie. But even the distraction of the Sugar Cane's rowdy bedlam could not dissuade her from thinking she'd made a terrible mistake. This thought only began to boil that much further when thirty minutes later, a whole half hour past their scheduled time for departure to that coveted dinner in the real world, Opal again and again repeated frantic glances at the ticking Timex, loose on her narrow wrist. Eight-thirty! Where was Charlie? "I'll see ya at eight!" he'd promised. "We're gonna have the time of our lives!"

Trumpet blasting, cymbal smashing mayhem continued to churn from the nightclub's small stage and dance floor. The mass of blissful, dancing couples seemed happily lost in the fog of their oblivion, Opal thought, aching for the same innocent ecstasy. *He'll get here. He better get here.* She struggled to distract herself by taking the cap from her bottle of root beer and spinning it like a top. But at each attempt, the spinning cap only careened into her half-empty bottle and fell to the floor. Three times she spun, three times she retrieved the cap, blowing off cigarette ashes from the ring of tiny metallic craters indenting the sphere. *Where is Charlie?* Opal anxiously continued reconfiguring the bottle cap's function, pressing it firmly into the palm of her hand to create a faint tattoo. Its sharp, spiky perimeter left a toothy imprint in the center of her palm, a raggedy but succinct full moon right over the start of her lifeline.

Branded for life, she mused, determined to think only of a supreme man who supremely loved her, tenderly running her fingertips along the cap's jagged, serrated edge, then enclosing it warm inside her palm. But an abrupt wallop to the back of her chair from a gyrating dancer forced the bottle cap to dig a little deeper. A bit of the ragged, tattooed circle on her palm now oozed bright red.

Branded with blood, she resolved, scooting her chair back to the table, *for life*. She gently massaged the droplet of blood into her palm, into the clear, curved line of demarcation of her skin that stretched from the center of her hand down to the tiny distension of purple veins on the underside of her wrist, believing her iconic little lifeline was receiving a medicinal balm.

Opal flipped the bottle cap in the air. *Heads, he loves me*, she waited, slapping it onto her wrist, *tails he loves me not*. She quickly removed her hand. It was heads. The faded yellow "*Hires*" font surely had confirmed absolute fact. The holy *Hires* root beer cap couldn't possibly lie, she concluded. Charlie loved her. But where was he?

Thunderous applause erupted near the stage. Then the house band, a trio of trumpet, stand-up bass and drums, launched into a crowd-calming soft ballad, and the once quaking dance floor began to gently sway. Opal sipped her now sour root beer and appraised the contented dancers gliding, and drunkenly stumbling to the placid rhythm of the love song. But they had nothing on her Charlie, she assessed. Charlie was a superb dancer. He could hold her in his arms and weave her through a packed dance floor like he was threading a needle, like she were lace, like precious silk, never once tripping on his feet nor stepping on her toes. Charlie held a woman like she was a gift. He danced with a woman like she was a cloud. Opal replaced the short, dark-haired white girl she saw dancing with a tall, blonde man, by inserting herself and Charlie into the scene, melting into Charlie's arms, dissolving into his embrace, waltzing across the floor. She sashayed her little bottle cap in a tango around the root beer bottle.

"All alone tonight, sister?"

Opal looked up to see a weasel-faced young man in a Panama hat. There was nothing familiar about his pinched, rodent-like dark eyes, nor his acne scars, nor the yellow stains glinting the sneer of his cracked smile, but the hat she somehow remembered.

"I have a date," she muttered, staring down to the table.

"Yeah?" grinned the weasel, his hands jingling change in his pockets.

"Yes, I do."

"Too bad. I figured we could get together, Baby. I had plans."

"No thanks."

"Don't be givin' me no brush-off, Doll," he said, laying his claw on Opal's shoulder. "We just met."

Behind him, two burly sailors suddenly danced by, knocking the Panama hat to the floor.

"Hey! Watch it, faggots!"

"You're pretty cute!" slurped one of the boys in Navy whites.

"Oh shut up, Tommy!" said his partner, "He's mine! Next dance, lover boy?"

"Fuckin' faggots!" snapped the weasel, retrieving his fallen hat. "I'd say shove it up your ass if I knew ya didn't like it!"

"Only with you, lover," crooned the sailor.

"Fuckin' fag and nigger joint!" the weasel snarled, and he stomped to the back of the club.

Opal prayed he would be stomping out through the back alley door never to return. She prayed Charlie would get there, and she wished her father had been sitting with her to fend off mashers. But Coney hadn't had more than a second to breeze by and just say hello. He'd been scurrying back and forth to the kitchen all night, toting heavy trays of beer bottles and wheezing through smoke wafting from the ever present *Lucky Strike* hanging off his lip. Opal had noted his coughing was getting worse. First thing, Monday morning, she decided, she'd take him to a doctor if she had to drag him there. Her father, for all his bad drinking habits, which were rapidly contributing to countless stupefied mornings when he could scarcely climb out of bed, she knew loved her. *Loved her*, and would walk on water for her if he could. That Coney had sanctioned, even encouraged her romance with a white boy was more than any daughter could ask from a father. That is, any black daughter from a black father. Coney was her treasure, but it was treasure quickly turning to rust from the plague of his cigarettes.

Again, Opal tried to turn her thoughts away from her terrors and toward the dance floor, toward the crowd of blissful couples trembling tenderly in each other's arms. She resolved not to think of anything else. She would not think of Panama hats, nor of her father's gasping gait, nor especially of the dank, dangerous nightclub where Charlie was working, where the intentions of the notorious mob-owners were always dubious, always deceiving, and where danger was their constant customer. Didn't Charlie say the men he worked for had already spent time in prison? For manslaughter?

But he'll be here soon, Opal determined, quickly dismissing these thoughts. She gently massaged the soft, flat side of the bottle cap against her cheek. *He'll be here, he's fine,* she promised herself, afraid to check her watch.

"Hi ya, Doll! I'm so sorry! You must be starved!"

"Oh Charlie, thank God!"

Charlie clasped Opal's hand, and his lips kissed it. "'You okay? You look like you got your head in a fog. Day dreamin' about me I hope! C'mon, let's go!" he said, tapping at the stogie wedged between his fingers.

"Charlie, where have you been?"

"Aww, it was nothin.' "

"What was nothin'?" Opal asked, getting to her feet.

"I was in Brooklyn, touchin' up a few things for my pal Angelo. He's got a little Italian joint that's a real dump."

"I was worried sick and I started to think--"

"And then all hell breaks loose, and I'm divin' under tables cause Angelo's nutty brother Sal comes in sprayin' bullets. What a mess!"

Opal threw her arms around Charlie's shoulders and buried her face in the tobacco-tinged cotton of his Oxford cloth shirt. Nothing was more sweet than the smell of a cheap cigar.

"What's all this? C'mon, Doll, let's get outta here."

Against her better judgment to venture past 135th Street with a white man, but longing for some semblance of a normal relationship, Opal ascended the Sugar Cane's dungeon steps to the street. *Normal relationship* had teased her like a tottering carrot over a ravenous nag, it tugged at her hopes and dreams and tempted her like the Christ thirsting in desolation. But it was truly more than temptation that summoned Opal from her desert on this night. In Charlie, she was certain she'd found her oasis. For one night, perhaps she would be a lamb led to shelter or to slaughter. But whatever the outcome, was it worth the risk? So on a misty, drizzly Sunday night in late September, Opal and Charlie set out walking the twelve blocks to the restaurant he'd picked out on 125th and Lenox Avenue. Lost in the rapture of their brave quest however, was any awareness that behind them stalked an angry, lean white man in a Panama hat.

Charlie was buoyant and bubbly beyond reproach. "This is gonna be great!" he beamed, sheltering his umbrella over their heads. "I found the cutest little Chinese restaurant with table cloths and candlelight and everything."

"It does sound great," Opal said, trying to sound cheerful, scanning the sidewalks. In the corner of one eye, she thought she saw a glimmer of white. The Panama hat! She turned around. But it was gone. The fear of strolling black and white together began to fester through her blood, her heart leaping from her chest. Fortunately, there were few people on 135th Street on a rainy night, and even if there'd been a crowd, with her head bent down under the shade of the umbrella, Opal hoped she wouldn't be seen. When they got to 133rd and stepped into Jungle Alley with so many rousing, posh nightclubs and cafes and hordes of people, she hoped she'd be discounted altogether. Indeed, Jungle Alley was hopping, even on a Sunday night. Limousines, and fancy cars and taxi cabs were lined up all along the curb, spewing swanky white gentlemen in elegant topcoats and glamorous white women in furs onto the crowded sidewalks and into the glimmering, famous nightclubs.

"Isn't it odd how my neighborhood can change so quickly?" Opal said, feeling a bit less fearful among the glamour. "One minute you're in a slum, then suddenly it's all high class"

"Nothing but high class for you, Doll," Charlie strutted, the rain coming down heavier. "Take a good look at all that sable and mink, cause Baby, I'm gettin' that for you too someday."

"I'd be happy if you and I could just go in to see one of these shows," Opal answered, as her place of work, Small's Paradise came into view, welcoming its chic patrons who scuttled in from the rain.

"Not a chance. Why would I wanna patronize a joint where my girlfriend waits on tables but ain't allowed to sit at 'em? But someday it'll change. You'll see. I'm gonna get that for ya too. We'll get to those shows."

Opal was doubtful of that. On the other hand, she thought, spying the splash of the giant *ETHEL WATERS APPEARING TONIGHT* across the marquee at Connie's Inn, it was truly amazing how things were changing for Negroes. She'd heard Ethel Waters herself traveled only in limousines, and she and Billy Holiday and Lena Horne also wore sable and mink like fancy white women. And hadn't she seen Duke Ellington and Louis Armstrong strutting from their shows at Small's in top hats and tuxedoes? Maybe Charlie was right. Maybe the world had changed. Opal raised her head up from the umbrella. After all, she thought, it was 1932, the modern world, things were bound to change. As she and Charlie glided beneath the towering sparkle of *ETHEL WATERS* beaming from the bright marquee, Opal could almost see a tuxedo trailing behind her beloved and felt the sable warm around her shoulders in a vision she believed was destined to come true.

But two swarthy white men in pinstripe suits stood just beyond the marquee, puffing on fat cigars. They salivated like hungry wolves as soon as they saw Opal.

"Hey, Palermo," one of them said, "give a look. Ya like white meat or dark meat?"

"Oh dark meat, definitely," leered his partner. "You too, huh Red?" he nodded at Charlie. "But I forget, which one do ya get to spread apart and make a wish? The legs or the thighs?"

"Let's get goin', Doll," Charlie whispered, urging Opal away.

But because she and Charlie had quickly hurried on, neither of them heard one of the wolves exclaim to the man in the Panama hat still following, "Well, if it ain't Joey the Pimp! Slummin' in Niggertown?"

And neither Charlie, Opal nor the two cigar smoking monsters were aware Joey The Pimp had already clicked open his new switchblade. Charlie quickly steered Opal toward Lenox Avenue, away from what he didn't know was about to take place in front of Connie's Inn, a flash of a knife that was meant for him.

"*Shakin' the blues away!*" he sang, "*If you are blue it's easy to shake off your cares!* Ain't that right? C'mon, Doll! Hey look, we're almost there!"

Opal said nothing, but bent as low as she could and inched closer to the center of the umbrella. The rain was now coming down in buckets. But she couldn't see the rain, hear the rain, nor feel it. She had gone absolutely numb. The cold reality of never becoming *ordinary people* was seeping into her bones like anesthesia.

Charlie stopped. "Opal! Look at me! Don't worry! We're gonna have a nice night. Let the rest of the world go by, ya hear me? Forget those creeps! Ya just gotta forget all the shmos of the world! They ain't nothin'! It's just you and me, kid. We don't gotta be beholden to nobody."

Charlie kissed her. On the lips. He really did. Right out in the open, right in public. Opal looked around hastily. There were flocks of people hurrying down Lenox to get out of the downpour. No one saw a thing.

Finally, at 125th Street, three doors from the corner, a gray, metal sign was creaking in the wind over a red door. "*YOUNG CHAN*" was painted on the sign in large, red block letters.

"This is it! Only Chan, he ain't so young. He's an old geezer about eighty. I think the 'young' is a joke. Get it? Egg foo *yung*?"

A clanging bell above the door shrilly announced their arrival. As they stood dripping at the entrance of a long narrow room with a line of tables on either side, Opal surveyed the conditions. The one aisle separating the tables was barely wide enough for the waiters to navigate without bumping into customers. Each table was bedecked in white cloth on which sat the stump of a wax candle stuck in a wine bottle. The walls were discolored, sporadically chipped white stucco, resembling any ten-cent chow house if not for an occasional, faded sepia photograph of the Great Wall or a Buddhist temple.

"I know it don't look like much," said Charlie, shaking raindrops off the umbrella. "I'm workin' on old man Chan to let me spruce up the joint."

Charlie closed the door behind them which sent the bell into another resounding clang. A few customers looked up. They were all Negroes who gave Opal a quick once-over and promptly turned away. A Negro waiter approached with two menus. He also gave Opal the once-over.

"This way," he growled. Although there were three empty tables at the front, he led Charlie and Opal all the way back to the very last table by the noisy kitchen.

As they sidled down the narrow aisle, Opal could feel each eye of every patron burning a hole right through the back of her raincoat. "Are you sure this is a Chinese restaurant, Charlie? Everybody's colored in here," she whispered.

"Yeah Chan's a class guy. He gets jobs for the locals, but all the cooks are Chinese. Who else would know how to make egg foo yung?"

The last table sat under a large window that opened into a steamy kitchen where indeed Opal could see two Chinese men in black skull caps clanging pots and pans and shouting to each other in their own language.

"Here Doll, you take this chair, so you can have the better view. I don't mind starin' at the cooks. I kinda like it. I wanna make sure they ain't servin' up a cat or somethin'," Charlie snickered. "Just kiddin'!"

Opal had a great view alright. She had a great view of two colored waiters standing at the front door, whispering and pointing back at her table. She had a great view of three different couples folding their napkins and leaving the restaurant before they were finished eating.

Charlie pulled the chair from under the window ledge and held it out for her. He did this, not their waiter, because their waiter, after tossing their menus on the table, went to the front of the restaurant to smoke a cigarette. Charlie took the opposite chair and sat, spreading out their soggy raincoats on the back of the chair behind him.

"That Won Ton soup sounds good to me," Charlie bubbled, perusing the paper menu, "and I'm gonna go with the Chicken Chow Mein. I love that stuff."

"That sounds fine with me too," Opal said, though she knew she'd probably not be able to eat a thing.

"I sure hope Chan's here tonight cause I wanna tell him what I got planned for this place. I see Chinese lanterns with red tassels hangin' from the ceiling, tapestries on the walls, gold leaf on all the baseboards and trim. I'll make a big pagoda at the entrance so when you walk in, you'll think you're right in China. Hell, I can turn this joint into a showplace."

While Charlie rattled on, Opal nervously picked bits of melted candle wax off the wine bottle, struggling to avoid the glaring eyes of everyone who remained in the restaurant. Though after twenty minutes of making a dozen little wax balls and watching the waiters smoke cigarettes, she wondered if they'd ever get to eat anything at all. It was clear no one would wait on them.

"I met Chan through his son Timmy, a real nice kid who's the dish washer at a joint I was fixin' up for Joe Masseria. It's funny, I wouldn't be caught dead in a place like this if it was an Italian joint. This kinda long narrow room is perfect for rubbin' out your enemies, know what I mean? You got this whole long path right to your victim. Just like tonight at Angelo's. Guys come in a room like this for lasagna and come out lookin' like linguini......."

Charlie rambled on, completely oblivious to the scorn and contempt, ridicule and derision shooting back at him and Opal like arrows. *What a waste,* Opal sighed, *and he looks so handsome tonight in his seersucker suit, so lively and happy. My poor deluded sweetheart.*

"....This other joint I been to in Brooklyn is notorious for that kinda stuff. Ya don't go in there after lunch if ya know what's good for ya. Otherwise, you'll be dodgin' bullets and divin' under tables quicker than you can--"

"Charlie," Opal interrupted, leaning in close. "I don't think we're going to be waited on."

"What? Whattaya talkin'?"

"I think all these colored folk are not happy with you and me being here."

"Aww, that's nuts. Here comes a waiter. Hey Buddy! Excuse me," Charlie's hand shot up, "we'd like--"

The waiter breezed past them and past the kitchen.

"See what I mean?"

"Nah, he's probably just goin' to the men's room or somethin'."

"I don't think so, Charlie. It's been almost a half hour since we came in, and there aren't any other customers left except for one old couple who's probably too nearsighted to notice us."

Charlie turned around and glanced at the elderly black man and woman who had finished eating and were drinking tea. "I am gettin' hungry," he said, turning back to Opal.

"I think we should leave."

"No way, Doll. We're gonna get a good meal and have a good time. We're fine."

Charlie rose up a little from his seat and turned toward the two waiters still standing at the front smoking cigarettes. "Hey pal! Can we order now?"

One of the smokers tossed his cigarette butt to the floor and snuffed it out with his shoe. He glided down the aisle between empty tables grudgingly, as if Charlie had just asked him to put his head in the oven. He came to their table with his hands thrust deep into his pockets. His hands stayed there. He didn't take out a note pad or card or anything to write down their order.

"Okay, I think we're ready," Charlie said. "We'd each like the Won Ton Soup and Chicken Chow Mein."

"Uh huh." The young man started walking to the front of the restaurant.

"See?" Opal whispered.

"Hey pal, the kitchen's the other way," Charlie directed.

The surly waiter turned and shuffled toward the kitchen.

"And, oh yeah, we'd also like a pot of hot tea please."

In a few minutes, a hand appeared at the window behind Opal and placed a pot of tea with two cups on the ledge. But no one came around to actually serve it.

Charlie got up and retrieved the pot and cups from the counter and brought them down to the table. "They're probably just short tonight."

He poured tea into Opal's cup and into his own. He took a big sip, but then tea exploded from Charlie's mouth back into the cup and onto most of the tablecloth. "This damn stuff is ice cold!" Charlie shot up and stuck his head through the window. "Hey kid, could you come out here a second"

Their surly waiter came back out with another cigarette dangling from his teeth.

"Ya want somethin'?" he mumbled.

"Yeah, if you wouldn't mind. We'd like a fresh pot of hot tea. This is cold as ice."

The waiter scowled then shuffled away.

"And sugar!" Charlie added.

The waiter turned back around. "Sugar?" he asked with an odd grin.

"Yeah, some sugar."

"What," the waiter leered at Opal, "your *brown* sugar ain't enough for you?"

Opal thought Charlie turned whiter than she believed any white man could. And she could feel her own skin turning blacker than night, blacker than coal, blacker than a tar baby, blacker than death.

"C'mon Opal, we're gettin' outta here!"

Charlie grabbed her hand, their raincoats and umbrella, then swooped up in a frenzy, storming through the restaurant and knocking over a few tables in the process. Charlie slammed the door so hard Opal thought its glass pane and all the windows in the restaurant would shatter into pieces. He quickly opened the umbrella and hurried to wrap the raincoats around their shoulders. It was still pouring. "You alright?" he asked anxiously.

"I'm okay."

"You sure?"

"I'm really okay, Charlie. I'm used to this. I'm just disappointed, that's all."

"Well, I'm not givin' up! Let's try somewhere else!"

"No darling, let's just go back to my place. I've got some leftover ham and beans. I can throw it together for a little supper."

"But I wanted to take you out! What the heck kinda man can I be if I can't take out my own girl!"

"It's okay. We'll figure that out some other night. We'll find someplace we can go. You know so many restaurant people, you'll find it. But I'm soaked and you're soaked. We don't have to be beholden to the world, Charlie, like you said, but tonight the world and the rain seem to have won this round. It doesn't mean we've lost the fight."

"Okay," he sighed, looking up and down the block. "Tell ya what. The dough I was gonna spend on dinner I'll spend on a cab. At least I can get us home in style."

They walked back up to Lenox Avenue where a steady stream of yellow taxis was feasting upon forlorn, soaked strollers, splashing through puddles and hailing cabs. Charlie pursed his lips and let out a whistle. A Checker cab slid to the curb.

"135th and Fifth," he bent down to the white driver.

"No problem," the driver answered in maybe a Polish accent. "No good night to be walking out."

Charlie pulled the back door handle and motioned for Opal to get in. But when he opened the door, the taxi driver took one look at her and smashed his foot to the gas pedal.

"Forget it!" the driver yelled, speeding away from the curb, and showering Opal and Charlie with a spray of gutter water.

"Bastard! That son of a bitch! That stinkin' son of a bitch! Who does that s.o.b. think he is! My money's just as good as anybody's! And we're soaked!"

"We were already soaked, Charlie. Let's go."

"What a goddam sucker I am! Soaking wet in a seersucker suit of all things! But I'm the seer sucker! One big God damn sucker!"

"No you're not Charlie. It's not your fault. How could it be?"

"Yes it is! Me and my stupid dreams. I musta been crazy. Completely God damn crazy! I should be locked up!"

They huddled under the umbrella. Charlie didn't say another word all the way back to Opal's apartment. They avoided Jungle Alley this time and kept to the murky, back side streets where the pools of rainwater reflected only the hems of dime store dresses and the cuffs of plain trousers not the diamonds and furs of 133rd Street. Opal didn't have anything to say either, nor the heart to. They even remained silent when they saw flashing red lights from police cars and ambulances near 133rd Street in front of Connie's Inn, where a crowd had gathered to watch two men in pinstripe suits be treated for knife wounds.

The rickety door up to Opal's third floor apartment creaked and clattered when they'd completed their sopping trek through the rain. Opal and Charlie climbed the musty staircase, heavy with the damp smell of wood-soaked mildew, their dripping shoes and coats adding to the dank mold. Remarkably, knowing she'd always been fearful of one day bringing a gentlemen caller upstairs to such a dowdy apartment, Opal noted that what was actually happening seemed not at all preposterous. Until now, no one had ever set foot in her apartment except for her own family, much less friends. And who had time for friends, male or female? However, considering their night's ordeal, drenched and dripping as she was, her squalid little flat seemed like a bountiful refuge. It didn't torment her mind for a fraction of a second that she was bringing a white man, any man, to her ramshackle flat for the first time.

"In here Charlie," Opal said, breaking the stony silence and turning the key. "I'll make us some hot tea." She stepped into the dark room and pulled the metal chain on a brass lamp. "Take your wet shoes off, sweetheart, I'll light the stove and get us some towels."

"Okay," Charlie muttered.

Opal went to the kitchenette at one end of the room, grabbed a stick match from the stove, threw open the oven door, and lit the pilot. She watched Charlie scan her tiny apartment. He looked absolutely miserable. Was it the frustration of their aborted dinner date or the despair of her threadbare apartment that was paining him so, she worried. Maybe he was having second thoughts about being with a colored girl in the solitude of her dreary flat. That alone could depress anyone, she agonized. Only one worn-out, overstuffed, brown velvet chair, one faded green corduroy sofa, and one wobbly pine table with a brass lamp underneath the one window draped by frayed sheer curtains were all that sat in the room. But there was the scuffed up Philco combination radio and record player standing against the back wall that seemed to impress him.

"Put on some music, Charlie, and I'll get us some dinner. It'll warm up in here soon. Papa and I try to save money on heat by just turning on the gas oven," Opal chattered nervously, then hurried to the washroom and fetched two towels.

"Sure," Charlie muttered again, perusing a few record albums lying on the floor.

Opal handed him a terry-cloth hand towel. "Here you are, dear, you're soaked to the bone."

"Yeah, so are you."

"Oh, I just have wet stockings. They're fine. But your trousers are sopping."

"I guess they are," he said glumly, staring down at his dripping pant cuffs. His trousers were soaked up to the knees. Charlie slithered off to the washroom.

He must think I'm nothing but a pitiable urchin living in a junkyard, Opal thought, rummaging through the ice box, a relic in itself, smelly and rusted from decades of stained, cheap ice blocks befouling the drip pan. Inside the ice box was a half empty bottle of milk she knew had started to turn, a two-inch cube of Swiss cheese, one egg, a pot of leftover baked beans she had heated up for breakfast, and a ham bone with maybe enough meat still clinging to it that she might scrape together for a meal. She'd make something halfway edible for her and Charlie, then send him on his way. Surely, she believed, he was more craving to leave than for an insufferable dinner.

Charlie came out of the washroom looking a little more crisp. "I had to take off my pants and wring then out in the sink," he half smiled. The ends of his trousers were completely wrinkled, but a comb had obviously been run through his wet hair. "I hung up the towel in there if that's okay."

"That's fine." Opal turned her back and grabbed a carving knife, tensely slicing up shards of meat and cheese. She made a pot of tea while the beans were warming on top of the stove. Charlie had put a Louis Armstrong record on the Philco, but the bouncy orchestrations and Mr. Armstrong's jolly warbling did nothing to brighten the mood. And no matter what attempts at gaiety that popped out of Opal's mouth, she was convinced it all just sounded silly and inappropriate.

"I love Louis Armstrong, don't you? I hope you like ham Charlie. Of course I know Jews don't eat ham, but I figured you did. Those wet trousers can't possibly be comfortable, Charlie. You should take off your pants."

"Huh?"

"I mean, I could get you a pair of Papa's to put on." she clarified, mortified. Oh God, did he think she meant something else?

Mercifully, her meager fare was finally cooked through, and she presented a plate to Charlie. They sat on the sofa with their plates on their laps, yet another mortification, for there was no kitchen table.

"Cause I'm a ding dong daddy from Dumas, babe,

And you oughtta see me do my stuff!
Why, I'm a clean cut fella From Horner's Corner,
Oooh, you oughtta see me strut!......"

Louis Armstrong chimed merrily from the Philco, but not one of his happy songs could clear the dismal clouds in Opal's front room.

"It's a nice Philco," Charlie finally said, raising a forkful of beans.

"Thanks. My brother Jonas got it for us. He said he bought it at a second-hand shop, but I don't know how he'd ever get the money to even buy something second-hand. He either stole it or made the money some way I don't want to know."

"I'm sorry."

How shrewd of me to make conversation about my degenerate brother! Opal thought. "Oh, that's okay," she stumbled along. "We do love having the radio. Of course, I never had any records until I started working at Small's Paradise. If one of the girls there hadn't've given me these old records, that turntable would be full of dust."

Charlie bit into his food. Opal choked down a spoonful of beans. Mr. Armstrong wailed in a background of howling trumpets, but the silence between Opal and Charlie was deafening. There was nothing else to do, she conceded, but put an end to a pitiful evening.

"I sure hope this sorry excuse for a supper tastes alright. You can just leave your plate in the sink before you go. I'll clean up later."

Charlie was scooping another forkful of beans, but plunked his fork back onto the plate. "Ya want me to go?"

"Well, I thought you'd want to leave," Opal stammered. "I didn't think you'd want--"

"Ya didn't think I'd wanna stay? Why wouldn't I wanna stay?"

"I don't know, Charlie, I just thought, that's all."

Now Opal was completely confused, one minute miserable, absolutely certain Charlie wanted to flee, and now scared to death he wanted to stay. She had a white man in her apartment. They were alone. She might be able to manage dinner, but then what? *Alone with Charlie,* she knew was not something she exactly feared, it was rather her own looming passion that was so terrifying.

"Up a lazy river by the old mill stream,
That lazy, hazy river where we both can dream,
Linger in the shade of an old oak tree,
Throw away your troubles, dream a dream with me........."

Even Mr. Armstrong now taunted her, daring her to dream of love as she sipped from her tea cup, praying her hand wouldn't shake. "You know, we could go back to the Sugar Cane, if you want, Charlie, the club's still open of course, and there's--"

"Wait--" Charlie interrupted, as one song ended and another began.

"Life is not a highway strewn with flowers, still it holds a goodly share of bliss"....sang Louis Armstrong.

Charlie finally brightened. *"When the sun gives way to April showers,"* he warbled along to the record, *"here's the point you should never miss!* I just made this record."

"What do you mean?" Opal asked, shoving her beans into little soupy corrals, she'd hardly eaten a thing.

"Though April showers, may come your way--" Charlie sang, his clear tenor voice harmonizing with Mr. Armstrong. "My pal Larry Porchnik, he's got a recording booth downtown, and he let me do a couple of songs, *'April Showers'* on one side and *'Swanee'* on the 'B' side. You'll see. I'll bring ya the record the next time I come over. *So if it's raining, have no regrets......*"

The next time! She almost gasped. *The next time he comes over?* But Opal never got to hear the rest of Charlie's song. She didn't hear anything at all except the volcano erupting inside her when Charlie sat his plate onto the floor, threw his arms around her and kissed her full on the lips. He kissed her hard, and she kissed back. They kept on kissing until *"April Showers"* had long been over, and the needle was hissing and grinding, stuck against the paper label at the spindle. Charlie's hands had pulled Opal's blouse out from the top of her skirt and was stroking the small of her bare back, inching his fingers up to her brassiere. Then he stopped.

"I wanna do this right," he whispered. "I'm a decent guy. I wanted to take my girl to a decent place and have a decent meal in a decent world. I wanna do things right, Opal, if you'll give me the honor."

She held out her hand. Charlie took it and helped her up from the sofa. She led the way to her bedroom door. Once past it, he lay her down on the feather mattress and unbuttoned her blouse.

"How could you think I'd want to leave? I never want to leave you," he whispered, swathing her neck, shoulders then chest with soft kisses.

Opal reached down, took his face in both her palms, and brought his lips to hers. The taste of his mouth was still tinged with sweet ketchup and molasses from the baked beans, but the taste of Charlie himself, she thought, was sweeter than honey.

All at once, in a wild frenzy of discarded clothes, groping fingers, desperate lips, and writhing passion, they made love, tenderly, obsessively, radiantly. Afterward, in the luxurious silence, Opal watched the glare of *LAUNDRY LAUNDRY* beating its harsh, rhythmic neon through her window, and pulsating upon the glossy freckles of Charlie's sweaty shoulders. But never again would that indifferent, spastic glower be a marauding moonbeam, she believed. Emblazoned on Opal's heart like a firebrand, the flaming, pink neon would now forever and only symbolize the pink of Charlie's skin, the rosy pink of his hair, the pink of his lacquered freckles, and the hot, amorous pink of the sheer iridescence of their love. Opal studied the cinnamon-colored down on Charlie's chest, thick and damp, and the silky soft hairs covering the forearm that held her so tight. Charlie was the color of spice, she thought. Even the pungent nutmeg scent wafting from his underarm was sweet and spicy like a warm muffin straight from the oven. She thought her own brown skin against his pink body seemed incongruous. He was glowing from the rosy blush of his exertion, radiant as a sunrise, while her skin, Opal believed, somehow seemed tarnished. She was the burnt butterscotch brownie that baked too long. And yet, she thought, butterscotch and spice could be a delicious combination. A soft chuckle escaped her lips.

"What's so funny?" Charlie asked, smoothing his hand across Opal's bare shoulder.

"Everything's funny, Charlie. Everything's wonderful, and amazing and completely carefree because I love you." She cuddled closer to him, feeling her eyelids droop, and lapsed into a dream where she was waltzing through a bakery filled with a billion cozy smells of fresh breads and butterscotch.

"And I love you, Doll."

Opal, as safe and happy as she could ever imagine, drifted off, with not a sliver of concern that Coney would be arriving home soon to pull down his fold-out bed from the living room wall. She'd just sneak Charlie past him early in the morning. For she had considered this proposition even as she'd first turned the key to her door an hour before.

She and Charlie, now bound by their enchantment, to a lullaby of honking taxi cabs, sporadic backfire from rusty mufflers, and drunken revelers on the street below, fell into a deep sleep.

Wide awake, however, was an angry, lean man in a Panama hat standing beneath Opal's window, simmering in the scathing neon, and seething that he'd broken, yet again, another blade to his knife several blocks back at Connie's Inn. Cursing his outrageous rotten luck, and with his claws cocked, the man in the Panama hat found a venue for his rage. Grabbing a heavy brick laying at his feet, he leapt upon the first thing crawling his way, a wheezing old colored-man, staggering toward Opal's building. The old man, coughing through a cloud of smoke that wafted from his *Lucky Strike*, would never make it to his door.

Joey   *1932*

With the tips of his sweaty fingers swollen from fire-red, gnawed-to-the-quick hacked nails, ground and spat out from weeks of infuriation, Joey "The Pimp" Rotollo eagerly caressed the new switchblade warming his pants pocket. But the sullied hands gripping his angry dagger felt no pain. The only feeling came from one dire impulsion churning through Joey's stomach, rapacious hunger. He skulked behind a lamppost on the corner of 135th and Fifth Avenue, and waited. *Oh how that sucker's gonna squeal like a stuck pig,* Joey drooled, envisioning the roll of big bucks he was about to pinch from Charlie Stark, that is, he thought, before the gush of Charlie's Jew blood could soak all those Ben Franklins and President Grants. A blustery wind shrieking through the dank night of Harlem fluttered the wide brim of Joey's Panama hat, but the hat was firmly clenched to his head, clenched like his fists. He believed all the wrath and rage of his twenty-one miserable years would soon be ventilated, the lifetime acid in his belly rushing through his veins and erupting all over Charlie Stark like a fire hose full of arsenic. It was all too fitting, he sneered, that Charlie Stark would reap the full-forced vengeance of his antipathy, fitting like a fist in a glove, like a drill to a hole, boring out each and every unnecessary scrap of Charlie's flesh and blood into thin air. *And I got the tool alright, for that Kike's hole.* Not for one second more of his grievous, disparate life would Joey let a Jew show him up.

As Joey expected, having trailed Charlie for three days, lurking in the alley behind the cheap gin joint Charlie was painting, suffering through unbearable nights with dumb Kikes at Benny Weinberg's Eighth Street Cabaret, eavesdropping on whatever conversations possible, finally, here came Charlie, strutting around the corner in a new seersucker suit to meet his nigger bitch at the Sugar Cane. Joey, stocked with a fresh pack of *Camels,* chose, however, to wait on the corner and smoke, letting the vapors of burning tobacco calm his lungs and sweeten his dark deliberation. *"I'll see ya at eight, Doll, It's only a short walk to the restaurant,"* Joey had heard Charlie say on the phone earlier that afternoon, his ear pressed to the basement door, behind which Charlie was slapping his pansy ass paint on the scummy walls of a flea-bag speakeasy.

"And this is gonna be your last walk ever, you asshole," Joey now whispered, blowing out a stream of thick smoke up to the old gaslight at 135th. Wafting into the dim beam of light, the heavy drag of cigarette smoke swirled in the wind, twirling into legs and arms, even a head, Joey imagined, the full bodied apparition of the ghost of a man, a mere specter of Charlie Stark disappearing into the night forever. Yet, Joey was content to stand and wait. He would smoke his whole damn pack, he snorted, before going back into that rat hole, fag-bag Sugar Cane. *Hoity-toity niggers dressed to the nines thinkin' they're so high class, like Charlie's black bitch, and all those filthy fags and dykes in there? Forget it.*

Four, hot, filter-less cigarettes later, when Charlie emerged from his rat hole with his bitch and took to the sidewalk, an ebullient Joey was practically salivating. The raptor in the Panama hat commenced his swoop. He slithered in between lampposts and in between raindrops which began to thunk against his Panama hat, forming a fine patina of reptilian slime across the brim. Vacillating from utter revulsion to gluttony, Joey glared at the happy couple out for a leisurely stroll, cooing and courting, hand in hand, completely ignorant of the circling shark just a few shadowy steps away. Patiently, menacingly, Joey followed close behind for several blocks, waiting for the perfect, pristine moment in which he'd open his fangs.

That moment presented itself when Charlie and his bitch turned onto 133rd. Joey felt the barbs in his trap constrict all the more tightly. For Jungle Alley was so jammed with people, *"No one's gonna see or hear a thing when my little rats start to choke,"* Joey murmured, a predatory palm gripping his blade, and he shifted gears into overdrive. As both the victims and hunter approached the grand marquee of Connie's Inn, a boisterous, chattering crowd was swarming, limousines and cabs blasting their horns for a spot at the curb. A screech of laughter erupted from the raucous crowd, shrieks that would surely stifle any cries of inflicted pain, Joey snickered. The cold drizzle that had begun a few blocks back was now drenching his face and neck, mingling with the searing sweat of his obsession. It was time to strike. Joey quickly hurtled toward the vile white man with his contemptible black woman seven steps before him, his heart pumping excitedly like it was Christmas. Then five steps from his unsuspecting prey, breathlessly ramming past the horde of tuxedos and furs peppering the pavement, then just three steps away, Joey lurched through the mob, clicking the switch to his knife with one remaining crag of a fingernail, and the razor flicked open.

"Well if it ain't Joey The Pimp slummin' in Niggertown," interjected one of two hulking bouncers guarding Connie's Inn.

" 'Must be lookin' for a piece of black ass, Tony. I mean shit, I hear his own hookers won't give 'im any."

With all 130 scrawny pounds, but slippery as a snake, Joey pointed his knife. *Swish.* A quick slice to the gut, a flash to the neck, all well and good for a couple of smart-ass roach bouncers, Joey deemed, but

WORLD ON A STRING

then, "Fuck! Another broken shiv!" he fumed, hurling bloody, jagged pieces into the gutter, racing from the screaming bystanders toward his bounty that was getting away. "But what's the fuckin' point of bird-doggin' that asshole and the nigger dame without a goddam shiv?" he raged.

His mood so inopportunely killed, he now doubted he'd be able to both knock off Charlie, pinch his wallet and/or poke the bitch at the same time without a weapon. Still, he bolted away from his lacerated victims crumpling at Connie's Inn to continue his pursuit, hoping to at least get some goods on Charlie Stark. Goods that just might one day come in handy. Goods like knowing for sure the mother fucker Charlie Stark was hording all his cash, Joey observed, watching Charlie take his bitch to a cheap Chink joint that must have cost him all of two bits for goat foo yung, when the fucker clearly had the dough to snag himself that fancy seersucker suit and treat himself to taxi cabs. Joey stuck close to his rats the rest of the night, ecstatic to unearth even better goods, like learning where the nigger bitch lived.

Hours later, dodging relentless raindrops beneath the bitch's window where he temporarily deferred his pursuit, Joey reckoned, "I can bide my time." He watched a light go on and then off from the window above, and wanted to throw up at the idea the two bedbugs were scratching themselves between the sheets. "But let 'em scratch," he simmered. "Enjoy your filthy fuck nights, pals. I ain't done with you."

And when a hacking, drunk old black man suddenly appeared, wobbling toward the bitch's building, Joey allayed his rage by discovering he was the beneficiary of a well-timed brick sitting at the edge of the curb. He grabbed the brick. Here came that drink nigger. A quick smash to the nigger's head evened the score for the busted night, Joey figured, though the bleeding black turd had nothing on him but two quarters and a bus token. But with an even score, for one night, Joey was satisfied to have sacrificed another knife and his corduroy suit to the rain.

The next day, neither the pursuit of a new switchblade, nor the sickly gurgle of two poorly digested sunny side-up eggs roiling inside his stomach could prevent Joey from budging one step away from his perch in a 52nd Street alley, hungrily scrutinizing the movements of Charlie Stark through a basement window.

It was late, almost noon. Joey defied the persistent brisk wind, and tugged the lapels of his corduroy jacket up around his bony neck, cursing himself for oversleeping, for staying-up way too late, stalking Charlie and his nigger the whole goddam stinkin' night. Now screened by a stack of boxes and wooden crates, Joey spied the son of a bitch Charlie Stark atop a ladder, smearing more paint on the walls of the basement speakeasy. But he could see this was no ordinary beer dump. To Joey, it looked more like a museum, all high class and ritzy with fancy furniture and shiny lights and paintings, like it was for sure run by high rollers. *Anyone with that kind of dough to make this butthole of a basement look like a palace must be rakin' it in,* Joey thought, his blood racing beyond patience, hurtling past urgency. But he desperately needed a weapon. And he needed the cash to get one, cash that was still pending from Johnny Hennigan who never paid up for the use of his three hookers, and from the hookers themselves who'd seemingly split town. Joey hadn't seen any one of them in over two weeks let alone get their action. *What a sucker I am for not fleecing those two asshole bouncers last night,* Joey stewed, kicking at loose bricks on the alley floor. But there'd been all that damn blood and screaming, and trailing Charlie Stark was the priority. *Another fuckin' broken knife!* Joey steamed. *What a goddam cheap shiv!*

However, the need to replace his knife was one thing, especially with no available cash, but the need to repay a half dozen loan sharks was quite another matter. His Uncle Carlo, in particular was a very treacherous matter.

"You'll get this back to me quite soon, ey little Joey Bambino?" Carlo had asked last week in the diffused candlelight from his regular table at *Villa Lucca,* a greasy meatball joint he owned off Mott Street. He'd just handed Joey a hundred dollar bill, the fourth hundred dollar bill he'd dished out to Joey in three weeks.

"Are you kiddin'? I'll make this back in a day, Carlo. I got Owney Madden in my back pocket slurpin' over my dames."

"Yeah? So what's another C note for, kid?"

"Gotta get me some new threads, Uncle. Maybe a pin striped suit. Hey, if I'm workin' for the big boys, I gotta look the part, don't I?"

Carlo, not really Joey's uncle but a ten-cent thug his mother used to shag between his pop's three week runs with the DT's, had not been surprised to watch Joey pocket the cash and slither out his joint, not to the men's haberdashery on the corner but toward the Bowery. There, Joey then spent most of an hour, haggling with the owner of the flop house on Allen Street where he usually sent his prostitutes.

"Just one fuckin' C note, Joey? Where's my other two hundred, you little pimp shit?"

Joey now anxiously jingled change in the unraveled threads of his pants pocket. The coins clanked frantically with no plush cushion of bills to soften the clatter. The breakfast Joey heard still rumbling through his intestines might be the last solid digestion he'd have for days, he brooded. He needed cash, and needed it fast. From his perch, he peered through the basement window, like a vulture over road kill, and continued ogling Charlie Stark on the ladder who was still fondling his stupid paint brush. Joey could see the place was completely empty. *Good! I'll have the bastard all to myself!* He just needed a plan.

A telephone rang. Joey watched the Jew bastard hop off the ladder to answer it. He began to savor Charlie's next phone call. "Next time, you fucker," Joey snickered, "that phone's gonna ring and ring and ring with no one to answer." The faint black hairs on his upper lip twitched at the prospects. But he *needed* a weapon. Joey kicked a pale, loose brick at his feet, and gouged out bits of caked mortar between the crumbling, faded red blocks. He ground the bits with the heel of his loafer, crushing, pulverizing each tiny pebble into dust, like he wanted to crush Charlie Stark.

"What the fuck I been thinkin'?" he smiled, lingering on the happy memory of last night's bleeding old nigger he had bashed so euphorically. He grabbed the loose brick at his feet. He'd wait for the son of a bitch Charlie to get back up the ladder, then sneak through the door, run to the ladder, and in one swift jolt, kick it over, watching the chump crumple to the floor. He'd smash the brick to the bastard's face, then trot way with easy money.

"Hang up, you dumb fuck!"

Finally, Charlie plunked down the phone. Joey dug his fingers into the brick, and made for the door, drooling for Charlie to climb the ladder. But the back alley door suddenly flew open.

"And life is a beautiful thing," Charlie sang happily, *"as long as I hold the string, I'd be a silly so and so if I should ever let go--- "*

Charlie danced up the three-step stoop. Joey and his brick quickly hid behind the crates. Another gush of the Canadian front blew from 52nd Street and whooshed down the alley, scattering trash and old newspapers, and swirling up clouds of dust. Joey held back a sneeze.

"I've got the world on a string--" Charlie peered down the alley. A rattling tin can and an envelope fluttered past him. "Perfect!" he said, snatching the envelope, *"--sittin' on a rainbow!* Charlie scampered back down the stoop into the basement.

Joey whisked dust off his Panama hat, let out a booming sneeze, and ground his fingernails back into the brick, hungrily anticipating Charlie's return to the top of the ladder. But instead, Joey watched the bastard linger near the bottom rung, mixing up colors, smearing paint onto the stupid envelope.

"C'mon, c'mon!" Joey whispered over the rasping wind, over the unrelenting rumble in his gut. He watched Charlie studying his new palette, then stepping back to study his work and lighting up a cigar. "Holy Christ!" Joey spat, "get your fuckin' ass up there!"

At last, Charlie began to climb the rungs. Joey straightened up, relishing the sheer kismet roaring through his veins, visualizing veins of gold now dazzling the once dark caverns of his dim life. "Jackpot!" he sniggered. Running a finger along a particularly jagged, chiseled edge of the brick, Joey mustered the engorged ferocity of his rage and snaked to the basement door. *"Whaa-choo!"* he sneezed again. But before he could wipe away the snot off the fuzz of his upper lip, he heard a voice.

"Bambino!"

And then he felt two familiar concrete claws swoop down upon both his shoulders.

"I'm so happy you cam to see *me*. Funny thing, my Little Bambino, I been lookin' all over for *you!* "

"Carlo! What are you doin' here?"

"Here?" Uncle Carlo raised himself up to his full six foot, two hundred pound frame, ran one hand over slick, coal black hair retreating from the gray in his temples, and sniffed the rose pinned to his lapel, all the while his other hand remained clamped to Joey. "This is my property you're crawlin' on, kid. Didn't ya know I'm about to open a first class joint the Jew Boy's fixin' up for me ?" Carlo gave a nod toward the basement where they both could hear Charlie still singing.

"What?"

"Jeeze, ya got a hearin' problem, kid? So how's your vision? Can ya see that fine gentleman down there?" Carlo yanked a thumb toward a tall, swarthy man dressed in a shiny blue silk suit leaning against the building at the end of the alley. "That's my business partner, Dominic, who just so happens to also be my mean ol' big brother. He looks after me, ya know? And Dom don't take too kindly to weasely little chumps double-crossin' his little bro."

"But, Carlo, I ain't doin' no double-crossin'---"

"Now now," Carlo interrupted, slapping his free hand over Joey's mouth, "ya don't gotta be explainin' nothin' to me. It's my brother who wants to meet ya."

Courteously, but with no obstruction of malice, Carlo escorted a feverishly squirming Joey out of the alley, twisting his arm behind him into a freakish pretzel, but taking great care to swab the dust off Joey's lapels and Panama hat.

"After all," Carlo said, "youse meetin' my classy big brother. I wancha to look respectable."

Charlie   *Sunday, September 25, 1932*

Every chance I got, I went to Harlem to be with Opal. Of course, not a soul knew about it, I made damn sure of that, for Opal's sake and mine. She had this crazy brother, Jonas, who was never around much, he sometimes worked as a stable hand up in Saratoga. But she told me he'd kill her if he ever caught her with a white boy. Her other brother Franklin was killed in the War, and her mom died when Opal was in grammar school. So it was just her and Coney, living in a cold-water flat four doors down from the Sugar Cane. It was strange, right in the heart of wild Harlem, smack dab in the middle of the well-healed big spenders at the Cotton Club, and among the sleazy clubs where the low-life sucked down booze and hemp till dawn, carousing, cavorting, raising the roof practically night and day, right in the middle of that crazy jungle, I'd found a precious jewel. My Opal, my little gem.

With my head in the clouds around the clock, I could hardly concentrate on the other girl in my life. My diva on the wall still waited for the breath of life from my paintbrush. On a cold morning in September with icy winds blowing like it was January, and me working in a basement with no heat, but thinkin' about my two gorgeous girls, I was warming up like it was summer. Thirty more minutes and my diva would step right into immortality. Thirty more minutes, and I'd be racing up to Harlem to be in the arms of a real life goddess.

"Ya know, I think you're jealous!" I laughed, dabbing my brush of cadmium red to my diva's cheek bones. "C'mon Doll! Would I two-time you?"

I head scuffling near the top of the stairs. *Oh well, what the hell,* I thought. *I always hear some kind of scufflin' in this joint. Ain't nothin' gonna spoil my mood today.* I didn't give one damn about the poor sucker Dominic was probably dragging down to rough-up. The creep just left me alone and let me paint. Besides, I'd dodged bullets before. Big deal. I had an angel sittin' on my shoulder, and an angel uptown. The last thing on my mind was the mischief of low-life hoods. I stood face to face with my beautiful diva, and sang out at the top of my lungs. "*I got the world on a string, sittin' on a rainbow, got the string around my finger! What a world, what a life! I'm in love!*"

My diva glared back at me.

"You're not smilin' at me like ya used to!" I said, laying down a glaze of red to a lock of her coal black hair. My diva just stared. I think she *was* jealous. "So who's been talkin' to ya about me, huh?"

She had plenty reason to be jealous alright. Just last night, for the first time, me and Opal made love. Nope, not just "made" love, we defined it in all glorious sense of the word. And what had been those crummy mere tumbles with all those other girls in my life had become pure paradise with my Opal, heaven on earth. She was soft and silky. Her skin was a gorgeous butterscotch bronze, a color I never could have created on any palette, a smooth shiny caramel that melted in my mouth. And lips and breasts and fingers and toes that also melted in my mouth. I thought I'd be nervous as hell. I wondered if I could go through with it. I wondered if I'd hear voices in my head saying it was wrong to be with a Negro as if there was something tainted about a colored girl. But when I watched my white freckled hand move up Opal's caramel sugar skin, I suddenly realized, *I* was the freak. This white bread freckled skin of mine wasn't the norm. The norm was the golden brown goddess in my arms.

"You are a true goddess," I'd whispered, kissing her.

"What?" she'd laughed. "Oh Charlie, no I'm not." And she kissed me back.

But she was. When I kissed her golden skin I felt like I'd pressed my lips to a sacred statuette, forged from precious bronze from a great ancient civilization, the ancient Africans, the Egyptians. I kept thinking she and all her generations were the one true mold for everybody else on the planet. Us white people were just the cheap hybrids. But far more important than that, Opal was the most gentle, the most kind person I'd ever met in my life. I was head over heels in love. If we had stayed up all night just talking, I still would have been in paradise.

"Don't you be jealous, my diva," I now whispered to the wall, "I may be in love, but you, I will make immortal."

The cadmium red blended perfectly, a gorgeous rouge on her delicate cheek bones to complete her utter divinity. Just one more little shmear onto her cheeks, maybe a tiny tinge more of red to her moist lips and she'd be done. I hopped off the ladder to study my masterpiece.

"Mark my words, Diva, some high roller's gonna come in here and wanna take down the whole damn wall to put up at the Met! You're gonna be famous!"

The mural really was a knockout. I could almost hear the flower peddlers, pitching their schpiel in the town square I painted. "Rosi! Fiori belli!" I could hear the whining screech of the organ grinder and practically smell the hanging garlics on the vegetable carts. And there on the marble balcony my diva overlooked it all with the same affection. Her lips were slightly parted in a smile, as if hungering for the juicy apples from the fruit peddler, or for a cool dip in the fountain, or maybe, just maybe, was I nuts, hungering for *me*. I climbed back up the ladder with a dollop of red on the tip of my brush, eager to moisten her lips one last time. We stood lip to lip. Her barely open mouth, was it awaiting my kiss? I almost wished I could kiss her. I had to laugh, I must be losing my mind, I thought. Nervous sweat was running down my armpits and the back of my neck like I was on a first date or something. Now *Opal* would be jealous! I started laughing right out loud at the idea of me plastering my lips to the brick, as if a simple kiss would dance my diva right off the wall and into my arms, like a princess kissing a frog to get her prince.

"Nope, better you should stay on the wall, Doll, than to hob-nob in this crummy two-bit joint."

I wiped my sleeve across my sweaty forehead and turned toward the one spotlight burning the back of my neck. The last thing I wanted was to shvitz like a pig all over my masterpiece. I jumped off the ladder and went to the left of the stage to turn off the spot. I still had enough light from the alley window to finish up. As I climbed back up the ladder though, I heard the front door open, a big iron door with a heavy latch. The door slammed with a bang.

Oh brother, here comes trouble, I thought.

"It's very dark," said a young woman's voice coming down the short steps into the club.

"It'll light up at night, Honey, I can guarantee that," I heard Minnie say with a nasty laugh. Minnie was the plump, bleach-blonde hostess, who always wore thick pancake make-up and even thicker ruby red lipstick, like a cheap kewpie doll.

I turned to look. Minnie, in a tight green dress that showed off every rolling ripple of flab around her bulging waist, waddled down the steps, taking quick deep drags from her cigarette. On her arm and shaking like a leaf was my friend Becky from my block on Third Street, a sweet, cute brunette who was always sending me roses. She couldn't have been more than fifteen, way too young for me. But what was she doing here? This was a place for whores. Her older brother, Abe, was a friend of mine. If he knew his little sister was trying to land a job in a speakeasy, he'd kill her. I stopped painting and laid low. I was glad I had turned off the spotlight. If Becky knew I'd seen her, she'd probably panic thinking I would squeal on her to Abe. Maybe I would, and maybe I wouldn't. I knew she needed the dough, everybody needed dough. But if she was my kid sister, I'd never let her out of the house again if I caught her in a joint like this. Just last week I had to read my own Katie the riot act.

At midnight she said she had to go out for Mom. At midnight? I don't care if it was for the Rabbi, forget it. Girls don't go "down the block" late at night. On Third Street, those who lived closer to Second Avenue were called "up-the-blockers," and if you lived closer to First Avenue you were "down-the-blockers." Lots of Italians were down-the-blockers. Good families mostly, but at night the Italian creeps were everywhere. If you wanted to keep your sister safe you didn't let her go down the block by herself at night, sometimes not even in the day time.

"Are you crazy?" I'd yelled at her. "Do you know what those guys could have done to you?"

"There weren't any guys around, Charlie. I had to get some soap for Mom, I had to!" she wailed.

"Soap? What was so important about friggin' soap? Nothin's that important to risk what you did. Ya coulda been ruined!"

She started to cry. "I spilled some shoe polish and grabbed the first thing I saw to wipe it up, and it was Mom's red table cloth!"

Jeeze, I knew about that table cloth. It was Mom's only memento from the ship she came in on. *The Statendam.* She told endless stories about her trip over on that boat, and her red table cloth had a picture of the ship right in the middle. She only used that table cloth for special occasions.

"There was shoe polish covering up almost the entire boat, and Mom was hysterical!" Katie sobbed.

"Where was Benny? He coullda gone."

"Oh c'mon Charlie," she sniffed, "he's always on the roof or in the alley shooting craps, and you're never home!" she'd bawled even louder.

Katie nailed me good alright. Working on my diva took up more time than working in the theaters. I was hardly ever home. And now with Opal in my life, I didn't have the time, nor wanted to make time, for nothin' else. But my brothers weren't around neither. Harry was a married man, and Hymie and Moe were grown up and never home, Benny was impossible, and then when poor Pop died, well, life in our meager little flat was hell for all of us, but especially hell for my kid sisters. So I was it. I was left to be the man of the house. I'd tried to take care of my family the best I could, I wanted to, but what a joke that was. I couldn't do jack. Like for Louie, I was never able to do one damn thing for him. I could only watch him rot away, like watching a cat get creamed under a truck. When my sweet baby brother finally died, his poor little heart so weak and his lungs filled up like a lake, I wanted to run away. I knew it wasn't my fault, he'd been sick since he was born, but I always felt I could have done something. Give more money to Mom for doctors maybe, spend more time with Louie trying to cheer him up. I couldn't do a thing but watch him shrivel up and fade away like one of my butterflies I kept in a jar.

And Pop, how can a guy take care of his Pop? I'd watched Pop shlep all over town my whole life, a scrawny guy like him haulin' a weighed-down pushcart that musta been two tons. Right, like I could've said, *"Hey Pop, take it easy! Slow down will ya?"* when he had nine kids to feed? A year after Louie died, the pushcart and Pop both keeled over in the middle of Orchard Street.

I know, I should've been takin' better care of my family. I should be takin' care of Becky too, and runnin' her out of this joint for good.

"Look, Honey, if you wanna work here, you put out or else," Minnie smirked, blowing cigarette smoke right in Becky's face. "You be nice to the customers, and they'll be nice to you. You can keep whatever jewels or furs you get, but the cash goes to me, and I split it up exactly fifty-fifty."

I wanted to throw up. Sweet Becky selling herself like that? How many sweet girls I knew had to resort to this kinda crap, it made me sick. But for that matter, how many guys I knew started bootlegging and racketeering for the same reason. Thank God I had my art work. If not, I probably would have been running booze and dames too.

I heard the girls go back up the stairs, and I returned to my diva, feeling kinda nauseous in my gut. Becky was such a good kid. *Was*. I felt miserable and angry all at the same time. *Damn it to hell*. I wanted to finish my mural with a good feeling, with pride. I wanted to feel good and go out to celebrate my masterpiece, grab a pastrami sandwich, a Schimmel's knish, a big kosher pickle, and then head up to Harlem. But now I didn't even feel like eating, let alone celebrating. I tried to blast these thoughts from my brain and concentrate on my diva, but then the damn phone started ringin' off the hook. I jumped off the ladder and grabbed it. Jeeze, would I ever get my work done?

"Yeah? Hello?"

"Charlie! It's me!"

Holy Smokes it was Opal. "What is it, Doll?" I whispered, though I was completely alone. "I told ya not to call here unless it's an emergency."

"It is an emergency! Papa didn't come home last night!"

"What? Where is he?"

"Charlie, I don't know. I got up late and saw he hadn't been here all night. But it's almost noon and there's been no sign of him!"

Her voice was so shaky, it scared the hell out of me. "Okay, calm down. I'm knockin' off here in just a few minutes."

"Please hurry, Charlie!" She stared to cry.

"We'll find him, Baby. Don't cry. He's probably just sleepin' it off somewhere. You'll see. In the meantime, do something to distract yourself until I get there. Sing a song, doll. C'mon, sing with me. C'mon, *I got the world on a string sittin' on a rainbow--*"

"I'll try Charlie, but I need to go. I'm going back to the Sugar Cane and ask around."

"Okay, but don't worry. I love ya."

I didn't know what else to say. I hung up, wondering if Coney had done something stupid. Too many times I'd seen the old coot staggering home from work counting his pay right out in the open, in the middle of Harlem for Chrissake, for some marauding leech to stick 'im up? Jeeze Louise, the man was stubborn. Couldn't tell him a damn thing. But I loved the guy. How could I not? He was father to my Opal. I climbed back up the ladder, feeling pretty worried too. When I'd left Opal early that morning, I figured I'd have to make like a mouse on my tip-toes to sneak past Coney snoozin' in the front room. But I saw the fold-up bed was still in the wall. I kinda wondered if something was up, but how the heck could I think about anything bad when I'd just spent the greatest night of my life?

The slime in the basement was already creeping me out, and now I had Coney to worry about. I just had to finish up quick and get goin'. Then I heard the iron front door open and slam again. I looked up and saw Dominic and Carlo lumbering down the steps in a big hurry. They were dragging in some poor sucker like a rag doll. I knew what was coming. I'd seen Dominic and Carlo break arms and bloody plenty of noses when guys didn't pay up or squealed or stole. It didn't take much for some poor shmo to be hauled in and get roughed up good by Dom especially, who had one hell of a nasty temper.

Of all the suckers, this particular sucker turned out to be that grease ball Joey "The Pimp" Rotollo. All I could think of was the last time I saw him, on my way to the People's Theater in the Bowery. I saw Joey trying to impress a John and his hooker by biting off the head of a rat. Blood went flying, and Joey just spat it out all nonchalant like it was chewing tobacco, right in front of the dame. He was that kind of guy, slimy, rotten to the core, and right off his rocker.

Dominic and Carlo threw Joey onto the seat of one of my nice blue velvet chairs I'd gotten for the club. *Okay, I'm outta here*, I thought. My mind was now focused on finding Coney. Who the hell cared what happened to Joey The Pimp?

Then I saw Dom smack Joey's chops with the back of his hand.

"No!" Joey squealed in that prissy high-pitched voice of his. It sounded just like the squealing rat when its head got chewed off.

But I'd had enough of the stinking side of life for one day, and started packing up my paints. I didn't care if I was finished with my beloved diva or not. I started down the ladder, again feeling lucky I'd turned off the spotlight so the boys couldn't see me. I tip-toed off the last rung and quietly started to swish my brushes in the cleaning water I had in a coffee can. But something bright caught the corner of my eye. I looked up. Dom had tied Joey's right hand to the arm of one of the side chairs, and what caught my eye was the gleam of an axe he held up high. I froze.

"No more excuses, Joey," Dominic sneered. "Now, instead of Joey the Pimp, you'll be Joey The Gimp!"

"I got the dough I tell ya!!" Joey screamed.

"Ha ancora il latte in bocca," Carlo laughed.

Dominic shook the axe at Joey's quivering nostrils. "Ya hear that, Little Joey Bambino? You still suckin' milk off your mama's tit? Innocent as a baby, huh? Ya know, Carlo, I bet right about now he's even wet his diapers."

"I got the dough!"

But the axe came down hard. Joey let out a blood curdling screech that raised every hair on my neck. I saw his hand fall like a potato to the floor. Blood was spurting all over the place. What came next, I don't know. I must have tripped over the coffee can cause it felt like water was everywhere, but all I saw was blood everywhere, and the water felt like it was blood running under my feet, and Joey was screaming and I heard, "Who's that? Who's in here? Get 'im!" And I heard guys running, and I tore out into the back alley as fast as I could run and run and run.

I ran down 52nd Street to Broadway and kept on running. Crazy things started flashing through my head, wild images of Dominic and Carlo tying me to chairs, the face of my sobbing mama, all my buddies standing over my coffin, cops grilling me under bright hot lamps screaming at me. *"Talk Charlie, talk! Who killed Joey the Pimp?"*

Just like in the movies. Maybe I had seen too many movies working in all those theaters, maybe my life was a movie. Nothing seemed real anymore. As I ran and ran, all the hoods I ever knew started flashing through my head, Joe Masseria, Bugsy Siegel, all of 'em, and they were all out to get me. But even crazier, when I was running down Broadway past a hundred movie marquees, all those mugs in my head started to look just like Edward G. Robinson. And they were all coming after me, a dozen Edward G. Robinsons with Tommy guns chasing me, trying to rub me out! Maybe I couldn't tell anymore whether or not real life and the movies were all the same thing. But hell, maybe I never even had no real life. What was real about the theater? What was real about the underworld? Had I been just some chump character in a crazy drama my whole damn life?

I had no answers, I just kept on running. Running and running and looking over my shoulder constantly and smacking into people and lampposts. Running so hard I could hardly breathe, and my mouth was so dry my tongue was sticking to the roof of my mouth. I had to stick my hand in and actually pull down my tongue. My chest was burning like it was in flames. I couldn't even tell if any air was getting in my lungs. And then I suddenly thought of my sweet brother Louie who'd felt like this every damn day of his life, having your lungs squeezed in a vice so hard every breath feels like fire, and knowing that your days are numbered. Memories of Louie raced through my head like hot lead, and I burst out crying. Shit! Now my days were numbered too!

Somehow I found myself on Fourteenth Street, and I ran into the alley behind the RKO Jefferson Theater. I fell onto some garbage cans and lay there, puking up my lunch until I thought I'd die. What the hell was I gonna do? The hoods would want to shut me up but good, that I knew. And if the cops got to me first they'd make me rat, and then I'd be dead meat for sure. I already felt like dead meat. There was not a breath left in me, and the nasty taste of vomit was stinging my throat. My mind, my body, my life, everything felt like I was sinking, like I was drowning in quicksand. Drowning in the blood of Joey "The Pimp" Rotollo. Sinking, drowning, throwing up, hell, dead or alive, my life was now changed forever.

Miss Wilson   **Sunday, September 25, 1932**

An apricot-glazed petis fors, a perfectly sculpted delicate cube of mint, honey and fruit, the color of warm spice, and a sweetly knolled cranberry scone straight from the oven, emanating succulent vapors, like a perfumed rose enticing a bee, passed by the nose of Miss Wilson on their way to the next table in the Gypsy Tavern. The waiter deposited these confections onto pink porcelain saucers, and presented two thick espresso coffees to Ben Shaun and Gifford Beal, both absorbed in conversation, unconscious of the impeccable service.

"You cannot be a total recluse like Ault," Shaun was saying, popping the petis fors into his mouth in one oblivious gulp. "It's a neurosis. You fester, you asphyxiate. And then you drink, and you end up blinded by bathtub gin of all goddam things! He's now completely blind! Is there anything possibly more pitiable?"

"I believe I have become too old for the sensational," the snowy-haired Beal frowned, smudging a slivered peel of lemon on the rim of his espresso cup. "But I confess, although in context with current affairs, I worry our representations on canvas are too often viewed as just that. Mere sensations."

"On the contrary my friend, are the twenty-three gouaches I just hung truly an adequate homage to the sad fate of Sacco and Vanzetti?"

Like the inebriated bee, Miss Wilson found herself sucked into the esteemed painters' alluring bouquet of banter, while she sipped at her teacupful of Earl Grey and diligently drafted two butterflies hovering among lilies on a page of her small leather-bound sketch book. As she eavesdropped on the artists' conversation, all the while mentally renouncing their naïve endorsement of Sacco and Vanzetti, two convicted murderers, Miss Wilson meticulously configured an ongoing daydream between sips of tea and swipes from her lead pencil.

"But wait!" Mr. Shaun would exclaim, clinking his cup to its plate with alarm. "Enough of our paltry discourse, Beal. We have another worthy artisan in our very midst!"

"Quite right, man! Madam! Your renderings are most intriguing. Would you honor us with the privilege of reviewing the other illustrations in your book?"

Miss Wilson examined her drawing. The butterflies were passable, she believed, though a bit too cherubic for her taste, but the Tiger Lilies, she feared, were excessively smeared with Number Two pencil. She applied her art gum eraser to the stalks and tried again.

"I must say, the curators at The Whitney have been strangely co-operative," Mr. Shaun went on. "Perhaps an adherence to social realism has finally surpassed their lust for profits."

"But we have been remiss not to inquire of the gentle lady's fine drawings, Ben."

Miss Wilson swept gummy crumbles of rubber eraser from her lilies, and continued to figure and reconfigure her drawing, which was much more soothing and benign, she righteously believed, than Mr. Shaun's scandalous exhibit exalting criminals. However, the growing frustration of noting how quickly her feeble sketch had become nothing more than a mass of cluttered stalks and leaves wallowing beneath two mere butterfly cartoons, a pitiful jumble of leaden lines and gray splotched smears, forced her to reconsider the afternoon's repose, and she peevishly closed her sketchbook. She closeted it inside her handbag to remain a private obsession, never to be revealed to a single soul let alone to the renowned patrons at the next table, an unremitting obsession never quite capable of muffling her father's disdain from long ago. *"Enough with this foolishness,"* haunted her memory, her father so emphatically dismissing a little girl's guiltless illustration.

Still, only mildly chagrined, Miss Wilson turned her attention back to the banner headline blackening her morning paper, which cheered her considerably.

"BEAU JAMES SAYS BON VOYAGE"

"Waiter!" she hailed the passing boy with an empty tray. "I'd very much like one of those delectable-looking petis fors," she whispered, " like you served to Mr. Shaun."

"Yes, Madam. Of course."

A celebratory flute of champagne might have been the preference for some, but for Miss Wilson, an apricot-glazed petis fors seemed more than an adequate tribute to the much anticipated demise of rogue mayor Jimmy Walker. She'd already left work early to celebrate, to savor the morning papers with a self-pampering luncheon of tomato aspic, endive salad, and poppy seed crescent rolls, now this indulgent, sweet delicacy would be a fitting extravagance to consummate the event. The detestable and decadent Mr. Walker, who'd been merely posing as her city's mayor, all the while shoveling hush money to his Tammany Hall cronies, the police department and gangsters, proposing the absurd construction of gambling casinos amid the destitute Hooverville camps in Central Park, blatantly disregarding morality at every turn and even sabotaging Judge Seabury and Governor Roosevelt's investigations of the mayor's office, had mercifully resigned.

"The two-year scrutiny of corruption, vice, and pending charges of fraud, embezzlement and collusion, which resulted in last month's

resignation of Mayor Jimmy Walker, reached a final chapter yesterday morning in New York Harbor when he set sail for Europe."

"'His self-imposed exile in no way concludes our investigations into the wide-spread misconduct within the mayor's office,' said Judge Samuel Seabury who has spent over six months challenging Walker's refusals to testify to allegations of corruption'."

Miss Wilson could barely contain a sardonic chuckle as she visualized those countless illicit flutes of champagne cracking beneath the batons of vice squad officers raiding the 30,000 speakeasies Mr. Beau James Jimmy Walker had personally sanctioned and authorized for so many insufferable years.

"Teeming with supporters, opponents, curiosity seekers, and reporters, seemingly all of New York Harbor anxiously awaited Mr. Walker's final remarks before sailing."

Miss Wilson contentedly read on. Though she'd already gorged herself on similar accounts in *The Times*, *The Tribune*, *The Daily News*, *The Herald* and *The Dispatch*, she devoured her morning *Journal-American*, cradling it between her fingers with near reverence.

"'Friend and foe alike,' Mr. Walker beamed, steadfastly adhering to his flamboyant style of dressing in top hat and tails for important occasions, 'you will at least remember me for saving this town one heck of a lot of money! At least in me, you got a deal! Think what it would have cost you if I'd worked full time!'"

Could there be a more glorious day, Miss Wilson relished, as her lips embraced luscious apricot syrup, and she bit into moist cake, savoring the café's bustling company of savants, the smells of fresh brewed coffees, and the golden autumn maples shining through the steamy windows from MacDougal Street.

"New York Governor Franklin Roosevelt said from his office in Albany, that he too would continue the investigation until all charges were...."

As Miss Wilson followed the instruction to turn to page two, she felt an abrupt jolt to the slats of her ladder-back chair.

"Please forgive me, Madam," said Mr. Shaun, who had risen along with Mr. Beal. "I so do apologize."

"Not at all, sir! Good luck with your exhibit!" she feigned approval. Not even Mr. Shaun's controversial choice of subject matter could dissuade the buoyancy of her mood. She turned the page of her happy newspaper. But the continuing article and accompanying splashy photographs on page two were not the items that suddenly snared her attention.

MASSERIA GUNNED DOWN IN CONEY ISLAND
"Giuseppe "Joe The Boss" Masseria, notorious underworld

kingpin of New York's organized crime syndicate, was shot to death last night as he dined at the Nuova Villa Tammaro restaurant in Coney Island. Charles "Lucky" Luciano, who had been seen with Masseria in the restaurant prior to the shooting, and rival members of the Don Vito Cascio Ferro gang are suspected to be likely perpetrators. Witnesses said three men rushed into the restaurant with machine guns blaring, just after Luciano had excused himself to the restroom. Masseria, in competition for the city's bootlegging and racketeering operations, was..."

Miss Wilson's paper and pastry both fell to the table, the apricot syrup in her throat already beginning to curdle. She tried to retrieve the sudden arrow that shot to her brain, feverishly scraping the fresh, gaping hole of her memory. Wasn't it Masseria's uptown nightclub her Charlie was painting? Or was it a restaurant in Coney Island? She scoured the rest of the article.

"...Besides Masseria, waiter Salvatore Lusco, 23, was also killed, while several unidentified bystanders were seriously injured by gunfire........"

Fingers trembling, Miss Wilson reached for the coin purse inside her bag, snatched a dollar bill, and pushed it under her plate before dashing from the Gypsy Tavern.

"Whattayuh think, Miss Wilson?" Charlie's voice rang through the wound in her brain, and she wondered if she'd ever hear that actual voice again, as she tightly buttoned the collar of her tweed jacket and raced through an icy wind down MacDougal Street, turned onto Houston and hurried for Eighth Street.

"Whattayuh think? Ya like it?"

She could still see Charlie atop a ladder in her beloved Gypsy Tavern, smoothing down the final aqua blue touches to the back wall beneath the mahogany molding. Having endured Charlie's rejections of all her counseling and cautions, she considered finding him employment at the Gypsy Tavern a momentary triumph. His refusal to study with Mr. Hawthorne notwithstanding, she at least hoped refurbishing her little cultured café would have its remedial affects. While the bistro's drab, gray walls evolved into a soothing soft blue with peach trim, transforming the Gypsy Tavern into the most radiant fruit on the vine, day after day Charlie mingled with the world's greatest minds. And the elite clientele of the Gypsy Tavern, Miss Wilson had so utterly delighted, took to Charlie like kittens to cream.

"Nice work, Charlie," Scottie Fitzgerald had extolled after his luncheon.

"Got a match, Charlie? Take a break and come smoke with me," Mr. Hemingway had offered, brandishing two fat cigars.

For three blissful weeks Miss Wilson had witnessed an elevation in both the boy's mood and intellect. His enthusiasm, she felt, was genuine, and not merely based upon his usual penchant for hobnobbing with celebrities. His interest had seemed so sincere, not only in learning more about the café's esteemed patrons, but also of their work. After showing Charlie the frequently scrawled verse on table linen penned by her favorite poetess, a threadbare edition of Miss St. Vincent Millay was seen stuffed into Charlie's back pocket.

But Charlie's expanding enlightenment at the Gypsy Tavern, and her own ardent attempts to keep him enlightened, had been cruelly thwarted by the enticing offers of hoodlums, and she'd lost him once again. She believed she'd been a complete and colossal failure at shielding him from the Jimmy Walker-tinged stench and slime, like fetid sewage it so permeated Charlie's sad neighborhood. Her empowerment as a teacher, she felt, had been entirely ineffectual. The competition with easy money was simply too powerful, too disproportionate. What could she possibly have offered? The promise that education could be fulfilling and lucrative when so many learned men themselves were festering in Hoovervilles? Tip change from the school cloakroom was inadequate compensation for Charlie even at fourteen. There was not one dime she could now offer the twenty-one year-old Charlie whom, she woefully learned, had eagerly accepted a fifty-dollar proposition from the deviant Joe Masseria.

"Extra! The People's Mayor heads for Paris! Jimmy says 'see ya!' "

The newsboy's holler momentarily stopping her torrid scurry up Second Avenue, Miss Wilson snagged the *Morning Post*. She furiously rifled the pages until, there it was--

"DINNER WITH LUCKY NOT SO LUCKY, JOE THE BOSS NAILED IN CONEY"

"With meatballs and customers dropping to the floor, Joe The Boss Masseria wasn't so lucky to escape the bullets last night at Nuovo's Villa......"

But the article made no mention of other victims at all. Miss Wilson tightened the straying, gray wisps beneath her barrettes and rustled onward toward Benny Weinberg's Eighth Street Cabaret.

"I'm creatin' masterpieces, Miss Wilson!" Charlie's voice hauntingly resounded. "Ya should come see!"

For years she'd certainly seen his masterpieces grace her school and the entire neighborhood, she'd even ventured to Mr. Schwartz's theater, though she couldn't comprehend one Yiddish word of the script, to view Charlie's craftsmanship. But under no circumstances would she ever patronize a speakeasy, not when countless naive customers had been poisoned to death from toxic liquids, or blinded like the painter George Ault, while the brazen proprietors were shamelessly profiting. There was no doubt Charlie was creating beautiful paintings and decor. She had no doubt his true masterpieces were rising from the blood and ash of the underworld's nocturnal caverns, but she had grave doubts her Charlie could continue resisting the allure of temptation. However, her greatest fear was not that Charlie would actually be converted to evil and violence, but that he would be relentlessly pursued by it. And now her nightmare was coming true.

She hurriedly turned off Second Avenue onto Eighth. Just beyond the brimming trash bins and litter-lined sidewalk of composted dinners tossed from the windows above, she spied *"Benny Weinberg's Eighth Street Cabaret"* painted in big, yellow block letters on the storefront's picture windowpane. The street held all the appeal of an engorged garbage scow, she thought, but without one hesitation she marched into the club. Not that she'd be capitulating her morality to enter Benny Weinberg's liquor club, for it had only been rumored to serve bootleg drinks, but regardless, this time her repudiation of such establishments must be sacrificed. She knew Charlie had recently made renovations there. The proprietors must surely know where he was currently employed, hopefully, she prayed, not in Coney Island, not by the late Joe Masseria.

"And a Jack for knobs, you schmuck! Are you blind or what?" barked a balding, middle-aged man at a cribbage table. "I should be takin' those points!"

"I ain't no goddam schmuck, I was gettin' there! Gimme time!" complained his gray-haired cribbage partner.

A beefy man in an apron wiped down the counter with a damp rag. "Hey, you two, watch with the language! We got a lady present! What can I do for ya, Ma'am?"

Miss Wilson elevated her chin and strode to the bar. "I am looking for Charlie Stark."

"I bet ya money the moishe kapoyer's two-timing this ol' broad!" whispered the bald man over his shuffling cards, but it was loud enough for all to hear.

The bartender shook his head. "Yeah, that's a good one, Ma'am. I been lookin' for the son of a gun myself. Look right here," and he leaned over the bar and pointed to a large half yellow, half faded-green splotch underneath. "See that? I been waitin' for the punk to finish paintin' my joint for over a month!"

"Well, I'm sure the boy has good intentions, sir. He juggles so many jobs at once."

"Now what could possibly be more important," smirked the

gray-haired card player, lighting a cigarette, "than working right here in this grand Tal Mahal, hey Herb?"

The two men split into guffaws.

The bartender wrung-out the rag "I'm sorry, lady, I got no clue where Charlie is. But if you spot 'im, lemmee know. I could wring his silly neck like this slop here." And he turned away.

With a noticeable huff she hoped would convey her disapproval, but not discourtesy, Miss Wilson marched out of the club.

"Okay, how 'bout this, he owes her dough!"

"Nah, she wants 'im to decorate her church!"

She crunched the door behind her to the unrelenting whoops of men laughing, and she hurried away. "Mongrels!" she boiled. She'd go back to Third Street. Surely locating Charlie at any given time, she thought, would be an easy endeavor given his popularity and near eminence throughout the neighborhood. From the customary loungers on his stone stoop, she hoped only a few questions would be necessary to trace the boy's whereabouts.

But when she finally turned off Second Avenue onto Third Street, her heels throbbing from raging blisters inside her hastening black Oxfords, there was no one lounging on the stoop at building 58. Two young boys in ragged knickers, one of them missing his front teeth, were kicking a can down the steps. On the adjacent sidewalk, a wizened, elderly shirtless man, oblivious to the Canadian wind, played mumbledy peg on top of a barrel, the flash of his pen knife nearly shearing the bare arm of the toothless boy racing down the step. Four flights up, some faceless, abhorrent misfit was urinating out a window.

"God damn ya to hell, Pinsky!" screamed the shirtless knife thrower. "Get your meshuginah old man away from the fuckin' window or I'm comin' up there and cuttin' off both your pricks!"

Miss Wilson curtly turned her back on Third Street and dragged her oozing blisters toward the wrought-iron gate of the Music School to wallow in the jaws of defeat. Battling encroaching visions of Charlie sprawled and bleeding on the dusty floor of some shameful, decrepit diner, and fraught with the decade-long agony of trying to protect him, she was near faint with the anguish of wondering if he were dead or alive.

I've truly lost him, she agonized. More excruciating however, was not the sudden comprehension that Charlie's life was beyond her control, but that it had always been so.

On the less-shredded balls of her feet, Miss Wilson gingerly stepped through the school gate, careful to fasten the heavy iron latch in its secure slot, believing steadfastly in the perception a mere bolt could shield her and her domain from a pitiless world.

Opal   *Sunday, September 25, 1932*

Even in the midst of a dazzling, sunny afternoon, the Sugar Cane remained as black as night. Only one dimly-lit brass lamp with a teetering shade sat on a table near the bottom of the staircase which Opal was descending in a great flurry. Save for a lanky, teenage boy lackadaisically sloshing a mop across the floor, the club was empty. And cold. The heat had been turned off. Opal hurried to the boy.

"I'm looking for my father, Coney Thomas," she said breathlessly. "He woks the late night shift. Have you seen him?"

"Nope. I ain't on no late night, and don't know no Coney," the boy said, not looking up.

"Medium height, always smoking cigarettes, he's got a nasty cough. Are you sure you haven't seen him?"

"Yep."

"Well, if you do see a man of that description, would you please tell the manager as soon as possible? He'll know how to contact me."

"Uh huh."

"The manager, Mr. Owens, is he here?"

"Yep. Boss Man's back there, drinkin' coffee. I'm the one that works."

"Thank you." Opal stepped over the mop bucket, and headed for the kitchen, where light beams were leaching through its swinging doors. She pushed them open to find Mr. Owens, a stocky, middle-aged Negro with a scarred lip, plunked on a folding chair, drinking a mug of coffee and reading the Sunday funny papers. The kitchen, nowhere near the commercial size of a real restaurant, but as tiny as a tug boat galley, was moderately heated by the half-open door to the gas oven. On a burner above, sat a perking tin percolator.

"Yes, Miss? Whatcha need?" the Sugar Cane's manager asked, inching his feet as close as possible to the warm oven.

"I'm Opal Thomas, Coney's daughter-- "

"Yeah, I know ya. I see ya around," he said, looking her up and down.

Opal cringed at her slapdash appearance, for in her haste to find her father, she'd only had time to throw on an old skirt and blouse, a pair of scuffed penny loafers, and a tattered wool jacket. "My father didn't come home last night, and I'm terribly worried. Have you seen him?"

"Not since he knocked off. I don't keep no tabs on my employees after hours. But how 'bout some hot java, Sugar?" he and his scarred lip leered.

"No thank you. But could you tell me what time he left?

The manager poured himself a refill. "How should I know? Lots of guys finish their shift then stay for the show, like your daddy. I see him sluggin' down plenty of my White Lightnin' 'most every night."

"But did you see him leave?"

"Now look darlin', I said I don't keep no tabs."

"Papa always comes straight home from work. I haven't seen him at all." Opal bit her lip to keep it from trembling. Unstoppable tears engulfed her lids. "You know we're just a few doors down from the club. Will you let me know if he comes in?"

"Yeah. I know where ya'll live," the manager stuck his nose back into *Dick Tracy*. "I'll be down there myself lookin' for Coney if he don't show up here tonight."

"Thank you very much," Opal murmured, and left the kitchen, angry tears spilling over. She plastered herself against the back alley door and sobbed. The space between her temples began to split with pain, throbbing with fury at her stubborn father whose habitual, nocturnal rendezvous with Monkey Rum she always knew would come to this, and throbbing with terror that Coney could be rotting in some cold alley coughing his last breath, or worse, laying in the city morgue.

Opal wiped at her nose with a handkerchief and tried to compose herself. *"He's probably just sleepin' it off somewhere,"* Charlie had said. She had to cling to that hope. Tentatively, she pushed open the back alley door. But she was relieved to see the alley was just an alley lined with metal trash bins, teeming with garbage being tossed by gusty winds shooting between the buildings. She kicked a tin can which careened and clanked into an empty beer bottle. That sound and the sound of her loafers scraping against the bricks were the only noises she heard, though every lobe of her eardrums strained to hear the snores of her anticipated slumbering father, snoozing peacefully behind a crate or dumpster. But there was nothing between nor behind the trash bins. No body lay sleeping or dead in the garbage in the alley.

Opal limped back home, ripping through the possibilities. Could he be with a friend? But Coney didn't have many friends. His job by day driving the meat truck was so solitary. And at night, the other waiters on his shift were mostly younger men. *I should have asked Mr. Owens about contacting those waiters,* she pondered. But they could live anywhere. Maybe Charlie could help her find them. *Right, like we're going to scour all of New York City?* she brooded.

Opal shuffled back home past the four doorways between the Sugar Cane and her apartment. She passed the chain-link security fence covering the appliance store, the boarded up wig shop with the "for sale" sign in the window, the shoe repair shop she knew was just a front for race horse bookies, and the portico to the old hotel, where the same drunk she'd seen that first special night with Charlie was curled up again in the doorway. Opal stopped and stared at the man so blissfully lost in his dizzy dreams, and prayed her Papa was also somewhere *just sleepin' it off*.

A screaming fire truck raced down 135th Street, cars and cabs honked and jockeyed for passing lanes, primly dressed neighbors strolled home from church or on their way to lunch, everything seemed so normal. But everything seemed so wrong. Behind her, the window above the appliance store was flung open with a crash. Clouds of bacon smoke wafted out and were instantly blown away by the cold, brisk wind. *At least Mrs. Pettiford got to have a happy breakfast and a normal day,* Opal noted. How she wished she too could be having a normal day, lingering over breakfast, reading the morning funny papers. She should go up and quiz Mrs. Pettiford right now, she thought. Maybe she had seen Coney. Opal glanced at her watch. Almost one-thirty. Charlie would be there soon. She didn't want to miss him. The remnant vapors of bacon billowed through her nostrils, so sweet and sanguine, it permitted her a momentary indulgence of thinking happier thoughts. *Charlie!* she sighed. Was it really just yesterday she'd experienced her truly greatest night with her greatest love, and now be having her greatest nightmare?

Out of the chilly wind, Opal staggered up the steps to her flat. The first thing she did was light the oven pilot for heat. Her apartment was freezing. The living room window was clattering from the relentless bluster outside, seeping tiny, frigid wisps into the room. She fetched a hand towel and folded it over the window sill to squelch the cold, puffing between wood and glass. But not once did she glance toward the bedroom where, yes, just last night she'd been so happy and warm. She sank into a chair. *Oh Papa, where are you?* She kicked off her loafers, noting the lack of coins in the penny slots for good luck. Opal stared out the window at the deep crystalline blue, cloudless sky and wondered why it looked so gray. *But Charlie will be here any minute. Charlie will help me find Papa. And nothing will be wrong.* Despite the sudden realization she hadn't checked the alley behind her own building, Opal fell into an exhausted sleep.

When she awoke four hours later, her silent, lonely room was toasty warm, but her blood was as cold as the icy wind still rattling the window. Together the crypt of silence and the clatter spoke identical, conspicuous truths. Now, both her father and Charlie were missing.

Charlie   ***Sunday, September 25, 1932***

The handkerchief in my back pocket was covered with wet paint, but I wiped the vomit off my mouth with it anyway. This was as bad as it could ever get. I had to come up with a plan. Fast. I got to my feet shaking like a leaf and crept out of the alley behind the RKO Jefferson. *Maybe I should just hop on a train and get the hell out of New York.* But I only had on me eleven bucks and two quarters. That was nothin.' I peered into the street. Everything looked normal, cars and trolleys and people everywhere, and no thugs seemed to be chasing me. I looked up at the RKO marquee and saw *"I Am A Fugitive From A Chain Gang"* in big letters. I'd seen that picture three times already. I didn't care. I turned toward the ticket booth and slapped down my two quarters on the counter. The guy handed me a ticket, a dime back, and I ran inside past the popcorn. No treats today. There would never be treats again, not in my life. My life was over.

The movie was in full swing. I hurried down the aisle and found a seat in the middle of the theater. I wanted to be surrounded by as many people as possible in case Dominic and Carlo came in after me, shooting. My shirt, soaked with sweat, was sticking to me like glue, and I was shivering. The theater was freezing. I didn't have time to grab my jacket from the club. I stared up at the screen into the wild dark eyes of Paul Muni watching his buddy shoot up a diner full of people. I knew what was coming next, I knew this picture like the back of my hand. Muni gets framed for the murders and gets sent to a prison camp. Just like I was gonna get framed too, but a cemetery would be my prison.

I had to think. Where could I go? Dominic and Carlo would figure out soon enough where I lived. So would the cops. It was easy to track me down, I was a popular guy. They'd probably go rough up Bernie Poster, go after my sisters, Mama. And Opal! Holy shit, not Opal!

I stood up fast.

"Down in front!" someone yelled.

I sat back down feeling itchy like my whole body was covered in hives. I tried to get control of myself and think my way out of this. I had to. It wasn't just about me anymore but about everyone I knew. I slunk down into my seat. At least there were people around and it was dark. I was safe as long as the movie was on. There just wasn't anyplace else to go.

On the screen, Muni was getting slapped into heavy chains, and I felt the chains too, only around my neck. How I wished my life was just a picture show where everything bad would be over in a couple of hours, where the lights would come on, and you could casually stroll home munching the last hard kernels in your popcorn bag, thinking about nothing else but the chase scenes. Or the love scenes. Opal! I had to get to Harlem and find Coney! But how?

Life wasn't fair. There was Muni rotting in prison. He shouldn't be there. He's not a killer. Why doesn't somebody help him? Help me? I wished I was back at Schwartz's theater where I first saw Muni, when he was still Meier Weisenfreund. I wished I was watching Muni in *Scarface* where he was tough and on top, not like this goyische fugitive who kept getting framed and suckered. I wanted Muni to be on top, and *I* wanted to be on top. I wanted to be *Scarface,* I wanted to be every hard-nosed movie character I'd ever seen, tough, in control, nobody messes with Charlie. I wished I could jump right inside some movie and go far away like to China with Charlie Chan or to Germany with Greta Garbo in *The Grand Hotel* "where people come and go and nothing ever happens." That's it! I could go to Germany, I thought. World War One was long over. I could be safe there. Berlin was a hot town with lots of clubs and cabarets. I'd find plenty of work. Yeah, Germany! I'd be safe in Germany!

But how could I get there? Not with just eleven bucks. I couldn't stay in the RKO Jefferson forever. But I was absolutely exhausted. My eyelids started to sag. I couldn't stay awake a second longer. And then suddenly I'm dreaming. I'm dreaming I'm in the Sunshine Theater on Houston Street with my big brothers Harry and Moe. I'm only eight years old. I'm laughing and having fun, and we're watching Elmo Lincoln in *Tarzan*. I'm so happy. This is my favorite cause I'm just like Tarzan when I'm climbin' trees in the cemetery behind my building. When I call my friends out to play, I shout from my window just like Tarzan, "*Ahh-eee-ahh-eee-ahh-eee-o!*"

Then my dream takes me out on the street, and I'm alone, running through all the neighborhood theaters. I'm at the Majestic Theater on Second Street, the New Law Theater on Fourth Street, the Public Theater on Sixth Street, the Commodore on Eight Street, the Orpheum on Ninth Street and Second Avenue, and then at The Casino on Tenth Street, and I'm happy and eating popcorn and drinking gallons of celery tonic. But then the dream shifts to The St. Mark Theater next to St. Mark's church, and I'm watching the silent "*Dr. Jekyll and Mr. Hyde.*" It starts to get real dark and scary. So scary the piano player stops, and everything gets eerie quiet. I look around in the dark, and I can hardly see a thing. I'm the only one in the theater. Then suddenly a big black cloud rises up forty feet high in front of the screen. The cloud is a giant ghost. It's the ghost of Peter Stuyvesant! He's rising up from behind St. Mark's where he's buried. He's standing over me with his big mouth open wide and screams into my face, *"AHH-EEE-AHH-EEE-AHH-EEE-O!"*

He gets closer! He's gonna eat me!

"AHH-EEE-AHH-EEE-AHH-EEE-O!"

And now Tarzan's on the screen and he's being eaten by tigers, gnashing their bloody teeth. Tarzan is helpless and crying. His arms are getting torn apart.

"AHH-EEE-AHH-EEE-AHH-EEE-O!" he screams.

The tigers' teeth turn into silver switchblades dripping with blood. And then it's me the tigers are eating!

"AHH-EEE-AHH-EEE-AHH-EEE-O!" I scream, tigers are clawing at my face.

"Help me, help me!" I scream at the top of my lungs, but no one in the theater will help me! The tigers chew off my hand and it falls to the floor! There was no doubt about it! *I'm gonna be eaten alive!*

Bernie   ***Sunday, September 25, 1932***

Through the sunny, sugar-mist window of his pop's candy store, where he was stuck shelving *Postum* cereal boxes and unpacking a case of *Luden's* cough drops until his father's return from Queens, Bernie Poster could only see Benny Stark's back leaning against the old gas light on the corner of East Third Street and Second Avenue, but he could clearly see it was Benny in full crowing mode.

'Wonder where he stole 'em? Bernie thought, eyeing Benny's new wide-brimmed white fedora, cream colored blazer, white linen pants, fancy snow white kid-glove leather shoes, and, thanks to undersized hems of the trousers, bright blue Argyle socks hugging his ankles. Benny was waving at girls and showing-off his new clothes by shifting back and forth on each kid-glove loafer so he could thrust out a hip or shoulder to accentuate the fabric. Disgusted, Bernie watched him fumble in his breast pocket, take out a pack of cigarettes, shake the empty pack, crumple it up and toss it in the gutter.

"Oh no," Bernie groaned, seeing Benny turn toward his shop. Shrouding the entirety of his 136 pound frame against the cash drawer, Bernie was in no mood for Benny Stark's shenanigans. Would he really try to slip some bills from the register if Bernie's back were turned? Maybe. Bernie thought he'd seen the gonif sneak packs of *Camels* and *Old Golds* almost every time he came in the store.

"Hey kid, whassup?" Benny said, though he was actually younger than Bernie, as his six-foot ornamented façade ambled through the door which he slammed to the clang of the overhead bell. "I'm in a rush, kid, gimme some of those *Lydia Pinkham* pills, will ya?"

"Whassup with you, Benny?" Bernie asked skeptically, refusing to move one inch from the cash drawer.

"The price of eggs, ha ha, but for me, plenty. I'm makin' it big."

What a joke, Bernie thought, believing at least three weeks of grunge festered underneath Benny's craggy fingernails while locks of greasy black hair straggled out from under the hat into his dusty blue eyes. *Him tryin' to look all sharp and spiffy like he's just stepped out of a Turkish bath? What a phony!*

"Uh huh," is all Bernie said.

"I'm tellin' ya, Bernie, eppes. Ain't you skivvy to what's goin' down with Charlie? He's rakin' it in! And I'm the tag-along little bro, remember?"

"What you talkin'?"

Bernie hadn't seen Charlie in weeks, and it had been years since he could call the mamzer even a pal. Charlie? Forget it. Something else or someone else was always more important than being with Bernie Poster. Unless you were working in theaters or for the owner of some nightclub, or for somebody he wanted to suck up to, you might as well be dirt. The last time he saw Charlie, the son of a bitch had the chutzpah to tell him about some other supposedly great candy store on Grand Street. *"Caramels, they got, Bernie, and jello squares covered in powdered sugar, and Turkish taffy. I could blow my whole paycheck there!"* Taffy shmaffy! Poster's still had the best halvah in town, Bernie knew, but Charlie didn't come around any more for that either.

"So him and Theo Palma got it figured out good," Benny bragged, leaning in close to the register. "They go up-state, up to Liberty. They gotta be makin' shit loads of dough, the lucky buggers. And ya know those Lucky Bugs gotta have some helluva sweet deal."

Bernie knew all about the Lucky Bugs, and was dumbstruck Charlie had actually let himself get hooked by those creeps. The "Lucky Bugs" were a gang of Italians from Chrystie Street who had opened a social club next to the Colonial Friends. They'd gotten their name from the "lucky bugger" they knew who'd held up Judge Seabury one night. Seabury and Tom Dewey were investigating Mayor Walker and some big time gangsters, so how the robber got off Scott free was anybody's guess. He was one "lucky bugger." So when the Lucky Bugs moved to Third Street under the stoop from the Colonial Friends, Charlie, of course, fixed up their club, painting and decorating and becoming one of their pals. They'd even started calling him "Starkarino" and made him their featured entertainer. Bernie heard Charlie had a regular gig at the Lucky Bugs club reciting *"The Kid."* He'd seen Charlie act out this poem many times at the Colonial Friends. *"The Kid"* was a dramatic boxing story about two friends who eventually became fighters. They went their separate ways, then wound up one day facing each other in the ring. They had once loved each other, had been the very best of friends, but now they had to fight. One knocked out the other, and he died. It was a real tear-jerker. Anyone could recite that poem, Bernie believed, but if you acted it out all dramatic-like, as Charlie did, you could get people crying their eyes out. It was no surprise to him one bit that Charlie could get the meanest Lucky Bugs bawling like babies, because practically every one of them had sparred a little down at the armory, or had a brother or an uncle or a father or a cousin who was a welter-weight or heavyweight. Bernie heard that Charlie got the Lucky Buggers so farklemt, it bordered on apoplexy and nearly qualified him for sainthood.

"You kiddin'? Charlie's got mixed up with bootleggers?"

"One of the Lucky Bugs' got a pick-up truck," Benny went on, snatching a long *White Owl,* Poster's most expensive brand, from the cigar box, and lighting up. "Theo Palma gets to use the truck once a week to make his run. 'Talk about sweet deals! He crosses the Hudson on a ferry at 125th, and heads to a sugar refinery outside Liberty. In the dead of night, he loads up bags of brown sugar, covers 'em up with a tarp, then hauls 'em off to his uncle's barn where they make the booze. Theo carries thousand dollar bills on him! Charlie says he don't see a dine, but that's gotta be bullshit." Benny plucked a horehound drop from the candy jar and popped it on his tongue.

"So that's how he spends his summers, huh?" Bernie rankled. *They had once loved each other,* his mind recited, and he kicked a box of *Postum* cereal across the floor.

Benny sucked hard on the candy, making loud smacking noises with his teeth. "I says to him, 'Charlie, tell Theo I wanna be invited.' But Charlie says, 'I'm tellin' ya Benny, I don't make a nickel. I just do it for laughs. Theo just wants some company. It's a long haul, we don't get back til four a.m.' Charlie says he don't even know where the barn is. For his 'protection,' Theo says, he drops off Charlie at a cemetery before he unloads the truck. Charlie says he just sits at the side of the road for an hour by a bunch of old tombstones waiting for Theo. Get this, Bernie, he sits there and smokes a corncob pipe so he can fit in with the locals. But I says, 'Who cares what the fuck you smoke? It's the middle of the night, for Chrissake. Get off your ass, and go help Theo and make some dough.' But no, my meshuggie brother, the world's biggest schlemiel, would rather sit in a goddam cemetery at three A.M. suckin' a cornball pipe. Every time he goes off with Theo he's gotta have that damn pipe. But he don't fool me with this bullshit. I'm tellin' ya, Charlie's gotta be loaded."

"You sure? He really goes up there every week?"

Benny spewed cigar smoke over the slurping candy, tobacco-tinged horehound drool at the corners of his mouth. "Sometimes twice a week."

Bernie opened a pack of *Beeman's* and chewed all five sticks at once.

"And the broads, Bernie! He's slept with every waitress at the Red Apple Inn!"

"He told you that?" Bernie remembered Charlie always being a gentleman. He never used to talk dirty about girls. But Bernie supposed that had now changed too.

"C'mon! How could he not? Him and Theo hang out at the Red Apple on every trip. Charlie says he knows all the waitresses. They give him free coffee. I'll bet you five he's got a little piece of ass at Grossinger's too."

"No way."

"I tell ya, the guy knows how to make connections. Theo's cousin is one of the cooks and gets 'em free meals, and Charlie says Jenny Grossinger might let him spruce up the dining room. Hey listen to this, Bernie. Charlie told me the best joke I ever heard in my whole life. He heard Henny Youngman tell it when he--"

"Can it, Benny!" Bernie snapped, grabbing the schpritzer guns for seltzer, and throwing them in the sink. He remembered the summer he practically begged Charlie to go to Grossinger's with him and his family, but no, Charlie said he was working for "Maurice." Yeah, like he and Maurice Schwartz were bosom buddies.

"Why the hell would I wanna spend a week with a bunch of alter kakers shvitzing in their food anyways, Bernie?" Charlie had said.

Not that he exactly relished the idea of being fifteen years old and spending a week with his parents, but Bernie at least figured he and Charlie could go off for some adventures like they used to. Without Charlie, the week had turned out to be just one big boring Jewfest. Staying in the hotel, Bernie had observed, was not a whole lot different than being on his own block. Grossinger's was teeming with Jews, just like the teeming tenements. In fact, Bernie had learned most of the Jews at Grossinger's, whether streaming out the hotel or lounging on the quaint porches of Snow White cottages, had actually once been streaming from the Lower East Side. But now they pranced around with their shnozzes in the air just because they had a new Brooklyn or Bronx address, and this suddenly made them big shots.

The only bright spot was that there must have been a million girls, and most of them on the make. Bernie didn't get to kiss one of them, though, try as he might. The closest he got was while swimming in the lake and grabbing Shelly Morganman under water. He had pulled her down and smacked her lips good, but she had on braces and his lip had bled like a pig. Who knew from braces? Everyone Bernie had ever known had crooked teeth. They probably would have crooked teeth forever, he'd supposed, unless they got to move to the Bronx. But If Charlie'd been there, he figured he'd have made out a lot better, returning to Third Street not with a bruised lip to show for it, but maybe at least with a couple of decent hickeys.

To make things worse, when Bernie had returned from the Catskills, and found him at the Music School shmoozing it up with Sylvia Frend, Charlie crowed a completely different tune.

"Little Bernie Poster! Back from the Borscht Belt so soon? I was just tellin' Sylvia, me and her gotta get up there for a few laughs."

"Boy, do I have some good jokes for ya, Charlie. Give a listen to this!" Feigning George Burns, Bernie had grabbed a chalk stick off the blackboard tray and struck a pose, tapping at the chalk like a cigar. "Okay, here it is. A doctor gives a man six months to live. But the man says he can't pay his bill. So the doctor says, 'Alright, I'll give you another six months.' "

Sylvia turned away.

Charlie had just rolled his eyes. "Jeeze Bernie, what a putz. Ya don't tell a Borscht Belt joke like that. 'Alright," he aped, but in an exaggerated, thick Yiddish accent, 'I vill give ya another seex months!'"

Sylvia cracked up.

"See baby? This ain't nothin'!" Charlie strutted around the room. "Think of the laughs we'll have when *I* take ya to Grossinger's!"

"Yeah, well, Myron Cohen told it better, and anyways you blew it," Bernie had lied. "If you had come with us, you woulda lived it up. We had a ball, swimming, and boating, and all the kosher food you could eat, piles of it. We saw Bennie Fields and Ted Lewis and Henny Youngman and his Swanee Syncopayters, and--"

"Bernie, will ya stop already with the celebrities? Ya forget who ya're talkin' to? Like I haven't seen these guys a million times? I've had coffee with 'em for Chrissake. Run along, Bernie, better yet, why doncha go down to your pop's store and get me and Sylvia some *Black Jack* and a *Mal-o-Mar*."

What a goddam schmuck! Bernie now churned the memory. *Up at Grossinger's, huh? Mr. Wise Guy, huh?*

And Charlie was no angel. Wasn't it his bonehead idea to dress up in KKK hoods and run up and down the block? Twenty-two years old and still acting like a dumb kid. He and Milton Krauss had raced into the store with sheets over their heads.

"Ya shoulda seen it Bernie." Charlie had cackled, racing into the candy store, Milton leaning on his shoulder also in hysterics. Both of them could hardly stand up, they were so out of breath from running and laughing.

"Yeah!" Milton had panted. "We ran into Breines's delicatessen and two old schlumps dropped their salamis!"

Charlie started screaming. He couldn't get the words out. "Get it?" he'd wheezed, tears rolling down his cheeks.

Bernie'd just kept wiping down the cigarette racks and schpritzer cans.

"C'mon, Bernie! Doncha get it? They dropped their salamis!" Charlie was buckled over. "Their salamis, Bernie! Like their dicks!"

He and Milton had fallen to the floor like a couple of spastics.

"Yean, I get it, Charlie. Very funny. It wasn't so funny for old lady Melnik." Bernie'd said, retrieving all the *Sen-Sen* boxes they'd knocked over. But Charlie and Milton just kept screaming with laughter and rolling on the floor.

"I said, it wasn't very funny for Mrs. Melnik!"

"Oh God! It's too funny!" Charlie hooted, trying to get to his feet. "What about Mrs. Melnik? Did she drop her salami too?"

And they went off again.

"No God damn it! She fainted!"

"Yeah? So?"

"She was passed out for half an hour! They thought they'd have to take her to the friggin hospital!"

"Well, I can't help it if she's some old yenta who can't take a joke."

"She fainted, you asshole, cause she thought it was a pogrom! Half the people on the block thought it was a pogrom! Ya can't go runnin' around like the KKK when almost every family down here was pushed around and beaten up in the old country! Are ya crazy?"

Charlie had grabbed Milton off the floor. "C'mon Milty, let's get outta here," was all he'd said. "Bernie's no fun."

And wasn't it Charlie, Bernie continued to stew, who broke Willie Heckleman's window for no good reason? Because of dumb Charlie, the poor delivery boys kept blowing out bicycle tires from all the broken glass, and couldn't make a dime for days.

Fuck 'im, Bernie continued to boil. Charlie had time for Milton Kraus, he had time for Theo Palma and Maurice Schwartz, he had time for any schmuck on the block, but not a goddam second for Bernie Poster. The hell with Charlie Stark.

"Charlie says they're openin' so many Jew joints up in Sullivan County they're callin' it 'Solomon County.' Get it Bernie? Solomon like the--"

"I said, can it, Benny!"

"Oooo! Touchy touchy! Ya know Bernie, ya gotta get outta this shop. It's makin' ya cranky. Hey, I hear Schoneberger and Noble's got jobs down at the Doctor Brown's factory. Ya should switch careers, pal. Nah, never mind, you get shicker on cream soda, doncha kid?"

"No Benny, you take the fuckin' job, and work for a change and get outta my hair!" Bernie tore into a case of *Nehi* grape soda bottles and tried to shelf them without breaking them all. Benny Stark, he simmered, couldn't do one goddam job if his life depended on it. The one time Bernie'd ever heard of him working, he blew it big tine. He'd become a delivery boy for Aaron Citron, shlepping ties to stores around lower Manhattan. But Benny's very first time out, some scam artist saw him leaving Citron's shop.

"I'm too weak to walk up the four floors to my friend's apartment," the bilker had said, carrying a big shopping bag. "Can you take this up for me? I'll give you a quarter, Sonny."

Dumb as a stone, Benny had left his box of ties on the sidewalk, took the guy's package, ran upstairs, then came back down to find the crook and all the ties had scrammed. What a nebbish!

"Nah, who needs to work?" Benny bragged on, ripping off a strip of candy dots like they were free. "I stick close to Charlie and I'm made in the shade. Hey, Charlie says Grossinger's got some crazy machine that makes snow. Can ya believe it? They're gonna make fake snow this winter. Charlie says he'll take me sleddin,' and that Jenny Grossinger told him she's gonna--"   "Shut the fuck up, Benny!"

"Jesus, what's the tsimmis, Poster? Alright, alright, just gimme those *Lydia Pinkham* pills and I'll amscray." He nodded toward the back shelf.

Infuriated, Bernie turned to search the shelf then stopped, and then realized Poster's didn't sell *Lydia Pinkam* pills. "You know we don't sell that stuff, damn it, go down to--"

And when he turned back around, Benny was sliding his grubby fingers out of another candy jar, pulling out a big handful of *Mary Janes* while his other hand pinched two packs of *Camels* off the rack.

"Fuckin' A, Benny! That'll be four bits you schmuck! Then get outta here before I call a cop!"

"Okay okay! Kush meer in tuchis, Bernie! Kiss my ass!" He tossed a dollar bill onto the counter. "Who needs your cockamamie stale candy anyways!" Benny casually strolled to the door and yanked it open. "Ya know I thought when you went off to Havana to work on that cruise ship you'd come back a macher, Bernie." He turned up his nose and wiped off the wide lapels of his blazer as if they'd gotten soiled in the store. "But you ain't no macher. You're just a putz."

"Zol dikh khapn bayn boykh, you son of a bitch! And I hope the pain in your gut grows into your fuckin' skull!"

The door slammed shut. "Slam, slam, fuckin' slam!" Bernie raged. "Every goddam time I turn around I'm gettin' slammed!"

Bernie yanked off his white apron and hurled it at the door. He followed the direction of the throw, stomping to the cardboard hanging on the door knob and angrily flipped it to CLOSED. "I'm slavin' away in this fuckin' shop," he grumbled, "while the schmuck Charlie Stark dances down easy street like Fred Astaire! How can that bastard be so goddam lucky?"

Sooner or later though, Bernie fumed, it would all catch up to him. *He'll see. No one cozies up to mugs and stays clean, or alive, for long. Not even Charlie Mother Fuckin' Stark.*

His blood boiling up from his chest to the throb in his temples, Bernie grabbed his hat and coat, and stormed out, slamming the door behind him harder than Benny Stark. He started walking. He didn't know where. He didn't care. He didn't care his pop would come back and find the shop closed on a busy Sunday afternoon. *Who cares?* Maybe he'd find a picture show, maybe go to a fight. Yeah a fight. What he'd give to get the gloves on and find Charlie in the ring.

"The mob kept tellin' me to land,
And callin' things I couldn't stand;
I stepped in close and smashed his chin,
The Kid fell hard... he was all in...."

A hook to the chin, a jab to the head. Charlie falls to his knees. The referee starts the count. "One.... two... three!....."

"The doctor turned and shook his head,
I looked again... the Kid was dead!"

"Eight... nine.....ten! Knockout!!"

They had once loved each other.

But yeah, who needs the bastard Charlie Stark? Bernie growled, stomping up Second Avenue. *And who cares if he lives or dies?*

Charlie   ***Sunday, September 25, 1932***

"AHH-EEE-AHH-EEE-AHH-EEE-O!"
"AHH-EEE-AHH-EEE-AHH-EEE-O!"
"Charlie! Jeeze fuckin' Louise, wake up! You're screamin'!"
I exploded from my dream, and felt a hand on my back, shaking me.

"What the heck's the matter with you?" asked my brother Benny. "Are you Tarzan the Ape Man being attacked by lions or somethin'? You're at the wrong picture, ya dope. This is your pal Muni."

I was not happy to be awake. The dream was horrible, but it was more horrible to remember gangsters were after me.

"What time is it?" I asked. My mouth was still vomitty. The rest of me felt like complete drek.

"Five-thirty"
"Five-thirty! Holy shit!"
"Shh!" someone griped.
"What the hell you doin' here?" Benny whispered. "I thought you'd seen this picture twenty times already."

"I gotta get outta here!" I had to get to Harlem fast. Opal must be worried sick. And maybe they got to her first!

"Shhh!"
"Jesus, Charlie, ya look like hell and smell even worse."
I bolted to my feet. "I can't talk about it! I gotta go to Harlem!" I said, racing up the aisle.

"Hey, wait a second!" Benny chased after me.
"No! Leemee alone!"
"Who's after ya, Charlie?"
"Shaddup! You're ruinin' the picture!"
"Ahh shaddup yarself, ya moron! Charlie! Wait the fuck up!" Benny followed me through the lobby.

When I got out to the street, the late afternoon sun was blinding me. I squinted through the traffic. Take a bus? A cab? What? I had to get goin' quick.

"Shit, I said wait up already!" Benny scurried out of the theater. "I can take ya to Harlem, for Chrissake!" He walked past the sidewalk, around the front of a shiny Stutz Bearcat parked at the curb. "Let's go!"

I about dropped my teeth. Benny opened the door to a 1920

gleaming, gold roadster convertible with big white sidewall wire wheels that lit up the street like jewels. There was mother-of-pearl inlay around the dashboard, and the creamy white leather seat up front was so thick and luxurious you wanted to sleep on it.

"I got it for the afternoon. Ain't it a 'beaut?" Benny said, sliding behind the wheel.

"Jesus, Benny! You stole a Stutz Bearcat?"

"Shit no, I ain't that stupid. Johnny Hennigan paid me twenty bucks just to get it washed. I was meetin' 'im in front of the RKO Jefferson, but he never showed, so I went in for the movie."

"That's not his car, you idiot! Where would Hennigan get the dough for that? He works for Owney Madden! This is Madden's car!"

"Yeah? So what?"

"You better stay right here and wait for Hennigan. You think I can get you off the hook from Madden *twice*?"

My meshuganah brother, just last month, had beaned one of Owney Madden's pigeons. It was a complete accident, but Owney Madden don't believe in no accidents. Of all the luck, I actually got to meet the guy and saved Benny's stupid neck when Madden and me both turned up at Philadelphia Jack Doyle's funeral. I'd been touchin' up Harvey Berman's place when some creep stormed in sprayin' bullets at Doyle. I dove off the ladder to the floor and fell on some guy who turned out to be one of Madden's boys. At Doyle's wake, Madden himself came up to me saying all syrupy-like in his thick, blarney brogue, "Thanks for savin' me boy, Red. 'Looks like I owe ya a favor."

I had one already picked out. Benny'd been hiding out from Madden in the Music School basement for five days.

"Big deal," Benny now shrugged. "If the car's Madden's, ain't that Hennigan's problem? He's the one who didn't show. I got time to take ya to Harlem," Benny grinned. "Ya meetin' up with your pal, Cab Calloway? Jeeze, Charlie, ya better change. Ya smell like fuckin' puke!"

I didn't know what else to do, so I climbed in. It was about as strange a day as I could ever imagine in my life. Joey The Bleeding Pimp, me pukin' my guts out in an alley, screaming in a picture show, thugs about to rub me out, Coney missing, me now sitting in the fanciest car I'd ever seen, and my crazy kid brother testing the patience once again of killer Owney Madden.

"And where the hell you get the duds?" I said, eyeballing Benny's new camel cashmere suit worth at least a C note.

"Don't ask!" And he slammed his foot to the gas pedal.

The Bearcat scampered down Broadway, purring like a kitten, hugging the road as smooth as a knife slicing through soft butter. What a car! It was more like a golden chariot. People were staring at us like we were royalty. *Oh jeeze! That's all I need*, I realized. *I'm stickin' out like a diamond in a pig pen.*

"Turn around!" I shouted.

"Why? We're heading uptown like ya wanted."

"I said, turn around!"

"What the fuck's the matter with you?" Benny careened the car around Fifteenth Street. "C'mon pal, ya can tell me. Who's chasin' ya?"

"Nobody! Just head for the Music School and go to the back alley!"

I figured if Benny could use the Music School basement for a hideout, I could too. At least for maybe an hour or so, long enough for me to cool my head and figure out what the hell to do in a safe place. Mr. Brown, the school janitor had a little cot in the back room behind the furnace. Nobody would find me there.

"Ya can't fool me, Charlie. I know a guy on the run. Like that time we saw Eddie Kepple when the Five Points Gang was after 'im. Remember? He slept in a different apartment every night for a month. Jeeze, and the poor bastard never even--"

I tuned Benny out. I was tellin' him nothin.' My brain just kept swirling. *But what's the point of me holn' up in the Music School? I gotta get to Opal!*

"And hey, wasn't it Eddie Kepple that broke into Churgin's drug store and spilled all that pomade and people kept slippin' and slidin' and ol' man Churgin couldn't pay off--"

But where the hell else can I hide? I can't go home, I just can't. And even if I hide out in Harlem, they'll find me sooner or later. They always do. Oh God, if it could just be last night! How could I possibly transport myself back to last night, when I was so safe and warm in the arms of my sweetheart? But what the hell was I thinkin'? I had to get to Opal whether I smelled like puke or not.

"Turn around!"

"Are you crazy? We're here already! Make up your mind, you shmo! I ain't no taxi driver!"

We had just pulled into the alley behind the Music School. "Make tracks, Benny! I gotta get outta here!"

"C'mon, Charlie. Can't ya just go across the street first, and have Mom run ya a bath or somethin'? You're a fuckin' mess!"

"Oh my God!"

"What now?"

"Benny! It's Rosh Hashanah! Mom's got dinner! I was supposed to bring rugelach!"

"Hey, I can't be worryin' about no dinner. I gotta get this car back to Hennigan."

"Holy shit, Benny! What am I gonna do?"

"Look, crazy man, I'll take ya wherever ya wanna go, but just make up your damn mind!"

"Okay, okay! Get goin' back to Harlem!"

"Jeeze Charlie, ya act like your hepped up on some opium thing. What is it with you?"

"Just head for 135th Street and shut the fuck up!"

"Alright, but I gotta tell ya, this is Eddie Kepple all over again."

I didn't say another word. Benny rattled on about God knows what, but I couldn't hear a thing, except for maybe the sound of a Tommy gun blasting through my brain.

Benny eased the car through the dark alley behind the Music School, but just as we were about to turn onto Second Avenue, something big and lumpy was lying on the bricks. "Jesus Christ! Who is it?" I screamed, for a second thinkin' it was me!

"Relax, Charlie, it's just a fuckin' horse."

There were hardly any horse carts clomping around my neighborhood anymore, but that didn't mean they couldn't turn up dead. Sometimes they'd rot and smell for days before the sanitation workers picked them up. This one was pretty fresh, but had a nasty sneer on its face like it could jump up any second and trample us. But maybe that wasn't a sneer on his face, I thought. Maybe it was a look of relief. No more hauling heavy loads on cold pavement, no more sleeping in some shit-filled horse barn behind a shit-filled tenement. Death had brought this old nag an escape. What a relief it could be for me too if I could escape the hell of New York. Benny had no choice but to roll the wheels of the Stutz right over the horse so we could get out. And I had to get out. Out of New York forever. I could hear the poor horse screaming when our back fender scraped across its hide. *Yeah, ain't it the truth? Like this poor nag, dead but still being hammered. The story of my life!* But I was getting out. How would I tell Opal I was leaving New York? Yet, how could I ever leave Opal? And if I stayed, maybe we'd both get a bullet in the head. There was no other option but for me to leave. There was no way my problems were gonna hurt my beloved.

Cruising through the East Village over to Broadway, me ducked down as low as possible, the city just mocked me. As much as I wanted to escape, the city kept luring me back. Warm, friendly smells, smells that could one hundred percent bring me to my knees, were teasing my nostrils. A dozen restaurants were cranking out Sunday suppers. I could smell beets simmering for borscht, warm breads baking, spaghetti sauces swirling with garlic, sweet cheese being stuffed into cannolis, seafood frying, beef and pork and chickens being smoked or stewed, and a million potatoes boiling and bubbling, waiting to be mashed with gobs of butter.

The sweet smells of New York food hovering like angels over the sidewalk were as close to heaven as the angels themselves. Those delicious perfumes wafting out of all the restaurants energized me somehow, and suddenly I got this crazy idea to beat my chest like Tarzan and go after the tigers. Every sniff of lasagna or kugel or pot roast and even stinky sauerkraut was a reminder this was *my* town. No one was gonna chase me away. Not a couple of dumb thugs like Dominic and Carlo. I'd show 'em!

Then a siren came blasting off Tenth Street from Hell's Kitchen, and here came two ambulances and three cop cars. *Shit, but I have to leave New York or wind up dead.* My brain felt like it was on the Loop-T-Loop, spinning crazy, tumbling upside down and all around, up and down, back and forth, over and over and over. Go? Stay? Live, or die? *What!?!* A cold wind roared into the convertible and through my open shirt collar. Oh God, I was going nuts! Soon I'll be just like Dr. Jekyl and Mr. Hyde, I thought, all bug-eyed and completely bonkers. Soon I'll be in a straight jacket or lying in an alley with a belly full of bullets or a belly full of maggots like that old nag. And who would give one damn? There was not one soul to help me and save me from the tigers. My city had abandoned me. I didn't fit in nowhere. I was a stranger in my own town.

"Now that you've read from the Torah, Ysrulic, you will tell me what it means."

Jeeze, I *was* goin' crazy. Out of nowhere Rav Meir, the old bearded Rabbi who always wore a black hat and black suit even in the sweltering summer, was in my head. My pop had made me go across the street to the synagogue and read just two sentences for my bar mitzvah. But why was this in my head now?

"Read it again," he had insisted.

"Moses agreed to stay with the man who gave his daughter, Zipporah, to Moses in marriage. Zipporah gave birth to a son and Moses named him Gershom, saying, "I have been a stranger in a strange land."

"Well?" Rav Meir had squinted at me over his thick glasses.

"Moses had been in a desert, so now he's in a strange country?" I'd guessed.

"Some texts say 'I have been a stranger in a strange land,' while other texts say 'I have *become* a stranger in a strange land.' Is there a difference, Ysrulic?"

I didn't have a clue.

"Ysruluic?" he'd kept calling my real name.

"I give up Rabbi. I didn't know there'd be a quiz."

"Very well," he had laughed, "but someday I promise, you will know. Now run along home. Your father has a new pair of pants for you."

Why was this in my head? I turned toward Benny. He was

puffing on his stogie and waving at dames in fur collars gliding into ritzy hotels across from Central Park. "Hey Doll! Wanna ride in a classy car?" he screamed.

Maybe Benny was the stranger. This moyshe kapoyer in a cashmere suit, did I ever really know him? Had my own brother become a stranger to me? Or had he been a stranger all along? I turned toward Central Park. Through the tall elms I could see lights twinkling on the lake. The last time I saw that lake was in daylight when me and Bernie had strolled to the subway cherishing a jar of minnows. But that was centuries ago, before Bernie Poster had also become a stranger.

Nothing was the same no more, not friends, not family not even the beloved village of my city. Maybe I was the stranger. *No one really knows me,* I thought. *No one's ever known me or my thoughts, my dreams or my desires. They just know what I've let 'em know.* So maybe it was me. Maybe I'd become a stranger even to myself. All the jokes, and pranks, and songs and stories, and combing the streets and cruising the rooftops, and hustling and conning and scraping and begging, hell, I was a damn machine, a machine lost in a fog. No, worse than that, a machine in a coma. Had I been asleep most of my life like some Rip Van Winkle? You wake up, and no one knows you at all. The answer to that question was simple. There *was* a difference between being a stranger and becoming one. I had to get out. I had to break out. I had to put my head down and charge and explode like a bull.

So I climbed out of the car.

"What the fuckin, hell?" Benny yelled.

I flipped myself over the door, hung onto it with one hand and shot my fist to the air, landing on the running board. "Alright! Come and get me!"

Headlights blinded my eyes like lighting bolts, but I saw everything as clear as day. I saw Alex Chertov bouncing me around like a yo-yo, I saw a seamy parade of motley mobsters hauling me from dive to dive by the end of my nose, not giving one shit about the masterpieces I was making, I saw a whole auditorium packed with school teachers nagging me to go to art school. I saw a rooftop full of frumpy dames sneering *"how much money is ya makin' Charlie?"* and I saw a planet full of bigots telling me who to love. Shit, I had been a stranger to myself! But no more! Enough was enough!

"I'm takin' ya to the loony bin! Youse gonna get killed!"

"No, Benny! I'm getting myself alive! I yam what I yam and that's all that I yam! I'm Popeye the Sailor Man!" I sang, glued to that running board like it was my magic carpet. I stuck out one leg and stretched my arm up to the sky, up to grab the stars. "I just ate my spinach, Benny!"

"Holy fuck! Will ya get in the car?"

"No!" The freezing wind raced down my shirt, but it felt like a Spring breeze. It even started to snow.

"Charlie! *Get* in the car!"

"No way!"

I'd finally gotten it. Everything was gonna be okay. I'd leave New York alright, but on my terms. No more tryin' to prove a damn thing to anyone else ever again. Hell, I'd survived the slums for twenty-two years and survived a thousand bullets shot through a thousand dumpy joints. I could survive anything. And I would. I had that angel on my shoulder, didn't I? And a four leaf clover in my pocket! I reached inside and shook the little matchbox. Even over the roar of that speeding Bearcat, I could hear the sweet rattle of those four little crusty leaves. Luck was with me for sure! No matter where I'd wind up. Thugs or no thugs, money or no money, bigots or no bigots, I was gonna leave this crazy madhouse of New York City and head for Hollywood. Why not? I'd show those phony movie people how to build a set. I was gonna do it! Really do it! And Opal was coming with me!

Mama   *Sunday, September 25, 1932*

"L'shanah tovah, Clara!" chimed Mrs. Zucker, grabbing a push-broom from behind the toilet at the end of the hall. "Stayin' home for the holidays?"

Detecting the hiss of a tiny tear erupting from the bottom of one of the two heavy paper bags she held tightly against her chest, Clara hurriedly fished through her coat pocket for the house key. "Yeah, me and the kinder. We'll be here. And you?

"My oldest brother, the furniture maven, he's taking us this afternoon to the Catskills," Mrs. Zucker answered, flashing a proud smile between the knots of her tied, white kerchief dangling behind each ear. "Brown's they got a big megillah."

The tear in Clara's bag was stretching toward a split. "How nice for you," she said, attempting to cradle her left hand under the ripping bag, and to jab the key through the hole with her right.

Mrs. Zucker, having plucked several rags and a *Sapolio* soap can from the bathroom shelf, extended the length of her ample five-foot frame to heighten her pre-eminence. "But first I gotta make with the spic and span before we go on our vacation, yes? Good yontev, Clara!"

"Good yontev to you, Mrs. Zucker."

And the two women hurried inside their apartments, just in time for Clara to clump her parcels on the kitchen table as the shredded sack sliced in-two. She lurched at three rolling eggs as they waddled out their cardboard crate toward the edge of the table.

"A klug auf Columbus!" she sighed. "They can make a box to hold eggs, but still can't invent a proper sack, ey, Louie?" she said, habitually disregarding the six year silence languishing from Louie's old room. Clara removed her fraying, gray tweed coat, draping it and her worn, black leather handbag on the coat rack hook. "Chicken, raisins, egg noodles, cottage cheese, cream cheese," Clara catalogued her purchases, rummaging through the intact bag and the shredded one. "The nutmeg? I should not have the nutmeg I paid for?" She threw aside the torn brown paper and found the small tin of spice. "Ahh! Here it is! Good! I will make one fine kugel for you kids!"

She pushed aside the groceries and turned to the iron sink, grabbing two ceramic mixing bowls and a wooden spoon from the overhead shelf. Returning to her groceries, Clara grabbed a small paper bag and dumped out a pound of golden raisins into one of the bowls.

"Could you believe the meshugie grocer tries to sell me purple raisins? Purple raisins for a kugel? Ay yi yi!"

She turned to the cast iron stove in the middle of the room, lifted the kettle to check its fullness, plunked it back down, and lit a match to the pilot. Back to the sink, she bent to grab a cooking pot underneath, filled it with water, then lit another burner on the stove. While the two vessels heated, Clara glanced at the ticking clock above the door. "One o'clock already!" she fretted, wondering how she could bake the kugel, and get it out of the oven in time to bake a chicken for an early holiday supper by four o'clock. She also wondered when her girls would get home to help her clean, God forbid the house should have dust on Rosh Hashanah.

"Loretta's social club got a real ram's horn for the shofar!" Clara's sixteen year-old Eva had chirped excitedly that morning, rushing to the "Happy 4692" party being sanctioned at the Music School, since the synagogue, though right across the street, only held services for paying members.

"And my club's takin' everyone to the East River for tashlikh, but Katie's more excited for the apples and honey, of course, the little pig. But I promise Mama, we'll all be home by noon," Loretta had pledged, scurrying out the door with her sister.

"Feh, and how many kinder are now floating in the farshtinkener river?" Clara said to the walls. She removed the wrappings from her remaining bundles and proceeded to obey the recipe inside her head for the perfect kugel, birthed by her mother and all their mothers who came before. "'Tashlikh, hah! Such a waste of good bread!' " your papa would say, ey Louie?" she chided, remembering her husband's aversion to the Jewish New Year practice of tossing bread crumbs in flowing water to cast away sins.

"Every day we should repent for our sins, not just once a year! And who can afford to throw out bread?" Sam would decree every September.

"Ahh Sam," Clara sighed, cracking an egg into the mixing bowl, wondering where the time could have possibly flown. It had been almost five years since Sam had left her, had keeled over onto the steaming, indifferent, summer pavement of Orchard Street like a cat falling from a rooftop.

"Thud! He just fell to the street like a stone, Clara!" Manny Gershman had sobbed, he so loved Sam. Manny, also a pushcart shlepper from Second Street, had worked alongside Sam for years. Up and down the Lower East Side into Little Italy, wherever they could make a sale, sales that had grown fewer and fewer thanks to the neighborhood Woolworth's and Kresge's and retail shops decimating the pushcart vendors and thrusting them into deeper poverty. He and Manny had to work-in twelve extra blocks a day. It was no wonder Sam's heart gave out, like Louie's. But thank God for Manny, Clara harkened back to that sad day. Had Manny not been there, who knew how long her Sam would have festered in that hot city morgue, alone, unidentified, forgettable?

"No, Mama, no, that's not true," her son Harry had said. "Everybody knew Papa. Everybody knew him and loved him. Papa didn't die alone."

Yes he did, Clara maintained after almost five years. *I was not there.*

Without measuring, Clara eyeballed her ingredients, stirred them carefully, then plopped extra wide egg noodles into the pot of bubbling water on the stove. Gone were the days of rolling out dough, cutting endless slices of noodles and hanging them up to dry.

"A klug auf Columbus," she muttered again, believing store-bought noodles were more reminiscent of dried paste then her own rich, egg dough, but at least they saved time. "Now I have so much time, ey Louie, for all my recreations!" she laughed, tearing off heavy wax paper from the capon she'd just bought from Breines The Butcher. "'Der raykher est ven er vil, der oremer ven er ken,' remember Louie? There goes your papa once again. 'The rich eat when they want, the poor when they can.' So we need to thank your brother for this nice fat bird, ey Louie?" She reached inside the capon and removed the giblets and several small globs of fat, throwing them into a skillet, lighting the burner, and shoving them around with a metal spatula.

"Come be at our table on Sunday, Mama. Margie insists," Harry had said that Friday when he'd stopped by with his weekly ten dollar contribution and a box of Sabbath candles. "It's not so far uptown."

"It's a kindness I appreciate, Harry, but the girls and your brothers will all be here. Charlie's bringing a big box of rugelach, he says. We will have a good time."

"Yeah? Charlie *and* Benny?" Harry had looked so skeptical. "You've got to be kidding. When was the last time you saw either one of them?"

"Charlie? Yesterday, he came to change a shirt. And Benny, okay, three days past. But he'll be here for my kugel, you can bet money."

Her eldest son, Harry, a true gentleman, she'd never heard an angry or foul word escape his lips, who had suffered from his own staph-infected childhood chicken pox, leaving his neck and arms badly scarred, had reached into his pocket, and handed her another ten dollar bill. "Go buy yourself a feast, Mama."

She'd burst into tears, taking Harry's pale cheeks in her hands, and covering his scarred face and the crop of thick black hair on his head with many kisses. She was so proud. How Harry could turn out so successful after battling the slums was anyone's guess. From Styvesant High School he'd put himself through Pace Institute and became a big accountant for R.K.O. All on his own! Her boy! And he married beautiful Margie and lived in a nice apartment in the Bronx.

"We will have a good time," Clara now assured herself, tasting the *al dente* of one dripping noodle. But she would have preferred joining her son for the holidays in the Bronx. Harry, Margie, her sons Moe and Hymie, they'd all be there. But how could she burden Margie with six more Starks?

Clara carried the pot of cooked noodles to the sink and drained them in a colander. Again she glanced up to the clock. "One-thirty! Such a potch I will give those rascals!" she said, knowing she'd never raised a hand to her girls their entire lives. She combined her mixtures, poured them into a long, rectangular metal pan and placed it in the oven to bake.

"Okay, Louie, what to do next?"

She set aside the capon, then the rest of the groceries were put away, the dairy in the old rusty ice box, and the kasha and other grains stashed into the free-standing cupboard by the one window in the apartment. From the cupboard's bottom shelf, Clara rummaged through her four neatly folded tablecloths. *Not the white linen*, her sister Annie had given her, *too fancy*, she thought. She'd actually never even used it. "Like I'm gonna cover an old board over a claw foot tub with nice linen, Louie? Feh!" She also rebuffed the giddy, green-striped cloth with the clusters of painted tropical fruits Loretta had given her for her birthday. Not that she disliked Ettie's generous gift, but it was a cloth for maybe a nice luncheon or a party, not for yontev. And the red and white checked cloth Charlie had brought to her came from one of those Italian restaurants he'd decorated in Brooklyn, not that she had anything against Italians, of course, but it just seemed so goyische for Rosh Hashanah.

"How can I eat yontev food with the Talyenas?" she laughed, pulling out her only option, unfurling a big, red tattered cloth from the shelf of linens. Reverently, she took it to the table and flared it over the board. It was the tablecloth Sam had given her on their trip to America. Gazing sanguinely at the ragged material draped over just a board on a claw foot tub, Clara stood with her hands clasped to her chest, with her heart wandering back to immigrant steerage on *The Statendam*.

"Eat this, Haika," Sam was saying, after she had thrown up her pregnancy over the lowest deck guard rail and had stumbled back to bed. Harry had certainly been no gentleman in the womb.

"Sha! You shouldn't be here in the women's quarters! You want they should throw us into the sea?" But she was hungrily snatching the thin cheese sandwich from her husband's fingers.

"This chozerai is all I could pilfer from second class. Second rate if you ask me, they just get cold sandwiches up there. Maybe I can make off with a steak if I can sneak up to first class. But you eat, Haika. You gotta keep up your strength."

"We are packed in like slimy sardines down here," Clara was saying between mouthfuls. "Is it this bad in the men's quarters? Packed in with a bunch of smelly Polacks and Italians and Irish? With their smelly Polack, Italian and Irish men always sneakin' down here for hanky panky!"

"I should be so lucky!" Sam was laughing. "But here, I bring you something to keep you warm." He was draping a cloth, tight around her shivering shoulders.

"What shmatte is this?"

"Yeah, just a shmatte for now. I take my cards and gamble for a coat, and this is what I get. A tablecloth for a souvenir, ey? But in America, Haika, I will buy you furs."

The aged, red cloth with its embroidered picture of *The Statendam* smack in the middle, three towering furnaces spewing thick smoke over a rolling sea and six loose threads, now featured a blotchy, dark smear across its hull, the vestiges of a teenage girl looking for a boot-black rag. A stain that would never come clean, like a husband that would never return, Clara pondered.

"Such a gambler, your papa," she mumbled, giving the giblets a stir, the room congesting with pungent clouds of fried chicken fat and livers.

Clara remembered Charlie had tried to scrub out that stain with laundry detergent, *Sapolio*, a crusty bar of *Lava* hand soap, even *Clorox* bleach.

"Not with the bleach! You want to erase the picture altogether and leave me with a hole?"

"But Mama, I wanna help. Ya been cryin' for two days," he'd said.

"You wanna help? Stay away from the crimulniks and stay home for a change! Help me with your sisters so they don't get into mischief with shoe polish and God knows what! And you're no better, Mr. Mischief Maker!"

"Me? What'd I do?"

"Hah! Don't think I don't know about you! I hear everything!"

"What everything?" Charlie'd said, scrubbing the stain with *Lysol* a second, futile time.

Mr. Wise Guy! Clara had fumed. *Like a mother doesn't know her son?* She knew all about the crazy pranks Charlie pulled up and down the street. He'd tie up a fire hydrant in a burlap sack, make it look like a shopping bag, and pretend he needed help carrying in groceries, only to have some poor shlub break his back trying to lift the thing. Or when Spiess the photographer had that loose camera wire lying around in front of Safran's piano store. You touched the wire and you got a shock. So Charlie would grab the cold end of the wire and slap the tush of some passing sweet young thing with the hot end, and she'd jump ten feet out of her shoes. Big laughs he got from the schmendrick kids on the block. And she still couldn't forget Heckleman's broken window. What was next? Breaking necks like his gangster pals?

With the giblets now crackling and Clara sizzling, she stepped toward a cardboard box under the sink, for the moment ignoring a dripping pipe. "Mr. Wise Guy and his meshuganah brother better be here for my supper or I'll wring their necks like that chicken." She plucked a china dinner plate from the box. But, she thought, maybe it was pointless to set the table just yet. Laying out six place-settings of good Passover china would just demoralize her that much further if only four were at supper, she thought, an encroaching wave of melancholy seeping into her bones, piercing her own giblets like a pitchfork. Beyond the simmer of hissing livers and the persistent *drip, drip drip* from the pipes, the severity of unrelenting silence within her four dowdy walls was deafening.

Louie, Sam, nebbishe Benny, Charlie and his gangsters, I have lost them all, she agonized. *Half a family is not a family.* She placed one, lone plate over the tainted smear on *The Statendam's* tarnished hull. *Benny and his shooting the craps, Charlie's gangsters breaking necks, maybe his neck. Charlie piddling with his pipe dreams to be a big macher when I got broken pipes! Where is my man in the house?* She could count on Benny and Charlie like she could count on that capon laying a golden egg.

"Oh Clara!" came a cry and loud rapping to her door.

Wearily, Clara crossed the room and turned the doorknob.

"I want you should have these since I'm goin' on my vacation," said Mrs. Zucker, pushing a bundle through the crack of the opened door, her kerchief having been replaced with a plump brown wig. A navy blue suit with a tapered jacket was hugging her abundant hips. "At Brown's we will fress like pigs, no? And anyways, who wants to come back to a bag of rotten apples?"

"Thank you." Clara took the bag, smoothing back strands of auburn-ash hair, conscious that she'd not worn her own wig in years. She shifted one leg behind her in hopes of hiding the drooping hem of her dress she never quite got around to mending.

"Already my brother is waiting outside! In a new Packard no less! Such mazel, ey! Good yontev!" she sang, and toddled down the hall, clutching a carpet bag as big as herself.

Clara closed the door and placed the bag of apples on the table. *Maybe the girls will have had their fill at their party,* Clara hoped, remembering she'd spent extra money on the big capon rather than honor the tradition of sweetening the New Year with apples and honey. She had no honey. And besides, this New Year just didn't seem all that sweet.

Louie, Sam, nebbishe Benny, Charlie the wise guy! Catskill vacations! Hah! Back to the skillet, Clara wandered through her isolation and shoved at the sizzling innards with a spoon, one fugitive tear dropping from her cheek into the oozing poultry fat. There would have been a deluge, a sea of tears seasoning the giblets with the stinging salt of her despair, if not for the redemptive, approaching twitter of her three girls' laughter, having passed Mrs. Zucker in the hall.

Miss Wilson   *Sunday, September 25, 1932*

Little Angelo Morelli tried again. His ten-year old chubby fingers gripped the neck of his violin, then he tentatively drew his bow across the strings. However, once again the horsehair squeaked across *G*. Not just squeaked, but screeched with a vehemence that would crack the crystal punch bowl, thought Miss Wilson. *Strauss is surly rolling in his grave. At least no one has the gracelessness to laugh,* she winced, surveying the tolerant faces of parents attending the semi-annual Music School junior violin recital. Relief was clearly palpable when Angelo concluded the *Pizzicato Polka* by plucking *D* instead of *A, E* instead of *G*. Yet the applause was strong and genial as the tenement boy in a clean white shirt shuffled back to his seat, being replaced by eleven-year old Connie Loucosto at the front of the recital room. Her rendition of Dvorak's *Humoresque* sang from her strings, certainly much less sophisticated than Angelo's Strauss, but at least much less offensive to the ear, deemed the school's librarian. For a few moments, Miss Wilson hoped to drift into a dream of transitory calm, and in those fleeting seconds allow herself to ponder only the rapture of music, melody and the impending promise of a budding artiste. She would not think about Charlie Stark, whose own promise had seemed to evaporate as emphatically as the defenseless snowflakes she saw melting onto the stone ledge outside the Music School's frosty windows.

Miss Wilson re-evaluated the postures of cucumber sandwiches and shortbread cookies upon their plates at the refreshment table, battling all marauding thoughts that, like the plummeting snow flakes, she too had been defenseless in protecting her Charlie. But she could not think of Charlie Stark who probably had indeed been caught in the wrath of Joe Masseria's mob gunfire, the blunt snare of an iniquity, a pestilence she could never, hardly, forestall. Was he crippled, bleeding, festering, worse? She flung away the reels of these projected images inside her head with a jerk of her chin toward Connie Loucosto's soothing violin. And with another jerk and a scornful pinch to her lips, she motioned to Tommy Loucosto he not even dare attempt to shoot that rubber band at his little sister.

"Who?" Tommy had said earlier that evening inside her library, when Miss Wilson attempted a final, desperate interrogation. But Tommy was only conscious of the upcoming world championship between the Yankees and Cubs, his nose submerged beneath the *Daily Post* sports page.

"Charlie Stark, Tommy. Surely you know Charlie. He lives right across the street. Everyone knows Charlie. Have you seen him?"

"Never heard of 'im. Sorry."

The same question was asked of Howard Fenster, hurrying to make his club meeting on the third floor. "Charlie Stark?" he had scoffed. "Ain't he a hood, Miss Wilson? Why ya wanna know about a hood like him?"

It's hopeless, Miss Wilson now sighed, sagging against the cold window frame. She shifted restlessly on the blistered soles of her feet, a reproving consequence, she believed, of an irrational pursuit. *For what could possibly be more irrational, than me scouring these endless slums all afternoon for a boy who could be anywhere in the city?* She fanned her recital program at tiny beads of sweat beginning to bubble down her burning face and neck, despite the frigid wisps escaping the window where she stood. She tried to focus back to Dvorak and not on a persistent urge to lapse into fear, the one strident terror, the unwavering, eternal dread that for all those years she'd been a consummate failure in protecting a child, nurturing her Charlie for greatness, and at the very least sheltering him from jackals.

Lively applause broke out all around. Connie Loucosto took her bows, bending so low, her long blonde curls caressed the tops of her waxed and shined patent leather pumps.

"Bravo!" cheered Miss Wilson, yanking all thoughts away from despair.

Little Jimmy DeLucca, his fresh crew-cut also waxed and shined, now faced the audience. He raised his bow and began to melt into Mozart like a swan drifting through still waters, Miss Wilson savored. A luxurious sigh escaped her lips, and she closed her eyes, believing this sweet stream of talented children, these blossoming neophytes, seemed to gush like a medicinal fountain, spewing an elixir for her soul, a tonic of hope that permeated her flesh like a vaccine. *No*, she would not think about Charlie Stark.

"I must thank you, Miss Wilson, for your last minute corrections to the program," whispered Miss Birnie as Jimmy's bow danced across his strings.

"Not at all, Miss Birnie," Miss Wilson, sighed again and kept her brightening beam at the children.

"I'd completely forgotten we'd scheduled our recital on the Jewish New Year. Though I certainly miss young Freddie Mandel's fine performance, I do understand why--"

"But of course! How could I be so stupid?" Miss Wilson blurted out, to the disapproving scowls of Jimmy DeLucca's parents, grandmother, Aunt Theresa and their parish priest Father Benito.

"I beg your pardon?"

"Oh yes! Quite right, Miss Birnie!" she babbled. "Straight away!" and Miss Wilson dashed to the opposite side of the room. In a manic whisk of self-assurance, Miss Wilson glided to the punch and coffee table in a state of sheer ebullience. *Of course Charlie is nowhere to be found! He's helping his mother with the latkes or lighting the Menorah and whatever else they do! He's probably across the street right now!* With not even a shudder, spying all the orange and grapefruit slices had been surreptitiously plucked from the punch bowl, she blithely scrutinized the platters of crystal cups. *Charlie is just fine!* She repositioned the row of folded napkins to make room for the sugar bowl and creamer, affectionately patted the punch bowl, and bent to plug the coffee urn to the wall. Jimmy DeLucca's little violin was soaring. He was clearly more proficient than Freddie Mandel, she mused. *Today the Music School, Jimmy! Tomorrow Carnegie Hall!* Miss Wilson swayed, permitting herself a fantasy waltz partner as she gripped the handles of the coffee urn. She watched the snowflakes, no longer glowering on the window ledge, they were positively glittering in their own happy waltz.

Rigorous applause exploded from the crowd.

"Bravo! Bravo!" Miss Wilson exalted.

The excited parents rose in a cluster around the young performers.

"Just one moment! Please everyone!" Miss Birnie announced. "First, I want to thank all these wonderful students for their hard work! These young virtuosos were simply divine! And now we want all of you to join us for a few refreshments before you leave. Miss Wilson will assist you at the refreshment table."

The sheen on the bubbling coffee urn reflecting the smile of her revived optimism, Miss Wilson happily stood back, absorbing the crisp aroma of fresh grounds awaiting their brew and the balmy chatter of proud parents and relieved students, as if they all exuded sweet perfume. *Charlie is just fine!* her mind repeated. An ethereal glow so enveloped the room, it seemed to her God's own angels were applauding and mingling through the crowd. She laughed right out loud. The snowflakes had suddenly turned to golden glitter right before her eyes, flickering like precious jewels leaping from the heavens. She bent toward the shimmering window pane and looked out.

But there were no jewels illuminating the snow. In the alley below, Miss Wilson saw a car pulling up to the school's basement door. And not just any car. It seemed to be a golden chariot gleaming through the snow like a lighthouse in fog, its headlights blaring up to her window, flaring like a dragon. The car crept to the back entrance, sneaking up in the dark like a snake, and there in the front seat she saw Charlie Stark and his brother Benny. They seemed to be arguing, but she could not make out any words. Charlie was clearly upset. *But, thank God! He's alive!* She clutched at her heart. But she couldn't help noticing Charlie looked terrible, dirty, cold, shivering in the wind without a jacket, his hair looking wild, his face even wilder. Was he injured? Miss Wilson clutched at her heart again. She saw no signs of blood or violence. Yet Charlie seemed hysterical. Something was wrong. Deadly wrong.

The car started to pull away but stopped. Something was lying at the end of the alley. Something big and dark and sinister. A body? she trembled. It wouldn't be the first time death was a mere deposit in her neighborhood like feces dropped from a horse cart, she grimaced. Wasn't it Joe Masseria who was said to be the perpetrator of Third Street's most recent stabbing? But Joe Masseria was dead. And Charlie, her Charlie, he was alive!

She felt a tap to her shoulder. "Miss Wilson?" asked Miss Birnie, "Shouldn't you be ladling punch?"

But she bolted past the school's director and hastened to the practice room next door where she knew there was a fire escape. There would be precious time to descend the steps and actually get to Charlie, but perhaps, if she could just climb out the window, call to him, lure him upstairs, get a jacket on the boy, something!

"What good performance tonight, Miss Wilson!" the immigrant Mrs. Loucosto said in broken English, stopping Miss Wilson's charge from the room. "My Connie, I so proud! The teacher recital, also nice. But not you? You no play with instrument?"

"No, Mrs. Loucosto," Miss Wilson answered, inching around the woman. "I do not."

"Pity."

Knocking down a chair and three music stands, Miss Wilson raced into the dark practice room to the window, thrust it open, sank her palms onto the cold window ledge and climbed out.

"Charlie!"

But the golden chariot lumbered over what she now saw was a dead horse frozen to the pavement, and Benny, behind the wheel, sped away.

"Hey Charlie!" someone shouted.

She saw Bernie Poster suddenly dashing through the alley.

"What the fuck!" he yelled. "Ya can't even answer me when I call ya? No, ya mother fucker! Ya don't even see me!" Bernie screamed at the tail pipe and bumper speeding away. "Ya never even see me at all, you son of a bitch! I'm fuckin' invisible!"

On the fire escape above, the Music School's librarian stood in the falling snow, unaware the wind was clattering the buttons on her red cashmere sweater and that the heel of her shoe was wedged into the grate of the top step. She watched Bernie stagger away toward Second Avenue. He was crying, and his cries clamored up between the buildings into the frozen caverns of her heart like the explosion of weary canons firing their last rounds in a battle long since lost. The battle was indeed lost, the war was over, she thought, sensing a knife cauterizing the hollows of each and every blood vessel sewn beneath her skin. But she was not the only soldier left lying in the field, she knew that now, watching Bernie turn the corner. The battlefield was visibly littered with the spoils of Charlie Stark. But was it really his fault? she wondered. *Probably not. He sees only what he wants to see, and doesn't see us at all.*

Miss Wilson wrenched her shoe from its trap and went back to the recital room.

"Are you ill?" Miss Birnie asked.

"Oh, I'm quite fine, Madam," Miss Wilson answered, astounded at how composed the words seemed to sashay off her tongue, as she replaced the director at the punch bowl.

"What on earth could have possibly torn you away from these magnificent children?"

" 'Thought I'd left my handkerchief in the practice room, yes," mumbled Miss Wilson, robotically ladling pink fruit punch into a steady stream of cups passing before her. "But all is quite corrected now. And yes, these are magnificent children."

"Virtuosos, I contend," Miss Birnie beamed," I can certainly see them all first chair, the hallmark of symphonies here, throughout America, throughout Europe. And why not?"

The Music School's librarian suspended her ladle to watch joyful students chomp handfuls of cookies, engulfed by the babble of their families' affection. "That's exactly how I see them as well," she said, aware her vision was suddenly as clear as the Waterford punch bowl, its crystals sparkling brighter with each depleting scoop. "It is the seeing of the thing that makes it so."

"Come again?"

"Anything under the sun is beautiful, Miss Birnie, if you have the vision," she explained, though her employer remained nonplussed. "I'm dreadfully sorry, Madam" she said, noting a catch in her throat and the sting of tears in both eyes. "I must retrieve something from my office. I'll be just a moment," and Miss Wilson handed back the ladle.

Her tiny workplace, though habitually cold and still, tonight offered soothing sanctuary as Miss Wilson entered and closed the heavy oak door behind her. Eyeing the pile of over-due book notices that needed her signature and a stack of Dewy decimal cards that should have been filed, she flopped against the door, just to savor the silence. *No, I do not play a musical instrument,* she sighed, scanning the walls of her bleak office, *I have no particular talent at all.* She crossed to the wind-driven, rattling window, where, nailed to the wall beside the molding, hung a small 10 X 10 inch canvas of two muscle-bound Africans hauling stuffed, bulging fish nets onto a scow.

"Anything under the sun is beautiful, it's the seeing of the thing that makes it so," was scrawled in the bottom left corner. *"CH"*

The painting, a gift from her friend Mr. Hawthorne, was the sole illumination in her dreary room, and yet it appeared as the supreme elucidation in her mind. There would never be a Charles Stark Retrospective at the Metropolitan Museum, Miss Wilson now conceded, there would never be the discovery of a talentless school librarian penciling portraits at the Gypsy Tavern, nor the likelihood of little Angelo Morelli soloing at the philharmonic. Yet, curiously, she observed, this seemed to feel acceptable. She gazed past the cold window pane at two ragamuffin boys on Third Street, tumbling in the snow.

And then, cognizant as the clarity of one six-pointed snowflake, delicate but fierce in its intricacy, Miss Wilson instantly comprehended the clear necessity to let Charlie Stark go, now and forever. It was that simple. It was time to not only emancipate Charlie from her obsession, but to emancipate the obsession itself. *The truth is,* she thought, returning to the shiny glaze of painted sweat on Hawthorne's toiling Africans and the shimmer of his majestic sunrise in the background, *my Charlie, just as he is, truly, is as beautiful as anything under the sun.*

"That's my eye, you shit!" she heard from below.

"Fuck you! I didn't do it on purpose!"

"Ya did too!"

"Did not!"

"Did too! I'm bleedin'!"

Miss Wilson turned back to Third Street, and affixed her numbing gaze to the combatants flinging snowballs. But then, something stirred inside her, something more than inspiration, something that felt altogether sanctioned.

"No, I do not play an instrument," she said, "but I can, and I will do--"

She shot an arm behind her. The arm reached for the handbag hanging from her chair. She hurriedly rummaged inside the purse for her sketch book.

"So fuckin' what!" came the cry from Third Street.

"But I'm bleedin'!"

Miss Wilson quickly flipped through her pad of drawings, past her barren winter elms, her desolate streetscapes, and her fruit bowl still-lifes to a clean blank sheet. Without hesitation, her flurrying lead pencil began to outline the images of two absolutely beautiful boys tumbling in the snow.

Charlie   *Sunday, September 25, 1932*

You shoulda seen the looks we got when the Bearcat cruised down 135th Street, shiny and golden in the snow, gliding up to the curb like we were giving Harlem a trophy. I bet folks thought it was the Governor or somethin' until they got a gander at me still flying on that running board. I was flyin' alright, flyin' straight to Opal, and then we'd both be soaring straight to Hollywood.

I hopped off and gave my little brother a smack to the head, "Thanks, kid, see ya 'round. Make tracks and get this baby back to Hennigan pronto."

"Hey! Where ya goin' so fast? Can I come?" Snow had already covered Benny's hat and coat in just the two seconds we'd parked in front of Opal's apartment.

"Hell no, I got business. Get goin,' Benny."

There was no trusting my kid brother to listen to a damn word I'd ever say, so I waited a second to make sure he pulled out, then I dashed upstairs. Three steps at a time.

"Opal!" I banged on the door. I could hear her radio blaring in the front room.

"It's okay, Lois! The cave is bigger than it looks!"

"No Jimmy! We need to wait for Clark!"

Great! She was still at home. I knocked again. But the cheap, soft pine just stared back at me. Nothin.' I pressed my ear against the door.

"Oh I wish Superman were here!"

There was no sound of sweet footsteps comin' to greet me. "Opal!" I banged again. "C'mon! It's me, Charlie!" Still nothin.'

What the hell? I thought. Weird pictures started swirling between my ears, Dominic and Carlo racing up there, Opal searching for Coney, snowflakes dancing in the headlights of a chariot, a cold, limp stub of a hand plopping in the dust of a gin joint. I turned and bolted back down the steps. The Sugar Cane was the only place she could be. I hit the sidewalk running, but four doors down, parked right in front of the club was that goddam Stutz Bearcat.

"Password, bub," barked the sentry, when I huffed and puffed up to the Sugar Cane's guarded door.

Jeeze, I had to think of a password at a time like this? Benny obviously got in. "It was 'Moxie' last week, right? Can't I use it one more time, fellah? I gotta get in! Be a chum!"

"Yeah, yeah," groaned the gatekeeper behind the iron-barred

window. "Go on in. By the look of ya and the smell of ya, ya seem pretty damn desperate."

The big steel door opened and I hurled myself down the steps. Yeah, I was a mess. I must have looked like I'd been dragged through the street by a garbage truck, but I could hardly think about my coiffure just then. My only thought was to grab Opal and get the hell outta Dodge.

As usual, the club was packed and rockin.' The kid, Artie Shaw, no older than me and already makin' records, was wailing his sax alongside two Negro trumpet players. The dance floor was so chock full of thrusting pelvises, I thought I'd be knocked down.

"Hey Charlie! Over here!" Benny waved his arms wildly from a table where he sat surrounded by jiving couples.

I snaked through the crowd, trying to peer past the jack rabbit dancers for my Opal. She had to be there. She just had to.

"This place is hotter than a pot belly stove!" Benny shouted over the music, thumping the table like a set of bongos. "Sit your ass down and let's have some drinks!"

"I thought I told you to amscray!" I said, trying to scan the tops of quaking heads. "And what about the car?"

"Are you kiddin'? I ain't goin' nowheres! I never seen so many hot dames! They all for real? Half this crowd's just a bunch of homos! *Oh, sweet and lovely lady be good, oh, lady be good to me!"* Benny sang, off key, to the music.

"I want you outta here Benny, now!"

"C'mon, Charlie! Ya need a drink, pal. The way you been actin'? Slam your butt down here."

"No, goddam it!"

And there she was. Back near the kitchen, engulfed by the mob, I could just spot my little Opal's red hat atop those sweet tight curls.

"Opal!" I waved my arms above the crowd.

She turned and saw me. We both fought through the swarm until we found each other and clamped our bodies in a vice.

"Oh God, Charlie! Where have you been? And what's happened to you! What happened to your clothes! What happened to--"

"Wait, just wait! I got so much to tell! But we gotta get outta here!"

"Why? What's going on? Oh Charlie, everything's horrible! Papa is still nowhere to be found. I've been asking everyone! It's been almost twenty-four hours! Where can he be?"

"Opal, listen to me! He's okay! I'm tellin' ya, he's dryin' out somewhere. Maybe he got picked up, and he's in the drunk tank till he sobers up! But we can't worry about that now. It's big, honey! We gotta scram!"

She looked at me in horror. "What happened?"

"Dominic and Carlo! Down at the joint, Joey The Pimp, him and the boys--" Jeeze, I couldn't get the words out fast enough. "I had to run, baby! And now we gotta run, cause I saw Dominic--"

Something smashed against my shoulder. I didn't want to look. But it was Benny.

"Hey bro! Who's the tomata?" he asked, squirming past two jitter-bugging sailors, arm in arm. "No wonder youse been actin' so funny, Charlie. I get it now. Hi ya, Doll!"

"Scram Benny!"

" 'Least ya can do is make the introduction. I'm Benny, Charlie's handsome little brother."

"I can see that," Opal said nervously, eyeing Benny's six foot frame, a good five inches taller than mine.

"I said get goin', Benny. Opal and me got business."

"Opal? Now that's a real nice name. I've had a few jewels myself, but not never no gem like you, Baby."

"Hey, don't you be talkin' to her like that unless you want my goddam fist in your goddamn teeth! Opal's a lady! And don't you ever, ever, and I mean *ever* forget it!"

"Okay olay! Jeeze, Charlie, I'm just havin' a few kicks. Let's go back to my table for some fun, huh gang?"

"Charlie," Opal said, looking like she was about to sob, "if you say we need to go, please let's just go."

"C'mon, Charlie, one lousy drink, pal. Live it up!"

"No!"

"I am so awfully misunderstood, so lady be good to me!"

I thought I was gonna faint straight away. I didn't have time for no drink, I didn't have time to be explaining a damn thing to my dumb brother, and I sure as hell didn't want to stick around that mob scene. Who knew who could be lurking in the crowd, lurking in the shadows?

"C'mon Opal!"

"Wait a second! The night's young!" Benny pleaded.

But I grabbed Opal's arm and started to scoot toward the back alley door.

"Hey, I said wait a second, Charlie! Someone's here to see ya!"

Oh God, no! I panicked. I turned around to the staircase. Of all people strolling down the steps, it was Cab Calloway.

"Wait up, Charlie!" Benny grabbed my arm. "It's your pal, Cab! Let's go sit at his table! Baby, I betcha don't know, but my big brother Charlie's practically a celebrity!" he grinned at Opal, who seemed completely bewildered.

Benny let out a whistle and waved his long arms above the

crowd at Cab. The Hi De Ho man, dressed to kill in his trademark white tuxedo, spotted me and waved back. Suddenly, all eyes were fixed on Cab and fixed on whoever he was waving to. *Great! I'm gonna be spotted for sure!* I stuck my nose right up to the hairs of Benny's stubbly chin.

"I said *no*, Benny! Leemee the fuck alone! I gotta get outta here!"

And then, just because it was already crazy on that perfectly insane Sunday night at the Sugar Cane, and just because I was already a mess, and just because trouble had already hounded me into the biggest trap of my life, the insanity became pure chaos when I saw three other guys coming down the stairs behind my pal Cab Calloway. The first was the same shmo I'd fallen on when Doyle was nailed, and I wound up saving Benny's neck from Owney Madden. *Holy fuck! They've tagged Benny and that goddam car!* I thought. But then, before I could worry even half a second about my kid brother, there they were, Dominic and Carlo strutting down the steps, puffing big stogies and checking out the room.

"Benny!" I yelped, practically swallowing my tongue.

"Yeah?" He was grinning like a school girl, still waving at Cab.

"Benny! The Lollywop!"

"What? Ya gotta be kiddin'? Now?"

Benny'd get his tuchis smacked good for stealing kids' candy with his meshugie "Lollywop," he called it. *"Hey kid, you're shoe's untied,"* he'd say. The poor kid would look down and before he knew what hit him, Benny'd lay into him, snatch the candy bag and scram. But that was years ago after one too many blistered hind ends from Mom.

"Now!"

"Who?"

"I don't care! Anybody! Just do it quick!"

"Okay, big brother!" Benny grabbed the sailor dancing next to him. "Hey buddy, your fly's open!" The gob looked down to his crotch. Benny jammed a fist to his groin. "Look!" Benny hollered, and pointed to the ceiling. "It's Ferdie Von Zeppelin!" The groaning sailor looked up and got another fist to his jaw as a reward.

All hell broke loose. Opal screamed. Every woman in the joint started screaming, fists and bottles of Monkey Rum went flying, and I went down to my knees. "Let's go!" I shouted up at Opal.

"Charlie! What's happening?"

"Hurry!"

She dashed through the rumpus toward the back door, with me racing after her on all fours like a mad dog. We scrambled out into the alley, into the wind and blowing snow. I stood up fast, saturated in the slime of cigarettes ashes and rancid pools of spilled booze, but the smell of me was the last thing on my mind cause at the end of the alley, parked in the street, were the swirling blue lights of three cop cars.

"Jesus Christ! Now they're after me, too! C'mon!" I grabbed Opal's hand and took off running for the fire escape under her apartment window. "I'll give you a boost up! Hurry!"

I practically pushed her up the steps, yanked open the window, and we both collapsed onto the floor, gasping for breath.

Her radio was still screaming.

"There's no reason to worry, Lois! Jimmy will be rescued."

"Bu, Clark! How will Superman find him? He's locked in a vault thirty miles away!"

"Trust me, Lois. Superman will find a way!"

When I could breathe again, I crawled onto Opal's lap like a whipped puppy. *Why couldn't there really be a Superman?* I wondered. *A Superman to come save me?* My throat wrenched, my eyes started to sting, I couldn't hold back no more.

"I'm the one who needs to be rescued!" I cried. I buried my face in Opal's dress and sobbed and sobbed like there was no tomorrow.

Hell, would there even be a tomorrow?

Opal   *Sunday, September 25, 1932*

Buckled on the cold hard floor with a frenzied Charlie in her lap, a half-dazed Opal threw an arm to the blaring radio and switched it off. "Charlie! For God's sake! Tell me what's happening!"

"I can't!"

"Charlie, please, you're scaring me!"

Charlie catapulted to his feet and ran to the window. He grabbed a pinch of curtain and peered out. "Thank God!" he panted. "At least the cops are gone! This is better! This is better!" he said frantically. He pulled a *Cremo* from his shirt pocket, didn't light up, but stuck the cigar between his teeth, and began pacing like a cat. "Who knows you're here?"

"What do you mean, Charlie?" Opal asked, getting to her feet, tossing off her red wool hat and coat. She switched on the brass lamp.

"No lights!"

She switched it off.

"At the club," Charlie ranted, pulling and popping every knuckle on each hand, "who knows you live here?"

"Nobody. I think just Mr. Owens the manager."

"Was he there tonight?"

"No, I saw him earlier, but he left."

"Good!" Charlie barked, continuing to roam her front room. He snatched the cigar from his teeth and pointed it with a menacing jerk at each of his next words. "Okay, here it is! But it ain't pretty!"

In the befuddled darkness, Opal sank onto the couch and gazed at the blinking pink flash of *"LAUNDRY LAUNDRY,"* framing the neon-lit silhouette of her beloved, who maintained his track across the floor and back again, commencing a rant that turned her blood as cold as the ice beginning to form on her window pane. Of all the million, mesmerizing stories Charlie had recounted for so many months, true or untrue, this one, she ached to be chronicled as fiction. But as she slowly assembled the shards of Charlie's stunning ramble, the naked truth of reality was as clear as the iridescent droplets of sweat propelled off his grimacing forehead into the scathing, lucid neon. Everything she had always feared, every nightmare that had ever crept into sleep, the desolation, the doubt, the terror of death, for her, her mother, her father, even for a wayward brother, was compressed into the inescapable reality of Charlie's violent tale. Who she was, who Charlie was, what they both lived night and day in this unforgiving city, this *absurd* reality, Opal now believed had always just been mocking reason all along. What in life was real anymore? she wondered. But, as she struggled to fend off excruciating visions of a man's hand falling to the floor, she suddenly understood the answer was as simple as the question. What in life, she asked herself again, could possibly be more real than an act of violence?

"So that's it," Charlie concluded, daring not to look at her. "So that's why we gotta get outta here. We're goin' to Hollywood, Doll. No one'll find me there. My pal Jimmy Durante'll get me a gig workin' in movies."

Opal rose from her dread, rose from the couch, and went to him. "But how do you know Dominic and Carlo are really after you? she asked, her grasp finally stopping the pacing Charlie in his tracks.

"How can they not be? They know I was workin' in their club! They know I'm a witness!!" He shook her off and flopped on the couch. "They were in the Sugar Cane! Why else would they go to a joint like that? They hate black people!"

"I think I did see those two men you described, Charlie, just behind Cab Calloway on the steps, right? But, I swear, the last time I saw them, they were cozying up to a couple of sailors. They were after something else, darling, not you."

"Don't be funny! This ain't no joke! Is your pop gone all night a joke?"

Opal turned to the stove. No, it was not a joke, she thought, staring numbly at the back burner, where, stuck to the grate, sat a rock-hard clump of scrambled egg she didn't have time to clean up from yesterday. But *yesterday*, she realized, might as well have been last month. Yesterday she could wake and dress and cook breakfast for her and Coney, and even slog to her job in a sweet swirl of precious sameness. How incredible, Opal thought, she'd now be coveting that day-to-day, humdrum grind as if it were a luxury, an indulgence, never again to be dreaded nor condemned. Oh, if she could just get back to *yesterday*, she ached, she'd forever celebrate that uninterrupting, delicious sameness when her father would light up his *Lucky Strike* and kiss her good-bye, and they'd both head off for work, and she'd have Charlie waiting for her that night at the Sugar Cane. But yesterday, she conceded, was gone. Yesterday was another lifetime.

"I'm sorry," Charlie recanted. I'm sorry for all of this."

Opal didn't answer. She took a stick match and lit the pilot.

"I said no lights!"

"Charlie. I am going to make us some tea," she said, trying to tug herself back toward anything routine. "I should probably be making you something to eat. Have you even eaten all day?"

"No," he moaned, his face in his hands. "Who can eat?"

"Charlie, darling," she came back to him and took his arm,

helping him off the couch. "I'm going to get you one of Papa's shirts. Go in the washroom and clean yourself up. You'll feel better. We need to think things through. I don't believe anyone's after you," she said, distinctly remembering two dark-haired, swarthy men in black suits, smoking cigars, and entwining themselves around two boys in Navy white bell-bottoms at a back table just before the Sugar Cane became bedlam.

"Yeah, well, I know better," Charlie grumbled.

"Go on now, you want me to be optimistic about Papa," Opal said, not at all feeling hopeful. She went to the closet and snatched a long white shirt off its hanger. "I want you to be optimistic too."

She handed Charlie the shirt and watched him totter toward the washroom. She watched the spasming neon and the flicker of flame beneath the tea kettle afford the only brightness in the room, while she sensed the light in her heart growing dark. *I will be an optimist*, she resolved, stuffing loose orange pekoe into a tea ball, for any conscious, articulate conception of losing both her father *and* her beloved was pure anarchy of the mind. Instead, she forced herself to focus on the menial simplicity of that sole and only instant, as if every tiny movement could be held prisoner in time. As if time could stop, as if time could stop the pain. She forced herself to absorb the very base mechanics of her palm grasping the kettle's iron handle, her finger crooked around a tin trigger, the steamy flow of boiling water splashing into a china tea pot, the sound of a baritone, tea-ball dunk into liquid, the affectionate click of a lid clasped into its ceramic slot. *I will think of nothing but this one solitary moment where everything is accounted for*, she struggled, *all eternity in the present tense.*

A door slammed.

"I'm okay," Charlie said blankly, exiting the washroom, Coney's long sleeves dangling past his wrists. "No one could possibly know I'm here if no one knows where ya live, like ya said," Charlie smiled half-heartedly, rolling up the sleeves, and slowly striding back to the couch.

"There you go, darling, I knew it would help," Opal heard herself say, but doubted its cheerfulness. She put cups on saucers and went to join him.

Charlie took the cup, slurped two sips and clanked it down. "Thanks, but no thanks, Doll," he sighed, laying back onto the sofa. "I don't need a thing right now, except maybe to sleep. My mind's gone. I don't know nothin' no more."

"Why don't you come lie down on the bed, Charlie? At least you won't have these old springs poking your back."

Opal grasped his hand and led him to the bedroom. Her sight

took-in the clear, cogent motion of their footsteps shuffling across a wooden floor, the deliberate movements of a man and a woman nesting upon a blanket, two lovers who in any other instant of eternity, she knew would be lolling in the blush of love. But instead, in that glare of angry pink neon, Opal could only gaze upon their two depleted bodies, fully clothed, but as naked and exposed and vulnerable as peeled pink shrimp.

"Let's get under the blanket, Charlie. It's so cold."

"Yeah, sure. Why not?"

"You want to keep talking?"

"No."

"Then just try to sleep, my darling."

"I don't feel like sleepin.'"

"Well," Opal started, she didn't know what else to say or do, "I suppose I could get some cards. We could play a game, but I confess, Papa's laced the deck with extra queens."

Charlie burst out laughing. Opal didn't think she'd said anything all that funny, but she began to laugh too, and they both collapsed into a fit of nervous giggles.

"It's not that funny," Charlie said, "on the other hand, everything's so bad, it's hysterical."

Opal seized upon the mood. "You've just got to believe you're okay. Whatever happened to that man Joey is not us, not about us. And Papa, well, I believe what you say, Charlie. In the morning, we can go down to the station and get him out of the drunk tank. Everything's fine. I'll believe you. You believe *me*, okay?"

He took her hand. "Everything's *not* fine, Doll."

For a man who didn't feel like talking, Charlie began to babble, uncorked like all the tension inside him had been bottled up not for just that one chaotic Sunday night. "Nothin's fine, not in this town. One minute you're flyin' high thinkin' you got the world on a string, the next minute you're a goddam cockroach at the bottom of a garbage can. Nothin' makes sense. I got friends who've become my enemies, I got enemies I thought were my friends."

Charlie ranted on about some hood named Joe Masseria, about dope dealers in the Bowery, about keeping his brother Benny out of crap games, about how there would never be a Grand Hotel.

Stop it! You're drunk! You're talking crazy! Just shat up! And hold me in your arms! Opal wanted to scream. But she let him rage on, about decent halvah, and making movie sets, and Paul Muni and palm trees.

"And that's why we gotta get outta here!"

Opal sat up. She smoothed back a curl of red hair wilting down his damp forehead. "You're right, Charlie. The whole world doesn't make any sense at all. But we don't have to run away."

"Yes we do! That's why we're goin' to California!"

"Charlie, for a minute I thought you might be hurt, or drunk maybe, I don't know what, but something's gotten in your head and made you delirious. You can't really believe we can go to California together?"

"Why not? I'll knock 'em dead out there in Hollywood."

"And what am I going to do in California? How can I leave Papa?"

"You can go to school and become a teacher like you always wanted. We'll make a little dough then send for Coney."

"But how could we travel together? If we took the train, I'd have to ride in the caboose with all the other colored people. We couldn't even eat together. And where on earth would we get the money for train tickets or have any money to find a place to live? And who would rent a place to a black woman and a white man anyway?"

She flopped back onto the pillow. She wanted to sob. The notion of sitting in a sparkling, white Pullman dining car, rumbling across the green American landscape, seemed like such a beautiful dream, but was such a childish fantasy.

"It is a wonderful thought," Opal whispered, stroking the thick, tawny hairs on Charlie's freckled forearm. "Maybe *you* should just go."

The silence in the room shrouded the two of them like an iron veil. Opal felt those last words stumble off her tongue, burning her teeth, her lips, her throat like hot coals. Had she really just endorsed the exodus of the only man she ever loved?

Charlie didn't answer. He stared out the window at the blinking pink neon. "Did I ever tell ya," he said, "that a blinking light was my very first memory? We were livin' in Brooklyn on Jerome Street when I was born, and over my crib was one little light bulb, hangin' from the ceiling. I musta been only six months old, but I remember that bulb blinkin' on and off. There musta been a short. Anyways, I remember wantin' to reach up and grab that light. Like if I could just get it in my hand I'd win a prize or somethin.' "

"Even then," Opal pressed her lips to his cheek, "you were so curious and wanting to create pictures in your mind, my darling, even as a baby."

"Maybe," Charlie said, taking her hand in his. He pulled up the wool blanket and snuggled it around her neck. "I do gotta create, Opal. But it's killin' me to make masterpieces for schmucks who don't appreciate nothin.' And the schmucks might just kill me for real."

"When will you go?" she incredulously heard herself utter, feeling worthless protection from the blanket, an icy chill permeating her every pore, a glacier enveloping her heart.

"Don't say that. I haven't decided to go anywheres."

"I think you have."

"Listen, if I leave New York, you're comin' with me."

"As what? Your maid?" she said, trying not to sound as cynical as she felt, thinking Charlie was wonderfully color-blind, but had no sight whatsoever of the rest of the world.

"You stop that right now! I don't *ever* wanna hear you talk like that! *Ever*. It don't matter if you're black or green or purple or what! You are smart and beautiful and you got more class than anyone I ever met! And you're goin' places! I'm tellin' ya!"

Opal felt a clamp suddenly latched to her throat. "But I'm not going with you," she was barely able to say.

"Listen, I got an idea. I'll go out west, make some dough, and send for the two of ya."

"Don't you need money to get there? It'll cost a fortune."

"I got eleven bucks in my pocket. I can get more. Plenty of guys owe me money."

"It's such a long way. I hear the train takes five days. What will you do for food?" *What am I saying?* Opal reeled. *I'm planning his trip? Packing him off with sandwiches?*

"Nah, if I go, I'll hitch hike. I got an aunt and uncle in Kansas City. I can stay a few days with them. I got this crazy idea to meet up with Roy Disney. Walt's in L.A. but Roy's still hangin' around KC. I wanna tell him about an idea I got. I wanna make a big amusement park, bigger than Luna Park and Coney Island put together. All the rides would be cartoon characters, like the roller coaster would have cars that look like Mickey Mouse, or the Loop-T-Loop would be a big Donald Duck. Wouldn't that be swell?"

The lock around her throat tightened. "'Sounds like you've already made big plans, Charlie."

"There ain't no plans, Opal, but if there were, all plans would include you, Doll. That's a promise. You hear me? That is my solemn promise. Besides, there could be six guys out on the street right now lookin' for me."

"There's no one looking for you, Charlie. Don't you know that by now?"

"Like I said, I don't know nothin' no more. I only know I'm happy and safe to be with you." He kissed her lips.

"I can't do a thing to keep you safe, my darling. You're the one with the four leaf clover."

Charlie reached into his pocket. He sat up holding a little matchbox in his hand and rattled the tiny remnant inside."It is lucky, ain't it?" he said, tenderly rubbing the side of the threadbare paper box.

He kissed Opal again, and she kissed back, and they held their kiss as if all eternity were the present tense.

"Because of you, I'm about the luckiest guy in the whole world."

Charlie slid open the matchbox and took out the crusted little clover. It showed no sign of ever being green, but whatever preserved it, the four tiny leaves had retained their distinct contour. Charlie held it to his lips and reverently kissed it, as if the fragile flower had never sat atop a remote hillside near a boys' camp in New Jersey but inside the shining chalice of the Holy Grail. He touched it to Opal's lips. She too kissed the little icon and silently, fervently, blessed it with all her heart, imploring, begging God to endow it with supreme holiness for the boy who would be carrying it away so many thousands of miles.

"Do you think you'll be able to sleep now?" Charlie asked, placing the clover back inside the box and sliding it shut. He circled his arm around Opal's shoulder, squeezing her tight to his chest.

How can I possibly sleep? she wondered, watching the pink neon flash against the ceiling in hypnotic rhythm. She begged to be lured into its spell, to be truly hypnotized into the oblivion of deep sleep, or maybe hypnotized into believing she were a bird to fly far, far away, or to be one of the snowflakes still falling beyond her window, blown far across the city, across the Atlantic, away from all thoughts of losing Charlie. And her father. Where was Coney? Would she really find him in the morning, snoring peacefully in a jail cell? Sleep, Opal now recognized, was just an extravagance, as extravagant as any notion of hope.

"It's awfully loud out there tonight," Charlie said, motioning toward the usual cacophony of honking cars and cabs on the street below.

"Drown them out, Charlie." Opal whispered, burrowing against him, believing if she could just remain within his grasp one more night, both the frost on the window and the frost in her blood would surely melt away. "Tell me a story, Charlie. One of your marvelous stories. Tell me a story about summer camp when all the boys and girls sat on the hilltop watching the stars twinkle on the lake."

"Okay, Doll."

A soft white shirt like the down of a gosling against her cheek, strong, able arms securely enclosing her, and the affirming heartbeat of her beloved serene in her ear, this, Opal believed would be her shelter in the storm for one moment in time, for one last night.

"…..Me and my very best pal Bernie Poster were on the hill above Highlands Lake when all the camps started playin' Taps on their bugles. Then the guys from the Newsboy camp started in on their harmonicas. And to cap it all off, the girls from Camp Cowina started singin' in one big chorus…."

For what else, Opal realized, could offer more complete and absolute perfection than the exquisite fullness of this one joyous moment?

"…….It was gorgeous, all those girls singin' in the tree tops, *all night, all day, angels watching over me, my lord…."*

The warmth of Charlie's body snug against her back, the sweet smell of his skin, and the gentle quaver of his song *were* perfection, she mused, sensing herself drift into a deep sleep. There was no apprehension nor regret, no past and no future, she now believed, only Charlie in her arms, an entire lifetime inimitably abiding in one sacred moment of pristine perfection. One perfect moment in time.

"……*All night all day, angels watching over me……."*

They both wafted into sleep. Assured of sympathy and sanctuary, they slept deeply, unaware that the noise on the street and the three police cars seen earlier, were the consequence of someone finding an elderly black man, dead, hidden behind a row of trash cans, dragged like litter to his obscurity, right in front of Opal's building. The unfortunate victim, having received a brick smashed to the back of his head, was found with a lifeless *Lucky Strike* still clinging to his lips.

The next morning, Opal blinked opened her eyes to solid white. *It must have really snowed,* she first thought, *up to the window.* The morning sun seemed to blaze everything in brilliant, glistening white light. She rubbed her eyes. In a patch of sparkling sunshine, a gleaming white shirt was what she was seeing, a gleaming white shirt draped over the chair next to her bed. *A white shirt!* She bolted upright and stared in frantic disbelief. Charlie was gone. He had put on his soiled shirt and left Coney's neatly folded on the chair.

Charlie *was* gone.

But nestled on her pillow sat his parting gift, the tender and unmistakable symbol of his solemn pledge: a frayed, but now blessed, little matchbox.

Mama   ***Monday, September 26, 1932***

Katie mumbled, coughed twice and turned over in her sleep. "I go to P.S. 79," she chirped dreamily.

"Shhh. Go back to sleep," Clara whispered, mistrusting the raspy breathing in her daughter's chest. From Katie's chin to tummy, Clara had swathed a half jar of *Mentholatum,* but at three A.M. she still listened and waited for more ominous symptoms than those of a mere chest cold. History had forced the habit.

Clara pulled the blanket more snugly to their necks and stared out the window at the falling snow. *Such a freakish snow*, she thought, *so soon in the fall, a bad sign for the New Year,* she sighed. *Already so many bad signs.*

Katie squirmed and kicked her mother in the small of her back. Clara jerked, and turned to face the sleeping daughter lying next to her, snoring little girl gasps of fitful, sick sleep. Clara reached to Katie's forehead. It was cool. *No fever, thank God,* she brightened. Perhaps, she could just turn back over and fall into sleep herself.

"Sam! Turn over!" an ancient memory sneaked into her head. "You're snoring! The paint's comin' off the walls!"

"What paint?" he'd asked. "It peeled off years ago."

Clara couldn't help herself and snorted out a muffled chuckle. She and Sam had laughed themselves right into a belly ache over that one. She jammed the edge of the cot's one pillow to her lips to mute her giggles, and glanced at Katie who, thankfully, remained snoring. Clara patted her daughter's soft brown curls, grateful to have a warm body with her under the blankets. Even with a chest cold, Katie's bony, thirteen year-old frame afforded soothing reassurance. Though Clara's craving for her most dear departed Sam to lie warm against her was powerful, to have her beautiful girl, the flesh and blood of a mother's love in intimate repose was equally potent. And though she could not quite express this in thought or word, Clara could only comprehend the easy, omnipotent calm of lying with her child, so warm and cozy on such a cold night. Too soon, Clara knew, Katie would be too old to sleep with her mother and would have to bed down with her sisters. *But three girls in one bed is too much.* It was okay for her boys to have packed the one and only real bed like sardines in a can, but girls needed their privacy. *Oh well, something has got to work out*, she sighed again, and labored for sleep over the persistent rumble of her girl's clogged sinus.

But Katie's clattering snores could hardly stifle the menacing, odd, shuffling feet Clara then heard swishing down the hallway toward her front door. She held her breath and listened. Now looming closer, ever closer, the sound of creeping footsteps stopped right at her door. And then with an ominous, slow creak, that door actually inched open into her dark apartment. Clara clutched at her heart. She clutched her sleeping child. From the dim light of the hallway, she saw a man's two black Oxfords stepping into the darkness. The door creaked again. It was a man! She was just about to scream.

"Mama, don't worry it's me."

"So how do you know I'm awake?" Clara gasped, her heart pounding, watching Charlie in the shadows, sneaking into the house.

"C'mon Ma, you always know when I come in late."

"Mr. Smart Tuchis, he thinks he's so smart, but not so smart to be coming home smelling like a brewery, huh? I can smell your stink from here!" Clara kept to a whisper, though Katie was dead to the world.

"I ain't been drinkin', Ma."

"So nu? You stink like you bathed in it."

"Nah, it's just on my clothes. Some mamzer spilled his drink on me. That's why I'm here, just to change clothes. Go back to bed."

"Fine. You come home at what is it, three in the morning, to change clothes and go back out again? What's the matter? You in trouble?"

"You kiddin', *me*?"

"I ain't believing nothing. And why should I? Three A.M. or three in the afternoon, such stuff comes out of your mouth, who knows what to believe."

This was old news. Her son, Mister Meshugie Story Teller! Once he'd come home saying if she'd turn on the tap, out would come root beer and celery tonic, saying he'd gotten jobs at the water works and a soda factory, and got confused where he was. Mister Comedian! And the tall tales he'd tell the girls? What garbage! Fairies lived under the sidewalk, dragons noshed on fire from the furnace in the Music School basement, he'd even told her girls they were all moving to Connecticut someday to live in a big house with a yard. Gevalt! Who could believe a single word from such a meshugana? Especially at three A.M.

"You didn't answer my question!"

Charlie tip-toed to her bed. "No Ma, I ain't in no trouble," he said, reaching beneath the cot and pulling out the metal trunk where he kept his clothes.

"Hah! You wear it all out on your sleeve. You don't fool nothing on me. And what kind of son stays away from home on Rosh Hashanah?"

"I didn't mean to," he whispered, snatching clothes from the trunk. "I planned to be here, honest, but somethin' came up. Is there any kugel left?"

"Feh on the kugel, like you care! Besides your meshugana brother ate the rest."

"Benny? He was here?" Charlie tried to keep his voice calm, not letting on for a second how glad he was to know his brother was alive.

"An hour ago, gorging himself on my food, then out again like you! I suppose it's some girl, huh? She's worth all this traipsing around at God knows what?"

At least that's what Clara hoped to believe. *He wears trouble on his sleeve all right!* she smoldered, *on his sleeve, on his collar, all over his pants. He's dripping in up to no good. Like the night Willie Heckleman's window just happened to break into a thousand pieces?*

Charlie said nothing but continued dragging out clothes.

"Okay, so it is a girl?" Clara demanded, folding her arms in a clench across her chest.

"Benny say anything?" Charlie asked.

"Say what? Who can hear a word over the pig noises he makes at the ice box. And you didn't answer my question!" she yelped, her voice up two octaves.

"Shh, you'll wake Katie."

"Let her wake! She also wonders why her brothers ain't never home!"

It was all too much, Clara fumed. Two schlemiel sons coming and going through her house like Grand Central, never knowing where they were, never quite knowing who they were anymore, for that matter.

"Kinder hobn iz laykhter vi kinder dertsten!" Clara muttered, with a wagging index finger pointed toward her son. "It's easier to have children than to raise them!"

Charlie pulled off his grubby shirt. "Oh Ma, I heard that one before."

"In the hamper, not on the floor! You want I'm supposed to touch that filthy thing?"

"Forget about it, Ma," he said, grabbing socks from the trunk. "Just go back to sleep."

"Answer my question. I know it's a girl. And what's with all these clothes you're taking?"

And then it hit her.

"Gevalt! You're eloping!"

"Shh Ma! I'm not eloping. I'm just goin' on a little trip. 'You know where Benny is? He owes me six bucks."

"He owes me ten! So where are you going?" Clara grabbed Charlie's arm before he could snatch more clothes. "And who is this girl?"

"There ain't no girl, Ma. I'm goin' by myself."

"Going, going, that's all he can say. Going where? And why are you going? You got jobs here, you're making good money. What's with this going? Talk to me!"

"Ma, let go of my arm. I just wanna get away for a while, that's all. I wanna have an adventure, like me and my pal Bernie Poster hiking up to the Palisades."

"What, you need a week's worth of clothes to go up to the Palisades? You didn't take this many clothes when you went to summer camp."

Charlie just snickered and stepped out of his grubby trousers.

"I said, in the hamper!" Clara snapped as his trousers went flying. She watched her son, in the dark, half naked. *Such a skinny boy, Little Bird Legs.* she thought. Charlie tugged on a clean shirt, and his little white bird legs, Clara saw, stuck out like toothpicks, *like the legs of a little boy not a man.* Her little boy, who'd hob-nobbed with Molly Picon and shlepped for the gangsters thought he was some big shot, but to her, he was just a boy.

"Charlie," she remembered, was it so far back? "Run to the butcher and get me a beef bone. I'll give you a penny for a Marshmallow Twist."

Then at least, he was always home, sprawled on the front room floor, drawing pictures, running in and out of the house with all the junk he'd found on the street, his "treasure" he called it. Ahh, but what could you do? You couldn't hold on to a boy forever. And make him a faygeleh? But when did the boy become a man? Clara wondered.

"Ma, come see the joint I'm doin' uptown!" he had said one day, with real whiskers growing on his chin. "It's a showplace! And hey, I can get you and Pop a little bootleg schnapps!"

A klug auf Columbus! Was he crazy? She wouldn't set foot in one of those lion's dens with the crimulniks, and cheap blonde tramps, and rat poison they passed for liquor. She'd get caught in a raid, wind up in a jail cell, or maybe even get shot with bullets in her head. Was Charlie completely crazy? Besides, what did she have to wear?

"Aww Ma, c'mon! Live a little!" he'd said.

" 'Aww Ma,' you want I should die a little?"

But she got no place with Charlie. Never could.

You can't say nothin' to this boy, Clara now sizzled, watching her son stuff clothes into a blue-checked gingham satchel. *And God knows what shiksa he's sleeping with.*

227

Charlie rattled something in the bottom of the trunk and plucked out a crusty old corn-cob pipe. He packed it down into his bundle, then changed his mind and stuck the pipe in his mouth.

"So many clothes, Ysrulic?"

"Yeah, Ma." He sat down on the bed, nudging her aside. "Ma," he hesitated, removing the pipe. "I'm goin' out west, to California."

"My God!"

"Ma, it'll be okay."

"What okay? You leaving your family is okay?" She felt the barbs of iron picks jabbing at a block of ice that used to be her heart.

"I'm gonna work in the movies, Ma. At first I thought I'd go to Germany with all those gorgeous cabarets they got over there. I'd get tons of work. And with the war long over I figured Germany was the best place to be."

"So go to Germany! It's closer!"

"But the movies, Ma! I'll be in the credits! Think about it. You and Pop sittin' in the Lowe's Delancey with all your friends, the picture gets over, here come the names scrolling down the screen, and there it is, big as life. 'Set design by Charles Stark'. "

"Feh on the movies! They can geh in drert! They can go to hell!"

"Mama, listen to me. I'll make big money. You know the ten bucks I give you every week? Imagine I give you a hundred bucks a week. Maybe a thousand."

"Oh God, such talk! That's all I ever hear from you! You and your meshugana stories! You gotta stay here, Charlie! You can't leave us!"

"Don't worry, Mama. When I make the big dough I'll send for you and the girls, and Benny too, if the schnook wants to come. Ma, you can live under a palm tree! It never rains! Sunshine all the time in California!"

Katie let out a snort and rolled over, taking the blanket with her. But Charlie snatched it back and gently draped it over his mother's shoulders.

"You can have a new life, Ma," he went on. "A better life than being in this old farshtinkener falling apart tenement, or on this farshtinkener block, or in this whole farshtinkener city. That's why I gotta go, and I'll get you out too, Ma. You'll see."

"A new life you say, huh?"

Clara thought he sounded like some Greenhorn, packing off to America. *Hah! That I did already!* And then she began to think back twenty-nine years when she was throwing-up from third class steerage into an endless, cold, vast ocean. *I suppose if I could leave my country and shlep three thousand miles, who am I to say Charlie can't create a life in California?* She watched her son at the edge of the cot, tugging on clean socks. If anyone could create a life out of nothing, she believed, it was Charlie. He could take a newspaper, or the wrappings from a chicken, or scraps from the street and they'd become pictures, and airplanes, and birds and toys. For twenty-two years, she'd seen him grab anything in the gutter, and make it beautiful. She supposed he could make California even more beautiful.

Still, Clara couldn't hold back her tears. "But it's so far!"

"There's telephones and letters. I'll be in touch every day," Charlie promised, trying so hard to keep himself from crying.

"How much you got?" Clara whimpered.

"Eleven bucks," Charlie answered. He got up, grabbed his clothes off the floor, and plucked a wad of cash from the pocket of his crumpled trousers, then dumped his dirty clothes into the hamper.

"Hmfph, and that's supposed to get you three thousand miles? What, you ain't gonna eat for a week?"

"I'm gonna hitchhike, Ma. I'll have plenty of money for food."

"Oh no you don't! You hitch hike and you get a club on the head from some crazy person who'll rob you of everything and leave you for dead!"

"Nah, people ain't like that, Ma."

"And don't you tell nobody you're a Jew! You'll get a club on the head for sure! They don't know from Jews out there in America!"

"That's not true, Ma. Anyways, I'm thinkin' of stoppin' in Kansas City for a coupla days and stayin' with Aunt Jenny and Uncle Max. See? They're Jews. Even in Missouri they got Jews."

Clara's tired, chocolate-brown eyes followed her son around the room, each retina inhaling his every tiny movement, one by one, frame by frame as if a movie projector had gone all ongepotchket and was running at the wrong deadly slow speed. He broke off and ate a piece of challa, he filled a cup of water at the tap and drank, he combed back his hair, and then he tied on his shoes to leave, all, to her, in deadly slow motion. But she was seeing without believing. This movie was all wrong. She watched her son tie up his bundle.

"You look like that bum Happy Hooligan off to jump a freight train," she admonished.

"Yeah?" Charlie smiled, snatching his jacket off the coat rack.

"Yeah," Clara sniffed. She could hardly believe her eyes. This couldn't possibly be real. Charlie off to God knows where and maybe out of her life forever? How could this be? She began to wonder if what the eye sees, the mind cannot truly comprehend. She remembered standing in a beet field with her mother and father as their eyes watched Russian soldiers burn their village to the ground, could she comprehend that? Or standing over an iron ship rail with her eyes bulging at an approaching, terrifying new land, or standing at her Louie's bedside with her eyes ripped apart by his choking in his own blood, until he choked and choked and had no breath. That too, her eyes were supposed to comprehend? *Standing on two legs,* Clara recalled reading one time, *is what made pre-historic humans different from the animals, standing above the ancient grasslands to see the world in a different way. But standing gave a curse,* she now decided. *We loom over everything and see the world for what it really is.* Though she was lying in her bed flat out, not standing at all, she could see what was sick-to-her-stomach *real* alright. Her Charlie was fastening his real belt and grabbing a week's worth of real clothes. He was pulling his real floppy old corduroy jacket over his head and was about to leave his family forever.

Charlie came to her and kissed her forehead. Clara could see the real bite he took from his lip so it wouldn't shake into a sob. She could hear the real taps of his shoes quietly heading for the door.

"Wait!"

"What is it, Mama?" he whispered, and when he turned, she could see the real shine of tears on his cheek.

"I want to kiss you back," she said.

Charlie crept to her bedside and bent down. She took his face in both hands. Her lips reached for her little boy's face, and her lips touched his tears.

"You need a shave," she said, her thumbnail flicking his scratchy stubble, and she wiped her nose.

"I don't got time for no shave, Ma," he wiped *his* nose. "And anyways, I'm thinkin' I'll grow a beard. A bushy red beard might make me look big and burly like a lumberjack, like Paul Bunyan or somethin.' Charlie Stark the Jewish lumberjack. I'll change my name to Paul Bunyanberg."

"Always with the jokes," she muttered, reeling that it was no joke never to see that red beard grow on her little boy's face.

Clara's forehead received another soft kiss, then Charlie walked to the door. Clara threw back the covers.

"Please, Mama, don't get up. You go back to sleep. Just know I love you, Ma. Tell the girls I love then too. And you can tell Benny I want that six bucks mailed to Kansas City."

The door opened. "I do love you, Ma." The door closed. Clara was left with only the girlish buzz-saw clamoring from her daughter's nose. Katie had slept through the whole thing, even with the cooter cats howling on the snowy fire escape, and a few carousing drunks on the street, and the down-the- blockers still up singing their opera. *But maybe it's better for her not to know just now her big brother has left forever.*

Thank God, Sam was already gone, she thought. *Cause this would have killed him for sure. This would have attacked his heart quicker than the pushcart.* Her own heart, she could feel, had already crumbled into a thousand, jagged pieces, even more than the broken glass from Willie Heckleman's window.

Clara reached over and put an arm around her sleeping daughter. She squeezed Katie's scrawny ribs to her chest to feel the genuine, clear beat of Katie's little heart. And then she began to feel the pigment in each follicle of each gray strand in her temples turn stone white. "Vos elter alts kelter," she whispered.

"Hmmmm?" Katie mumbled.

" 'The older one gets, the older one gets.' "

"What, Mama?"

"It's nothing, Katie. Go back to sleep."

"You got a bad dream, Mama?" Katie whispered, half-conscious.

Clara didn't answer. She could only think that at three A.M. her son was out in a blizzard, on the cold street somewhere in the night on his way to God knows where. *And I will never see him again.* She wanted to think he was just off to the Palisades with Bernie Poster. She did not want to think he was with some hoodlum, hanging on the running board of a speeding car with bullets flying. That, she could see as real as day. She could see everything. After all, she thought, *I am a standing human even if I am flat on my back on a bed with broken springs.*

"Yes, Katie. I was dreaming," Clara finally said. "It's all just a dream."

"Go back to sleep, Mama." Katie coughed, squeezed her mother's hand, and rolled over.

And sleep I must do, Clara sighed. *I should cry forever?* Tomorrow she knew she'd have to make a stew, feed her family, wash the clothes, and mop the floor. *What else is there?* She prayed the rest of them didn't get sick like Katie. But she also prayed Charlie would figure out his life, and soon, and come back to her. And he would, she resolved. He was no longer a boy, but a grown man.

Clara stared at the blank wall next to the bed and begged for deep sleep. And then, she had to laugh. "Ahh Sam!" she chuckled. Even in the dark she could see the wall was cracking with peeled paint.

On the street below, the grown man with a corn-cob pipe between his teeth, hopping down his stoop all six steps in one leap, bounded onto the sidewalk, forgetting to scan the block for his enemies.

"Oh I come from Alabammy with my banjo on my knee...." he began to sing to the waning snowflakes, and headed for the Bronx. Bent on waking his Uncle Abe to open his second-hand shop so he could dump the satchel and buy a real canvas knapsack with leather straps and many zippered compartments, Charlie couldn't wait to get to his first night's camp along a railroad track, where, by the side of the hobo's blazing fire, he figured he could sit and write Opal his first astounding installment. But Charlie didn't head for the Bronx just yet. He continued west on East Third Street toward Washington Square. For more central to his thoughts was finding a fallen branch on which he'd tie-up his over-stuffed satchel. Then, and only then, with the stick and bundle bobbing shamelessly upon his shoulder, would he travel the streets of New York and head to California like his hero Happy Hooligan.

"And I've gone to Loo-zianna for my true love for to see.............."

END

Clara's Kugel

Ingredients:

12 oz. package extra wide egg noodles
½ lb. cream cheese
8 oz. cottage cheese
5 large eggs
1 C. milk
¼ C. sugar
½ box golden raisins
½ tsp. nutmeg
½ tsp. cinnamon
1 tsp. vanilla
two sticks butter
pinch of salt

1. In a bowl of hot water, soak the raisins until they're soft.
2. Melt the butter.
3. Cream together the two cheeses. (Cream cheese should be at room temperature.) Add eggs, milk, sugar, vanilla, cinnamon, nutmeg, salt, and the melted butter. Mix well.
4. Cook and drain the noodles. Noodles should be *al dente.* Put in a large bowl.
5. Add cheese mixture and drained raisins to noodles, and blend thoroughly.
6. Pour kugel mix into a greased, 11 X 9 baking pan. Sprinkle on a little more nutmeg and cinnamon on top. Cover with foil and bake for 90 minutes at 350 degrees. (For a crunchy top, remove foil after 1 hour.)

Serves the whole meshpocheh.

NOTES

Karen Stark is a writer and artist who lives in North Carolina.

Cover design by Lisa Creed.